The
ANTIOCH
TESTAMENT

The ANTIOCH TESTAMENT

A novel about the lives of the apostles
after the Resurrection

Donald Joiner

Seraphina Press • Minneapolis, MN

SERAPHINA
PRESS

Seraphina Press
322 First Avenue N, 5th floor
Minneapolis, MN 55401
612.455.2293
www.SeraphinaPress.com

ISBN-13: 978-1-63413-630-3
LCCN: 2015909992

Distributed by Itasca Books

Book Design by B. Cook

Printed in the United States of America

Also by Don Joiner

Antebellum Churches in Georgia

Faith of Our Fathers

To the Christians in the Mid East who have been persecuted for their faith down through the centuries. And in our own time have suffered the destruction of their homes, their churches, cruel torture and death. All of them, past and present, have been: "…afflicted in every way, but not crushed; perplexed, but not driven to despair; persecuted, but not forsaken; struck down, but not destroyed." 2 Corinthians 4:8-9

CHAPTER 1

Suddenly, he was awake. Had it been an incoming round? No, he didn't think so; just a dream. There had been plenty of "incomings," however; enough to keep most of the third battalion alert and watchful. According to his watch it was 0520 a.m. Out here when there was an opportunity to sleep, soldiers learned to sleep lightly. The insurgents took every opportunity to lob mortars into the base at night and had done so with increasing regularity. Though still tired, he knew more sleep would be impossible. A couple of hours was about his limit these days, so he got up, dressed, and prepared to meet the day. Things were not going as well as they could here at Forward Operations Base Winslow in Iraq's Diyala Province during the first several weeks of January 2014. The base was frequently under mortar fire by Iraqi militants, requiring constant vigilance and the loss of much sleep.

The cold wind hit him as he opened the door to his hut—another reminder of the many surprises Iraq had in store for all American troops, but especially for the new guys. It was a reminder even in this, his second deployment, that if it wasn't hot enough to fry eggs on the sand, it was cold enough to make guys burrow deeply into their sleeping bags. He leaned forward into the wind as he made his way toward the headquarters hut for Company A, anxious to get started with the day's tasks. The evenings, for him, were bleak and long; he was tired of the long hours spent in his bunk reading fiction, and he took no interest in the poker games that sometimes lasted all night. He had to face it: seventeen years in the army and, for the first time, he was homesick. Here he was, Master Sergeant Will Foster, thirty-seven years old, a veteran of the first Desert Storm and now working on his second Iraq tour, and he was as homesick as an eighteen-year-old rookie.

The long and short of it was he missed his family with even greater intensity than he had on his first deployment. His son had made the high school football team as a freshman last year, but the season was over before his first deployment ended. Now Will Jr. had completed a second year on the team, and Will Sr. had yet to see him play. And Katie, his daughter, had started middle school this year. Middle school! Katie! Where had the time gone? It seemed only yesterday he was teaching her to ride a bicycle.

Foster reached the door to the headquarters hut as a gust of wind stung him with a spray of sand. Sand! Here in this country, everyone lived with sand. It found its way into all clothing and managed to penetrate every crease and orifice of a person's body. In the mess hall, one could feel the grit with every bite. Sometimes he wondered if his teeth would have any enamel left by the time this tour ended.

Once inside, Foster hung his jacket on a hook by the door and turned to see that Appleby, the duty sergeant, was at his desk. He was talking on the phone and, with a face turned beet red, he shouted a few obscenities to whoever was at the other end of the line and slammed down the receiver.

Aware now of Foster's presence, Appleby turned to him and said in an obviously angry voice, "It's like pulling teeth to talk to those jackasses at regimental supply. I've been on the line more than half an hour and have talked to three nitwits who don't know the difference between pens to write with and pins to stick in a bulletin board. Twice I've ordered potable water for the kitchen, and twice they've dispatched river water in tankers to wet down the sand."

"Did you send the river water back?"

"Hell, no! Who wants to look a gift horse in the mouth? We sprayed the water around the offices and the hospital and reordered more drinking water, but those imbeciles had the same tankers pick up another load of river water and bring it back here."

"Well, there you go," replied Foster. "Obviously, the gentle folk in supply are convinced this fierce band of warriors likes nothing better than to eat bad guys and wash them down with untreated river water."

"You leave the water problem to me, Will. I'll handle it," said Appleby. "Captain's been up and about since 0400 hours. He's not alone, and he wanted to know right away when you came in. I'll tell him you're here."

Foster frowned as he watched Appleby walk toward the captain's door. It wasn't like Captain Rogers to be up this early; as Foster knew, Rogers preferred to stay busy at work until the wee morning hours before turning in. He was usually the last one in the office in the morning, having been the last one at work the day before.

Appleby tapped on the captain's door and announced that Foster was here. As he entered and saluted the seated captain, Foster noticed that Khadum, one of the battalion's interpreters, was seated in a visitor's chair.

Returning the salute, Rogers said, "Have a seat, Sergeant Foster. Our friend Khadum has interesting information to share, and I'd like your take on it. Now, start at the beginning, Khadum. Tell us what you've found out."

Foster looked at the swarthy Iraqi. The man's dark eyes, hooked nose, and thick black mustache reminded the sergeant of the Republican Guard soldiers he'd fought during Desert Storm I. Brave and loyal, many had died rather than surrender to coalition forces. Though Foster was aware Khadum had been an officer in Saddam's army, he and the others who knew kept quiet about it because the man had consistently furnished the command with accurate information; and besides that, he spoke excellent English, a rare talent among Iraqis.

The Iraqi turned toward Foster, smiled a greeting, and began, "Sergeant, you will remember a man I've told you about who travels about the area selling cloth and needles to rural households named Abu Ahmed? Though he has provided me with much that I consider only gossip, I continue to listen, for he has, on occasion, revealed a tidbit or two of worthwhile information. He travels all over this area and is considered so insignificant that men speak openly within his hearing. Yesterday, he cautioned me to wait, and when no one was around, he told me he overheard young men talking about a planned attack on the Christian church in the village of Batufa. He might never have reported this information to me except for the fact his wife's family is Christian, and he knew I'd pass this along to the battalion."

Foster thought for a moment. He knew the battalion had standing orders to avoid sectarian conflicts among the Iraqis. He also knew that much misinformation was being spread, hoping to draw American forces into unfamiliar ground to be more easily ambushed. Batufa was a village of about sixty Sunni families, lying thirty kilometers from FOB Winslow. It was also located five kilometers from a paved road where an American convoy had recently come under fierce attack.

Captain Rogers broke the silence. "Well, Sergeant, what do you think? Is this yet another attempt to draw our patrols out God knows where so a band of insurgents can send our boys home in body bags? Or do they have another purpose in mind?"

With a glance at the Iraqi, Foster replied, "I can think of only three reasons why this info was meant to get back to us, Captain. If an ambush is intended, there are few places better than Batufa to give it a go. That's mostly flat, sandy country, but there's a gully near the village big enough to conceal any number of hostiles, and our troops would be sitting ducks for the bad guys."

He stopped and thought for a moment before continuing. "I think there's another reason, Captain. Perhaps someone is wise to Abu Ahmed and is looking to confirm this suspicion by waiting to see if a patrol is dispatched to the village on the strength of Ahmed's info. If this is the reason and one of our patrols shows up, Abu Ahmed will most likely lose his head."

Remembering his last patrol outing where the troops had come across the mutilated body of a Christian Iraqi, he added, "I can think of a third reason. Maybe the bad guys do intend to attack the church or its members. After all, our military hasn't made it easier for the Iraqi Christians in this country. The Muslims call us 'crusaders,' among other things, so I'm sure the Iraqi Christians now have an even bigger cross to bear inasmuch as they share our religion in this Muslim country. To tell you the truth, though, I didn't think there were many Christians in Batufa."

"The sergeant is right, Captain," the interpreter responded. "In more normal times, Batufa had only a small number of Christians, but now in these unfortunate days, the country is awash in refugees. After all, Iraqis are tribal people, and they're frustrated and angry and are prone to taking this anger out on strangers who have no large tribal base to defend them or extract revenge. Who better than the small minority of Christians to bear the brunt of the people's anger?"

Rogers rose from his chair, a signal the others took to mean the meeting was over. He said, "Good job, Khadum. As always, what you bring us has value. Keep your eyes and ears open, and meet with me whenever something comes along that you think I need to know about. But now, it's time for breakfast. Come on, Sergeant; let's see if our esteemed cooks have at last learned how to make a decent cup of coffee."

Braving the windblown sand, Rogers and Foster made their way to the Quonset hut that served as a dining facility. Entering, they took their place in the short line awaiting service. While waiting to be served, Rogers spotted the chaplain, Major Charles Monroe, sitting alone at one of the tables. When their breakfast was served, they made their way over to his table.

"What's up, Tom?" Monroe said, lifting his coffee mug in greeting as the two men sat down. "It's kind of early for you, isn't it? Being a nighthawk, I thought you didn't emerge from your blankets 'til the sun was full up. After all, most of your intelligence arrives during the night shift, doesn't it?"

Major Charles Monroe was a native of Savannah, Georgia. His grandfather was originally from Detroit but had accepted a management position with a large insurance company headquartered in Savannah. He first became president and then chairman of the board, and his son, Charles's father, followed him in insurance management. Now Charles's father was president of the company.

Charles's older brother, Ken, was an investment broker, had two unfortunate marriages, was now divorced, and lived in Atlanta. His sister, Louise, had died tragically in an auto accident when she was sixteen. She had been only one year older than Charles, and her death had a profound influence on his life. When Charles was a senior in high school, he announced that he was going to study to be a minister. His family at first welcomed the idea since they were stalwart members of the Episcopal Church and expected him to attend an Episcopal seminary. When he declared that he planned to attend the Methodist Church and apply to Emory University, they were much less pleased. Many arguments followed, but Charles stubbornly maintained his position, and the next year he was a member of Emory's freshman class.

By the time he became a senior, the family reluctantly accepted the fact that he was set on becoming a Methodist minister. Three years later, with degrees in political science and religion, he accepted an appointment to a small Methodist church in Glynn County.

During his second church appointment, he met and married Anne Blanchard, daughter of a prominent Savannah dentist. They had three children, Blake, now a freshman in high school, and Dorothy and Sam, seventh-grade twins. Six years ago, he had been accepted as an army chaplain. He'd served in Iraq for the past two years.

Rogers looked at Major Monroe and replied, "What's 'up' is multiple choice, Parson. You can take your pick. We get enough information during the night to send out dozens of patrols in all directions, but with most of it meant to get our boys out in open country so they can be picked off by the bad guys. Even if they lose ten of theirs to get one of ours, they go back to their villages with great honor since they've killed another hated infidel.

"You know what they call us, don't you, Parson?" Rogers continued. "Crusaders. And here I'd thought the crusades were over a thousand years ago. Guess stuff in people's minds never ends, does it? A thousand years! Talk about holding a grudge."

"Chaplain," asked Foster, "I can understand the reason why many Iraqis would hate us 'cause we whipped their backsides twice in the space of ten years, but to blame us for what happened a thousand years ago, I don't get it. What's with all this Crusader talk, anyhow?"

"Hope you're ready for a long answer, Sergeant, 'cause a short one just won't do. First of all, the Crusades were a series of religious wars organized by the pope to win back the Holy Land from the Muslim conquerors. You see, the Muslims had taken it from the Christian Eastern Roman Empire four hundred or so years before. A sore point for the Christian Europeans was the fact that the Muslims occupied Jerusalem, the holiest Christian site, and had more or less instigated a practice of harassing, torturing, imprisoning, and killing Christian pilgrims who sought to visit the holy sites there."

He paused for a moment, remembering the importance his old history professor Dr. Imlay had placed on the struggle between

Christians and Muslims in that long-ago era. "When the Egyptian Muslims took control of Jerusalem in 1065 AD, an estimated three thousand Christians were slaughtered. The Egyptian commander ordered that all Christian churches be destroyed. All of these atrocities contributed to Christian outrage in Europe, which simmered until the Eastern Roman emperor in Constantinople appealed to the pope for assistance in fighting the Muslims. You see, the Muslim Turks had driven the emperor's Christian forces back almost to the walls of their capital, Constantinople."

He thought about the excitement in Dr. Imlay's eyes when he described the gathering of Christians to hear the pope's call for action to retrieve Jerusalem. "Finally galvanized into action, many Christian Europeans rushed to join the armies that promised to reclaim the Holy Land and drive the Muslims out. The Christian soldiers who set out toward the East had red cloth crosses sewn to their clothing and were called Crusaders because they set out to retake the Holy Land. The name stuck, and many Muslims to this day call Europeans 'Crusaders.'

"This first Crusade was surprisingly successful, and the Christian forces conquered Jerusalem, tragically, with much blood and slaughter. Sad to say, many innocent civilians—Muslims and Jews—were ruthlessly killed in this conquest. In Jerusalem the Crusaders established a Christian kingdom that lasted for about a hundred years."

Foster was still not satisfied. "I hear what you're saying, Chaplain, but I still don't get it. What you're telling us took place hundreds of miles from Iraq in distant Judea and, as far as what I'm hearing goes, involved Muslims and Europeans. I could see Muslims in Jerusalem calling us Crusaders, but not Iraqis. They weren't there."

Monroe smiled as he responded, "Sergeant, maybe this will provide a little insight into the Islamic mindset. Many Muslims tend to believe any lands that were ever conquered or occupied by

Muslims, no matter how briefly or for how long, are always considered to be the rightful inheritance of Muslims. Any non-Muslim power entering Islamic territory, no matter for what reason or for how long, is considered to be an occupying infidel force."

"If that's the case, Chaplain, I've been to Spain and have seen the buildings constructed by Muslims hundreds of years ago when they controlled the place, so what you're saying is the Muslims, even though defeated and driven out of Spain long ago, still lay claim to that country," replied Rogers.

"Well," replied the chaplain, laughing, "perhaps not claimed so openly, since they're not in position to occupy Spain at the moment, but the belief is pretty solid in the Muslim world. Once territory has been conquered by Muslims, it's considered to be Muslim property from that time forward. Any people occupying the land afterward, like the Spanish, no matter how much time has gone by, are considered interlopers. But, back to the matter of us being referred to as Crusaders, let me continue.

"In recent years, it's become politically convenient for certain Muslim leaders, especially the more radical ones, to encourage the use of the word Crusader whenever European or American forces have acted to restore order in this part of the world. You have to keep in mind that many elements among the Muslim population owe their status in the community to shifting the blame for whatever hardships or natural calamities the people have suffered to the despised Westerners, who are all considered infidels. Like it or not, deserved or not, we're the latest Crusaders and are seen by many as hated infidel occupiers of a Muslim land."

Wanting to be absolutely fair in describing the history of the ongoing struggle in the Middle East, he continued, "Of course, I have to balance that with the sad fact that a hundred years ago, Western powers in Europe were in global competition to extend their commercial empires over many lands, including scores of Muslim territories. This period is so fresh in their minds that any foreign military engagement in their part of the world, no matter the cause, is viewed as a prelude to colonialism, especially when drummed into their heads at every service by the imams at their mosques."

Sergeant Foster sipped his coffee before saying, "Given that everything you mentioned is true, Major, why don't the imams tell their people we Americans were never a part of the European colonial occupation and don't intend on staying here when our mission's done? After all, Saddam was a butcher; he killed thousands of his own people and threatened his Muslim neighbors. There's no telling how many Iranians or Kuwaitis he killed while he was in power. Seems to me we should be welcomed as the guys who freed Iraqis from a cruel dictator, not seen as hated occupiers in a land no American in his right mind would give two cents for."

"You've identified the real crux of the problem we face, Sergeant. Sure, there are some Iraqis who appreciate what we did to remove Saddam's regime. There are even some who look forward to a true Iraqi republic, governed with the best interests of all Iraqis at heart, but I'm afraid those are few and far between. Like several other Muslim countries, Iraq is composed of two distinct Muslim sects, Sunnis and Shias, who despise and hate each other. To complicate things further, Iraqis belong to a number of tribes that have first call on their members' loyalty. The tribe is family, and anyone outside the tribe who harms a 'family' member is the subject of vengeance for the whole tribe."

Realizing he ran the risk of boring his listeners with so much detail, he added, "I might be telling you more than you wanted to hear, but this is a complicated situation. The split between Sunni and Shiite Muslims goes back to the time soon after Muhammad died in the seventh century. The vast majority of his followers supported Abu Bakr—Muhammad's friend and the father of one of the prophet's wives—to be the caliph or leader; they're called

Sunni. The minority thought the leader should come from among Muhammad's kin, and these became known as Shiite."

Pondering the centuries-old religious animosities existing among the two major sects of Iraqis, he said, "Today, approximately eight out of ten Muslims are Sunni. Since the seventh century, virtually all political power was in the hands of Sunni Muslims. All Muslims worship Allah as their only God, and all honor the Koran as their sacred scripture. Sunnis tend to follow the teachings of Muhammad, while Shiites tend to rely on their religious leaders, the ayatollahs, for spiritual guidance.

"Here, it's important to remember, even though the vast majority of Muslims worldwide are Sunnis, the Sunnis are a minority in Iraq, and Saddam came to power from a Sunni tribe. His brutality toward Shiites created an enduring animosity that frustrates the allied coalition's efforts to rebuild the country. There's no trust between the two sects. The best we can hope for is to encourage a degree of acceptance among them that will allow a functioning secular government to go forward."

Captain Rogers took one last sip of his coffee, stood up, and said, "Much as I'd like to hear more of your take on Iraqi history, Parson, I've got an in-basket full of problems waiting to be dealt with at my desk, and I'm afraid the CO's patience will be worn thin if I don't get busy working on solutions."

The office complex was barely visible in the blowing sand. When Rogers entered the building, he took a moment to stamp the sand from his boots and shake it out of his hair before heading to his office. Corporal Wilcox had the desk duty and handed him a Post-it note with a message that said Major Andrews, the CO, wanted to see him right away. For Bob Andrews to say "right away" usually meant there was trouble brewing in FOB Winslow's zone. Foster wondered if this summons had anything to do with the information Khadum had provided about the danger to the Christians in Batufa. He'd sent on this info marked URGENT to the major at first light. Crumpling the Post-it note, Rogers knocked on Andrews's door, opened it, and walked in.

Major Robert P. Andrews was a short, stout redhead completing his eighth year of service. "Come in and sit down, Tom," said Andrews. "I've received intel that verifies the information Khadum provided concerning the Christian refugees in Batufa. Seems that a large contingent of insurgents is gathering in and around the town, and they're particularly interested in exactly where the Christians are located. Threats have been made, and our intel people advise we can expect trouble at any moment."

Rogers replied, "I had another conversation with Khadum this morning, Major, and he reports that there's much talk in the town about a proposed attack on the church there. He's now out trying to gather more details."

Major Andrews stood and walked toward the office's single window. Looking out at the sand blowing around, he said, "I don't like it, Tom. It sounds too much like a tactic designed to get one of our patrols shot up, but on the other hand, unarmed Christians are easy targets, and attacks on them by militants are applauded in many Muslim communities."

Rogers stared at the floor for a moment before looking at the CO and saying, "Major, we seem to be caught between a rock and a hard place. Our standing orders are to stay uninvolved in civilian Iraqi affairs, but at the same time, move against armed militants before they can cause damage to us or civilian interests. The question is, are the bad guys armed, and do we risk getting ourselves caught up in a civilian ruckus? And if the civilians complain, seems like the powers that be are much more apt to listen to their voices these days than to ours."

"Yeah, I know, Tom," replied Andrews. "There are always risks involved; especially now, with a new Iraqi civilian government in the process of being installed, any action on our part will be under the microscope, but I've got a bad feeling about this situation. I want you to take a patrol into Batufa, and let's see if we can nip this event in the bud. If you run into problems, gather the Christians and get the hell out. Let me know, and I'll go up the chain to Baghdad for advice on our next step."

Rogers stood and said, "Perhaps I'd better take a reinforced patrol on this trip, Major. There are several places between here and Batufa that lend themselves to ambush, especially that hilly section and the big gully outside the town. I'll want Sergeant Foster along on this ride; he's got a knack for smelling out trouble."

"Take as many men as you need, Tom. I agree. Foster needs to be there. He'll be happy to be out in the field rather than here, stuck behind a desk. I'd feel better knowing he was with you. Oh, one more thing. Take Khadum with you. You well might need an interpreter on this trip."

CHAPTER 2

As the three armored vehicles carried the patrol toward Batufa, Captain Rogers was more than glad he'd brought Sergeant Foster along. Foster had asked permission to select the men for the patrol, and Rogers was only too happy to agree. Foster himself was in the lead vehicle and frequently stopped to reconnoiter those obvious places where an ambush could be set up. Several times he walked ahead of the vehicles scouring the area for improvised explosive devices, the dreaded IEDs.

As it was, with this cautionary approach, the patrol arrived at the dry gully several kilometers from the town at around three p.m., where they dismounted from the vehicles. After silently surveying the area and leaving three men to guard the vehicles, the patrol set off for the town.

Corporal Morris Nix stole silently ahead of the patrol. Aware of the danger he faced as the point man, he cast a furtive glance at every clump of brush along the uneven path they followed. How he hated these excursions into the desert. Troopers never knew when a clever ambush awaited, set up by the insurgents who seemed to grow more venturesome and cunning by the day. Around any bend one might expect to be met by the deadly chatter of AK-47 gunfire or be torn apart by the force of a roadside bomb, but he knew why Sergeant Foster wanted him and his squad on this patrol. They were good, extremely good, at what they did.

It was only last week that his patrol had set out to rescue a military convoy being attacked by insurgents fifteen kilometers south of their base. He chuckled when he recalled how they had come up behind the insurgents, who were preoccupied with shooting up the trucks and, before they knew what hit them, five bad guys were down, and the two remaining had thrown their hands up in surrender. When Sergeant Foster heard their story, he told them they were heroes and he would keep his eyes on them. Heroes! He had kept his eyes on them all right. Twice since last week he'd sent his "heroes" out on patrol, and here they were again, pounding sand toward the unknown.

Nix was a tough twenty-year-old from New Orleans. In fact, he'd celebrated his twentieth birthday last month and was now three months into his second Iraq tour. Wiry and strong, he had grown up in the projects, the only child of a single mother who was indifferent toward him. As soon as he was seventeen, his mother was only too glad to sign the papers for him to enlist. The army was the first real taste of discipline he'd ever encountered and the first home he felt comfortable in. He planned to make it a career, if he survived this tour. Serving as point man wasn't his choice; Sergeant Foster said he was good at it, so he drew this duty more often than not. Once, when he complained, Foster confided that most times the hidden insurgents would let the point man pass so they could zero in on the rest of the patrol that followed. That made sense, but Nix wasn't entirely convinced and asked Foster if he was trying to "snow" him. Foster looked at him with those calm blue eyes and said, "Nix, I put you at point 'cause you're about as good at spotting the rag heads as I am and, besides, do you really want to live forever?"

His reverie was interrupted when he caught a quick smell of something burning. Ahead, he saw a column of smoke drifting upward in the general direction of the town. He raised his hand to stop the patrol as he crawled forward up a small incline to get a better view, keeping his M16 rifle clear of the ever-present sand. Of course, nothing stopped the sand from getting into his boots, his armored vest, his jacket, and his pants, as well as in every crease in his skin, but he was used to it.

As he reached the crest of the hill, he saw the dun-colored walls of the town's houses. Slowly, he opened a case and brought his binoculars up to his eyes. He felt the presence of Foster, who had crawled up beside him. "What do you see, Nix?" the sergeant said. Nix swung the binoculars toward the smoke at the extreme left of the town and looked carefully before replying.

"One of the buildings in the town is on fire, Sarge. If our map is right, I think it's the church," Nix said as he handed the glasses to Foster, who quickly scanned the area with them.

Foster raised his hand and motioned the patrol to fan out along the small ridge around him. Captain Rogers crawled up beside the sergeant, and Foster told him it appeared the church was burning. Then he added that he'd spotted several men looking through the windows of the burning building and that the men were armed. Except for the smoke and the two men standing outside the burning building, nothing else looked to be out of place.

Suddenly, Foster tapped the captain on the arm and pointed to the road leading toward the patrol's location. They saw a pickup truck loaded with people speeding rapidly in their direction. Right behind the pickup were three other vehicles, including a jeep armed with a machine gun. The machine gun on the jeep fired at the pickup as it swerved along the road.

Rogers quickly ordered two of his troops to lay down covering fire not at, but in front of, the pursuing vehicles. When the pursuers saw the soldiers firing toward them, the vehicles slowed and came to a stop. The machine gunner aimed toward the soldiers and fired a defiant burst. Looking down, the captain could see the pickup laboring up an incline with steam pouring out from under the hood.

Keeping an eye on the three vehicles that had been in pursuit, Captain Rogers sent five of his men down the slope where the truck was laboring, with orders to have the occupants dismount and join the patrol on the ridge. He could see that other armed men were leaving the town on foot and running in the direction of the stopped vehicles.

Foster, again using the binoculars, pointed toward the church. Rogers saw at least a dozen armed men swarming down the slope toward the patrol's position. It was obvious the insurgents were trying to flank them. The captain sent two men to lay down covering fire while the soldiers he sent to the now-stalled pickup were hurrying the terrified occupants up the incline toward the patrol.

"Bad guys in the vehicles are moving again, Captain," said Foster. "I suggest we discourage them. With your permission, I'll have Nix and Murphy delay them while we get those refugees sorted out. We're not in an easily defended position here, so I'm thinking we ought to make tracks back the way we came and call in support from copters should any be nearby."

"Be sure Nix and Murphy first try to discourage the insurgents by firing overhead, Sergeant," said Rogers. "If the Iraqis keep on coming after that, then our boys can take them out. Have Peterson contact base and get us air cover. Be sure he tells them we're under fire. Now, let's get those refugees moving."

Isaiah Murphy was a tall, skinny, twenty-something, one of the unit's most recent additions from the hills of West Virginia. Although he was a fairly new soldier, he had proved to be an excellent shot. Foster often kidded him about using his rifle to discourage revenuers back home in West Virginia. The young man was cool under fire, and the sergeant didn't hesitate to pair him with Nix when the patrol was threatened on its flank. In the few months Murphy had been with them, he'd gained the respect of the men due to his marksmanship with a rifle.

The soldiers who had gone to rescue the people fleeing from the village brought back an old man in a stretcher along with the other occupants of the truck. When all the refugees were temporarily safe among his troops, Rogers sent reinforcements back to the ridge in support of Nix and Murphy, after which he ordered the rest of the patrol to begin deploying back toward their vehicles.

He asked the interpreter, Khadum, to question the refugees to find out what had happened in the town. When they reached the patrol's parked vehicles, Khadum reported, "They said they're the last remaining Christians in Batufa, Captain. The rest were trapped in the burning church."

He reported that the refugees had come to the town from the mountains in the north, but found the long-time Christian residents of Batufa had already fled several weeks earlier because of the threats made to kill them and burn the church.

Early this morning, as the refugees gathered at the church for a final prayer service before continuing their journey, armed men began to stone them, and when their leader protested, one of the insurgents stabbed him. The men forced the Christians into the church, spat on them, cursed them, and set the church on fire.

Unseen by the insurgents, several of the Christians took the wounded priest and led a few of the others through the smoke to escape out the rear door of the church. While the insurgents were celebrating the burning of the church, one of the refugees managed to steal the truck. The refugees who had managed to escape the burning building got in the truck and fled for their lives. Surprised by the escape, the armed insurgents rushed to their vehicles to follow. The escapees reported they saw the flames attack the roof of the church and heard the pitiful cries of their fellow refugees still trapped inside.

Sergeant Foster reported that Murphy and Nix had temporarily stalled the insurgents with accurate covering gunfire, but more armed men were gathering, and it wouldn't be too long before they would feel strong enough to advance on the patrol. Captain Rogers told him to recall the two men, turn the vehicles around, load the refugees aboard, and be prepared to leave for the base.

Two of the soldiers who had carried the wounded priest in a stretcher reported that the old man refused to leave behind a heavy bundle to make the stretcher easier to carry, and they were quite put out about it. "That bundle must weigh fifty pounds, Captain," one of the men complained. "I just about dumped him 'cause of his stubbornness, but he's wounded pretty bad, so we went along with it." Even now several of the troops were arguing with the priest's companions because the old man refused to hand over his bundle while they were putting him into one of the Humvees.

Khadum went to the vehicle and spoke to the refugees crowded around the old priest. "Captain, this old priest is in a bad way, "he said. "He's bleeding heavily from that knife wound and the medic doesn't seem to be able to stop it. He insists that he must see you now."

Nix and Murphy climbed in their vehicle. Upon hearing the distinct sound of helicopter motors in the distance, Peterson contacted the pilots, giving the coordinates both for the patrol and for the insurgents. Foster signaled that the patrol was ready to move out, and Rogers decided to ride in the vehicle with the refugees and Khadum. Looking up, he saw two copters veer in the direction of the insurgents, and the guns aboard both of them began their deadly chatter. Taking a last look around, the captain pointed in the direction of the base, and the convoy moved out. Turning toward the wounded man and his companions, he asked the interpreter to question them and find out more about this group, where they had come from, and when.

For the next few minutes, the Iraqi interpreter and the refugees engaged in animated conversation, punctuated with a great deal of hand waving. Rogers could see that the priest truly was in a bad way, and, despite the medic's best efforts to stop the bleeding, his blood soaked through the blanket they had wrapped him in. Finally, Khadum turned toward him and said, "Captain, he wants to know if there's a priest at Winslow. I told him there was no one of the Syriac Christian faith anywhere within miles of here, but an American Catholic priest came to the base once a month. I also told him the Americans had a Protestant chaplain there all the time. He said that would be acceptable, for he knew he was getting weaker and might not live long enough to see the priest. Because I am Iraqi, and he assumes of the Muslim faith, he was reluctant to say more, but believing he might not make it back to the base alive, he went on to say the bundle he has carried with him contains an old religious book he rescued from a monastery in northern Iraq before it was sacked by Muslim insurgents, and he wants you to swear on your honor you'll deliver it to the chaplain."

Rogers asked Khadum to try to get more details about where the refugees had come from, so the interpreter turned to the old man and the other refugees. Khadum then explained, "Captain, the priest and his party are from a village near the Turkish border. When the fighting between the Kurds and Saddam's army reached the outskirts of the village, the Christians decided it was time to leave the country. Since the Turks and a few breakaway Kurds were still fighting in the mountains, they headed south toward Mosul and were on the road for many days.

"It was after the Americans began deploying in Iraq that they came to the Monastery of Saint Yacob, where they intended to spend the night. They said this monastery had been virtually deserted by the monks who had fled to Syria after their abbot and three other monks were killed by Iraqi soldiers shopping for food in a nearby village one day earlier. The only monks left were an ancient gatekeeper and his young assistant.

"The old monk told the refugees it would not be safe at the monastery, for the soldiers were former members of Saddam's Revolutionary Guard, and, since Saddam had been toppled, they had become thieves and murderers. He explained that these former soldiers thought it great sport to plunder and kill Christians. The monk went on to tell them he would prepare supper for them, but they must not attempt to stay overnight, as it was far too dangerous. He advised them to continue southward and get far away from the monastery."

Pausing as the copters opened fire on the insurgents, the interpreter then continued, "While they were at supper, they heard gunfire coming from the direction of the village, and the young monk hurried to the bell tower to investigate. Almost immediately he returned, and in a terrified voice announced that a party of soldiers was on the way up the hill and would be at the monastery gates in less than five minutes.

"The gatekeeper hustled the refugees out into a corridor leading to the rear exit, but before arriving at the exit, he stopped at the monastery library, unlocked a cabinet, and returned with the bundle the old priest now seeks to leave in your care. He told them this mysterious item was of great antiquity and had long been the most treasured and closely guarded secret possession of Saint Yacob Monastery. He was afraid it would be desecrated or destroyed by the soldiers.

"When the refugees reached the rear exit of the monastery, they could hear a splintering crash of wood coming from the front entrance as the soldiers forced open the massive wooden doors. The gatekeeper quickly opened the rear gate, saying he would try to buy time for them to make good their escape. When they had been on the road fleeing south less than fifteen minutes, the refugees looked back in horror to see the ancient monastery engulfed in flames. Since that moment, they've been traveling more than two months, depending upon the generosity of fellow Christians, until they were betrayed in Batufa by a former Christian who had renounced his faith."

As the vehicles sped back to the base, Rogers looked at the old man and his companions and saw that all of them were waiting for his response. The old man coughed, and a thin trickle of blood rolled down his bearded chin. As the priest grimaced in pain, Rogers nodded his agreement to the priest's request, and the old man strained to remove the bundle from beneath the blanket while the interpreter reached over to help him. What emerged was a large, scuffed, leather-bound book, obviously of great age. With a glance at the priest, Khadum handed it to the captain, who was surprised by the book's weight. After a prodding from the old man, the interpreter retrieved a leather satchel from the old man's stretcher and motioned for Rogers to put the book in it. The priest smiled at the captain and started to say something, but only managed a coughing spell before beginning to spit up blood. Sighing softly, he lapsed into a deep coma.

Upon arriving at FOB Winslow, Rogers sought out the chaplain and found him in his office. He carefully removed the leather-bound manuscript from the satchel and laid it on top of the desk, then told the chaplain about the incident at the church in Batufa, about the plight of the Christian refugees, and how the old priest had insisted that the book be delivered into the chaplain's hands.

"I don't know what it is or what's in it, Parson, but it was mighty important to the old priest, and it was his request before he went into a coma that I deliver it straight to you."

Leaning forward in his chair, Monroe opened the scuffed leather binding and immediately recognized from his studies at Emory that the manuscript was written in a form of Aramaic and that it was incredibly old. "Did the old man tell you anything about the book, like where it came from or why it was so important?"

Captain Rogers looked at the chaplain for a long moment, then replied, "Major, we were somewhat preoccupied at the time trying to dodge bullets. Conversation in those circumstances was somewhat brief. Whatever the priest said was interpreted by Khadum, who told us only that old man wanted to be sure the book was delivered directly to you. We were told it came from a monastery up north and that it was highly valued by Iraqi Christians. The priest and his companions were afraid that if the Muslims got hold of it, they would vandalize or destroy it. That's it. I will say this, however: after what those folks went through, the fact that they thought only of keeping the book safe is a testimony to its importance, at least to them."

Accustomed as they were to treating combat injuries, the medical staff made short work of treating the refugees' wounds. Major Monroe was able to talk further with Khadum, but what Foster had told him apparently was almost all anyone knew. The other refugees told him the old priest had been the guardian of the book during their long trek down from the monastery to Batufa. He had told them it was an ancient Christian treasure and they must safeguard it at all costs. More than that they didn't know, nor did any other member of their small group.

Pondering what he had been told about this mysterious book, Major Monroe made his way back to his office where he again opened the book, wondering what it contained that caused the old priest to be so concerned that it not fall into the hands of the Muslims. What should he do with this old book? The army had a standard policy that any recovered item of historic significance was to be turned over immediately to Iraqi authorities, but the Iraqi authorities he had met wouldn't hesitate to sell anything of value to the highest bidder, and that included items of historic significance. So what was he to do? Who might advise him? He needed to talk to someone familiar with Iraqi culture, someone he might reasonably trust. The only one who came to mind was Khadum, but could he trust the man?

Could any man who had served as an officer under the brutal dictator Saddam be trusted? With a sigh the chaplain concluded that he had little choice. Khadum spoke excellent English, was well educated, and certainly was familiar with the culture of his countrymen. He spoke to the corporal on desk duty and asked him to send word that he wanted to see the interpreter right away.

Shortly after, he heard a light tap on his door. Monroe invited the interpreter to come in.

"You summoned Khadum, Major?" the Iraqi inquired, coming in and closing the door.

"Summoned is the wrong word, my friend, but it's true, I did ask for you, and I appreciate you coming. Please, have a seat. I'd like to ask your advice about something that's troubling me, and it has to do with the culture of your country and the possible discovery of a thing of historic value yet not appreciated by the vast majority of Iraqis. In fact, I'm concerned many would look forward to tearing this book apart and selling it piecemeal in the antiquities market."

Before he could continue, the interpreter raised his hand and said, "Chaplain, what you're inquiring about has to do with the ancient book that the dead priest wanted you to have. I believe his Christian companions are being processed for evacuation right now to a safer region of the country."

Surprised at the extent of Khadum's knowledge of ongoing affairs here on base, Monroe responded, "I was aware that you knew about the book, my friend, and that is precisely the subject I'd like to discuss with you and ask your advice about. The book seems to arouse the emotions both of those who treasure it as well as those insurgents who seek to destroy it. The problem I have is what to do with it. If I turn it over to the Iraqi authorities, what will they do with it? Will they put it in a safe place, a museum perhaps, or will they do something else with it? What are your thoughts?"

For a long moment the Iraqi was quiet, then he responded, "Chaplain, you are generous when you mention 'Iraqi authorities.' In my humble opinion, those who are in authority now are Shiite scum, and they would thank you profusely for rescuing a valued Iraqi treasure. Then, once out of your sight, they would immediately offer it for sale. That's what they've done with virtually every museum relic turned over to them since the American military put them in power."

"Khadum, my friend," said Monroe, smiling as he replied, "as a former member of Saddam's army, I know you have negative feelings about the new government and its Shiite majority. I'm not going to try and change your mind about them. I understand there's bad blood between Shiites and Sunnis and has been for centuries. What I want from you is your best advice about where the book properly belongs—who will safeguard it and preserve it."

After a long pause the interpreter said, "Although you call me friend, Chaplain, you do not know me, so you misunderstand what I have said to you. It is true, of course, that I did serve in the Iraqi army when Saddam was in power. I served on the front lines during the long years we were at war with Iran. I was wounded and hospitalized during the first Gulf War. And I fought you Americans when you invaded Iraq and overthrew Saddam. Like Saddam, I am a Sunni in a land that is predominately Shiite, but I am a secular Sunni, not given to follow the rants and hysteria of the mullahs who control the mosques. I consider myself a man of the world.

"You Americans believe that exposing Iraq to democratic principles will result in the Iraqi people demanding a democratic government. I think you are deluded. What you fail to understand is, first of all, we Arabs are a tribal people, and the tribes are generally commanded by strong and ruthless leaders. It is natural that we look to strong leaders when we form a government. Once you Americans leave, there will be chaos here until a strong leader appears. And make no mistake—a strong leader will, ultimately, emerge.

"My advice to you, Chaplain, the advice of this humble man of the world, is to take the book with you when you leave my country or, rather, get it out of the country as soon as you can. It is a Christian book, and in the present circumstances it is an object of derision here, worth only what someone would pay for old manuscripts. I'm sad to say the Christians are leaving Iraq as fast as they can. They are terrified, and rightfully so. They know they have no future here. The mullahs inflame the hatred and passion of the people, so they now persecute the Christians, who once were their neighbors. When the Christians are gone, the Shias and the Sunni can focus their hatred and animosities on each other. And when they have bloodied each other to the point of exhaustion, a strong leader will appear, and history will repeat itself."

Sad, but all too true, mused the chaplain. The Iraqi was being brutally honest, and what he said reflected Monroe's own view of the situation in Iraq. This was indeed a fractured nation, and outside the relatively few areas under control of the coalition troops, chaos, slaughter, and confusion were the norm. What order there was existed only due to the coalition's military presence. Withdraw that presence, and death and destruction would soon follow.

"I thank you for your thoughts, Khadum," Monroe said as he rose to open the office door. "I pray you're wrong about your assessment of the future of this country, but my fear is you may be right."

As Khadum walked to the door, he turned and said, "I know your heart is good, Chaplain, but you Americans believe everyone thinks as you do—that a little exposure to your own democratic values will cause a mass movement to a democratic government here. You truly do not know our people. Here they look first, not to the government, but to the tribe. They want a leader who can protect them, feed them, and crush their enemies. Iraqis will bide their time until you and your allies are gone, then the struggle for leadership will begin anew. The Christians have no future here and they know it, and that's why they are leaving in droves. Take the Christian book with you or it will be sold to the highest bidder." He then turned and walked away.

Monroe returned to his desk and thought about what the former Iraqi soldier had said. The man was certainly right about the Christian exodus from Iraq. Though they represented only 3 percent of the country's population, they made up more than 20 percent of the refugees seeking to leave Iraq. Since most of Iraq's fashion stores, grocery outlets, and music stores were owned and operated by Christians, they were the targets of the radical Muslims who forced them to shut down their businesses. Deprived of their income, objects of their neighbors' scorn, victims of religious persecution, and targets for murder, these businessmen and their families were eager to move to the West.

Iraq was a mirror image, reflecting what was happening throughout the Middle East. In Israel, the three cities most closely associated with the Christian faith—Jerusalem, Bethlehem and Nazareth—for almost two thousand years had majority Christian populations. No more. The Christians were now a small minority in each of them. Faced with the same kind of pressure from their Muslim neighbors as the Iraqis, they were leaving for the West as fast as possible.

Eighty years ago Turkey had more than two million Christians, but today there were only a few thousand left, and little Lebanon, once the most carefree and prosperous of Arab countries, had a majority Christian population as late as the 1930s. Now, with its cities lying in ruins after a brutal civil war, Christians numbered less than a third of Lebanon's residents.

Monroe stared at the ancient manuscript lying on his desk. Bits and pieces of its old leather binding flecked off and surrounded the book. It certainly had suffered, as did those who had lovingly cared for it. What did it contain? Who had written it? Why had the old priest defended it with his life? And why was it his dying wish to see that it remained in Christian hands? Suddenly, the chaplain made up his mind. He would send the book home. He would say nothing to his superiors, who would insist it remain in Iraqi hands, those hands which, according to Khadum, would sell it to the highest bidder. Once it was safe in America, he would find answers to those questions.

That evening, he found out that a friend—Phil Longstreet, one of the doctors at FOB Winslow—was leaving the next day to fly back to Atlanta. At supper, Monroe told him about the strange journey of the book and shared with him Khadum's gloomy outlook for its future should it remain in Iraq. Longstreet, an amateur historian as well as a skilled surgeon, was intrigued with the antiquity of the book and agreed to deliver it to Monroe's home in Augusta. Later, Monroe sat at his desk to write a letter to his wife, Anne, to accompany the book on its journey to America.

My dear wife, the love of my life,

You can't know how much I miss you and our children. I find myself staring at the calendar, counting the days remaining until I leave this place and return home. Home! The sound of it makes my heart beat faster. To think of sitting at the breakfast table in the morning with you and looking out at the green leaves and beautiful flowers in our backyard is what sustains me in this drab and dreary place. I can assure you, I know exactly how much longer I'll be away from you—exactly two months and three days! By March 20th I should be sitting at your breakfast table drinking my third cup of coffee!

Is Blake still excited about going out for football in the spring? He'll need to put on a few pounds before the knocking starts. And what about Miss Dot, still thirteen, going on eighteen? Does she still camp out on the telephone? And Sam, ever so serious Sam. Have you gotten used to having a musical genius for a son? And does his trumpet practice still make the dogs howl? Tell all our guys their old dad can hardly wait to see them.

My friend, Doctor Phil Longstreet, has agreed to deliver an ancient Christian book to you to keep until I return. I know little about this book except that it is of great age and it was lovingly cared for by a small group of Christians who were fleeing from Muslim insurgents. The central figure among the refugees was a priest who guarded the book and insisted that it be given to me and kept out of the hands of the Muslims. Regrettably, that was his dying wish, for he had been badly wounded by the insurgents before our troops rescued the group.

Once home, I plan on finding an expert in ancient Eastern languages to examine it so we can know what it contains and when it was written. Until then, I want you to put it away in a safe, dry place and don't discuss it with anybody, for I'm not sure of its legal status or mine for having sent it out of Iraq. We'll sort all these things out when I get there. I've got to rush and get this letter in today's mail bag. Kiss all our brood for me. Remember, two months and three days!

I love you,
Charles

One week later, Major Charles Monroe was a passenger in a Humvee returning to FOB Winslow from the army supply depot when his vehicle was struck by an IED. The driver was killed, and the chaplain lost both his legs and had other extensive injuries. After emergency surgery at Winslow, he was flown out of Iraq, headed to the military hospital facilities in Germany. Anne, his wife, had received his letter the day before she was notified that he was grievously wounded.

CHAPTER 3

She wasn't the pretty little thing she'd been twenty-odd years ago. In fact, she admitted that someone describing her would have to honestly say she was a tad overweight, and that description would come from her friends. Others would say she was short and dumpy. She knew she hadn't aged well. Mary Rogers was, as she told her closest associates, "on the south side of fifty." They never asked which was the south side, and for that she was extremely grateful. Had they asked, she would have smiled and lied.

For more than twenty-five years she had worked for Brinkley and Todd Investments, and for most of those years she'd been passed over when newly hired investment brokers selected their personal secretaries. They always seemed to be interested in the young pretty things in the secretarial pool. She had been resigned to a fate of being interviewed only because of her seniority when Ken Monroe joined the firm seven years ago. To her great surprise, and she was sure to the vast astonishment of her younger and prettier counterparts, he selected her.

She found him to be a no-nonsense broker, and that suited her perfectly, for she herself was obsessed with the brokerage business. Her respect for Monroe had grown steadily through the years and, at her request, he had taken over her own modest investment portfolio, and she had seen it prosper beyond her wildest calculations.

Though he was only in his mid-forties, senior management had realized early on that they had a true prize in Ken Monroe. So they did what they needed to do to keep him—they made him vice president, and now he supervised all the firm's senior investment brokers in addition to managing the portfolios of many of the firm's wealthiest clients.

Ken's personal life was an entirely different matter. He didn't share the religious convictions of his parents and his brother, Charles. Before he finished high school, he became the rebel in the family. In a heated argument with his father, Ken said he not only didn't plan to attend any more church services, but that he didn't believe in God at all. From that moment on, he refused to discuss the matter of religion, despite the earnest entreaties of his father or Charles.

In college, he didn't fare well in the humanities, but in math and economics he excelled. In fact, he did so well that he won a scholarship to graduate school in finance at the University of North Carolina. While there, he met Audrey Matthews, a beautiful blonde senior who was a member of the gymnastic team. After two dates, Ken was utterly smitten, and when they both graduated that summer, they eloped, to the chagrin of both sets of parents.

Ken's first job was with a brokerage firm in New York. At first, they were both excited about going to the Big Apple, but soon after arriving, it became crystal clear that Audrey, the daughter of a wealthy Raleigh attorney, hated New York, and while Ken prospered at the firm, the arguments at home intensified. Ken explained that he had a contractual responsibility to remain with the firm for two years, but Audrey remained adamant. If Ken was going to remain in New York for two years, it would be without her. Less than three months after arriving in Gotham, Ken returned to their apartment one evening to find a note saying that she was flying to her parents' home in Raleigh and wouldn't be returning to New York under any circumstances.

The next weekend Ken flew to Raleigh, where he met with Audrey to discuss their situation. No matter what he said to try to resolve this problem, she said if he wouldn't break his contract and leave New York, she would divorce him. Ken asked her to think over what she was asking, because if he were to break his contract, it would destroy his reputation in the financial world. Shortly after he flew back to New York, he received notice that Audrey had filed for divorce.

Having little or no personal life, Ken devoted all his energies to his career in finance. When the divorce was finalized less than a year after they were married, he kept his dates with several attractive women casual, resisting any effort to become seriously involved. To those women who desired a closer relationship, he explained that he was "married to his work" and that would have to be understood. Meanwhile, his reputation in the financial world continued to grow, and he was mentioned as a rising star in several financial journals.

After working for five years in New York, he accepted a position with Brinkley and Todd in Atlanta and began a rise to the top within that firm. Then he met Susan Darnley. Despite his intention to keep his female relationships casual, this one moved from casual to serious in a surprisingly short time. She seemed everything that Audrey was not—a tall, willowy brunette who loved the world of finance. She was vice president of a local bank dealing in commercial construction. She was lively and spontaneous, the complete opposite to the often sullen and exasperating Audrey.

Not only did they share a mutual interest in finance, they also found a common appreciation for antique shopping. Rarely did a weekend go by that they weren't in some small town attending an antique auction. Within six months of their first meeting, they were married, and Ken bought a house in a trendy area of North Atlanta as a showplace for their antique collection.

At first, they appeared to be a perfectly happy couple with many shared interests and friends, but suddenly, at the end of their second year of marriage, Ken filed for divorce, and neither would talk about it with their mutual friends. Though they were both often in attendance at financial activities, they avoided each other by design. Ken redoubled his commitment to his career, and his firm prospered mightily as a result.

Today he was scheduled to meet with three of his special clients, doctors who planned a new business venture with a surgical device that could potentially be worth millions. Mary had prepared for the meeting by providing the necessary refreshments and was in the process of arranging Monroe's financial analyses of the proposed venture when his private telephone rang. *Odd*, she thought, *no one but his family and closest friends have that number, and since his recent divorce, it's rarely in use.* When she answered, a sobbing woman identified herself as Anne, Ken's sister-in-law, who said it was urgent that she speak with him.

Just then, Ken returned from meeting with Cyril Todd, president of the firm. Mary explained that he had an urgent call on his private line, that it was his sister-in-law, and she was obviously upset.

"Anne?" he answered, hearing her sobs. "What is it? What's the matter?"

"It's Charles, Ken. He's been seriously wounded, and it's touch and go. He's in Landstuhl Regional Medical Center, an army hospital in Germany, and I've been told I need to be there as soon as possible. Mom will stay with the kids, so I'm flying to Atlanta at one thirty today to connect with Delta's flight to Frankfurt at six o'clock this evening. I know you're busy and have a lot going on, but I'm so afraid, Ken. Charles was due to return in two months." Anne paused for a moment before asking tenuously, "Would it be possible for you to get away and go with me? I know its quick notice, and I'll understand if it's impossible."

"Anne, of course I'll go with you. Don't say another word. Pack and concentrate on getting ready. Don't forget your passport. I'll meet you at the Delta Sky Club at the international concourse in

Atlanta. Tell the attendant you're with me. Now, try not to worry so much. Charles is a tough old bird. I'm sure he'll be okay."

Obviously, he was anything but sure his brother would be okay. He was as worried as his sister-in-law, but he had things to do and plans to make before leaving for Germany.

"Mary, contact Doctor Williams and tell him I can't meet with his group today. You can tell him my brother is in critical condition in an army hospital in Germany, and I'm flying out there tonight. Check my calendar for the next several weeks, and explain my situation to those concerned. I'm off to Cyril's office to brief him on a few upcoming matters before heading home to pack. I'll be meeting Anne at the airport."

He also instructed Mary to make reservations through his client Jay Andrews, an executive at Delta, for the evening flight to Germany, hotel reservations for both of them, and to confirm all this by giving him a call at the Delta Sky Club at the airport.

Hartsfield-Jackson International, considered the busiest airport in the world, lived up to its reputation as Ken made his way through the crowds. Even at four p.m., the place was filled with people. It was only as he made his way to the international concourse that the number of people began to decline. When he arrived at Delta's Sky Club, he spotted Anne sitting alone and staring out toward the runway through a large window. She didn't see him until he sat beside her and put his arm around her shoulder, and when he did, she turned toward him and wrapped her arms tightly around his neck.

"Oh, Ken," she said, crying softly, "I've lived with this fear since Charles became a chaplain. He's had this insane desire to be right where his 'boys' are, even if that's in the middle of a war zone. I've tried to tell him the children and I need him and want him close to us, but he stubbornly insisted his calling was to be with the troops. Now look where that got him. Bruised and broken and next to death in an intensive care unit in Germany!"

He held her close and let her talk it out until her sobs and tears diminished. He held her until she pulled away and looked into his eyes, studying him intensely. There was something of Charles in his eyes, but Ken was taller, bigger, and more ruggedly handsome than her husband. She knew he kept himself in shape through a rigorous weight lifting routine, and he never passed up an opportunity to play soccer, a sport he excelled in at college.

"Ken, I'm embarrassed not to have spoken to you since your divorce. I always liked Susan, and I'm sorry things worked out the way they did. I know Charles worried about you all the time, almost like he were the older brother, and the only thing stopping him from going to you was his tour in Iraq and the needs of his 'boys' there."

Ken smiled as he remembered how his brother had always wanted to know how he was getting along and what he was up to. Though he hadn't thought about it before, Charles's concern for him was indeed more typical of an older rather than a younger brother. He had shared few details about his divorce from Susan with Charles, letting him know it was a subject he didn't want to discuss.

Because he wanted to relieve the tension he knew Anne felt about Charles's condition, he sought to distract her by confiding particulars about his divorce that he had refused to discuss with anyone else. He told her that Susan had met golf pro Vince Harwood, who had the time and put in the effort necessary to get Susan's attention. She had been unfaithful, but Ken and Susan had parted, if not as friends, at least on amicable terms, and Susan was now presumably the happily married Mrs. Harwood.

"Ken," Anne said, "whatever will I do if I lose Charles? The uncertainty of all this is unbearable. The kids know their dad is in a bad way, and I won't be there to comfort them. Our own little part of the world has absolutely been turned upside down."

"It's only natural for you to worry, Anne," Ken responded,

"but I think you're concentrating too much on a worst-case scenario. The army has the best surgeons in the world, and I'm sure Charles is getting great care at Landstuhl, so try to focus on those things you're involved with at home and the things the kids are doing. That's what Charles will want you to share with him when we get there. You and the children are his world, Anne, so concentrate on sharing those things with him."

Although he had said this with a calm and reassuring voice, those were emotions he didn't feel. He didn't know the extent of his brother's injuries, and he feared the worst while he worked hard to convince Anne otherwise. Finding out his sister-in-law hadn't eaten a bite all day, he insisted they go to a nearby food court. There he ordered for her and made sure she ate.

During the long flight, Anne asked him a tentative question about his divorce, and he readily answered to keep her focus momentarily away from Charles's injuries. He told her intimate things concerning the divorce he would never have mentioned in different circumstances. He told her Susan had been unfaithful to him for several months with the golf pro, a person he had considered one of his good friends, but he'd been so absorbed in his work he'd never had an inkling anything was amiss.

He told her that when Susan admitted the affair, she also told him she wanted a divorce. He conceded he was surprised at how little he was bothered by her confession. He had agreed, and one month after the divorce was finalized, Susan married Vince Harwood, the man who had taught them both the intricacies of the golf game.

Getting little sleep, both Charles and Anne were fully awake when the plane began its descent over Germany. After clearing customs in Frankfurt, Ken rented a Mercedes, and they headed toward Landstuhl, about an hour's drive away. Ken had called the medical center from the airport, but was told patient information couldn't be discussed by telephone. They stopped at a restaurant for breakfast, where again Ken insisted that Anne eat something. Shortly thereafter, they were on their way, and Ken was determined to keep Anne from dwelling on her husband's injuries.

Drawing on his previous business trips to this area, he recounted the history of the region. He told her Landstuhl was an ancient town of Celtic origin and that the local museum contained artifacts verifying the presence of Roman soldiers in the area. He explained that this part of the country was annexed by Napoleon to the French Empire, but after his defeat at Waterloo, it became part of the Kingdom of Bavaria, which it remained until the end of World War I.

Seeing that he had her attention, if only for a moment, he told her that at the beginning of World War I, Bavarians eagerly followed the lead of the German Empire and enlisted in the German army, but mounting casualties, chronic shortages of civilian goods, and hunger over the next four years caused the kingdom of Bavaria to attempt to sign a separate peace treaty with the victorious allies in early 1918, but the effort failed. When the war finally ended later that same year, the kingdom of Bavaria ceased to exist and became what it is still called today, the Free State of Bavaria, a part of the German nation.

By midmorning, they arrived at the huge Landstuhl Regional Medical Facility. A guard directed them to the parking lot for the hospital complex. Upon entering the waiting area, a young female army corporal politely asked them the name of the patient they were there for. Within ten minutes, they were met by a short man in his early forties, who introduced himself as Major Gordon Fry, one of the surgeons familiar with Charles's injuries. He was dressed in his scrub greens and told them he had recently been in surgery. He asked them to follow him, and they walked down a long hall to a small, private waiting room. Once inside he invited them to be seated.

"Mrs. Monroe," the doctor said, "I'm going to be perfectly frank with you. Your husband has been badly injured. As you may know, after emergency surgery in a base hospital in Iraq, he was airlifted here and spent over ten hours in surgery. Twice while in ICU, we had to readmit him to surgery and, I'm sorry, I have to tell you his condition is still critical. He's lost both legs, and he may yet lose his right arm. I need to warn you not to be shocked when you see him. His right eye is gone, and he received other extensive injuries. Now, all that being said, he's receiving the best medical care possible; we've got a pretty good track record here, and we'll do all within our power to aid his recovery."

"When can I see him, Doctor?" Anne asked, her face betraying the anguish and exhaustion clearly present.

Major Fry said, "He's under heavy sedation right now, but if you'd like, I'll take you up to ICU for a quick peek. After seeing him, I'd suggest you go to your hotel for rest and refreshment, and come back tomorrow for a longer visit."

The three of them went out to the hall and to the elevators. After another long walk, Captain Fry led them through the ICU area, where the rooms faced out to a central nurses' station. He halted before one of the rooms and stood back, motioning for Ken and Anne to step ahead. What they saw was a patient lying completely still on a bed, totally covered in bandages, with several tubes connected to him and an oxygen mask covering his nose which, as best they could tell, was the only part of his body not swaddled in gauze. When Anne followed his body contour downward and saw that it ended above the knees, she turned with a gasp and buried her face on Ken's shoulder.

Guiding her out of the room, Ken said, "Thank you, Doctor Fry. I think we'll heed your advice and head for the hotel. We're staying at the Novotel Kaiserslautern. I'll call the hospital desk and confirm our room numbers so you can reach us if needed." He gently led Anne down the long corridor to the elevators.

During the drive to the hotel, Ken attempted to engage his sister-in-law in light conversation, but she was unresponsive, and he noticed she kept wiping away tears. Seeking once again to distract her, he said, "This is an interesting part of Germany, Anne, with such a rich cultural and historic background. Though the city itself dates from the ninth century, it got its name because it was the favorite hunting ground for the ruler of the Holy Roman Empire, Frederick Barbarossa. The city still preserves the ruins of the emperor's castle, which is located in front of city hall.

"When I was here on business several years ago," he continued, "I was told that Barbarossa was one of the first rulers to raise a huge army to participate in the Third Crusade to retake the Christian Kingdom of Jerusalem after it fell to the Muslims under Saladin in 1187. Historians tell us the emperor's army of over one hundred thousand men marched overland to Asia Minor, where they defeated the Muslims twice, but the old emperor was not fated to enter the Holy Land. When a bridge over a river was crowded with soldiers slowly marching across, the ever-impatient Barbarossa decided to swim his horse to the other side, but he drowned in the attempt. He was so beloved by his German soldiers that they lost heart to continue in the crusade. Instead, they turned about, reversed course and returned to Germany.

"An ancient legend long held by Germans says that Barbarossa never died, but is asleep in the mountains of Bavaria, dozing on his throne along with his sleeping knights. According to the legend, when Germany needs him most, the old emperor will awaken and lead the nation back to greatness." Lost in her thoughts, Anne did not respond.

When they arrived at the hotel, a valet parked the car while Ken and Anne were escorted to the desk by a doorman. Greeted cordially by the desk clerk, they received their keys and went to their rooms. When they reached Anne's room, Ken told her to run a hot bath and take a refreshing nap; he'd call her later, and they would have supper.

The next few weeks were hard. Charles didn't awaken from the medically induced coma until the second week. Ken and Anne devoted all their time and attention to the badly wounded man. Anne was with him from sunup to sundown, and Ken took over for her during the night hours. It wasn't until the end of the third week that Charles was completely awake and responsive. When he realized that his brother had been at his side for two weeks, he adamantly insisted that Ken return to his work in Atlanta.

"Anne is here with me, Ken. Her mom is looking out for the kids so she can stay with me. Doctor Fry has arranged for her to stay in guest quarters here at the hospital complex for as long as necessary. You've got a business to run, and I insist that you go home—no ifs, ands, or buts about it. Go home. We'll be on the way to America soon enough according to Doctor Fry."

Though he protested, Charles remained stubbornly insistent, so Ken booked a flight back to Atlanta the next evening. When he got back to his office, there were a thousand things to catch up on, and he quickly became absorbed in his work. Anne called each evening to keep him up to date on Charles's status, and as the days and weeks passed, Anne became more cheerful and told him Doctor Fry had announced Charles would soon be ready to fly to Walter Reed Hospital. Six weeks after his arrival at Landstuhl, Charles had made enough progress to be airlifted back to the USA.

CHAPTER 4

The healing and rehabilitation of Major Charles Monroe was a long, slow, and painful process. He underwent four separate operations to remove fragments of the explosive device, and he suffered frequent severe headaches from his head wounds. He was comforted by the steady devotion of Anne, for she spent every minute she could with him.

Bob Healy, an accomplished pilot and wealthy client of Ken's, insisted on flying Anne in his private jet from Augusta to Washington and made this a regular practice. Bob had served in the air force during the Vietnam conflict and was active in veterans' concerns. He was an affable character and repeatedly told Anne he'd "romp and stomp" all over the army if Charles ever got slighted during his hospital stay.

On several occasions, Bob flew down to Augusta, swept up the children, and brought the whole family to Washington. He had a condo in nearby Maryland and insisted that Anne and the family stay there while visiting Charles. When Anne told Ken she was troubled about so much reliance on Bob, he laughed and said, "Bob Healy would rather fly than eat, and he loves the excuse to fly down to Augusta to bring you and the kids to Washington. After all, he'd rather be in the pilot's seat than anywhere else; and don't for a minute concern yourself about staying in his Maryland condo. He only uses it on rare occasions when he's in Washington to lobby on behalf of his fellow commercial builders or to browbeat some poor congressman who didn't vote right."

On a more somber note, he told her that Bob's middle son was a Special Ops soldier stationed in Afghanistan, and his oldest was a marine fighter pilot currently stationed aboard a carrier in the Persian Gulf. He told her Bob Healy was heavily involved both as a VA hospital volunteer in Atlanta and as an advocate for wounded and needy veterans.

The day finally came, six months after his arrival at Walter Reed, for Charles to go home. A VA hospital in Augusta could continue his rehabilitation. Bob again insisted on providing transportation and even arranged with one of his flying buddies to borrow a bigger private jet to accommodate the entire family.

When they boarded the plane, Bob asked Charles's son, Blake, if he'd like to sit in the copilot's seat during the return trip, and they all had a laugh as they watched how quickly Blake ran to the front to grab the seat before Bob could entertain second thoughts.

Ken picked up his brother and carried him down the narrow aisle to his seat. As he gently put him down in a window seat, Charles leaned over and said, "Sit by me, Ken, on the way home."

Charles looked in surprise at Anne, but she simply nodded and indicated Ken should do as his brother requested. When the plane attained altitude and the passengers began to unbuckle seat belts, Charles told Ken for the first time about the mysterious book the old priest had insisted on giving him. He shared his initial concern about bringing the book home, but the interpreter, Khadum, had described the probable fate of the book if it remained in Iraq.

Intrigued by the story, Ken asked, "How in the world did you manage to get the book out of the country?"

Charles told him about his friend, Phil Longstreet, who had agreed to take the book to Augusta with him since he was being rotated home within a few days. He went on to say, "As soon as Phil got home, he took the book over to our house and gave it to Anne, who put it where she always puts things that don't have a regular place—in the closet in the guest bedroom—and it's been sitting there all this time. I couldn't leave it in Iraq under those conditions, Ken."

After thinking about it for a moment, Ken turned to his brother and said in a quiet voice, "What do you plan to do about the book, Charles?"

"I plan to do everything in my power to find out what this book could possibly contain that would cause a man, a Christian priest, virtually with his dying breath, to insist that I take possession of it. I never got to talk to him, and those companions of his, fellow Christians, apparently knew nothing about its contents, though they told us he guarded it carefully on their long journey south."

"But didn't anyone at your base, perhaps an Iraqi, have even a tiny idea about what it contained?" asked Ken.

"All I know, Ken, is that the book isn't written in Arabic or any other current Middle Eastern language. I believe it's an ancient form of Aramaic, the language Jesus spoke, or perhaps a Persian or Turkish dialect, but that's supposition. I don't know, and I only had the book a short while before my encounter with an IED, so I didn't get far with any kind of investigation.

"The only thing I can say with any assurance is the book is written in an ancient tongue and that it's old and extremely vulnerable in present-day Iraq. What's intriguing, Ken, is that the old priest was so absolutely determined to keep it out of the hands of the Muslims. According to his Christian companions, he never told them anything other than the book was holy, and he always kept it with him, close by his side as they journeyed south.

"What I can see clearly now is that the book was so meaningful and precious to him that he protected it with his life, and when he knew he was about to die, he insisted that the book be given to me since there was no priest available in the area. Now it's up to me to unravel the mystery."

"Charles, I shouldn't have to say it, but it seems obvious to me your first and greatest priority to yourself and to those who love you is to concentrate on your program of rigorous physical rehabilitation. That's what Anne, the kids, and I want most for you, and each of us looks forward to being personally involved in whatever it takes to get you strong and healthy."

Ken continued, "You owe it to yourself and to your family. There's no way in the foreseeable future you're going to be able to go traipsing around the country investigating an old book. Your emphasis has to be on regaining your health. You're now out of Walter Reed and due to reenter the hospital in Augusta. It shouldn't be rocket science for you to see you're not ready for this kind of activity, and won't be for a while."

Charles looked at his brother fondly, smiled, and said in a gentle voice, "I know that, Ken. Believe me, no one is better able than I am to know my physical limitations. I've got a huge mountain to climb, and I've got to start climbing quickly if I want to improve; and you're right, of course. I owe it to my long-suffering family to continue this rigorous rehabilitation plan prescribed for me at Walter Reed, and I assure you I intend to. What I need, Ken, is a surrogate—someone to begin this investigation for me until I can get back on my feet, so to speak." He laughed at his own pun as he finished speaking.

Ken couldn't help smiling as he responded, "And do you have such a surrogate in mind for that task?"

Staring at his brother and becoming serious, Charles said, "Why do you think I asked you to sit in Anne's place on the way home? I was praying you had figured it out by now. Who else could I trust with this mission?"

Surprised, Ken exclaimed. "Wait a minute, brother. Hold on. While you'll be in the warm embrace of your family and involved in rehabilitation in Augusta, I plan to be back in Atlanta advising folks how to preserve and increase their fortunes. These folks are not only smart; they're fickle. If I'm not there, they'll find someone else. I don't have the luxury of time for that kind of venture, Charles."

Charles maneuvered to place his only remaining useful hand on Ken's wrist and quietly asked, "Ken, will you give me a week of your time? I've thought about this book all during the long months at Walter Reed, and, through Anne, I've been in touch with several of my former theology professors at Emory on a number of occasions and shared what little I knew about the book. Doctor Knox Coleman, my former faculty advisor and good friend, has even visited me at Walter Reed, and we've discussed the situation at great length. Because we're uncertain about the legality of my having the book, it was important to locate someone proficient in ancient Middle Eastern languages who would be discreet. Doctor Coleman has identified a party he believes would fit this category. What I need is someone to make this contact. Can't you do this for me, Ken?"

Ken didn't answer immediately. He thought about the situation. This book, whatever it contained, was of great importance to Charles and had more than likely sustained him during his darkest moments, the long weeks and months of agonizing therapy at Walter Reed. Perhaps the mystery of the book was one of the few things that diverted his attention away from his physical limitations. Now that his brother would be in the loving embrace of his family, he wanted him to concentrate on regaining health and strength. And, after all, what was Charles asking of him? Was it too much to spend a week at this task? And now, even though he was not a believer, his own curiosity had been stirred over this ancient book.

Turning to look directly at his brother's war-ravaged face, he said, "All right, Charles. I'll spend a week taking the book wherever you say, but you've got to promise me that, in return, you'll immediately begin your rehab, no matter how painful; and I'll have Anne and the kids to verify whether or not you keep to the schedule.

One other thing: after I've spent a week with this book and the interpreter, that's it, I'm done, but you've got to continue with your therapy, no matter how long and no matter how hard. Deal?"

"Deal," Charles replied.

For the rest of the flight and later, when they were home in Augusta, Charles shared the discussions he'd had with Doctor Coleman concerning a possible plan of action in regard to unraveling the mystery of the book.

"Doctor Coleman mentioned during one of our conversations that a few years back he had met the abbot of a small Syrian Christian monastery, a certain Mar Isaac, who, along with a handful of monks, had emigrated from Syria twenty years previously to West Virginia, where they established a monastery. He counts the abbot among his close friends and converses with him frequently about religious matters. Doctor Coleman has invited him, on several occasions, to address seminarians at Emory when early Christian history is being explored.

"Doctor Coleman went on to say that, during the course of their conversations, Abbot Isaac mentioned the great pride he and the Syrian community took in the growth and development of the monastery library that now housed one of the most complete collections of Eastern Orthodox Christian writings to be found in this country.

"It appears that many Christian families who emigrated from the Near East found the monastery library to be an ideal repository for the ancient and revered family manuscripts they brought with them from their native lands. Though he hasn't talked with the abbot recently, Doctor Coleman said he would be glad to give him a call if I decided this was the place to start an inquiry."

Ken couldn't help but notice the excitement so evident in his brother's voice whenever the subject of the book came up. *It's the only thing that sustains him,* Ken thought, *the only thing that succeeds in keeping his mind off the pain and rigors of the long healing process yet ahead, and he needs to be involved in this quest as much as his limitations will permit.*

"Okay, Charles, I'll leave it up to you to contact your Doctor Coleman and arrange a date and time for me to visit this monastery. While you do that, I'll head back home in the morning and take care of a few things at the office. Remember, our deal is that I'll worry about the book for a week while you concentrate on your rehabilitation."

Ken flew back to Atlanta the next morning. When he arrived at his office, he brought Mary Rogers up to date on his brother's health and rehabilitation and told her he was taking a week off to complete several business errands for Charles. He went to Cyril's office and told him about the mysterious book and his promise to Charles. Cyril agreed that Ken should undertake this effort for his brother and encouraged him to take longer, if necessary.

Knowing how involved Cyril was with the project he and the doctors were engaged in, Ken reviewed some complicated business strategies Cyril might use when he met with them in Ken's absence. Shortly after four o'clock, he went home and packed his bag with a week's worth of gear. Several hours later, he was on a connector flight to Augusta, and before midnight, he had taken possession of Charles's book and booked passage the next morning on a flight to Charleston, West Virginia.

CHAPTER 5

Hakim hurried down the alley on the outskirts of Tikrit a hundred or so miles northwest of Baghdad. Thus far, he'd avoided the numerous American armored patrols that frequently crisscrossed the streets in this restive city, but soon the sun would set, and darkness would render him safe. He knew the Americans pulled their patrols after dark to avoid the IEDs planted by the city's numerous insurgents. The absence of the Americans allowed the members of the dominant insurgent group, his own beloved group, Martyr's Revenge, and their imam to meet without fear of arrest to plan new strategies for driving the despised infidel from the land.

Hakim hated the American invaders of his homeland. As a member of the Sunni minority, but especially being a resident of Saddam's hometown of Tikrit, he and his family had profited greatly during the years Saddam's Baath Party ruled the country. Now, with Saddam's downfall, he had not only lost his privileged position as a highly paid government employee, he and the other minority Sunnis were frequent targets of majority Shiite revenge. Even here in Tikrit, where Sunnis were predominant, a great sense of loss of power and prestige was all-pervasive. The infidel Americans were responsible, and for this reason, Hakim had sought out and joined this, the most radical of the Sunni insurgent groups, and had fallen completely under the spell of the group's imam, Zaid al Rifia.

After the planning session was completed and various members were given their specific orders about continuing the struggle against the invaders and the cursed Shiites, Zaid motioned for Hakim to remain after the others departed.

"Hakim, son of Gabir, are you and your family well?"

"Yes, beloved of Allah, we're as well as can be in these difficult days. My brother is with the faithful in Afghanistan, where our struggle with the infidel Americans goes forward, and my father continues to provide information about their military dispositions around our city."

The Imam Zaid smiled as he said, "I know the faithfulness of your family, Hakim. I know we've always been able to count on you when important matters need to be resolved, but I asked you to remain behind, for I have a much bolder operation to share with you that's above and beyond whatever has been asked of you in the past."

"You have only to command, beloved of Allah. I exist to serve the Martyr's Revenge in whatever capacity you desire. Tell me what you want me to do."

"You will recall our lessons from the Hadith, the recollections of the Prophet—may peace be upon him—where we discussed the personalities of those so-called Christian apostles, those fishermen companions of Jesus, and how they lied and exaggerated as they composed their scriptures in order to deceive the world."

"Yes, I remember well, most worthy Imam, how the Prophet Mohammed—may his name be blessed among all the faithful—said these men were under the spell of the Evil One, and they wrote such things as never happened that still beguile and mislead Jesus's followers to this very day. Jesus was a prophet, but these blasphemers declared he was the Son of God."

"Hakim, you must know what I'm about to tell you is of great importance to our true believers, those who wish to rip away the veil of ignorance and lies that prevent millions of Christians from embracing our true faith. What I say to you now is told only to those who will be leaders among the faithful. One major hindrance exists that prevents us from introducing the longed-for caliphate that will bring justice into the world through means of Sharia Law. Are you ready for this revelation, my son?"

"Yes, my Imam. I am prepared to give my life in the struggle to pave the way for the glorious return of the caliphate," replied Hakim.

"Listen closely to what I have to tell you. It has come to us through the drunken remarks of a former Iraqi officer who works for the hated Americans that a few months ago, an ancient Iraqi manuscript held to be priceless by the Christians was stolen from our country and transported to the USA. One of the infidel American doctors took it with him to Augusta, a city in the state of Georgia. From what we understand, it's possible this book will reveal matters that will strengthen the Christian faith even though it's built on lies and distortions. Whatever it contains, once it is revealed, it will postpone the reintroduction of the caliphate, and that simply must not happen.

"Our brothers who live in America, faithful to Allah and to the cause of the caliphate, have been put on notice to observe and report on where this manuscript is and what is being done with it. This matter is extremely important to our leadership and has been designated a top priority operation."

"But, beloved of Allah, why should we be concerned that an old Christian manuscript has been stolen? Better such rubbish leave than to remain and contaminate our land with lies and distortions. How does it being in the land of the infidels affect us?"

"How does it affect us, little one? An infidel Christian monk revealed under torture that this book will glorify Christianity at the expense of Islam. He said it would annul once and for all the Islamic argument that Jesus' apostles were deceivers and liars. If this manuscript of ancient age make a great revelation that strengthens

Christians in their belief or in the integrity of those who were Jesus's followers, what do you suppose that will do to our centuries-old effort to demonstrate those followers were liars and deceivers who led men astray? It is our intention to do all within our power to prevent this book from seeing the light of day while we work diligently to destroy the Christian faith.

"Admittedly, many followers of the Prophet, those not blessed by Allah with insight into these weighty matters, go about the business of daily living blissfully unaware that the resurrection of the caliphate is the key to our final victory over the infidels. They are ignorant sheep. You, however, are one of the blessed ones on whom Allah's favor rests. It was Allah himself who led you to the Martyr's Revenge.

"Remember, Hakim, the caliphate will not be restored as long as the infidels in America are majority Christian believers. The Americans are the worst of the lot, inspired by Satan. Our dream will remain unfulfilled unless we are successful in removing the props that sustain Christian belief in America.

"It may surprise you to learn that Martyr's Revenge has many faithful sons in America. I am entrusting you with the task of leading them to find and destroy this book. No matter the cost, we must absolutely prevent this cursed book from being translated and printed in English. Should, Allah forbid, we prove to be unsuccessful in this effort, the issue of the caliphate will be delayed. The supreme leaders of the united groups formed to expel the infidels expect only success from you, Hakim.

"Upon news of your success in this matter, you will be embraced by the leadership and given a role of great responsibility. Money will be no problem, and members of the Martyr's Revenge now in America will be instructed to provide you with every assistance. You will communicate with me each Tuesday at precisely ten o'clock pm EST on the cell phone that will be given you before you board the plane in Jordan. Now these are most important instructions. You'll never refer to me by name. My code name for this mission is 'Amir,' while you will be known to our associates and in communication only as 'Sentry' for as long as you're in the land of the infidels. The book will always be referred to as 'package,' never by any other title. You must never mention the word 'book.'

"Arrangements have already been made for you to go to Jordan and board a flight to America. When you arrive in New York, you will be met by one of the Martyr's Revenge officers, who will have been informed about your mission. He will bring you up to date on what our agents have discovered about the book's whereabouts. He will also provide you with funds for this undertaking. You'll remain with him until further notice, communicating with me only at the appropriate time and only by the name 'Amir.' This is an imperative mission, my young friend. Many important individuals will view your progress with great interest. Now, if you have no further questions, go to your home and prepare for your departure. Tell no one, not even your parents, about your task."

CHAPTER 6

It had been an early morning flight. Ken had picked up his rental car at the airport in Charleston and was headed for the sparsely populated mountain area east of the capital, not far from the Virginia state line. He'd been told the trip to the town of Harkins Corner would take several hours, but he wasn't worried, for his appointment with the abbot arranged by Doctor Coleman was flexible.

The farther east he traveled, the less traffic he encountered, and the hills grew higher and the road more winding. Taking his time, he enjoyed the wild beauty of the land, and he didn't stop to eat until after one o'clock. The last fifty miles took him deep into the mountains, and by two fifteen, he rounded a curve and was in the town of Harkins Corner. He stopped at the Chamber of Commerce, where he was given directions to the monastery. The road that took him to his destination curved sharply upward until he finally saw the rustic sign proclaiming he was entering the grounds of Saint Matthew Orthodox Monastery, and visitors were always welcome.

He parked next to the only other car in the small parking lot and walked toward a gate in the cream-colored wall that seemed to completely enclose the monastery. As he entered the enclosure, he noticed a sign for a gift shop and started toward it until he was stopped by a young man dressed in a black robe.

"Excuse me, sir. Are you Mr. Monroe from Atlanta?"

When Ken said he was, the young man introduced himself as Brother Thomas and said he'd been asked to accompany Ken to the abbot's office. They walked through a walled courtyard filled with the rich scents of summer flowers. Hummingbird feeders were attached to several posts, and several of the tiny birds were fiercely occupied in driving their cousins away. Ken and the young monk walked up a set of stairs that led to a long corridor running along the side of the building.

Halfway down the corridor, Brother Thomas, who hadn't said a word during their walk, knocked on an ornate wooden door, opened it, and motioned for Ken to enter. As the door closed behind him, Ken saw he was in a secretarial alcove. Immediately ahead, a door opened, and a tall, bearded man walked toward him. Smiling, the man held out his hand.

"Mr. Monroe, I'm pleased to meet you. I am Mar Isaac, and you are most welcome to our monastery. Doctor Coleman called again this morning to remind me you were on the way. Many here in the West prefer to call me Abbot Isaac or Father Abbot, whichever is more comfortable. I trust your flight today, as well as the long drive, did not tire you unduly. Please, come into the office. Can I get you a cool drink or a coffee? Would you like a bite to eat?"

As Ken sat down, he replied, "Thank you, Father Abbot. No, I'm not tired, but a cup of coffee would be most welcome if it'd not be any trouble."

As the abbot walked to the outer office to get the coffee, he turned toward Ken and said he always looked forward to coffee when he returned from one of his frequent trips.

While both men sat back enjoying their coffee, they exchanged small talk about Atlanta, which the abbot visited from time to time when connecting to overseas flights. Ken told him about his investment firm there and explained what his role entailed with the company.

The abbot spoke about his long acquaintance with Doctor Coleman, Charles's professor at Emory University, and about their mutual participation in a number of religious gatherings through the years. He mentioned that on several occasions, he'd been invited by Doctor Coleman and the faculty to lecture at Emory's School of

Theology. He said that Doctor Coleman had visited the monastery on a number of occasions and frequently called on the resources of the monastery librarian for assistance with his own historical research.

As the abbot spoke, Ken took advantage of the time to study his host. The man had an olive complexion, a deeply lined forehead, and a beard that was long and almost pure white. Over his black robe he wore a wooden cross suspended on a gold chain. His eyes were dark, almost black, and he spoke with a trace of a foreign accent. Ken guessed him to be in his late sixties.

The office itself was sparsely furnished. It contained a large walnut desk with absolutely nothing on it, a walnut desk chair, and a matching credenza. A large painting in the Byzantine style of a saint was hanging on the wall behind the desk, and there were two mismatched guest chairs. That was it; no other paintings, bulletin boards, or anything else.

"I must admit that I am curious, Mr. Monroe," said the abbot as he placed his empty coffee cup in its saucer. "Doctor Coleman told me that he would rather have you explain in person how we here at Saint Matthew could be of assistance to you. It seemed a little out of the ordinary that the good doctor would have so little to say about your proposed visit."

Ken had wondered whether Charles had urged Doctor Coleman to be discreet in making this contact. Perhaps the lingering and unresolved matter of the book's legal ownership had prompted his brother to do so, but Charles had told him before he left Augusta to feel free to share whatever information he felt appropriate with the abbot.

Ken had already made up his mind that full disclosure was the best approach, so he proceeded to tell the abbot about the book— how it was so highly valued by the priest in Iraq, and how, before he died of his wounds, the old man had insisted the book be delivered to Charles because he was the Christian chaplain at the base. He also described Charles's injuries and present incapacities and how Ken had been asked to initiate the investigation. He had the book with him now and hoped someone at the monastery would be able to describe its contents.

After expressing his sorrow for the wounding and suffering of Ken's brother, the abbot said, "Tell me, Mr. Monroe, are you at all familiar with the Eastern Orthodox faith?"

"I confess, very little, Father Abbot," replied Ken. "I've visited orthodox churches in the past, both in Atlanta and Florida, but those were Greek churches, which I assume are somewhat different."

The abbot smiled as he said, "Yes, they are quite different, Mr. Monroe. Do not be embarrassed, for most Americans, as well as most Europeans, are, if you'll excuse me, dreadfully ignorant of Christianity east of Jerusalem. Inasmuch as our linguist, Doctor Bankkour, might be working closely with you and your brother to decipher the contents of the book you brought with you, permit me to share something about my ancient church, its accomplishments, its traditions, and sadly, its tragic history.

"The greatest early church historian, Eusibius of Caesarea, writing in the fourth century, tells us that the prince of the apostles, Saint Peter, established the church in Antioch and was himself its first patriarch. Church historians are in accord that Antioch was the first and the oldest Christian church, and Holy Scripture tells us it was in Antioch that its followers were first called 'Christians.' From Antioch, Christianity spread to other lands.

"The language spoken by our Lord and his disciples was Aramaic, which is more commonly referred to as Syriac today. So the earliest Christian writings and liturgy were in the Syriac tongue west of Jerusalem while east of the Holy City the writings were in Greek.

"Christian historians concur that Syriac scholars were instrumental in the study and interpretation of biblical literature. Once the Bible was translated into their language, Syriac scholars enriched the great libraries of the world with many commentaries and documents of great historical value. Tragically, during the Muslim persecution of our church down through the centuries, many of these ancient and irreplaceable manuscripts were destroyed.

"I am pleased to say, however, even with the loss of so many of our early Christian Aramaic documents, a number have survived and are among the oldest written manuscripts in existence. Today, they are the most treasured possessions of the world's greatest museums. In fact, the British Museum in London has the world's oldest known copy of the Gospels, written in Aramaic and copied from an even older manuscript at least sixteen centuries ago.

"Here's another fact the world knows little about, Mr. Monroe. Syrian Christians were among the first to obey our Lord's command to carry the Gospel to the farthermost corners of the world. From Antioch and Edessa, they went north, south, and east, converting countless thousands of Persians, Indians, Arabs, Armenians, Huns, and Chinese. Among these people, Syriac became the liturgical language used in their worship services. Archaeological expeditions in these lands continue to turn up religious articles with Syriac inscriptions to this day.

"I trust I'm not boring you, Mr. Monroe, but I wanted to ensure you understood at least the rudiments of Eastern Orthodox Christianity and its contributions to the Christian experience. Here in the West, Christians have so little knowledge of the spread of early Christianity in the East."

"Father Abbot, I must apologize. I simply had no concept, no idea of what you have described about the growth of Christianity in the East."

"Please, Mr. Monroe, there is no need to apologize," the abbot said with a smile. "From this little discussion, you now know more about the Eastern Orthodox Church than ninety percent of the Americans, and the Europeans as well. I thought a little insight might be helpful now and down the road in your quest for answers. I wanted you to understand we here at Saint Matthews are not novices when it comes to ancient manuscripts. By the way, since we've mentioned ancient manuscripts, you did say you have this mysterious book with you, didn't you?"

"I have it in the trunk of the car. It's a rather cumbersome bundle, old and fragile, so I thought it best to leave it there for the moment. Would you like for me to go and get it now?"

"Let me send for our Doctor Bankkour first. He not only teaches, catalogues all our books and documents, and serves as our valuable manuscript librarian, but he is a noted Middle Eastern linguist and quite an accomplished historian as well. I know Doctor Coleman values his work highly and no doubt anticipated his involvement in your quest from the start."

The abbot picked up his phone, dialed a number, and said something in what Ken assumed was Syrian. He placed the phone back into its cradle, stood up, and asked Ken to accompany him to the parking lot where Doctor Bankkour would join them. When they got there, waiting for them was the librarian, a handsome, dark-featured man who appeared to be in his early fifties.

"Mr. Monroe, this is Doctor Malik Bankkour, a most valued member of our faculty here, as well as our librarian and the custodian of our most treasured documents," said the abbot as the men shook hands. "I trust you will be staying with us while Doctor Bankkour studies the manuscript, Mr. Monroe? We have anticipated you would and have prepared our guest quarters for your use."

"That's kind of you, Father Abbot, but I didn't mean to intrude on your hospitality beyond the review of the book. I was quite prepared to stay in a local motel."

"Nonsense," responded the abbot. "We've looked forward to your visit and consider you an honored guest. You would do us a great favor to partake of our hospitality."

With that, the matter was settled. Ken thanked the Abbot, who excused himself, leaving Ken with Doctor Bankkour. Ken opened the trunk of his car, retrieved the bundled manuscript, and followed the librarian inside the building and down a long corridor. Doctor Bankkour opened a door and indicated Ken should enter before him into the large room that held a long walnut conference table surrounded by a number of upholstered chairs.

"What I've been told, Mr. Monroe, is that you bring with you an antique manuscript that's journeyed all the way from Iraq. I can understand your concerns about its fragile nature due to its presumed great age, but you'll be pleased to know we're now in a climate controlled room designed for situations such as this. I hope you won't be alarmed when I tell you most of the books brought to me are not nearly as old as their custodians might believe. Most, in fact, are from the past two centuries. May I ask you to place the manuscript on the table for our initial review?" said the linguist as he put on a pair of white cotton gloves. Then he looked at Ken, smiled, and said, "Please, don't worry about its condition or our handling of it. From this point onward we will observe all conservator amenities as though we were examining the Declaration of Independence."

After Ken placed the book on the table, Doctor Bankkour gently removed the cloth wrapping Anne had covered it with back in Augusta. Ken peered closely as the book was uncovered, for this was the first time he had seen it. Flecks of leather were left on the cloth wrappings as the linguist went about his task. Ken could see that the book was about twenty-four inches tall and eighteen inches wide. He estimated it to be twelve inches thick. From the beginning he had been amazed at the book's weight; in fact, it weighed more than the suitcase full of clothing he'd brought with him on this trip.

As he opened the book and examined the writing on the first page, the librarian smiled as he said, "The book is clearly written in a form of Aramaic. Do you know of this ancient language, Mr. Monroe?"

"All I know is that Aramaic is supposed to be the language Jesus spoke," replied Ken.

"Indeed, he did. Jesus and virtually everyone else in Judea at that time wrote and conversed in Aramaic," said Bankkour. "Do you know how ancient this language is, Mr. Monroe? It was the language used by the Assyrians when they established their empire almost three thousand years ago. It continued to be the language of choice used by the Babylonians, who succeeded the Assyrians, and by the Persians, who ruled the great land mass that stretched from Ethiopia all the way to India. For a great many years, Aramaic in these lands was the preferred language of choice, much as English is in the modern world today."

"Then I'm glad you've already determined what language the book is written in, Doctor. Perhaps by tomorrow we'll know what it's all about," said Ken.

Doctor Bankkour smiled as he looked at Ken. "It won't be quite that fast, Mr. Monroe. Let me tell you something about this ancient tongue. I think it might help you understand that our task could be rather complicated.

"Scholars have long determined there are at least four separate and distinct time periods for the Aramaic language. Each period contains significant changes in meaning that occurred in the spoken as well as the written language. These periods are generally referred to as Old Aramaic, Imperial or Assyrian Aramaic, Middle Aramaic, and Modern Aramaic, which is still in limited use in our own time. Now, those are the major time divisions and cover the three thousand years of the language, but the situation is even more complex than that. There are also different dialects to be considered as well. There are so many variables to consider, I don't know how long it might take to interpret the book, but it certainly might not be quickly done."

The linguist glanced at his watch and said, "But the hour grows late; it will soon be time for supper. I'll call one of the brothers to escort you to our guest quarters so you can freshen up after your long journey. If you'll give me your car keys, I'll also have someone bring your suitcase to your rooms."

Doctor Bankkour picked up the telephone, said a few words in what Ken guessed was Syrian, and within a few minutes a young monk appeared and asked for the keys to Ken's car. Shortly thereafter, an older monk, who introduced himself as Brother Gregory, asked Ken to follow him to the guest quarters. Doctor Bankkour said he would come to escort Ken to the refectory within the hour.

After another long walk and a climb up to the second floor, Brother Gregory opened the door to a surprisingly well-appointed apartment located at the end of the hall. After the monk departed, Ken explored his new surroundings and was pleased to find a small but comfortable living room, a bedroom overlooking a courtyard, and a bath with a large, walk-in shower. Shortly afterward, a knock on his door reminded him that his suitcase had arrived. After the young monk left, Ken resolved to snatch a quick shower before supper.

When they arrived an hour later in the refectory, Ken was invited to sit between the abbot and Doctor Bankkour. After the abbot led the community in prayer, one of the brothers walked to the lectern and began to read. The abbot leaned toward Ken and told him in a whisper that this ancient custom allowed the community yet another opportunity to read and hear the lessons in their ancient Syriac tongue. The meal was plain but good, with fresh vegetables that Ken learned were grown on the monastery farm. The reading ended ten minutes after it began, and the murmur of conversation among the fifteen or so gathered in the refectory encouraged Ken to ask a question.

"I hope you will forgive my ignorance, Father Abbot, but I had always thought the monastic life was a Western Christian custom. I did not realize it was practiced in the East as well."

The abbot laughed as he responded. "You are indeed forgiven, Mr. Monroe, for you share the views of most Western Christians. The truth about monasticism in Christianity is that it first flowered in the desert wastes of Egypt during the third century among the Copts, an Eastern Orthodox denomination. From there, it advanced eastward through Judea, Syria, Iraq, and even into the Persian Empire, long before Saint Benedict founded Western monasticism in Italy sometime in the sixth century.

"In the East, our churches have always considered monasticism as the most glorious form of the Christian experience, but there are clear differences between the Eastern practice of monasticism and its Western counterpart. The Western monastic way of life for most monks could be characterized by their withdrawal, either fully or in part, from society to devote themselves to a life of prayer, solitude, and contemplation. In the East, those who practiced monasticism were first and foremost missionaries, whose priority was to obey our Lord's command to go to the whole world and preach the Good News to all people. To be sure, they also led lives of prayer, solitude, and contemplation, but these were practices meant to educate and fortify them for their missionary ventures."

"And is that still the intent and purpose of Eastern monasticism? Here at this monastery, as well as at others?" asked Ken.

The abbot looked away for a moment before he responded. "That is still the purpose of this monastery, Mr. Monroe. Sadly, this is one of the relatively few Eastern Orthodox monasteries still operating, out of the thousands that once flourished. At one time Eastern Christian monasteries stretched all the way from Syria through Turkey, Iraq, Persia, and into China and southward from the Caspian Sea into southern India. Those who have hated us because of our Christian faith have succeeded in driving us out of most of these lands, including the land of my birth. Fierce and relentless persecution over the last five hundred years has reduced Eastern

Christians to a mere remnant of their former number, but we here at Saint Matthew Monastery still prepare and send our monks out to places in this country to minister to Christian refugees from the Near East in areas where they have settled."

"Now I'm confused," Ken replied. "You said persecution during the last five hundred years had dramatically reduced the number of Eastern Christians. I believe you must be referring to Muslim persecution, and since Mohammed, the founder of that religion, was born sometime around 600 AD, are you saying there was no persecution for the first several hundred years after Mohammed died?"

"No, I am not saying that at all, Mr. Monroe. There are things you need to know about Islam and those who follow that religion in order to understand the suffering and persecution of Eastern Christians through the years," said the abbot. "During Mohammed's lifetime, he and his followers were preoccupied with establishing Islam in the Arabian Peninsula. At this same time, the Christian faith had, for many years, been predominant in what we now call Syria, Turkey, Iraq, Judea, Lebanon, Egypt, and North Africa. There were even many Christians in Persia and China during this period as a result of the labors of Eastern missionaries.

"Shortly after Mohammed died, his followers embarked on a campaign of ruthless conquest that swept all the way into France before it was stopped. Syria, Judea, Egypt, North Africa, Turkey, Persia, and Iraq all fell to the Muslim conquest. Only when the Christians in those lands surrendered was peace declared. Until their surrender, Muslim armies carried on a jihad, or Holy War, against all unbelievers. After surrender, Christians and Jews were allowed to continue practicing their respective religions only by payment of a special tax called Jizya, but terrible restrictions applied.

"Christians and Jews, for the most part, were treated with contempt as second-class members of society. Christians were forbidden to build new churches or to even repair existing ones, so it would be fair to say that Muslim persecution for us began shortly after Mohammed's death, but the tempo of persecution picked up dramatically five hundred or so years ago. Before then, the persecutions were of a more local and intermittent nature."

"Then what caused the persecution of Christians to accelerate around five hundred years ago? We're talking about the time period, roughly, of Columbus's discovery of America."

"There were two developments that spawned the intense maltreatment of Christians that took place in this time period, Mr. Monroe: the conversion to Islam of the Mongol tribes in Asia, and the advance of the Muslim Turks through Asia Minor in what is now Turkey. With the collapse of the Byzantine Roman Empire five hundred years ago under Muslim assault, former Christian lands were devastated. Christian inhabitants were slaughtered by the tens and hundreds of thousands. Churches and monasteries were looted and destroyed, and many ancient and invaluable Christian and secular manuscripts were lost or destroyed. Perhaps the manuscript in your possession is one of the few to survive this desecration. Let us hope this proves to be the case.

"In the decades that followed after Constantinople fell to Islamic forces, hundreds of Christian dioceses in Muslim-dominated lands simply vanished. In Turkey alone, almost four hundred dioceses were reduced to three.

"Even within the last one hundred fifty years, the world has witnessed one atrocity after another committed against Christians by Muslims, and, sadly, the world has remained largely silent. It is a well-documented fact that more than ten thousand Christians were slaughtered in what is now Lebanon in this period. Many thousands more were murdered in Syria at the same time.

"Mr. Monroe, did you know that barely over a hundred years ago, more than a hundred thousand Christian Armenians were brutally slain by Turkish Muslims? Even as late as World War I early in the twentieth century, more than half a million Armenian Christians died at the hands of Turkish Muslims.

"In Iraq, the land where your book was found, thousands of Christian Iraqis were slaughtered by Muslim Iraqis in the persecutions of the 1930s, well within my lifetime. These persecutions continue, Mr. Monroe, and the world still remains largely silent. Our own ancient Eastern Orthodox congregation, founded by the Apostle Peter himself, once numbering in the millions, is now a mere shadow of its former self.

"The exodus of Christians from Iraq since Saddam was overthrown has accelerated dramatically. Virtually every Christian in a Muslim country wants to leave his native land. Isn't it ironic that today there are more Eastern Orthodox Christians in Europe, Australia, and America than there are in their original homeland?"

"I had no idea about the extent and recent history of these persecutions," Ken replied. "I don't believe I've ever heard or read about these terrible oppressions."

The abbot looked at Ken with sadness in his eyes as he responded. "You did not know, and the American people do not know, because the American media chooses not to publicize the persecution of Christian minorities by Muslims, Mr. Monroe. For reasons of their own, the media chooses to portray Muslims as the victims of Western aggression and thirst for oil. Forgive me for asking, Mr. Monroe, but would you mind telling me, are you an active member of a Christian denomination?"

Ken sighed and looked down at the table. "No, Father Abbot, I am not an active participant in any church organization. In fact I am an unbeliever, a religious skeptic, if you will. I'm only involved in this enterprise because my brother is not physically able to take part. He is a Methodist minister, an active Christian, and I might add, a good man. On the other hand, I'm the 'black sheep' in the family, much to my family's distress."

"I will pray for you, Mr. Monroe. I believe faith is a precious thing, easily lost, but not as easily regained. You say you are the 'black sheep.' I would remind you, I serve a risen Lord who goes out of his way to find lost sheep. But here I am, forgetting my role as host. I know you must be tired from your long journey today, and I am keeping you from your rest."

With a signal from the abbot, Brother Gregory appeared and motioned for Ken to follow him, and they walked back to the guest quarters. Once settled in, Ken called Charles and told him about the day's events. He revealed Doctor Bankkour's assessment that the book was indeed written in Aramaic as Charles thought, but mentioned the man's caution that the translation was dependent on which version of Aramaic was used in the manuscript's construction. He also repeated the linguist's warning that not all manuscripts were as old as people thought.

Ken said that he would stay at the monastery for a few more days, but after that he would need to return to Atlanta to tend to business matters, leaving the book in Doctor Bankkour's hands. He told Charles he was impressed with the linguist and believed him to be a capable scholar.

Charles asked Ken to express his personal appreciation both to the abbot and to Doctor Bankkour for their willingness to undertake this project. After promising to keep his brother posted, Ken realized he was more tired than he had thought so he ended the conversation and turned in for the night.

The telephone woke him. Looking at the clock on his bedside table, he saw it was only five fifteen a.m. Rubbing the sleep from his eyes, he picked up the phone and was greeted by the obviously excited voice of the linguist.

"Mr. Monroe, I'm sorry to disturb you at this early hour, but I have exciting news about the book that I think you will be interested in. If you could be ready in ten minutes, I'd like to have you join me for an early breakfast."

Catching the linguist's excitement, Ken was ready in seven minutes, and was eager to learn what had caused the excitement when the man knocked on his door three minutes later. Putting his finger to his mouth to indicate silence, Doctor Bankkour led the way down to the corridor and past the room where Ken had left the book the day before. Stopping at the next door, he opened it and motioned for Ken to enter. It was obviously an office, but the desk had been swept clean and now served as a table complete with coffee and sweet rolls. The linguist poured two cups of coffee and asked Ken to help himself to the rolls, then both men sat down.

"I do apologize for the early wake-up call, Mr. Monroe, but I confess I could wait no longer. I had no idea your manuscript was anywhere near as religiously startling and historically important as I have come to discover in one short evening's work. You don't know the depth of my emotions whenever I come across something that even approaches the rare quality of the manuscript you have brought with you.

"To my complete surprise, the manuscript is written in what scholars refer to as Modern Aramaic and is in the Antiochian dialect, so I could begin the translation faster than I originally thought when we talked yesterday. I could hardly wait for our supper to be over so I could hurry back to the book, and by one a.m. I had a rough translation of the first few pages. You have without question a wonderfully rare and religiously important find, Mr. Monroe, one that has the potential to excite Christian scholars throughout the world if it contains what I think it does and if it is deemed genuine."

Ken was visibly perplexed as he said, "I don't understand your excitement, Doctor. You have told me that the book is written in Modern Aramaic, so why would something that is in a modern language be of much interest to Christian scholars?"

The linguist smiled as he replied. "Let me explain, Mr. Monroe. When I say Modern Aramaic, I am referring to the latest Aramaic, but Modern Aramaic can be dated as far back as 600 AD. I believe this book could well have been written as early as that and, moreover, it more than likely could be a copy of an even earlier work now lost to us."

"Now you have gotten me excited. Tell me what it contains that might rouse the interest of religious scholars," said Ken. "I know you didn't wake me at this hour and invite me to an early breakfast just to tell me we had an old book on our hands."

"What I am about to share with you, Mr. Monroe, is based on a preliminary review of the first few pages of translation. I believe I can estimate the age of the book, but I can't verify the contents as being genuine. In fact, I doubt anyone could, for what I believe it contains is unique and has never before been revealed. This is a rather convoluted explanation, but it is crucial to what I believe could be contained in the book.

"This is what excites me, Mr. Monroe. The book appears, on the surface, to be an early Christian writing that describes in great detail the missionary activities undertaken by the first Christian disciples after Jesus's Resurrection. That is as much as I feel comfortable in saying at this moment. Much examination and testing remains to be done before it can either be verified as genuine or exposed as a fake."

Taken by surprise, Ken said, "A fake? How could that be? Could those terrified Iraqi Christians who risked their lives to keep this old book out of the hands of the insurgents have possibly considered it as being a fake? Did the old priest die protecting a manuscript he knew to be phony? Why didn't they give it up instead?"

Doctor Bankkour responded calmly. "Mr. Monroe, I never intended to imply that those brave souls who brought the book down from the mountains ever believed it was anything but genuine. I'm certain they thought it was worth every sacrifice, even of their lives, but scholars who spend their days examining old documents recognize that there are at least five forged documents for every genuine one that comes to them. Forgers are clever rascals. Considering the vast amount of money chasing ancient artifacts, a few of the brightest and most skillful of these forgers can manufacture a manuscript that even our most astute museum curators can be taken in

"You're right, Doctor. Now that I think about it, I should have considered that the survival alone of something apparently this old defies all the odds. For a manuscript written countless centuries ago to have lasted into our day seems to me to be pretty incredible. So tell me, at this moment do you honestly believe the manuscript could have been written more than a thousand years ago yet remain unknown and undiscovered for all these years?"

For a few moments Doctor Bankkour remained in silent thought. Then he replied, "The Dead Sea Scrolls remained hidden in a cave in the Judean Wilderness for two thousand years before being accidentally discovered by an Arab shepherd boy looking for a lost lamb. The famous apocryphal Gospel of Thomas, written in the second century, was found buried in pottery in the sands of Egypt eighteen centuries later. Fragments of a Roman library, charred and buried by the eruption of Mount Vesuvius in the first century of the Christian era are being carefully restored and translated in Italy. A century ago historians found important ancient Christian manuscripts that no one knew existed in an obscure monastery in the Sinai Desert.

"I say all of this lends credence to the age of this book. Anything's possible, Mr. Monroe, but I suggest we move cautiously and with discretion until we can get a better handle on what we have here. Let's reserve judgment for now and see what further translation and examination reveals. I'm cautiously optimistic, however.

"With your permission I'd like to invite several linguists and biblical historians to join me in this examination. They're all good and true friends with impeccable scholarly reputations, and we've collaborated on a number of projects over the years. What is more important, they'll work at no charge should they be allowed limited and specific commentary rights. I'm confident they will agree on absolute secrecy, for they know that premature publicity would seriously impede our research. I trust them and their scholastic integrity.

"Verification can be a long and laborious process, Mr. Monroe, and their skill and talent will allow us to shorten the investigation time considerably. When we have made progress in our research, perhaps we could all meet to bring you and your brother up to date. If not, we can always use the monastery. Would this be satisfactory to you?"

Ken considered the linguist's suggestion. Actually, there were few other choices. Months of scholastic research lay ahead. He knew he needed to get back to Atlanta where his work was piling up. He also thought that Charles should profit from the months of rehabilitation ahead and, hopefully, would get some measure of his strength back. The scholars could meet in privacy at his office, and he was sure Bob Healy would jump at the chance to fly Charles to Atlanta.

Ken reached out to shake the linguist's hand. "That works for me, and I will arrange for us to all meet at my office in Atlanta at a mutually agreeable time if that is convenient for your team."

Doctor Bankkour smiled and said, "Then shall we have a second cup of coffee?"

CHAPTER 7

At precisely ten o'clock p.m. on the first Tuesday of the month, a phone call was placed from New York to Tikrit, Iraq.

Amir: "Yes?"

Sentry: "I am reporting in from New York as instructed, Amir."

Amir: "I trust your trip was pleasant and not too tiring."

Sentry: "Thank you, it was an uneventful flight. I also thank you from the bottom of my heart for this opportunity to retrieve the package that should never have been exported. The friend you told me to expect was waiting for me at the baggage claim when I arrived. He and his associates have managed to trace the package to Augusta as you had indicated. It seems that an infidel American doctor brought the package to this city. We have purchased tickets to Augusta and will fly there on Thursday to try to trace the package to an address. Several associates from Atlanta are already on the way to Augusta to perform a preliminary investigation."

Amir: "Then have a safe journey to that city, and let me hear from you next week. Important people have assured me of their interest in your quest."

CHAPTER 8

A t eleven a.m. on a windy day in October, Bob Healy landed his plane at Fulton County Airport. When Ken and Charles exited the plane, they found, to their surprise, a specially equipped van there to meet them. The driver informed them that Cyril, Ken's boss, had insisted on providing this vehicle to transport Charles to the meeting. Since the group wasn't scheduled to meet until two p.m., Ken instructed the driver to take them to Mary Mac's restaurant on Ponce de Leon Avenue.

"You rarely get to Atlanta, Charles," he said to his brother. "Now that you're here, get ready for a true culinary experience. Their fried chicken is to die for."

Charles looked at his brother, grinned, and said, "You forget that yours truly spent over six years at Emory. Did you think that during all those years of prowling around Atlanta I never ran across Mary Mac's? That place is an Atlanta landmark if there ever was one, but, hey, I'm surely not arguing with you. Let's go. You couldn't have picked a better place."

The meal was everything they could wish for, but Ken most enjoyed spending the time with his brother. It was all too easy to observe the physical results of his injury. Although he had gained back a small amount of weight, he was still many pounds short of where he should be, and his face showed nasty pink scars where shrapnel had struck him. Ken could see that Charles was excited about their meeting, and that was a good thing. Anything that would take his mind off the grueling drudgery and pain of his rehabilitation was well worthwhile in Ken's book.

Later, when they were back in the van and headed to Brinkley & Todd's to meet with the scholars, Charles put his hand on his brother's shoulder and said, "Ken, I don't know how to thank you for bringing this all about. If you hadn't pitched in and been willing to take charge of this investigation, that book would still be sitting on a shelf in my closet back in Augusta."

"Well," Ken replied, "I certainly don't see myself as having been in charge of anything. I was simply filling in for you until you were ready and able to take over, which, by the way, you'll soon be set to do, and then, on the day you step back in, I'll be more than ready to step aside. I'm a financial advisor, Charles, not a biblical historian, minister, or a linguist. This is your adventure, not mine. I've simply been your substitute, and that's been my purpose from day one. In fact, I've told Doctor Bankkour, the monastery linguist, on several occasions not to divulge information about the project to me, but rather to bring us both up to date at this meeting. It's your baby, Charles, and what we hear today will be brand new to both of us."

When the van pulled to the curb on Peachtree Street at their destination, Charles reached over, grabbed his brother's arm, and said, "I'm nowhere near ready, Ken. The medical team in Augusta has outlined a series of operations that entail extensive rehab, but we can talk about this on the way back to Augusta. For now, let's put that aside and meet the experts. I'm excited about whatever it is they're prepared to tell us."

They took the elevator to the third floor where Brinkley & Todd had a large conference room. As the door opened, both Cyril and Mary came forward to greet them. Each of them had met Charles before he went to Iraq and were anxious to make him as comfortable as possible for this meeting. It was with no small degree of pride that Cyril stepped forward to open the doors wide while

Ken pushed Charles's wheelchair into the conference room. The room itself was, in a word, elegant. No expense had been spared in its furnishings, and Cyril was reminded yet again of his successful argument with his partners that their customers deserved no less than the best in accommodations.

The five men at the conference table turned to face the new arrivals. Doctor Bankkour, the monastery linguist and Ken's recent contact, quickly got up to shake Charles's hand. "And this must be Reverend Monroe, who risked so much to bring this ancient manuscript to safety here in America. On behalf of thousands of Eastern Christians who have sought sanctuary in America and Europe over the years, I thank you, Reverend Monroe, for this truly miraculous rescue of what appears to be an irreplaceable Christian treasure.

"In a few moments, we'll begin to grasp how important this find is, but for now, please, make yourselves comfortable in this beautiful room. We are truly appreciative that Mr. Todd has made this excellent room available for us. Now, permit me to introduce these eminent gentlemen, scholars all. I'm sorry your former professor and mentor, the esteemed Doctor Coleman, could not be with us at this meeting, but he has so many scheduled commitments that we fully understand."

Ken wheeled Charles to the head of the table, then seated himself to his brother's left. Mary and Cyril excused themselves and closed the doors behind them as they left the room. Doctor Bankkour stood at the other end of the table facing Charles and proceeded to introduce the men seated along both sides of the table.

"Seated to my right is Doctor Gabriel Sabha, formerly of Damascus University in Syria. Since coming to this country five years ago, Doctor Sabha is professor of ancient languages at Saint Cyprian's Theological Institute. He has written extensively about the Aramaic language, and his works are currently indispensable textbooks in several American universities."

Doctor Sabha was a short, overweight man in his fifties with a receding hairline and a thick grey beard. Ken thought that except for his physical size, he bore a remarkable resemblance to the abbot.

"Seated next to Doctor Sabha, we have Father Michael Fyvia, who's an internationally recognized archaeologist and whose most recent excavation was the Roman fortress several miles south of Izmir in Turkey. He is dean of Orthodox studies at the McLaughton Institute for Christian Research, as well as professor of New Testament studies. He's only recently returned from the Vatican library in Rome, where he was called upon to take part in interpreting an ancient Syriac manuscript that had only recently been discovered among the many items that have yet to be brought to light there."

Father Michael smiled and looked embarrassed at his introduction. He was a tall, elderly man, probably in his late sixties, with long white hair and a full white beard. He was dressed in the black habit of his priestly calling and fingered a small golden cross hung about his neck.

"On the other side of the table, sitting opposite Doctor Sabha, we have Doctor Allen Morse, Regent Professor of Oriental and Near Eastern history at Thomas Wallace College and Fellow of the Augustus Fillmore Museum of Near East History in Maryland."

Doctor Morse was a short man of small, even delicate physique, probably in his middle forties. He apparently shaved his head to disguise his natural baldness and seemed to be of a nervous disposition, for he kept tapping a pencil on the table during the introductions.

"And last, but certainly not least, we have Doctor Martin Szabo, formerly dean of Fine Arts, Basra University in Iraq. Doctor Szabo currently serves as special advisor in cultural affairs to the US government and consultant to the national government of Iraq. He recently completed a monumental study of the Muslim conquest of the Persian Empire which is being translated into four languages at last count."

Doctor Szabo was a surprisingly young man, tall and swarthy, with a winning smile. If he had to guess, Ken would put his age in the mid-thirties. He was certainly the most flashily dressed of all present, wearing a yellow shirt, gold tie, and a purple sports coat.

"I apologize for the somewhat lengthy introductions, but since this is our first get-together as a working group, I wanted Reverend Monroe and his brother to know something about the scholars present who have worked so diligently on transcribing the early chapters of this ancient document. All of them are nationally recognized in their respective fields and are well-qualified for the work at hand. Each has generously provided a great many hours of intense research at Saint Matthew's, enabling us to disclose the fruits of our labor to you, Reverend Monroe, and to your brother.

"We'll make every effort today to be clear and concise in describing our work up to this point. I call on Doctor Sabha, our senior linguist, to open our meeting with his explanation of the Aramaic used in this manuscript. Doctor Sabha, the floor is yours."

The Syrian professor turned toward the brothers and said, "Before discussing the language of the manuscript, Reverend Monroe, I want to express my sincerest appreciation for the courage it took to get this book out of the carnage that's Iraq today. You made the right decision, and we have you to thank for preserving it for this study. Had you not made that monumental decision, I fear the book would have fallen into far less sympathetic hands and, more than likely, it would have either been destroyed by fanatics or illicitly sold to unscrupulous antiquities dealers who would have dismantled it and sold its separate pages to equally unscrupulous buyers. In any case, as an historical and religious document, it would have been lost to the world forever.

"Now, about the book. There are a few things you should

understand as we begin this work. Although lengthy, it is necessary to go into a bit of detail about the language we will be dealing with so you might better understand what a treasure you have rescued.

"As you already know, the manuscript is written in Aramaic, an ancient Semitic language that goes back in time more than three thousand years and probably much further back than that. Did you realize that Arabic, Assyrian, Ethiopic, and Hebrew are all derived from Aramaic? Historians tell us that the ancient Assyrian, Babylonian, and Persian empires that stretched all the way from India to Abyssinia utilized Aramaic as their official language.

"What is not commonly known is that for many years Jewish scholars employed Aramaic rather than Hebrew in their writings, and for several centuries, Aramaic remained the predominant language utilized by the Jews in their religious practices. Scholars have known for many years that more than two hundred verses in the Old Testament were originally written in Aramaic rather than Hebrew.

"Of course, you're familiar with the Dead Sea Scrolls concealed in caves in the Judean wilderness for two thousand years and found in the 1940s by an Arab shepherd boy. While most of the world assumes that all the bits and pieces of manuscripts discovered there were written in Hebrew, the truth is that many of the fragments were written in Aramaic.

"Until recent years, biblical scholars had thought that the New Testament was first written in Greek, then translated into other languages. Now, a growing number of scholars argue that the earliest Christian manuscripts, including the New Testament, were first written in Aramaic, then translated into Greek. Linguists tend to refer to Christian Aramaic as Syriac, and one of the earliest known Christian Bibles is written in Syriac and is called the Peshitta. There are literally thousands of Syriac manuscripts that are treasured possessions of many of the world's greatest museums.

"Reverend Monroe, I see you have a question?"

"Doctor Sabha, I understand that Aramaic has been around for millennia, and I assume there are probably definite historical age classifications for the language. If this is so, what estimated age is the Aramaic used in this book?"

The Syrian smiled as he answered. "You are correct, Reverend Monroe. Actually, there are at least ten or twelve unique historical divisions of Aramaic that have been identified by linguists through the years, but for simplicity's sake, we'll consider only the four major classes of the language.

"The first of these is called Ancient Aramaic, which was in use between 900 BC and 700 BC; then there is Imperial Aramaic, the official language of the Assyrian, Babylonian, and Persian empires during the period 700 BC to 300 BC. Next came what is known as Middle Aramaic, the language used in many of the Dead Sea Scrolls and in the earliest Christian writings from about 200 BC to 200 AD. This was followed by Late Aramaic, in use from about 200 AD to around 800 AD, and last, there's Modern Aramaic, which has been in use since around 800 AD. Modern Aramaic, Reverend Monroe, is still the language of choice in small isolated communities in Turkey, Syria, Iraq, and Iran.

"To specifically answer your question, the Aramaic used in your manuscript is a version of Late Aramaic, but I must defer to our historian, Doctor Morse, who has worked diligently to establish a date for this document. Please, forgive my intrusion on your time, Reverend Monroe. Perhaps I'm regressing into a typical and tiresome college professor's role, but I wanted to present you with the historical and religious background of this ancient language before discussing your manuscript and the place where it probably was written."

Still fidgeting with his pencil, Morse stood and looked at Charles as he said, "The short answer to your question about the time frame of the Aramaic found in your manuscript surprised us. It is definitely Late Aramaic, as Doctor Sabha has stated. All of us are in agreement on that score. Furthermore, the evidence is convincing that the manuscript was written at the famous school which was located at Diar Mar Elia, the Monastery of Saint Elijah near Mosul, Iraq.

"This monastery was founded around 500 AD. We know that Baselius II, the abbot at Saint Elijah around 800 AD, was a Syriac theologian of great renown who attracted many scholars to the school, which became a center for learning throughout the Middle East. We're familiar with other manuscripts that originated from that school, each with a unique wording and certain inflections that has led us to agreement on that issue. The school at Saint Elijah was, for many years, referred to as the Mother of Bishops since so many future Eastern Christian bishops received their education there.

"Now, as to its preparation. Are you familiar with vellum, Reverend Monroe? That's the animal skin the ancient writers employed as a writing surface before the advent of paper. It was and is to this day a time-consuming, labor-intensive process. It requires the cleaning, bleaching, and stretching of the animal skin on a frame, and then the meticulous scraping of it with special knives to remove all the flesh.

"To create tension, the craftsman has to alternate between wetting the skin with water and allowing it to dry numerous times. The finishing process usually includes lightly roughing it with pumice, then adding lime or some other substance to allow it to accept writing. Of course, the durability of vellum depends, first of all, upon the care in which it was prepared, and secondly, upon the type of animal skin used. This manuscript, though we believe it to be over one thousand years old, is in unusually good condition, solid evidence that it was prepared by experts and cared for lovingly down through the centuries. We believe it's written on sheepskin vellum, which is one of the better sources."

Ken, knowing his brother would be interested in communicating with the monks who might tell him more about Syriac manuscripts, raised his hand and asked, "Is it possible for investigators to visit that monastery and its school in Mosul?"

"Unfortunately, Mr. Monroe, Saint Elijah, the monastery and its school, now lie in ruins. They were first destroyed around 1750 when Persian ruler Tahmaz Nadir Shah led his Muslim army to the place, killed many of the monks, and demolished the monastery buildings. Though it was partially rebuilt around one hundred years ago, it was badly mauled again in the recent war when American forces learned that Saddam had hidden a number of his tanks there. They thoroughly bombed the area, and the destroyed tanks now litter the grounds that once were carefully tilled gardens of the monks. The monastery grounds now house a US army outpost." He smiled at the other members of the group as he added, "I don't think visitors are welcome at the site these days."

Turning toward Charles, Morse continued, "To briefly sum up, our research tells us, because it was written in Late Aramaic, the manuscript was completed before 900 AD, more than likely at the library of the Monastery of Saint Elijah in Mosul, Iraq. At a later time, we surmise that it was sent to another Iraqi monastery sometime before the destruction of 1750, where it probably remained, according to the Iraqi Christians who brought it to you. From these facts that we know or believe, and from the subject matter in the book, we can draw a few tentative assumptions. We've come to the conclusion, after much discussion and study, that the manuscript is a ninth-century copy of an even older manuscript going back at least to the late first century AD."

Ken could see the excitement on his brother's face and thought that, in spite of his physical handicaps, this meeting was so good for him. It took him, if only for a brief spell, away from the constant pain of his injuries which were enhanced by his dogged determination to faithfully perform the strenuous exercises of his ongoing rehabilitation.

Charles leaned forward in his wheelchair and eagerly asked, "But what exactly is this book about, Doctor? What does its text tell us? I can see excitement in your eyes and the eyes of all of you in the room. You wouldn't be here today if this was merely an old, pious book. No, your eyes give you away, so tell us, what has so excited you?"

Doctor Bankkour laughed as he responded. "Ah, Reverend Monroe, you sense the exhilaration we all feel, and you're now inquiring about the thrill each of us feels about the contents of this book, the reason we so-called experts have suffered each other's idiosyncrasies during our long hours together, the glue that has held us together. To provide the answer to your question, I'm compelled to call on my distinguished religious colleague, Father Michael Fyvia. Father Michael, tell them why we're so animated."

The old priest was slow to rise from his chair, but when he did, he directed a question to Charles. "Reverend Monroe, I know from your studies at Emory that you're well versed in early Christian history. Tell me, what do you know of Saint Ignatius of Antioch?"

Charles thought for a moment, then said, "I recall that Saint Ignatius is one of the earliest of the Fathers of the Church. I believe he was rumored to be an associate or disciple of the apostle Peter; that, in later life, he was condemned by the Roman emperor and sentenced to die in the Coliseum in Rome."

"You're absolutely correct, Reverend Monroe. Please be patient with me as I introduce the author and subject of the manuscript. Perhaps you also know that the Eastern Syrian Christians believe their denomination dates from the time of the Apostle Peter and that Peter himself was the first bishop of Antioch, one of the most important cities in the Roman Empire.

"We Syriac Christians believe Saint Ignatius was Antioch's third bishop, appointed by the Apostle Peter himself to lead the church in Antioch. Saint Ignatius lived from around 40 AD to sometime during the early years of the second century when he died a martyr to the faith in Rome.

"In the Eastern Orthodox church we have always venerated him and call him Ignatius the Illuminator because he himself was a brilliant light in the spiritual darkness of those years when Christians were persecuted by the Roman authorities.

"Historians tell us that when the Roman Emperor Trajan celebrated his victories over the Dacians and Scythians sometime around 110 AD, he commanded that all the people in the empire were to worship the gods of Rome in thanksgiving for Rome's victorious campaign. Anyone who ignored or failed to obey the emperor's decree was subject to the penalty of death.

"When Trajan visited Antioch, Ignatius was summoned before him and accused of defying the emperor by not worshiping the Roman gods. When asked by the emperor to reconsider, Ignatius refused, saying he worshipped only the One True God and his Son, Jesus Christ. For that, he was condemned to die and was taken in chains to Rome, where he was to be displayed as an enemy of the state in front of the crowds in the Coliseum before being thrown to the lions for the Romans' entertainment.

"You no doubt remember from your seminary days, Reverend Monroe, that Saint Ignatius left us a series of epistles to the various churches as he was being transported to Rome. These letters were of great importance, as the theology of the early church was still being formed, and they are quite valuable, for Christian manuscripts of this era are so rare. Our link to those days in written form is provided only by the Gospels and Epistles contained in the Bible and the letters of Saint Ignatius and Saint Clement, plus a handful of fragmentary lines from a few other church notables.

"Today most Christian scholars are in agreement that Saint Ignatius was a disciple of the apostles, and his name is closely associated with Peter, Paul, and John. There's an ancient tradition that Ignatius was a fellow countryman and companion of Saint Luke and that Ignatius corresponded frequently with him.

"Let us return for a moment, if you will, to the Monastery of Saint Elijah in Mosul. In 1743, Persian invaders gave an ultimatum to the monks to convert to the Muslim faith or die. They refused, and around one hundred fifty were slaughtered on the spot. Since that time, the monastery has been virtually abandoned and, except for a brief time of limited repair a hundred years ago, had fallen into decay as described by Doctor Morse. I tell you all this to introduce your manuscript, Reverend Monroe. We believe it was produced there in the ninth century, based on an inscription found at the beginning of the book.

"We feel scholastically comfortable with the inscription on the first page of the book left by a monk we believe to have been closely associated with Ephraim, known to have been the abbot of Saint Elijah Monastery around 850 AD. This notation is inscribed in the upper left margin of the first page of the manuscript, as it is in several other ancient works we have knowledge about, no doubt having been so ordered by that abbot. We have translated it as follows:

I, Elias of Sumayi, senior scribe in the library of the glorious Monastery of Saint Elijah, do hereby declare and affirm before my abbot, the venerable Ephraim, that I have faithfully and reverently transcribed and translated from the Greek the testament of the Blessed Ignatius of Antioch, successor to the chair of the Blessed Apostle Peter, and that the translation I have prepared contains no embellishments or ornamentations. These are the words of the Blessed Ignatius the Illuminator rendered now in Syriac."

"Excuse me for interrupting, Father, but you said this notation was known from other manuscripts. Does this mean Saint Elias was distinguished for its library in ancient times?" Charles asked.

"It's long been accepted by Middle Eastern scholars that the

Monastery of Saint Elijah was renowned for its splendid library associated with its school, and it produced many worthy Syriac manuscripts used in Eastern churches and monasteries until its destruction by the Persians. The school was highly regarded throughout the Middle East, and many scholars from distant countries received excellent training there. It was in this monastery that many ancient Greek texts were translated into Arabic for the Muslim rulers. Because of its scholarly reputation in the early years of Muslim rule, the monastery was protected by the caliphs, and many of the scholars associated with the school were employed by Muslim leaders in high government positions.

"Perhaps I should advise you, Reverend Monroe, that like all trained linguists, we have taken small idiomatic liberties to make the translation relevant and meaningful in English. Other than those, what we're about to share with you comes directly from the ancient pen of Brother Elias, written about twelve centuries ago and, even then, we believe, were translated from a Greek text that must have been written some eight hundred years earlier. Just think, what we are about to hear are the words written by Saint Ignatius in a series of letters to a woman who was the daughter of a man named Theophilus. You will recall that Theophilus was the person Saint Luke dedicated his Gospel to in our New Testament over two thousand years ago."

CHAPTER 9

"**I** am honored and privileged to be able to stand here and read the first chapter of this precious document to you." Father Michael began to read aloud to the group.

My dear daughter in Christ, Dorothea. How my heart rejoices in these troubled times to hear from you. I think often of the kindness and generosity of your dear late father and the happy hours I spent in the company of believers in his household. And your letter brings back fond memories of another visitor in your esteemed father's home, that of our dear brother, Luke. I can hear his golden voice even now, dear Dorothea, so many years since he left us, proclaiming the glorious Resurrection of our Lord and Savior Jesus Christ to the entire world. And I am reminded of the wonderful friendship that developed between Luke and your late father, Theophilus, whose quest for enlightenment and truth for himself and his entire household is, to this day, used in our churches as an example for all believers.

That same household is now a bastion of faith in this sinful world, and you, dear daughter, with your magnificent gifts, have sustained the believers here in Antioch in these evil days, when out of ignorance and inspired by Satan, misguided men conspire against the truth of Christ.

You have reminded me yet again that you and the believers in your household have longed to know what became of those first disciples and followers of the Lord as they set out to obey his final commandment that the Good News be proclaimed to the ends of the earth. Even during my last visit to your home, when I explained that I never once heard Peter, John, nor any other apostle mention their own personal struggles while discussing the fruits of their missionary endeavors, you insisted that it would be important for future generations of believers to know what happened to our Lord's first followers.

At that time, I believed, like the first disciples, that their own journey in faith was not important so long as the Good News was proclaimed everywhere they went. After all, in those early days of the faith, most of us believed that Judgment Day was imminent. But, with the passage of time, I see more clearly that we erred in this thinking, and your request for information about their later lives is a noble one, and I will make every effort to comply with what you desire.

I regret that difficulties with the authorities brought about by the lies and connivances of unbelievers have prevented me from writing to you sooner. As it is, I will turn my full attention to the task in loving memory of my beloved friend, Luke, and your dear father, Theophilus, and as you suggested, to honor the memories of those first disciples of our Lord, whose only desire was to spread the word of truth to the multitudes before the approach of Judgment Day.

You, of course, are aware that I was blessed by our loving Savior to be counted as a companion of those beloved disciples Peter, John, and Paul when their labors brought them close to Antioch. Luke was a physician long before he accepted the faith, and I saw him frequently when his travels brought him to Antioch. I met Barnabas once when he was in Paul's company as they visited old friends and converts in Antioch. The disciple Thomas came to Antioch and stayed a week on his way toward the east, and when I was no more than a boy and a child in the faith, I found him to be a wonderful companion and a good teacher.

Before he gave his life for the Lord in Achaia, Luke sent me documents he had gathered while working on his accounts of Peter's and Paul's missionary journeys. It was always his intention to add to this history and to include the miraculous works and activities of other disciples, but age, infirmities, and persecution prevented it. I have reviewed his documents and have included this information in my letters to you. Since much of our information is rather lengthy and I am getting old, I have prevailed upon my younger assistants in the Lord's work, Aristarchus and Tychicus, to assist me in this endeavor.

More than eighty of the earliest disciples were present when the Holy Ghost descended on them at Pentecost. Many of these, inflamed with the spirit, accompanied the apostles as they set out to proclaim the word of God to the world, and their children and grandchildren still labor in the vineyards of faith in distant lands.

It is fitting that I first write of the later ministry of our beloved brother in Christ, Paul. You will no doubt recall that in the record that Luke left us, Paul had been under arrest in Rome. He was confined in a house under guard until his case could be heard. Even there, the Lord continued to work through him, and several of his guards became followers of the Way. A number of the leaders of the Jews visited him during his confinement, and two of these leaders were converted.

Sometime later, Paul was summoned before the Praetorian prefect, Afranius Burrus. When the prefect called upon witnesses to bring charges, Turtullus stepped forward and said, "Distinguished and noble prefect, peace and tranquility should prevail in our land. This man, above all others, inflames the people with his radical teachings and is counted as a leader of the Nazoreans, a despicable sect that owes fealty to another king other than to Caesar. Noble Prefect, only with this renegade's death will Judea continue to enjoy peace and tranquility."

The prefect then turned to Paul and said, "What is your answer to these charges?"

Paul replied, "Excellency, I know you will judge fairly when you have heard all the facts. The one they rightly say I owe fealty to was crucified years ago in Jerusalem during the reign of Emperor Tiberius. This Jesus, I believe, sits at the right hand of God.

"Noble Prefect, I have never once counseled anyone to disturb the peace and tranquility of Judea or any other place in the empire. I say to you, with great respect, that I have committed no crime either against the emperor or against the Jews. I stand before you in this court simply because I preach the resurrection of the dead who will live again by virtue of the Lord Jesus's death on the cross, and for no other reason."

"Why, then, do these men so hate you that they braved a journey across the sea to bring these charges against you?"

"Excellency, these men know full well that I was once authorized by their own Jewish Sanhedrin to apprehend the followers of Jesus and bring them before that Jewish court in chains for trial and punishment. The Sanhedrin was so pleased with my work that they commissioned me to go to Damascus and arrest the Nazoreans there.

"It was there, before the gates of Damascus, that this Jesus, the one I follow, appeared to me and changed my life. I became his devoted follower. It is because I now no longer persecute the followers of Jesus, but rather serve them in his name that the Jews have such hatred for me."

The prefect then turned to the Jews and asked, "Does he speak the truth? Did he once persecute those he now befriends?"

Tertullus replied, "Noble Prefect, he did at one time perform such a service, but now he incites the rabble. He is a turncoat who deserves only death."

"How does he incite the people?

"He blames us for the death of this Jesus, who was a blasphemer. Moreover, this man teaches that Jesus was the Messiah and the son of God, and that is blasphemy, for which he deserves to be put to death."

The prefect said, "This is a purely religious matter that concerns only you Jews."

Tertullus responded, "In Judea we Jews worship but one God, and men dare not blaspheme."

Afranius Burris rose and said, "This man is a Roman citizen. If I thought this man was responsible for the turmoil in Judea, I would be quick to condemn him. You Jews are a restless and quarrelsome people; take care you do not burden the emperor again with your absurd religious disputes. This case is dismissed."

Once Paul was freed, he and his companions boarded a ship bound for Barcino. While at sea, terrible storms caused the passengers to fear for their lives, but Paul calmed them and promised that all would be well. Damage to the ship, however, forced the captain to seek shelter at Massilia so that the ship could be repaired.

While in Massilia, Paul was invited to address the Jews. In the synagogue, Paul stood before the assembled Jews in Massilia and reminded them that the prophets had foretold the coming of the Messiah. He proclaimed that Jesus of Nazareth was the Promised One who had been crucified in the fulfillment of Scripture.

One of the members suddenly shouted, "I know who this man is! My cousin, who recently came from Jerusalem, told me all about him. He would have you believe that a carpenter from Galilee is the Promised One of Israel. Those who believe that this Jesus was the Messiah are heretics, outcasts who deserve to be stoned."

Many in the synagogue shouted that Paul should be beaten, but the leader stood up and spoke. "My brothers, I asked this man, Paul, to speak to us. Let him leave this place in peace."

Paul said, "It has long been my practice to preach the message of repentance and salvation taught by Jesus to the Jews first, but if you will not listen, the Gentiles will, and the salvation intended as your inheritance, but refused by you, will be theirs instead."

A man came up to Paul and said, "Sir, I am Nemonius, a merchant from this town, and I was a fellow passenger with you aboard the ship from Ostia. Those things you told us about the Nazorean have remained steadfast on my mind. Would you come with me and share more about him with my household?"

Paul fell to his knees and declared, "O Lord, blessed be thy holy name. For the message spurned by the Jews has become the treasure of the Gentiles!" Then he arose and accompanied Nemonius to his home.

Paul told them how Jesus had willingly paid the terrible price of crucifixion so that all who believed in him would abide with him forever. He shared with them how Jesus had appeared to him before the gates of Damascus and changed his life.

On the next day, Nemonius invited several neighboring families to join his household to hear Paul. Nemonius's young nephew, Ariston, stood up and exclaimed, "I want to be a follower of Jesus!"

Paul replied, "Jesus said, 'If anyone wants to follow me he must not consider his own well-being. Day after day he must take up his cross and walk with me. Anyone who fears for his own safety will be lost, but if one forgets himself in service to others, that one will be truly saved and will live forever. What does one gain even if he wins the whole world at the cost of his immortal soul? Whoever is ashamed of me or of what I say, I, in turn, will be ashamed of him when I return in glory to judge the world.'

"Truly, I tell you, it is not easy to be a follower of Jesus. The world hated him and despises those who follow him. Know that I and other disciples of Jesus have been beaten, stoned, and imprisoned. Do not say hastily, 'I want to be a follower of Jesus.' Can you indeed pick up your own cross daily and follow him? Can you face the scorn of the world for his sake?"

Paul's companions were astonished that so many Gentiles came to hear him preach and wanted to be baptized. During the days and weeks that followed, Paul and his companions continued to proclaim the Gospel. Many Gentiles were won over for Christ in the days that followed.

One day, Paul said to Nemonius, "You have heard my teaching over these past weeks, and you have learned much about our Lord from my companions. Now the time has come that I must leave you and go where the Lord sends me. Hold fast to the love of God through our Lord Jesus Christ, and remain steadfast to the Gospel I have preached. If anyone comes to you preaching a Gospel different from the one you have heard from me, send him on his way.

"Endure in the faith, and you shall reign with the Lord and his chosen ones. Lead a blameless life, a model for others to imitate, for that is how the Good News is spread. Give no cause for the governing authorities to find fault with you. Be mindful the Lord has set them in authority over the people. Remember also that the Lord has set you and your companions apart as his people for the purpose of increasing his kingdom by sharing the Good News with all who will listen."

After boarding the ship for Spain, Paul raised his hand in blessing for Nemonius and the believers who had followed him to the dock. "Be at peace with all men. Remember to do good even to those who hate you, for you have been ransomed from the world by the blood of Jesus Christ. Remain true to what you have been taught. Uphold Nemonius, and be guided by his example. Remember, the path to salvation is narrow while the road to damnation is wide. Love one another as your Lord loves you, and pray for me constantly, that I might continue to be used by the Lord."

When they were in sight of Spain. Paul prayed, "We give you thanks, O Lord our God, for bringing us to the far western reaches of the world. By your grace we have been allowed to accomplish the will of our Lord and Savior Jesus that the Gospel be preached even to the ends of the earth. Grant, then, that your servants might strike a responsive chord in the minds and hearts of the people of this land so this Gospel will become their joy and inspiration as it has been ours, for we ask it in the name of Jesus. Amen."

Paul sought out the Jewish leaders and they, being eager for news, invited him to speak in the synagogue. "My countrymen, for these past thirty years, I have traveled to tell those of the circumcision the glorious story of God's love for his people.

"For three years, Jesus the Nazorean shared his message with the people who came to hear him in ever increasing numbers. He restored sight to the blind and healed the lame. Many believed in him, including several among the Jewish leaders. Many more marveled at what he said, declaring that no one had ever spoken like this man.

"Those who held power were jealous of his esteem among the people, and so they resolved to be rid of him. Many were convinced he was the Promised One, the Messiah.

"Crowds in Jerusalem turned out in great numbers to welcome him, and they hailed him as king. But that same week one of his followers betrayed him to the Sanhedrin, and he was condemned by the Romans to be crucified. He had many times predicted he would die, only to rise again within three days. By God's grace, he rose from the tomb, and many in the city saw him and have borne witness that he lives. And much later, I was favored by God's grace to have seen him, and, where once I persecuted those who followed him, I now am his devoted servant."

Several of the Jewish leaders became alarmed at the number who became believers, so they went to the governor to complain about Paul, but they were told the governor took no part in religious disputes. The leaders of the synagogue then told Paul he was no longer welcome to speak in that place. As was his custom, Paul informed the Jewish leaders he would now take the Gospel to the uncircumcised.

Marta, a Gentile convert to Judaism and one of the town's leading citizens, invited Paul and his companions to meet in her house. She introduced Paul to her household and asked him to share the Good News with them.

After six months had passed, more than one hundred had been baptized, and Paul gave thanks to the Lord Jesus for those who had been saved. As the number of believers continued to grow, Paul had a dream in which the church communities he had established earlier cried out to him to return and reinforce their faith. For three nights, this same dream was repeated, so Paul announced to his companions that they should remain in Spain spreading the Good News while he must return to the lands of his earlier ministries.

Paul learned that a ship was planning to depart with a cargo for Corinth. He pleaded with his followers to keep pure the faith he had taught them. He raised his hands and blessed those he left behind.

When they arrived in Miletos, Paul was pleased to find the church there prospering under the leadership of Hesoid, one of the first he had baptized in that city years ago. He commended Hesoid and the presbyters of Miletos for their righteous diligence and prayed with them that it would continue to thrive and prosper.

He had been in Miletos for two months when a letter reached him from Diodotus, the bishop in Corinth, urging him to come quickly, since dissention had once again split the congregation. Paul immediately left for Corinth.

When he first laid eyes on the apostle, Diodotus fell to his knees, embracing Paul's feet. The bishop explained that foreigners claiming to be believers from Judea had begun teaching the church members all sorts of strange things, professing they had been granted a higher understanding of what God required of true believers. Among those teachings, they had told the members that God understood the natural appetites of men graced by God with higher learning, and approved when those appetites were indulged. Accordingly, they had demanded costly food and superior accommodations to be provided at the expense of the congregation

.Paul rebuked Diodotus for his weakness in ever allowing these men to address the members. "Where are those Corinthians to whom I first introduced the Lord Jesus Christ? Does anyone in this room remember having heard of Christ and his wonderful works before I preached his Gospel to you? Were any of you aware that God had sent his only Son to die on the cross for your sins before I announced this message of salvation to you? Does anyone in this room dispute my credentials as your first teacher in Christ Jesus? No? Then, hear me now.

"When I first came among you and preached Christ and him crucified, I warned that men would come like wolves among sheep, with strange and different teachings, hoping to lead you astray for their own selfish ends. I also warned you these men were servants of Satan, whose sole purpose was to deceive and rob you of your heavenly reward. Now I see that such men are here among you. They pose as believers, but their teachings betray them as sons of perdition, and they will only be satisfied when you join them on the road to destruction.

"Have you remembered so little of that which I taught you? Where is the strength of your belief in Christ? If you are led astray so easily in the days when I and the other apostles are around to correct you, what will you do in the days ahead when we, the apostles who know and preach the truth no longer walk the earth? Who will be your guides then?

"These deceivers have made of you a mockery and a stumbling block to those of your companions who seek the truth. They subvert the Lord's teaching when they teach you to abandon self-control concerning your physical appetites. Have you so soon forgotten that the Lord Jesus taught men to be willing to cut off the hand if it is the instrument that causes them to sin?

"If you elect to honor these liars with positions of respect in your midst, then I want no part of you. You do not desire the light of truth, but prefer the darkness of deceit."

Two leaders of the congregation, Dionysius and Micah, stood up and vowed to expel the false teachers from their midst and implored Paul to forgive their ignorance and transgression. The entire congregation stood up in support, and Diodotus was instructed to inform the newcomers that they were no longer welcome. Heeding the pleadings of the people, Paul remained in their company for several months, strengthening their faith.

Sometime later, disturbing news reached the congregation in Corinth that a great fire had destroyed much of Rome and that Christians were being blamed for this tragic event.

A few weeks later, a ship arrived, having on board a number of believers escaping from Rome, and the Corinthians were distressed to hear that authorities in Rome were arresting and persecuting Christians in the capital. Believers told of mothers being forcibly separated from their children and shackled in chains before being led off into captivity. The Corinthians gladly shared their homes with the new arrivals and comforted them in their misery. Paul cautioned the Corinthians to expect persecution and prepare for it since Jesus had predicted it would come to those who followed him.

Soon it became apparent that the arrest and conviction of Christians was being extended to the other major cities in Italy, and fear grew that it would expand to additional Roman provinces, for the Roman people shared the emperor's animosity toward Christians.

As this was taking place in Rome, news arrived that Jews in Judea had risen in open rebellion against the Roman authorities. In Jerusalem, independence from Rome was declared, and coins were struck to commemorate the occasion. Hundreds of Roman merchants and their families were slaughtered in the uprising, and, as the most radical elements of the Jewish Zealots gained power in Jerusalem, persecution of Christian believers increased, and cruel torture caused many to renounce their faith.

In Rome, Emperor Nero ordered his general, Titus Flavius Vespasian, to restore Roman rule. When he arrived in Caesaria in Palestine, Vespasian marched east, forcing the Jews to retreat to Jerusalem. The influx of Jewish refugees, the shortage of food, and the increasing power of the Jewish radicals compelled the surviving Christian believers under the leadership of Simeon to leave Jerusalem for the cities of the Decapolis. Shortly afterward, the Roman army surrounded Jerusalem, and many Christians believed God had withdrawn his favor from the city.

Meanwhile, Paul visited the cities and towns of Achaea, strengthening their faith and warning them of the persecution soon to come. While in Corinth, Paul received word that Peter had been imprisoned and condemned. Paul went to a wooded area to be alone, fell to his knees, and prayed for guidance.

After determining what he must do, Paul addressed the congregation, "Dear friends in Jesus Christ. From the beginning, when you first took infant steps in the Gospel of your salvation, I warned you that the faith you now possess, bought by the Lord's sacrifice on the cross, could only be maintained through constant prayer, dedication, and persistence. You are not only witnesses to the power of that faith, but also to my repeated warnings that the evil forces of this world would conspire against you. Bear witness now to what I say. The day has now arrived when you must be prepared to suffer persecution, for the dark forces of the world are now arrayed against all true believers.

"Our brothers in Rome already suffer grievously for their love for the Lord. Many have been tried and condemned for the burning of the city, a crime for which none of them are guilty. Be assured, the world hates us for the testimony we give that Jesus Christ is Lord of all. Once you crossed the threshold of belief in our Lord Jesus Christ, you were marked men, doomed to the perpetual enmity of the world and of its sovereign ruler, Satan and all his minions; but take heart. Keep your eye on your heavenly prize, for the time of persecution is but a short moment, while your heavenly prize is eternal.

"The time has come when I must leave you. And in my heart, I know that I will never see you again in this world. I have written to Timothy and have asked him to come to you from Ephesus. I have also asked him to contact the brothers in Italy and tell them to be expecting me. Timothy will be a comfort to you as he has always been for me. Now, I ask you to sustain me with your prayers, for I must go to Rome. Our beloved Peter is in the hands of the authorities, and the church in Rome is being brutally tested without his firm hand to guide it.

"My heart tells me Rome is my final destination on this earth. Do not cry for me, for I welcome it. My race is nearly over, and I hope to receive the laurel wreath of victory from the hands of our Lord and Savior, Christ Jesus."

Paul sailed to Italy and was met there by Aulus and Galerius, members of the church in Rome. Both men were fearful to discuss church matters while they were surrounded by strangers. It was not until they were safely behind barred doors that they felt secure enough to tell of the horrors occurring to the brothers and their families in the capital city.

"The wickedness of this persecution is beyond belief," Galerius said. "The emperor has ordered his soldiers to arrest all followers of the Way. Men and women, even those who are not of our faith, are beaten unmercifully until they divulge the homes and hiding places of believers. Mothers and fathers are torn from their crying children, who are left destitute. Those who are arrested are crammed into filthy cells. No food or water is available, and, when they are judged, they are given one opportunity to renounce the faith and worship the emperor. Those who do so must first disclose the whereabouts of other Christians. Those who refuse are given over to the managers of the games, where they become prey of wild animals to amuse the crowds.

"Peter was apprehended while preaching in the underground tombs of the city. He was shackled and led away to the dread Mamertine prison, where he languished for many months. Then, during the consulship of Lucius Telesinus and Suetonius Paullinus, he was tried and condemned by the imperial court and crucified like our divine savior."

Aulus and Galerius urged Paul to leave Italy immediately, to save himself so he might provide leadership to believers in hiding.

Paul said, "All through my ministry, I have faced danger at every turn. I have been stoned, spit upon, cursed, lashed, imprisoned, and left for dead. Now I see clearly that here in this place, the center of the empire, my race has run its course. Be assured, I have no fear of whatever lies ahead, for I am anxious to meet our risen Lord face-to-face, but my personal desire must be put aside for the moment. With our beloved Peter gone to his reward and the persecution gaining in intensity, I must continue on to Rome and give what comfort I can for as long as God permits." Reluctantly, the brothers agreed to accompany him to Rome.

Galerius escorted Paul to the home of a fellow believer named Baram. Baram secured the door and led them to a room at the rear of the house. He said, "No Christian home is a sanctuary these days. Christians are being tortured to reveal the names of fellow believers.

"I have sent my wife and three daughters north to Ancona, hoping they would be safe there, but word has reached us that the persecution is spreading beyond Rome to other parts of Italy. Nevertheless, I plan to follow them as soon as I complete the sale of my business." Paul and the brothers left Baram and continued on their way to Rome where they were to meet in Durio the barber's house with a frightened group of believers.

More than a dozen terrified Christians gathered in Durio's house to welcome the apostle. He asked the barber's wife to bring him bread and wine. "Brothers and sisters in the Lord, these are perilous days, days of misfortune and suffering for God's chosen ones. But all life is filled with pain and suffering, even for the rich and powerful who rule the world. But for you, rightly called the elect of God for in God's great unfathomable mercy, he has selected you out of the multitudes that inhabit the earth for the priceless gift of salvation. You, the precious few, are chosen to abide with him forever.

"Remember what Scripture tells us: 'My heart is glad and my soul rejoices; my body abides in confidence; because you will not abandon my soul to Hell. You will show me the path of life and fullness of joy in your presence and I will abide in the delights of your right hand forever.'

"On the night before he died, our Lord gathered his disciples around him, blessed and broke the bread, and gave it to them, saying, 'Take this and eat, for it is my body.' Then he blessed the wine and gave it to them to drink, saying, 'This is my blood to be poured out on behalf of many.'

After they had consumed the bread and wine, Paul said, "On this same night in Jerusalem, our Lord also told his disciples, 'Let not your hearts be troubled.' I say to you, do not be fearful of the acts of men who are inspired by Satan. The Lord declared those who loved and followed him would be hated as he was, and this has come to pass in our day. Take heart, then; be bold, and love the Lord with all your strength!"

Over the next several weeks, all who heard Paul were empowered with the spirit of God.

One night, when the believers had once again gathered at

Durio's house, the residence was surrounded by soldiers. The officer in charge marched in and announced that all in the house were under arrest by order of the emperor. As the soldiers tied the hands of the believers, the officer demanded, "Which of you is the man named Paul?"

Paul stepped forward and said, "I am Paul."

"As the leader of this rabble, we have special orders for you. You are to be taken to the Mamertine in chains to await the pleasure of the Praetorian prefect for judgment in accordance with the emperor's edict."

Paul was taken to the Mamertine prison and fastened to the same pillar that blessed Peter had been chained to months earlier. The others were taken to the Circus Maximus where they were tried, condemned, and separated, either to be burned alive or to be prey for the wild animals in the arena.

While languishing for more than two months in the Mamertine, Paul continued to testify on behalf of Jesus. He told his jailors that Jesus bore the sins of many on the cross at Calvary. One of the jailers, Crispus, was convinced by Paul's testimony and asked to be baptized. Despite his chains, Paul joyfully baptized him and welcomed him to the elect of Jesus Christ.

Paul was brought under armed guards to the Castra Praetoria to be tried by the Praetorian prefect, Sophonius Tigellinus. This man had been the first to advise Nero to blame Christians for the fires that had ravished the city. Crispus was assigned to accompany the apostle to the Praetorian headquarters.

Having been told that the Christian leader was to be brought to trial, the people gathered by the roadside to jeer and hurl insults at Paul. All along the Via Sacra, throngs lined the way, heaping verbal abuse on the prisoner.

Crispus and the soldiers kept the taunting crowd away from the apostle. Paul said to the converted jailer, "Those who were there told me the crowd was screaming like this in Jerusalem years ago when our Savior carried his cross on the Via Dolorosa to Calvary, there to be crucified. Praise God, I will soon be with him in paradise."

Paul and the escort were admitted to a large courtyard where they were met by a company of Praetorian soldiers. The Praetorians took custody of the apostle and marched him to the Shrine of Standards, where the trial was to be held. More than one hundred people were present, mostly members of the imperial court, including senators, former governors, rich merchants, leading actors, and high-ranking military officers.

The centurion announced, "Attention, all who are present. By command of the emperor, Nero Claudius Drusus Germanicus, the Praetorian Prefect Sophonius Tigellinus is directed to preside at the trial of Paul of Tarsus, a Jew and leader of the despicable Christian sect held responsible and fully accountable for the fires that so recently devastated our beloved city."

Facing Paul and the assembled audience, the prefect said, "This man standing before you is a known leader of that sect called Christians who refuse to acknowledge the godhead of the emperor and who are known to be responsible for setting the horrible fires that so recently devastated our city. This man has a long history of rabble-rousing and troublemaking. He was first brought before Roman justice in Judea during the Consulships of Petronius Turpilianus and Caesennius Paetus, accused of causing a riot among the Jews in that accursed province. Because he claimed Roman citizenship, he was sent to Rome for trial.

"Because our emperor is a most merciful and benevolent ruler, this man was granted his freedom, yet he continued, to stir up the Christian masses to set fire to both public and private buildings in Rome. Now, after months attempting to hide from lawful pursuit, he has at last been apprehended and is here before the emperor's court.

"Paul of Tarsus, do you have anything to say to this court in your defense?"

Paul replied, "It is clear to me as well as to all present, Honorable Prefect, you have already determined that even on these false grounds, I must die. I have been ready for this moment every day of every year I have labored for my Lord Jesus Christ. I will not appeal your decision, but I will speak on behalf of my fellow Christians who are blameless of the crimes lodged against them. Not a single one of them has set fire to any building. Not a single one has disobeyed any of the just laws put in place by the emperor or his governing authorities.

"Do your spies not inform you I have always proclaimed that those who are Christians are to obey the government authorities, for God is the one who allows the government to exist? And do they not bring you word that there is no government that God has not placed in power? Do they not tell you I caution all Christians to obey the laws of the government since those who refuse to obey the law are refusing to obey God?

"No, Honorable Prefect, these people you hold in your cells are the most obedient of the emperor's subjects, yet they have been cruelly mistreated, starved, and have been condemned to death. Do with me what you will; I am old and have run my race, but restore these innocents to their homes, where they might continue worshiping in peace, never offending the emperor or any of his subjects."

Tigellinus replied, "You claim that you and your followers broke none of the emperor's laws, but this is a complete lie. The Senate has affirmed the imperial edict that all who reside in the empire must honor the emperor's person with solemn oaths of worship, yet you Christians refuse to do so. This alone is sufficient to merit the death sentence."

"Honorable Prefect," Paul responded, "God grants emperors, kings, and princes the right to govern the affairs of men, and Christians honor this right by their obedience, but God reserves worship unto himself alone, and no man can assume or share that which God has reserved for himself alone. As Christians, we are bound to follow God's command, and he is the sole object of our worship."

"Believe what you want about your God, but in all the lands where Rome has sent her legions, the emperor's will is to be obeyed. Jews in the province of Judea have risen in revolt and pray to your God for deliverance. Now they will face one of Rome's greatest generals and the might of Rome's legions," sneered Tigellinus.

"Wise men do not mock God, who created all things, Prefect," responded Paul. "Great and powerful kings through the ages have declared themselves to be divine and have vainly attempted to usurp the power of Almighty God. Where are they now? Today, they are all dust and lie beneath the feet of common men. Many are raised to high estate to govern the affairs of men, but the prudent among them recognize that their power comes from God, and that he alone is worthy of worship."

Tigellinus turned to those in attendance and said, "Do you see, my fellow countrymen, how obstinate this fellow is who dares to withhold worship from the emperor? He and his followers think that they have the right to determine which of our laws to follow and which to discard. He is no different from his fellow Jews in Judea, who have become traitors desiring to set themselves apart from allegiance to the emperor and to Rome. They are renegades, and we will destroy them."

Looking around at the assembled crowd of nobles, Paul said, "Romans, for many years you Gentiles were allowed to live in darkness, reveling in all kind of wickedness. Because you were ignorant in your sins, you were not held accountable by God like the Jews to whom he had given his holy Law. This Law demanded that God alone be worshipped; but now a glorious light has come into the world—Jesus Christ, the Son of God—and Jew and Gentile alike have been invited to participate in the redemptive power of Jesus Christ's sacrifice on the cross.

"Because Jesus came to us, Jew and Gentile alike, the gates of heaven have been thrown open to all who confess that Jesus Christ is Lord, and God alone is worthy of worship. But with this great gift comes responsibility. As you Gentiles no longer have to live in darkness, you also no longer live without accountability. What was forgiven in the past because of your ignorance in darkness will now be held against you since you are now free to embrace the glorious light of salvation. Mark well how you live and what you do, for on the last day, Jesus, the one who was crucified by you will judge each man according to his actions."

Tigellinus rose and said, "By your own mouth you have condemned yourself. By order of this court and in the name of the emperor, you are to be put to death. Were it not for the fact you claim Roman citizenship, you would be taken to the arena to entertain the crowd by your death there. As it is, your head will be severed from your body. Guards, take this prisoner away!"

Paul was led away in chains to the Ostian Gate. The Praetorian escort bade him to kneel. Paul looked up toward heaven and said, "Lord Jesus, forgive these men who commit this act in ignorance. Now, at last, my work in your service is done, and I long to be with you." The Praetorian raised his sword, and the sentence was carried out.

CHAPTER 10

Doctor Bankkour put the report back in his briefcase and called on Doctor Morse to discuss this chapter.

"There are a number of observations I'd like to make regarding the Roman judicial process," Morse said. "First of all, historians have long believed that Roman emperors deputized others to conduct trials of ordinary persons accused of criminal activity. Many times these were midlevel officials. It is intriguing to read that, in Paul's case, men as high up in the emperor's service as the Praetorian Prefects Afranius Burrus in his first trial and Sophonius Tigellinus in his second and final trial would be named judges. A few traditions report that Nero himself condemned Paul, but it seems more likely the emperor, during the latter years of his reign, would designate others to act in his stead. After all, he despised taking time away from his acting or singing lessons to become involved in government affairs.

"Burrus had been a long-time close associate and advisor to Nero. He had been selected by Nero's mother, Agrippina the Younger, wife of Claudius Caesar, to ensure that Nero was named Claudius's successor, and even though it's suspected that Burrus later had a hand in Agrippina's murder, he and Seneca were chief advisors to Nero during the early years of his reign."

Morse continued, "Rome, by all accounts, was governed well while these two men advised the emperor. The Roman philosopher

Seneca and Burrus managed to thwart most of Nero's dangerous tendencies during those early years, and many thought the 'golden years' of Emperor Augustus had returned. All too soon, however, the real Nero emerged.

"In 62 AD, Burrus died. Historians say he was murdered by order of Nero. In any event, the first trial of Paul in Rome had to have taken place before or during 62 AD. After Burrus's death, the emperor appointed Tigellinus as Praetorian prefect. According to the historian Tacitus, Tigellinus 'introduced Nero to every form of wickedness.' He was known to be the emperor's most trusted confidant, and he is thought to have profited greatly by arranging audiences between his own clients and Nero.

"We know that Tigellinus accompanied the emperor to Greece in 67 AD. During Nero's absence from Rome, Tigellinus's co-prefect, Nymphidius, was placed in charge of the government, and that individual used this time to consolidate his influence with the emperor at Tigellinus's expense. It is believed that when the imperial party returned to Rome, Tigellinus's position with Nero had been greatly weakened.

"Because he had lost his influence at court and was no longer a close companion of the emperor, Tigellinus managed to save his life during the upheavals in the last months of Nero's reign. When the legions under Governor Supicius revolted and marched on Rome, Nero fled the city and committed suicide.

"Tigellinus was safe for the moment, but when Nero's successor, Galba, was murdered after ruling less than a year, the next emperor, Salvius Otho, ordered Tigellinus to commit suicide, which he did."

Doctor Morse smiled as he admitted, "I know I'm going on and on, and I apologize; historians are inclined to get carried away, but the point I'm trying to make is that both Afranius Burrus and Sophonius Tigellinus were Praetorian prefects under Nero at different times and could well have been designated judges on the emperor's behalf. The contrast between the characters of each man based on their description in the manuscript seems to accurately reflect their history.

"I'm also impressed that Ignatius followed the common practice among the citizens of the Roman Empire of that era in describing specific years by naming the consuls who were elected for one-year terms for that particular year. This throws a little light on dates that these important events occurred, dates that we haven't been privy to before now.

"Ignatius describes Paul's first trial in Rome during the consulships of Turpilianus and Paetus, which was in 61 AD, and the condemnation of Peter during the consulships of Telesinus and Paullinus, which was in 66 AD. Thus far in history, the dates for these occurrences have all been speculative at best."

After Doctor Morse sat down, Doctor Bankkour called on Father Michael Fyvia. The elderly priest stood, smiled at Charles, and said, "Reverend Monroe, you must be as surprised as I was that the manuscript definitively declares that Paul indeed undertook a mission to Spain. Although several ancient traditions hint at this journey, this is the clearest indication we have that Saint Paul ever completed his long-desired missionary voyage, and I had never read any account nor heard of any tradition concerning the apostle's journey to Massilia, which was the Roman name for Marseilles. That visit makes sense, though, as an intermediate destination point on an ancient sea journey to Spain.

"I'm sure the citizens of Marseilles will be surprised and pleased to learn that Christianity was first brought to their ancestors by the apostle to the Gentiles, but bigger by far is the fact that Paul did indeed undertake a journey to Spain. I think this will gratify those biblical historians who have long held this view. Paul spoke about his desire to visit Spain, and here we have Ignatius's confirmation that he did.

"But I must return to the first part of the manuscript. Tradition in the Eastern Church has always been strong that Saint Ignatius the Illuminator was a companion of Peter, Paul, and John. Ancient Syriac tradition tells us he was consecrated the third bishop of Antïoch by blessed Peter himself, and Luke's *Acts of the Apostles* remind us that Paul and Barnabas were active missionaries in that city, and for extended periods of time. Ignatius could have been one of their converts, or perhaps a son of a convert.

"I'd never heard, though, nor read anything that stated the Illuminator knew or was acquainted with any of the Seventy, the first disciples and followers of our Lord in addition to the twelve apostles; not only that, but according to the manuscript, he kept in communication with a number of their descendants. Biblical historians will certainly be interested in this newfound information."

The priest continued, "Here's something else I believe will be of great interest to historians. I know of no tradition that tells us that Ignatius had access to any of Saint Luke's notes or letters. What a treasure trove that would have been! Just think, to have before you notes having to do with all those witnesses Luke interviewed while compiling his Gospel and the *Acts of the Apostles*, to say nothing of quotes from St. Paul during their long days and months spent together at sea and in the towns and cities they visited in the course of their missions.

"Think of it, Reverend Monroe. We now have evidence that Theophilus, a mystery man in the New Testament, the one for whom Luke wrote both his Gospel and Acts, was a distinguished citizen of Antioch; that he and his family were Christian converts and he had a daughter, Dorothea, for whom Ignatius now agrees to write about the further missions and destinations of the apostles. Ignatius also confirms what several early traditions claim, that Saint Luke was martyred in Greece. All in all, gentlemen, what we have is a fantastic glimpse into apostolic times that has remained hidden for two thousand years."

Charles asked, "Hasn't church tradition always been consistently strong that Paul was put to death during Nero's persecution, Father? And wasn't this the first of the great persecutions the early church suffered?"

"There is credible evidence that Nero's predecessor, Claudius, initiated the first of the Roman persecutions," replied the cleric. "We have a statement from the Roman historian, Suetonius, who wrote that, since the Jews were constantly causing disturbances at the instigation of Christ, Claudius was forced to expel them from Rome. This might be referred to as a 'soft' persecution, one in which households were forced to move, but probably accompanied with little physical force.

"The real intense and physical persecution, though, did begin with Nero. I happen to have with me the description of that era written by the Roman historian, Tacitus, who was a boy when these events occurred. If you'd like, I'll share that with you now."

"I'd like to hear it, Father," Charles responded.

Father Michael then reached into his briefcase and extracted a notebook. "You will, of course, remember that in 64 AD, Rome had suffered through a terrible fire that raged uncontrolled for six days and destroyed about three-fourths of the city. The people of Rome suspected that Nero himself had ordered that the fires be set because of his well-known desire to rebuild the city in imitation of his ancestor, the great Augustus. It was in order to blunt these accusations that the emperor laid blame for the fires on the Christians. His henchmen arrested several of the believers who, under terrible torture, gave up the names of other believers and implicated them, so all Christians in the city were held responsible for the fires."

Adjusting his glasses, the priest referred to his notes and began to read, "The Roman historian Tacitus described the matter as follows:

To stop the rumor that he had started the fires, Nero falsely charged with guilt and punished with the most fearful tortures, the persons commonly called Christians, who were hated for their enormities. Christus, the founder of that name, was put to death as a criminal by Pontius Pilate, procurator of Judea, in the reign of Tiberius, but the pernicious superstition, repressed for a time, broke out yet again, not only through Judea, where the mischief originated, but through the city of Rome also, whither all things horrible and disgraceful flow from all quarters, as to a common receptacle, and where they are encouraged. Accordingly, first those were arrested who confessed they were Christians; next on their information, a vast multitude were convicted, not so much on the charge of burning the city, as of hating the human race.

To their deaths they were made the subjects of sport; they were covered with the hides of wild beasts and worried to death by dogs, or nailed to crosses, or set fire to, and when the day waned, burned to serve for the evening lights.

Father Michael closed the notebook, putting it back in his briefcase. Then he concluded by saying, "A number of scholars estimate that Nero's persecution resulted in the deaths of about five thousand Christians."

Doctor Bankkour then asked Charles if he had any further questions or any remarks about what he'd heard.

"What I'm compelled to say, Doctor, is how profoundly impressed I am with the work all of you have done. Just think, we now have been privileged to witness the final journey of Paul; to be present when he was twice tried, when he was condemned, and to be there when he suffered martyrdom. And to think we are the first individuals in two thousand years to have concrete evidence of what became of the great apostle."

"Concrete evidence, Reverend Monroe?" Doctor Bankkour replied. "A word of caution, if you please. No matter what we who are involved in this project believe about this document, we must look at it as critics will see it. What we have is an ancient document that claims to be an account of the lives of the apostles beyond those mentioned in Holy Scripture. It is believed by most historians that the last book of the New Testament was written sometime around 90 AD. We know that Emperor Trajan condemned Ignatius during his visit to Antioch, which took place around 110 AD. We believe, further, that Ignatius was a contemporary of the apostles and was in personal contact with several, including Peter.

"We must remember that the manuscript claims to be a Syriac copy of a lost Greek original. We've dated this book at having been written around 850 AD. This alone makes the manuscript one of the oldest Christian writings in existence today, but it does not prove the authenticity of its contents. After all, more than eight hundred years separate this document from the lost original.

"Scholars are acutely aware of the many ancient documents purporting to be genuine that later proved to be, in fact, pious frauds. Whether or not this manuscript is a genuine account of the latter actions and deeds of the apostles might never be proven with absolute certainty. As we study it more closely and apply historical criticism, we might be in a better position to judge its authenticity.

"No matter how much evidence we produce, though, there will always be critics. We must remember that, for a number of reasons, there will always be skeptics who will deny the manuscript's legitimacy.

"But in spite of all the obstacles scholars or skeptics will attempt to put in the way, those of us who have been involved in this enterprise from the beginning are persuaded that the document is genuine. Who else at that time would have been in a better position to gather the evidence of the comings and goings of the apostles than the learned Ignatius? After all, the historical record acknowledges he was the head of the early church in Antioch, a major crossroad between the east and west, one of the most important cities in the Roman Empire.

"Most scholars accept that Ignatius was personally acquainted with Peter, Paul, Luke, and John and was their companion early on in their missionary endeavors. He also more than likely knew a number of the early disciples as they passed through the city to spread the Good News to the east as well as to the west.

"We believe that of all the early church fathers, Ignatius was the only one who had the resources and the knowledge and the staff in the form of the seventy original disciples commissioned by Jesus as well as their descendants to assemble this information; and in Dorothea, the daughter of Luke's Theophilus, we have a compelling reason why Ignatius would have taken the time to compile that information.

Doctor Bankkour could see that Charles was visibly tired so he concluded by saying, "But we've been at this business for more than three hours, and we don't want to unduly tire you on this our first session. I wanted you to meet all the members of this scholarly team. In addition to their work on this document, all of them have demands on their time that require their attention. For our upcoming meetings, I would suggest that in most of our future sessions, Father Michael Fyvia and I bring you and your brother up to date as our translations progress with, of course, any of the team members who might be available. Does that sound satisfactory to you?"

Obviously relieved by the suggestion, Charles agreed, and after shaking hands with the team and thanking them again for all they had done thus far on the project, he and Ken left the building and returned to the airport.

On the flight back to Augusta, Charles asked, "So what do you make of what we've heard so far, Ken? What do you think about this team; do you think what we've seen and heard thus far is worth all the time and effort?"

Ken thought for a moment before he responded, "The team seems well qualified, and they seem to be working well together.

Though I'm certainly a novice at this, I don't see how the breadth of talent could be improved upon. One thing, though; I want to explore the copyright regulations governing a work of this nature. I want you and your family to have full custodianship of the final product when all this is concluded.

"Is it worth the time and trouble? I guess only time will tell, but we're certainly off to a good start."

Six weeks later, Doctor Bankkour called Ken and asked him when it would be convenient to schedule the next meeting. "I think I detect a certain excitement in your voice, Doctor," Ken said. "Am I right? Would it be acceptable for us to meet at my brother's house in Augusta? This hasn't been a good week for him, I'm afraid, and travel right now would be a hardship."

"Of course, Mr. Monroe. I'm sorry that Reverend Monroe is not progressing as well as we had hoped. You're most perceptive about our enthusiasm, and I believe you and your brother will share this excitement, for our team has completed the translation of the next chapter of the manuscript that tells what happened in the later ministry of the prince of the apostles, Simon Peter."

Ken offered the team air transportation from Atlanta to Augusta via Bob Healy's private aircraft. Doctor Bankkour thanked him and said he and Father Michael would look forward to the meeting in Augusta.

Several days later, the two scholars met with Ken and Charles in Charles's home. When they gathered in the chaplain's study, Doctor Bankkour indicated that Father Michael had expressly asked to present this session. The priest began with a prayer. "Lord God, Father of all mercies. In every age you raise up champions to defend and nurture the true faith. Now, in your infinite wisdom, you have seen fit to roll back the curtain of two thousand years and reveal to us in this sinful generation the later works and life of the blessed apostle Peter, a tried and true champion, the one your only Son, our Lord and Savior Jesus Christ, named to lead the church in the earliest years. Make us worthy instruments of this revelation, we ask in Christ's holy name. Amen."

Then Father Michael looked at Charles and said, "Reverend Monroe, I thank you from the bottom of my heart that you were the first instrument the Lord God utilized to rescue this wonderful manuscript from the hands of those who wished to destroy it. Years in the future, men will remember the name Charles Monroe whenever they read an account of how it came to be preserved. Now, without further delay, hear what Ignatius tells us about Simon Peter."

CHAPTER 11

One week after the first international phone call had been made, another call was placed, but this time from Augusta, Georgia, to Tikrit, Iraq.

Amir: "Yes? Were you successful in your search?"

Sentry: "It took most of the week, but we were successful in determining that the package was initially delivered here to the address of an military officer who was injured, praise Allah, in our homeland, and is now undergoing rehabilitation in an Augusta military hospital. An associate was able to discover from a nurse at the hospital that a medical doctor returning from our native land brought a large package to the soldier's home shortly before that soldier was wounded. We have since discovered that the soldier is an infidel Christian minister.

"Another of our associates who was watching the soldier's house believes the brother of the soldier now has custody of the package. The brother is a financial manager and lives in Atlanta, so the New York associate and I are flying to Atlanta tonight to investigate this further."

Amir: "It would seem you need extra resources in order to complete this task. I charge you to think of time as an enemy in this search. You will tell your associates that nothing in their lives is more important than the successful completion of this mission. The fact that a Christian minister is involved with this package is most disturbing."

Sentry: "I will tell them there will be no rest or family gatherings until we complete our assignment."

Amir: "Very well. Keep to the phone schedule. I trust you will have greater success in Atlanta. The leaders in our group are increasingly anxious that the package will be found and returned. More of our resources in America are being devoted to this search. You may expect to hear from them shortly."

CHAPTER 12

"Reverend Monroe," Father Michael said, "It is such a blessing to be able to read what Ignatius writes about the leader of the apostles and the first bishop of Antioch." The priest then began to read aloud.

When I speak of the blessed apostle Peter, I do so with great fondness, for it was under his inspiring witness that I first heard about our Savior and Lord, Jesus Christ. As you know, Dorothea, Paul and Barnabas were the first to minister to the residents of Antioch and, by the grace of Almighty God, their efforts resulted in so many among the Gentiles becoming believers that word spread throughout the city; and my father, who was an official in the government, determined to hear for himself what his friends and clients were telling him about the wonderful words and acts of Jesus.

It was at this time, during the consulship of Antistius Vetus and Sullius Nerullinus, that Paul and Barnabas resolved to go to Jerusalem and present the evidence of the extensive conversions among the Gentiles taking place in Antioch and to resolve a controversy involving keeping the Jewish Law after baptism.

Many among the Jewish Christians maintained that the new Gentile converts were obligated to undergo circumcision, but Paul and Barnabas believed that wasn't necessary. During the absence of the apostles, Amplias, an early convert and friend of my father, was left in charge of the Christian believers. When Paul and Barnabas returned with the wonderful news that the leading figures in

Jerusalem had ruled in their favor, there was much rejoicing among the Gentile believers, and I had occasion to hear Paul preach to the believers. Despite my pleas that we become followers of the Way, however, my father insisted that we obtain more information before being observed in public with a congregation of believers.

After Paul and Barnabas departed to go to other mission fields, Amplias was again left in charge of the believers, but being of advanced years, he wrote to Peter and appealed to him to come and organize the church in Antioch. Almost from the moment Simon Peter arrived in the city, many among the Gentiles became believers, and my father invited Peter into our house to tell us more about the Way. Knowing that the Roman authorities were skeptical about this new faith, my father hesitated to commit himself or his household without further information, despite the power of Peter's preaching. It was then that Peter introduced my father to Luke, a physician and historian, who was a recent convert and was at that time interviewing those who had been eyewitnesses during the ministry of our Lord.

Even though my father continued to fear the reaction of the authorities should he become a follower of the Way, I prevailed upon him to allow Peter to baptize me, for I desired nothing other than to serve the Lord. Peter continued to visit in our home, and he asked me to accompany him as he visited the sick and infirm among the believers.

About this time Amplias went to be with the Lord, and Evodius, a holy man and a diligent worker, was appointed by Peter to lead the church while he traveled throughout the provinces of Galatia, Pontus, and Cappadocia, winning many to salvation by the power of his preaching. The apostle bade me assist Evodius in furthering the Lord's work in Antioch while he was away, and we ministered to the sick and destitute among the believers.

Peter frequently returned to our city and would confer with other disciples about their labors for the Lord; then he would determine where they were most needed and send them on further journeys to spread the Gospel. There was a great sense of urgency in those days, since most believers expected the end of days to be near.

Simon Peter was a natural, inspirational leader. His decisions were well thought out and were received with reverence by the disciples. I never heard anyone question him about any decision he made. He was extremely loyal to the disciples, and they considered him their great friend, as well as their unquestioned leader. His calm reassurances strengthened the elect when times were trying. I recall that his brother Andrew was of great assistance to Peter when decisions were made concerning pairing the disciples for various missionary endeavors.

Peter's reputation for impassioned preaching opened many doors. He had the kindest eyes I ever saw in a man, and this quality captivated large numbers of citizens who were seeking religious truth in those days. Many found it at the feet of the leader of the apostles.

Unfortunately, the controversy about circumcision did not end with the declaration made in Jerusalem. Many of the Jewish converts in Antioch still demanded that Gentile converts be circumcised to be accepted into the church. Among those who insisted upon circumcision was Baram—a Pharisee, a wealthy merchant, and a leader of the Jewish converts who had embraced the Way. Baram had opened his large residence for Christian services, and Peter was frequently present.

One day a large contingent of Jewish converts gathered in Baram's home to hear Peter speak on this subject and to voice their concerns. Baram began the discussion by saying, "We are aware of the declaration made in Jerusalem concerning the Gentiles and circumcision, and we believe this declaration was made in grievous error. As you were a companion of the Lord throughout his earthly ministry, we want to know if, at any time, he accepted Gentiles among his followers without requiring that they submit to the Law of Moses."

Peter stood before them and replied, "My brothers, hear me. During the three years I was with him, our Lord and Savior insisted that his ministry be first directed to the people of Israel, and for that reason, he forbade us to visit the towns of the Decapolis where the Gentiles were the majority; but among the crowds who came to hear him were Gentiles, and on more than one occasion I heard him marvel that, among the Gentiles, he found those whose faith in him was greater than was to be found among the circumcised.

"You have all heard that our Lord died on the cross but rose again from the dead. Indeed, his Resurrection is the reason you have elected to follow him. When he first appeared to his disciples in Jerusalem after his Resurrection, he said to us that all people in every nation must be told in his name to turn to God to be forgiven. He made no distinction between people of the circumcision and Gentiles. Scripture tells us that a great light will become known to the Gentiles, and I declare to you that great light is the same Jesus Christ you have elected to follow. Since the Lord makes no distinction between people, the circumcised and the uncircumcised, neither do those who follow him."

In all his travels to distant places, Peter always spoke to the circumcised first, then to the Gentiles. He instructed the disciples to do this in imitation of our Lord, but despite this practice, conversion among the Jews declined, and this decline was attributed to the decision made in Jerusalem and reinforced by Peter in Antioch that Gentile believers did not have to submit to circumcision.

Throughout his ministry, Peter would first exhort his listeners to be obedient to the governing authorities and to be matchless examples of good behavior in the midst of unbelievers. In spite of his exhortations, however, those in government, no doubt inspired by Satan, remained suspicious and were wont to accuse followers of the Way whenever civil discord took place.

I accompanied Peter on a mission to Comana in Cappadocia,

and when we arrived there, Esdras, the leader of the synagogue, invited the apostle to speak to the Jews. When we entered the synagogue on the appointed day, Esdras introduced Peter as a prominent member of the Way and asked him to provide evidence that the Messiah had come.

Peter took his place in the center of the building and said, "Fellow Israelites, you have asked me to give you evidence that the Messiah, the Promised One from ages past, has appeared during our time. I can and do testify that Jesus Christ is the Messiah, but you might say, 'Peter, you are deluded' or 'Peter, you lie.'

"During the time of his earthly ministry, I witnessed the many miracles that Jesus performed. With my own eyes I saw the lame walk, the blind see, and the lepers cured. Yes, I even saw the dead come back to life, all through the majesty of the power granted him by God.

"It is a far better thing for me to allow Holy Scripture in the words of the prophets to present the evidence so that you can judge for yourself whether or not Jesus is the Messiah. For I know, brothers, that you deem these ancients to have been inspired by God. I believe in my heart that they were led by God to prophesy those things that were to take place in our own time, and in the person of Jesus Christ.

"Ages ago, Zechariah foretold that thirty shekels would be given as a reward for the capture of the Messiah. When the one who was to betray him, Judas Iscariot, appeared before the Sanhedrin, he asked how much they were willing to pay him to deliver Jesus to them. They spoke among themselves, then offered him thirty shekels.

"The writer of the Psalms tell us, 'For it is not an enemy who approaches me, but it is you, my companion and friend, we who had fellowship together.' On the night Jesus was betrayed, this Judas Iscariot, one the Lord had selected and trusted as his friend, went up to him, kissed him, and said, 'Hail, Rabbi!'

"Jesus said, 'Friend, do what you have come to accomplish,' and Judas signaled for the temple guards to arrest and bind him.

"Zechariah said, 'Strike the shepherd that the sheep may be scattered; and I will turn my hands against the little ones.' My brothers, I confess to you that on the night the temple police came to arrest him, I ran away. Yes, we all ran away, my companions and I, all who had sworn to die with him, ran away, scattered like sheep.

"Isaiah tells us, 'He was oppressed and he was afflicted, yet he did not open his mouth; like a lamb that is led to the slaughter.'

"When Jesus was accused by the Sanhedrin, he remained silent, and when Pilate said, 'Do you not hear how many charges they bring against you?' he remained silent; he did not answer even to a single charge.

"Isaiah prophesied, 'He was pierced through for our transgressions. He was crushed for our iniquities. And by his scourging we are healed.' When Pilate saw that the Sanhedrin would not relent in their determination to have Jesus executed, he ordered that Jesus be scourged and condemned him to crucifixion.

"Another of the Psalms says, 'They divide my garments among them. And for my clothing they cast lots.' Now when he arrived at Golgotha, the soldiers wanted to divide his garments among them, but his outer garment was a seamless robe, so they decided to cast lots for it. In another place, one of the Psalms says, 'They pierced my hands and my feet.' When Jesus arrived at Golgotha, the place of execution, he was stripped of his clothes, and they nailed his hands and his feet to the cross.

"The Book of Amos says, 'And it will come about in that day,' declares the Lord God, 'that I shall make the sun go down at noon, and the earth will be dark in broad daylight.' I do testify, my friends, that on the day my Lord Jesus died, the sun disappeared, and the earth was in darkness, and men cried out in great fear. There are many still living who were present on that day, and you can ask them whether or not I testify to the truth."

Then Peter sat down, and there was much discussion about what he had told them. Several present said they had been in Jerusalem on the day our Lord was crucified and that Peter's testimony was true, that the earth had indeed become dark at around noon.

All through Cappadocia, Galatia, and Pontus in the synagogues of the towns, Peter preached much the same sermon, and a number of the Jews became followers of the Way. The Gentiles, however, were even more receptive, and many were baptized during Peter's ministry in those days.

At another time I accompanied the apostle when he was invited to address the synagogue in Adana. After he had spoken, several began to question whether new Gentile converts were required to abide by the Mosaic Law.

Peter rose and said to them, "My brothers, listen to me. All along, it has been God's plan that I was meant to bring the good news to the Gentiles as well as to the Jews. God has made it clear to me and to my brothers in Jerusalem, those who were our Lord's companions, that he loves all men, Jew and Gentile alike, and that he makes no distinction between them. This he demonstrated by giving the Holy Spirit in equal measure to Jew and Gentile alike. Since he has plainly shown that he loves Jew and Gentile equally, my brothers in Jerusalem and I have agreed that no further burden be placed on the Gentile believers than that they refrain from eating food dedicated to idols, meat that has been strangled, and that they refrain from illicit sexual encounters."

When several among them still argued that all converts should be required to abide by the Law of Moses, Peter answered and said, " Who even among you is able to keep every jot and tittle of the Law? My Lord and Savior Jesus Christ said that one was to love God with all his heart, all his spirit, and with all his mind, and to love his neighbor as himself. Beyond this, he laid no greater burden, and neither do we."

The first visit Peter made to Rome took place during the consulship of Volusius Saturninus and Cornelius Scipio at the invitation of the centurion Cornelius, who had been transferred at the emperor's command from Caesarea to Rome. You will recall that Cornelius and his family had been the first Gentiles to be baptized by Peter.

It seems that this same Cornelius had become a trusted companion of Claudius Nero Germanicus, the reclusive grand-nephew of Augustus Caesar. The many physical infirmities of Claudius left him with few friends and close associates, but because of their shared interest in Roman history, he and Cornelius became friends and worked together on several scholarly pursuits.

Shortly after Claudius surprised everyone by being named emperor, he ordered Cornelius to Rome to discuss the deteriorating political situation in Judea. Claudius was so impressed with the centurion's grasp of events there that he desired to promote him to general. Cornelius thanked the emperor profusely, but declined because of his advanced age, then retired from the army to his wife's estate outside Rome. Because of the emperor's hostility toward the Jews, he immediately began ministering to them in secret as well as the followers of the Way and arranged for them to meet in the catacombs near the Via Salaria.

The Holy Spirit looked with favor on Cornelius's work among the Jews and the Gentiles, and many desired baptism in the Lord's Way. He continued this work after Nero ascended the throne, and it was at this time that Cornelius wrote to Peter and begged the apostle to come to Rome.

Peter was working and baptizing many in Pontus. Churches had recently been established in Comana and Trebizond, and the apostle was on his way to Sinope when Cornelius's letter reached him. He was reluctant to interrupt the work of the Holy Spirit in Pontus, but decided it was important to visit with Cornelius, even for a short time, to strengthen the young church in Rome. Taking John Mark with him, he traveled to Rome.

When the disciples arrived in Rome, Cornelius welcomed them into his home. Peter was overjoyed to see that the sons and daughters of Cornelius were firm in their faith and how eager they were for Peter to recount for them what Jesus had said and done.

Cornelius explained that Nero had become increasingly despotic. For several months, the mood of the Roman public had turned against the Christians, lies had inflamed the crowd, and the emperor had noted the disposition of the public concerning the Christians. Cornelius revealed that Christian services were now held in secret in the burial chambers of the city, the catacombs.

Peter and John Mark were amazed when they saw how the Holy Spirit was at work among the people. Then Peter preached and John Mark interpreted, and many were baptized. They stayed for one month with Cornelius and his family, and Peter worked diligently to reorganize the administration of the church in Rome. He shared much of what he had heard the Lord teach while he lived among them; then the apostle blessed Cornelius, and he and John Mark set sail for Antioch.

While he was in Antioch, other apostles and disciples met with him to plan missionary journeys in areas where the Way was unknown.

I was with him in Paphlagonia when word reached him that certain teachers from Jerusalem were sowing confusion among the believers. Straightaway, we traveled to Amarchia.

"My brothers," Peter said, "when you first heard the wonderful news that the Messiah, the Promised One, God's son, had come and that he had accomplished many great miracles, your hearts were filled with joy. When you heard he had died as full payment for your sins, and by that act, had opened the gates of heaven for those who believed in him, your joy was complete.

"Filled with wonder, you pleaded with those who brought you this incredible message to share with you the things the Messiah had said and done during the years of his earthly ministry.

"You were told how he healed the sick and the lame and how he miraculously fed the multitudes who came to hear him speak. You were told how he drove the moneychangers out of the temple and chastised those who mistreated the poor and helpless.

"Your hearts overflowed with joy when you heard what Jesus said and did; and who were these messengers who brought this wondrous news to you? I was one, and I testified from the standpoint of having been a witness to these things he had said and done. Paul and Barnabas, though not being physical witnesses during his earthly ministry, were, nevertheless, through God's grace, spiritual witnesses, and they were inspired to testify to all these things. In your joy, you believed what we testified to and committed yourselves to follow the Way.

"What has happened to your joy and to your faith? Now men from Judea have come to you, posing as teachers with a different message, and your beliefs have been shaken. What you heard from me and from Paul and Barnabas has been challenged by these who claim to be righteous teachers; believe me, brothers, your salvation is at stake.

"Carefully examine what these so-called teachers have told you, and vigilantly ponder the consequences. What is the purpose of these ravening wolves but to devour your faith? They have said that Jesus was a holy man, perhaps a prophet, but he was not the Messiah, the Promised One, the Son of God. If what they claim is true, then Jesus was a most deluded man or a great liar, for I testify that I have heard him say on many occasions that he was the Son of God and that he was sent by his Father to bring salvation to those who believe in him. My brothers, he proved this claim by performing miracles that no man had ever seen in ages past. If he was not who he said he was, I and the other apostles have testified to a great lie.

There was total silence in the synagogue. All eyes were on the apostle. Peter continued, "Consider the great joy you first received when we brought this good news to you. Was this great joy the product of the evil one, the father of lies, who seeks only your downfall, or was it by and through the grace of Almighty God, who is your loving Father? Do these so-called teachers who proclaim a different message from ours have your spiritual welfare at heart, or do they seek to delude you for their own selfish purposes? I say to you that it was men such as these who shouted 'Crucify him!' when Jesus was brought before the Roman governor, and the truth is not in them. They are nothing but mists of the night, soon to be dissipated by the light of the sun, thieves who would steal your faith and deny you the Lord's gift of salvation.

"Come to your senses, dear brothers. Let no man mislead you. You are heirs of Almighty God, for unto you he gave his only Son. You were washed in the blood of this Son, and by this act, your sins were forgiven, and a place was prepared for you in paradise, an eternal home for all who believe and persist in this belief; but be forewarned. These wolves are merely the first to try to lead you astray. Others, even more dangerous, will come, for Satan has many slaves to do his bidding, and the Son of God is his most implacable foe."

Peter was tireless in his ministry. I could barely keep pace with him, and he was many years my senior. It was at this time he resolved to return to Jerusalem to meet with James and to determine what could be done to alleviate the suffering of believers being persecuted there.

The party of the Zealots was creating much havoc in Judea, and Christians were the objects of much scorn and ridicule. Upon his arrival in the Holy City, James informed Peter that the Sanhedrin had ordered him to be arrested on sight. He urged Peter to leave Judea immediately which the apostle reluctantly agreed to do.

You will recall, dear Dorothea, blessed Matthew's account of the Savior's life records that the angel of the Lord appeared to Joseph in a dream and told him to arise quickly and take Mary and the infant Jesus and flee into Egypt, for Herod was seeking to find and destroy the child. Joseph took the mother and child and fled into Egypt. They settled in a small village called Babylon until Herod died and they were able to return to Judea. It was to this same place that John Mark persuaded Peter to visit after the apostle's short stay in Jerusalem.

Upon their arrival in the fortress town of Babylon, Marcellus, a Roman officer, asked Peter to speak to the soldiers under his command who had expressed an interest in knowing more about the Way. He invited Peter to address the soldiers in his home and about ten gathered there to hear the apostle.

"My friends," Peter began, "you have heard that God long ago made a covenant with the Jews and declared them to be his chosen people. He promised to abide with them so long as they remembered to honor and worship him alone. He confirmed this bond by leading them out of slavery in Egypt and on to Judea where, under their kings, David and Solomon, they built a temple to worship him; but they proved not to be trustworthy and began to honor false gods made of stone and metal. Because of their sins, he chastised them and caused them to again be taken into slavery in distant lands, but he promised to send them a Messiah who would redeem them when they turned away from these false gods and remembered their covenant promise.

"Throughout all the years of this covenant, prophets had foretold that one day, God would send the Messiah, and the people longed for this day for many years. All their hopes for the future were grounded in this promise.

"My friends, I testify that God kept his promise and sent the Messiah, Jesus, but his own people did not accept him, even though he miraculously healed the sick, the lame, and the blind. Even though his signs and wonders were seen by multitudes, still, the religious authorities refused to accept him and conspired to bring about his death. The governor ordered Jesus to be crucified, but death could not hold him. On the third day, he rose from the grave as he said he would, and he has made it clear to me and his other disciples that God desires salvation for all men, Jew and Gentile alike, who believe that Jesus is God's only begotten son."

For several months Peter and John Mark preached to increasing crowds of soldiers and a number of them sought baptism. The conversion and baptism of the Roman officer, Marcellus had stimulated much interest among the members of the legion stationed in Babylon. It was at this time that a letter from Rome once again altered the apostle's work.

The letter was from Cornelius, the former centurion, to Peter, informing him that Simon Magus the Samaritan was in Rome, posing as the Messiah and leading believers astray.

You will recall from our beloved Luke's report, dear Dorothea, that Simon Magus, a performer, asked the apostles to sell him the power to call upon the Holy Spirit. Peter and John severely chastised Simon and exclaimed that the only price acceptable to God was faith.

Cornelius reported in his letter that Simon had convinced many of the believers that he was ordained by God with the gift of superior knowledge of divine matters, and the congregation was now divided, a few following Cornelius and others following Simon.

To Cornelius's distress, Senator Marcellus had fallen under the sway of Simon Magus. Cornelius reported that the Christian believers meeting in his own home had dwindled to less than twenty, and Simon Magus, with the help of Marcellus, had attracted ever larger crowds to the senator's home. Cornelius urged Peter to hasten to Rome to restore order among the believers.

When the apostle and John Mark arrived in Rome they met with Cornelius and almost immediately the three set out for Senator Marcellus' house which was located near the Tibur River. Cornelius had informed them that at that moment Simon was demonstrating his remarkable powers in the Senator's house.

When they arrived there, Simon, under the spell of Satan, deluded himself into thinking that Peter and his companions were there to honor him. He performed several magical acts, drawing exclamations of praise from the crowd. "My friends, I welcome Peter to this company for he above all others is due honor and respect for his actions in my honor. I endorsed him to lead my followers when the Sanhedrin in Jerusalem sought to take my life. I am the mirror of God, the Christ. In Samaria I was known as the 'Father' while Gentiles knew me as the 'Holy Spirit'; but in all Judea I am known as the 'Son.' Before, you knew me as 'Magus,' but I stand here before you this day to tell you I am the manifestation of the Godhead, the Supreme One, and if you only believe in me, you will have life forever in heaven."

Peter stood and began to speak in a loud, clear voice. "Romans, hear me. Even in a distant land, word came to me that Simon Magus had said and done many amazing and astonishing things. It was because of these things I heard that I am here with you this day, but what I heard from Simon's own lips is the most astounding claim of all. He claimed to be the reincarnation of Jesus Christ! And he has beguiled you with magic to cloud your judgment to make this absurd claim appear true.

"I assure you, I have known this man and his diabolical works for a long while. He pretended to accept Jesus Christ as Lord and Savior, but the truth is not in Simon Magus. When we placed our hands on the heads of those who had accepted Jesus as Lord and

Savior, the Holy Spirit entered them, and Simon Magus begged us to sell him this power. We told him then that the power of God was not for sale at any price and advised him to pray earnestly for forgiveness.

"Now he has appeared in your midst with the same magical trickeries. He is no manifestation of the Godhead; he is no resurrected Christ; he is an agent of Satan, the deceiver. He is a monstrous boil that, if not lanced, will infect the whole body with deadly poison, a charlatan with cheap tricks fit only for gullible men. He claims to be the risen Christ, but he is unfit to even trod the ground on which our Savior walked. He claims to be divine. He is a mere man like all of us, and the eternity he will inherit is the fire of an everlasting hell, along with Satan, his master."

Peter turned to Simon. "You claim to be the Christ, then prove it and not with cheap deceptions. Christ died on the cross and arose from the dead three days later. If you are who you claim to be, prove it here and now before this audience or take your foul trickeries elsewhere."

Simon announced that he would repeat the Resurrection. He demanded to be buried in Marcellus's garden on that very day and claimed he would rise again on the third day as he had done before. Simon called out to the people to come forth and observe his burial and return on the third day to witness his resurrection.

"So that the weak among you will be strengthened in your belief in me, I will be buried here for three days. After the tomb is filled, go to your homes and pray for enlightenment, then on the third day and at this same hour the tomb will be opened and I will come forth before your eyes."

Simon carefully arranged his robes and lay down in a coffin his assistants had provided. The lid was sealed, and the household slaves lowered the coffin into the ground.

Peter and his companions had left before the burial, but within the hour, they appeared at Marcellus's door.

"Marcellus," Peter said. "Come with me to the grave in your garden. There, the truth will be revealed."

"But, Demos, Simon's servant has told me that I must not leave this room and must remain in mourning and prayer until the appointed hour on the third day."

"Marcellus, you are being deceived yet again. Come with me and see for yourself."

They walked out into the Senator's garden and watched the gravesite from behind a tree. They observed Simon's assistants down on their knees; dirt from the tomb had been shoveled hurriedly aside, and the coffin was wrestled out of the ground. The assistants hastily removed the lid and pulled a clearly uncomfortable Simon from its confines.

Peter and the indignant Senator Marcellus walked up to them, and Peter said, "Simon Magus, your so-called resurrection is three days early. You expected people to return three days later to find you already 'resurrected.' You are now exposed here in Rome as you were in Samaria, and Marcellus will proclaim the truth of your 'resurrection' to those whom you have deceived. You have no place among true believers in our Lord and Savior, Jesus Christ so take your trickeries elsewhere.

Peter continued to minister to the Romans. He laid his hands on Cornelius and pronounced that henceforth the former centurion would serve as the community's bishop; then he laid his hands upon members of Cornelius's household—Sergius, Licinius, and Trebonius—and charged them with extending the Lord's work to the outer suburbs of Rome and beyond.

One day Cornelius said to John Mark, "We implore you to write down all Peter has said in the past, that we and other Christians might use his wonderful recollections of the Lord's sayings and actions when we speak to unbelievers."

John Mark agreed and began soon after, dear Dorothea, the manuscript that has been so helpful to those of us who never knew the Lord in the flesh. It was at about this time that the terrible fire broke out in the shops around the Circus Maximus destroying much of Rome and giving rise to the story that Nero had purposely set the fire. To avoid personal blame, the emperor put out the word that the fire was started by the Christians and ordered his soldiers to round up the Christians for judgment.

In the mass trials that followed, Tigellinus, the Praetorian prefect, convicted all the captive Christians—men, women, and children—as arsonists as well as atheists and sentenced them to a humiliating death as entertainment for the public.

Cornelius and his companions had taken Peter aside and persuaded him to flee to Perusia and take shelter among the Christians there. But as he traveled north on the Via Flaminia, Peter suddenly halted, fell on his knees, and wept. "My friends, the Lord has spoken to me and has made it clear that I must return to Rome. I heard his voice say to my shame, 'Who will comfort the sheep when the wolf appears if the shepherd runs away?'"

So Peter returned to the city with John Mark as his only companion, while Cornelius and the others were directed by the apostle to continue on to Perusia. To the frightened believers in Rome, hiding as they were in the catacombs beneath the city streets, Peter's presence brought a measure of consolation and his words comforted them.

He reminded them of the promise the Lord had made to those who followed him on the last night he was among them. "Even on the night that he was to be betrayed, our Lord said to us, 'Do not be afraid, for I go to prepare a place for you in my Father's house, that where I am, you shall be also. And in that house there are many rooms. So do not be afraid of anything evil men bring against you. As they hated me, so shall they hate you. You are my beloved. Be not afraid.'"

The believers were heartened by Peter's words and gave thanks that they were among the Lord's elect, but as the persecution increased in intensity, Peter decided that John Mark should leave Rome and return to Egypt to continue spreading the Good News there. A short while later, the Praetorian Guard raided the catacombs, arrested Peter along with many Christians gathered there, bound them, and brought them before the Prefect Tigellinus to be tried.

Recognizing that he had in his custody the leader of the Christians, Prefect Tigellinus said to Peter, "How dare you Christians deny worship to the emperor! What possessed you to set fires that have so devastated our city? You are an accursed people and an insult and disgrace to the people of Rome. Speak, and do it quickly, for I tire of you and all your deluded followers; but perhaps you have reconsidered and desire to worship the emperor after all. Speak!"

Peter answered, "Noble Prefect, you know full well that no one among our brothers set fires in the city. The reason for this persecution is that we believers worship only one God, the creator of the universe. Our Holy Scripture, in existence before Rome was ever settled, puts it plainly, 'The Lord alone is God! There are no others!' How, then, can we worship the emperor, a man like ourselves, when the Lord alone is God?"

Tigellinus made a show of covering his ears and scoffed at this claim, saying, "You are the leader of those cursed and deluded men who claim that a condemned criminal was king of the Jews. You call the one who was nailed to the cross, 'Lord.' All of you wretches who brought this foolish belief to Rome deserve to die exactly like your so-called king."

"You are correct. We do acknowledge Jesus, the one you crucified, as Lord and King, but he rose triumphant from the grave, Prefect, and he sits at his Father's right hand in glory. I know this because I have seen him with my own eyes as have many others. Those who believe in him will share eternal life with him."

"Silence! I've heard enough of this outrage!" cried the prefect, again covering his ears. "I will hear no more! Guard, take this man to the Tullianum where he might come to his senses and worship the divine emperor. Remove him from my sight!"

Peter was taken to the Tullianum, the dreaded Roman dungeon, and chained to a pillar in that dark and fearsome place. There he remained in chains for many months, each day being asked by the guard if he had reconsidered and was prepared to worship the emperor, but his answer was ever, "The Lord alone is God. There is none other before him. He sent his Son to die for me. He alone do I worship." All during this time, he remained chained to that pillar, and the guards marveled at his endurance for he was unable to lie down because of the chains. Indeed, several of their number, including the detail commanders, Martiniam and Processus, were so impressed with the apostle's faithfulness in such adversity that they became believers and secretly asked him to baptize them.

Later, when Tigellinus heard that even the guards had become admirers of the apostle, he realized that Peter would never worship the emperor and ordered the guard to take the prisoner to Vatican Hill and crucify him.

Processus, who was in charge of the guard, walked alongside the apostle and whispered to him, "Peter, we can overpower the soldiers, remove your shackles, and help you escape."

But Peter replied, "Many years ago, my friend, after his glorious Resurrection, the Lord Jesus told me that a day would surely come when I was old and grey that men would lead me where no man wants to go. I now see that day has come and, where once I denied even knowing him, I now proclaim him my Lord and Savior. How I have missed him! Rejoice with me, for this day I will meet him in his Father's house just as he promised."

Peter asked the soldiers to nail him head downward on the cross, saying he was not worthy to die as his Lord had so long ago in Jerusalem. Processus ordered them to comply with the apostle's wishes. So it was that Peter, the one Jesus named to lead the apostles, died serving our Lord even to the end.

CHAPTER 13

When Father Michael finished reading aloud, he looked at Charles, Ken, and Doctor Bankkour, all of whom seemed completely lost in thought; then the priest gently spoke, "Gentlemen, I dislike having to interrupt your meditations, but the good Doctor and I have a plane to catch shortly, so we need to proceed with our report."

Doctor Bankkour answered, "Forgive me, Father. I was truly lost in thought. Every time I read or hear Ignatius's account of Peter's ministry, his life, and the terrible price he paid for his faith, I'm overwhelmed with the awesome new information this discovery brings to us. Now, as I had promised, it's time to analyze what we've heard, and I'd like to begin by pointing out that Ignatius seems to validate what historians could only speculate about as to the date the first Church council was held in Jerusalem. My notes tell me that C. Antistius and M. Sullius Nerullinus were counsels in the year 50 AD, so that, apparently, is the date Paul and Barnabas presented the case for Gentile converts before the others in Jerusalem. Also, I find it intriguing that Ignatius tells us Peter was the one to introduce Luke to Theophilus, Ignatius' father. Think about it. Ignatius, as a boy and young man, had already met Peter, Luke, and probably several others of the first Christian followers of the Lord."

"And if I may add," said Father Michael, "it's no less intriguing to find that Ignatius confirms what we Syrian believers have long maintained, that Evodius was indeed the first bishop consecrated by Saint Peter in Antioch. This has been a long-standing tradition of the Eastern Church, and I know our brothers at the monastery and indeed throughout the Eastern Orthodox community will rejoice in this confirmation.

"It is also fascinating to learn that Peter actively used a number of Old Testament Messianic prophecies in his preaching to substantiate the claim that Jesus was beyond question the long-awaited Messiah. I feel sure that the other apostles must have used this same approach in their ministries.

"Perhaps the most exciting news of all is the revelation from Ignatius that Centurion Cornelius, featured in Luke's book of Acts, is one of the founders of the church in Rome. To the best of my knowledge, no information about this has been previously discovered."

"Not only that, but Cornelius is described by Ignatius as being a friend and companion of Claudius before he was elevated to the imperial throne," said Bankkour, after apologizing for interrupting Father Michael. "And it's certainly possible that Cornelius's friendship with the future Emperor Claudius may have allowed the Church to prosper and grow during the years Claudius ruled the empire. Perhaps it was this friendship that prevented a more harsh persecution of Christians during Claudius's reign."

Father Michael smiled as he looked at Charles and said, "You see, Reverend Monroe, the great excitement of this project causes scholars to chatter like schoolboys, each of us so anxious to share what we've learned with you that we can't wait for the other fellow to finish before we jump in."

He paused before adding, "We know that Paul had to deal with what he referred to as false teachers among the faithful as reported in his Epistles. What we hadn't known until this discovery was the apparent widespread activity of these false teachers during the early years. Ignatius tells us of Peter's hurried trip in Asia to confront these men and their teaching probably not too long after the first church council meeting in Jerusalem. It would seem that Peter, as well as Paul, had to spend a portion of time going back to the churches to repair the damage caused by these men.

"It is certainly possible that some of these were Gnostics," continued the priest. "Gnostics maintained that the most important teachings of Christ were meant only for a select few. It would seem that both Paul and Peter were anxious to proclaim that the fullness of the Gospel was to be freely preached to all believers."

Father Michael hesitated for a moment, then, smiling broadly he said, "And what about the news of a Roman fortified outpost in Egypt called Babylon? There has always been rampant speculation about the use of the name Babylon as it's associated with Peter. Some scholars believe the apostle traveled to the city of Babylon during his years of ministry, yet others dispute that and claim he used the name as a code word for Rome. Ignatius tells us that Peter, in fact, visited the small fortress town of Babylon in Egypt—the same area that the Holy Family settled in when they fled Herod's wrath.

"Historians tell us that after Augustus conquered Egypt, he established a military fortification there because of the site's strategic location near the Nile. From this fort, the legions could respond to any efforts of rebellion from the conquered Egyptians with the added factor that it was an ideal place to collect tolls from craft plying the waters of the Nile."

Doctor Bankkour drew the group's attention to Ignatius's account of the news about Christian persecution in Jerusalem, news that caused Peter to journey there to give comfort to the believers, only to have James, the brother of our Lord, warn him to leave the city.

"This was, apparently, around the year 62 AD, for most biblical scholars believe that James himself was martyred later this same year by allies of the high priest, Ananus."

The linguist continued, "All Judea was in turmoil during those years leading up to the Jewish rebellion against Rome. The Zealot party of the Jews was intolerant of any but the orthodox Hebrew faith, and it's known that the Christians suffered greatly since they were viewed as heretics by the Zealots. It was only a few years later that open rebellion broke out, which ultimately led to the slaughter of thousands of Jews by the Roman legions and the enslaving of thousands more when Jerusalem and the temple fell to the Romans in 70 AD."

Then Father Michael said, "You'll remember, Reverend Monroe, that the *Acts of the Apostles* tells us in chapter eight about the confrontation Peter and John had with Simon Magus in Samaria. Simon wanted to purchase the ability to call down the Holy Spirit but was rebuked and sent packing by Peter and John.

"Ignatius explains that after being overcome in Samaria by the apostles, Simon journeyed to Rome, where he apparently picked up quite a following, even among the believers, by his magic acts. Early church tradition refers to Simon's adventures in Rome, and a few even describe Peter's victory over him there, but Ignatius's letter explains in much detail how Peter unmasked the magician at the senator's home.

"It is indeed amazing that so many early church traditions are verified, at least in part, by Ignatius's account. One of the more fanciful versions of this confrontation had Simon Magus soaring above astonished Romans by means of hidden cables before the prayers of Peter caused the cables to part, dropping the magician to an ignominious heap in front of a laughing crowd."

Charles then asked, "What about Ignatius's claim that Peter was chained up for months in, what did he call it, the Tullianum? Do any of the traditions support that claim?"

Bankkour responded, "The Tullianum is another name for the Mamertine, one of the most notorious prisons in ancient history. It was constructed around 700 BC in the Forum in Rome originally as a cistern, but became a prison for the most high profile prisoners of the Roman Republic, then for the Roman Empire.

"You might recall from Roman history that Cicero had the Cataline conspirators executed there, and Julius Caesar had the Gallic chief, Vercingetorix, and many other Gallic chieftains confined there for years until they were forced to march in Caesar's triumphs. Afterward, these prisoners were taken back to the Mamertine to be executed. Years before these events, the African ruler Jugurtha, captured by Gaius Marius, was imprisoned there. For one to be sent to the Mamertine was a death sentence. Prisoners were either strangled or starved to death.

"There is an early church tradition claiming that both Peter and Paul were imprisoned in the Mamertine. Visitors to the prison today are shown the pillar to which the apostles were chained, but most scholars haven't placed much credence in this tradition. Ignatius confirms it, however, and I feel sure historians will argue about it for years to come.

"Paul, of course, wrote about his own imprisonment several times in his Epistles. Most scholars believe his first confinement in Rome was simply a matter of house arrest. The second one could well have been in the dreaded Mamertine.

"We don't know what date the Mamertine was abandoned as a prison," continued Bankkour, "but at least since medieval times, the site has been used for Christian services. Today, visitors to the site are shown an altar containing an upside-down crucifix as a reminder of the way Saint Peter was martyred. Beside the altar is a slender column said to be the one to which both Peter and Paul were chained."

Father Michael then added, "One of the most interesting and intriguing aspects of Ignatius's account is his report that the former centurion, Cornelius, persuaded John Mark to write down the substance of Peter's sermons in Rome with the clear implication that this later became the Gospel according to Mark."

"I was struck by that, too, Father," Charles said. "In my seminary days at Emory, I recall reading that some of the early church fathers considered Mark's Gospel to have been Peter's recollections of Jesus's ministry."

"It is true, Reverend Monroe, that early Christian tradition connects John Mark to Peter as Peter's secretary in Rome. It certainly makes perfect sense that Peter, who most probably spoke only Aramaic, would need an interpreter when preaching to the Romans, who more than likely wouldn't have understood the Aramaic tongue. John Mark, who, like Paul, must have spoken Greek as well as Aramaic probably stood beside the apostle translating what Peter was saying about his years with Jesus. I can well imagine the Roman congregation eagerly waiting for John Mark's Greek translation of Peter's recollections. Then, all too soon, Peter was arrested, tried, and condemned, and the marvelous memories he shared of Christ's life and works on earth would have been silenced if not for Mark's writing about them.

"Sadly," the priest continued, "we no longer have the written early Christian history of Papias, a first-century Christian writer, but we do have a fragment of his work preserved by the great church historian Eusebius in his own church history. According to Eusebius, Papias wrote that Mark had become Peter's interpreter and accurately wrote down what he remembered the apostle said, but not necessarily in the order it was said.

"So it seems reasonable to me," continued Father Michael, "that the Romans, and according to Ignatius, Cornelius himself, would prevail upon John Mark, Peter's long-time companion in ministry, to write down what he remembered of the sermons of Peter that he had so recently interpreted for them.

"Most scholars consider the Gospel of Mark to be the first of the four Gospels written, and they consider that the other Gospel writers drew heavily upon Mark's work as these later books were developed. Ignatius tells us that we owe so much of what we know about what Christ said and did to Cornelius and the other Romans who successfully prevailed upon Mark to record Peter's sermons.

"It would seem that John Mark was a figure of much greater prominence than I had thought," Charles said. "And I don't recall reading about his missionary journey to Egypt."

Father Michael replied, "Here's an interesting bit of news. It seems there's newly discovered archaeological evidence in Israel revealing that bits and pieces of what we call 'Mark's Gospel' written in Aramaic have been found among the thousands of fragments scholars have pieced together from the Dead Sea Scrolls. Furthermore, they've dated these fragments as having been written no later than 50 AD. This would mean that the first Gospel to be written was completed less than twenty years after Christ was crucified. Should this be the case, it would mean that the first Gospel was written while many eyewitnesses were still alive who could verify the events as having taken place as recorded. Most scholars believe that Peter led the young man John Mark and his mother to Christ around 44 AD. We know the apostle affectionately considered John Mark his son in the spirit, as mentioned in First Peter.

"As to John Mark's journey to Egypt," continued the priest. "Remember, according to Ignatius, Mark had already worked to spread the faith there after Peter had assigned that country to him early on. We can speculate he had made long and enduring friendships with converts to the faith there who kept him appraised about conditions in that land. The Coptic Christians in Egypt have a long-standing tradition that Mark went back to Alexandria in Egypt around 65 AD. The evangelist no doubt brought his completed Gospel written in Greek with him when he traveled to Egypt. This makes perfect sense, for most of the people in Alexandria either spoke or were familiar with Greek."

The priest smiled wistfully as he continued speaking, "The

Egyptian Coptic Christian tradition tells us that the Greek-speaking people of Alexandria, alarmed at the rapid growth of the church under John Mark's leadership, put out rumors that the Christians were about to destroy the pagan idols. Thus incensed, a furious mob descended on the Christians while they were celebrating the Lord's Resurrection from the grave. Mark was roughly seized, a rope was placed around his neck, and he was kicked and spat upon while being dragged through the streets of Alexandria behind a team of horses. Finally, after hours of this brutal treatment by the angry pagans, he died of his injuries."

As they prepared to leave to return to the airport, Doctor Bankkour turned to Ken Monroe and said, "You've been so quiet during our presentation, Mr. Monroe. You must excuse our enthusiasm, but we who spend our lives delving into ancient religious manuscripts rarely, if ever, are privileged to be acquainted with such a monumental discovery as Ignatius's work. It will be the center of discussion among scholars for decades to come, but I realize this might not be nearly so exciting for those not in our line of work. Please forgive us if we're boring you."

Ken, taking Doctor Bankkour by the arm and leading him down a hall away from his brother's hearing, said, "Quite the contrary, Doctor. Please don't mistake my silence for lack of interest. You know, when I first became involved in this business, it was only because of Charles's injuries. I admit I had little personal curiosity other than being of assistance to him, but as we've progressed in this task, I've become more interested in the revelations of what those first Christians accomplished and the tribulations they endured.

"I'll confess, Doctor, when this project began, I expected to be bored. I'm not. I find that I'm beginning to be more involved than I would have ever thought possible. My concern now is about Charles. His health is not improving as we had hoped. He has continued to lose weight, and his strength seems to be waning. I don't know how much longer he'll be physically able to make these trips, no matter how much he wants to."

Six weeks later, Ken met alone with Doctor Bankkour and Father Michael to review the translation of the next chapter of the manuscript by the team. Ken indicated his brother had shown only a slight improvement. After expressing his concern about Charles's lack of progress, Bankkour began by saying, "This next chapter deals with the ministry of both Andrew, Peter's brother, and Matthias, the only apostle not personally called by our Lord during his lifetime. Matthias, of course, was the one selected to replace Judas Iscariot after his treacherous betrayal."

CHAPTER 14

A phone call was placed from Atlanta, Georgia, to Tikrit, Iraq on a Tuesday evening at precisely ten o'clock p.m.

Amir: "Hello."

Sentry: "I trust you are well, Amir."

Amir: "Very well, thank you. And what have you to report? Has your search been fruitful?"

Sentry: "We seem to be a step or two behind, even with the additional resources you have assigned us."

Amir: "Then enlighten me as to what progress you've made. I need to inform those important people who are following this project closely, and I have to tell you, their patience is wearing thin. Several prominent members have said the quest should have been completed by now and that the package should already be on the way back to where it came from."

Sentry: "I promise you, and hope you will assure them, that all of us involved in this matter have worked day and night, but have been frustrated at first by the absence of the minister's brother from his workplace in Atlanta. When we discovered that he had left town, we used this opportunity to enter his home and search for the package. It was not to be found anywhere, and several of our associates are capable searchers. The next evening, we even managed to enter and thoroughly search his workplace, but the package was not there, either.

"When the minister's brother returned from his trip, we

managed to enter his home once again, the following evening, but as before, without results. We even entered the workplace again, thinking he might have left it there, but the package was not to be found.

"When we met at the home of one of our associates, we discussed all the details of our stay in Atlanta. We have concluded that the brother must have either sent the package somewhere by express or he must have personally delivered it while on his trip out of town. Fortunately, while we were in his office, I observed that he had written the words 'Saint Matthew Monastery, West Virginia' on his desk calendar. After talking to you, I am planning to call one of our contacts in Charleston, West Virginia and ask him about this place."

Amir: "Then get on with it. I need not tell you that the important personages in our organization are beginning to have second thoughts about the capabilities of you and your associates. I hope you will have something meaningful to report next Tuesday."

CHAPTER 15

"Before we begin, Doctor," Ken said. "There's another matter I'll share with you though I don't think it has any bearing on our project. It appears that an intruder has entered my house in my absence. Nothing seems to be missing, but still, it's a bit disconcerting to know someone has violated your privacy."

"I can well imagine your concern. And I hope it's as you say, unrelated to our project. Have you notified the authorities?"

"I did call the police. They came, made out a report, and informed me there's been a rash of similar incidents in this neighborhood lately. But please, it's a matter of little consequence. Let's drop it and continue with your latest translation.

Doctor Bankkour looked at his notes and began to read aloud.

Another of the Lord's first followers I came to know personally and admire was Andrew, the brother of Peter. Even among the saintly apostles, dear daughter in Christ, Andrew was known as a man of great spirituality who spent long hours at prayer. This intense spirituality appeared early in the life of Andrew, who, as a young man, left his home in Capernaum and journeyed many miles south, where he spent a year studying with the Essenes, a small austere Jewish sect who disavowed contact with the Sadducees and Pharisees that they considered to be too worldly. The Essenes hid themselves away amid the mountains of the Judean Wilderness near the Dead Sea.

When John the Baptist appeared out of the desert proclaiming that the Day of the Lord was near and calling on the Jews to repent and be baptized, Andrew heeded the call and became one of John's followers. For over a year, he assisted in the preaching and baptisms conducted by John along the banks of the Jordan River; then, when the Baptist saw Jesus and proclaimed him to be the Son of God, Andrew immediately left John and became our Lord's first disciple. Among the apostles, he was always referred to as the First Called, and that holy title followed him for the rest of his life.

Andrew was an able administrator and organizer, and he used these talents to help his brother Peter plan the ministry travels of the disciples. He was extremely devoted to Peter, and I never heard him argue with anyone, friend or foe. He was calm and forthright and was an excellent judge of men and their capabilities.

I first met Andrew when he joined his brother Peter on a mission we had undertaken to Amisus in Paphlagonia. He was accompanied by Matthias, the one chosen by the apostles to succeed the traitor, Judas Iscariot. They had arrived after almost a year spent establishing churches in Thracia. While they had been successful leading many to the Lord in Appollonia Pontica and Thynias, especially among the Gentiles, they had been brutally opposed by the Jews in Byzantium, and Matthias had received a serious head injury as a result.

While Matthias recovered, Andrew joined us for several weeks as we labored in the Lord's vineyard in several towns along the coast in Paphlagonia. In Sinope, the leader of the synagogue, Esdras, said, "My brothers, these men have come to us with a message concerning events that took place in recent memory in Judea."

Andrew spoke. "Men of Israel," he said, "you have no doubt heard about a great commotion in the land of our fathers in recent years. A man known as John the Baptizer came forth with a stirring message, claiming that the Day of the Lord was near. Many of our brothers came to hear him, and a number of them submitted to his baptism as a symbol of their desire for salvation. The authorities, anxious about their control over religious matters, began to plot ways to silence John, but in the meanwhile, Jesus of Galilee came to John to be baptized, and when John laid eyes on him, he shouted, 'Behold, here before you is one whose sandals I am unworthy to latch! He is the Son of God!'"

One of the congregants said, "Our fathers have always told us what sets us apart from the Gentiles is our belief that the Lord our God is one. Where is it written that God would have a Son? Why would the Baptizer utter such blasphemy?"

Andrew replied, "Do you recall what King David said a thousand years ago in the Psalms? 'The Lord said to me, "'You are my son; this day I have begotten you.'" The prophet Isaiah said, 'For unto us a child is born, a Son is given; and the government will be on his shoulders.' And the prophet Micah foretold the place of his birth when he said, 'But you, Bethlehem Ephrata, though you are tiny among the many places in Judah, yet from you shall he come forth, the one who is to be ruler in Israel, one whose life has been foretold from ancient times.'

"My friends, John boldly declared that Jesus, the man in their midst, was the Lamb of God. And Jesus himself frequently spoke of God as his Father. Jesus said no one approached the Father without first coming through him, and for making that claim, he was condemned by the Sanhedrin and crucified at their urging by the Romans.

"And where were we, his friends, when the Sanhedrin's guards came to arrest him? Where were those of us he had chosen to be his followers? Where were we, his companions, who had pledged to defend him or die with him? Why, we were so frightened, we ran away and hid in the cellars of Jerusalem, and our frantic hope was that somehow we could escape the Sanhedrin and return to Galilee.

"Yes, my friends, I confess we were desperate, frightened men. The one we called 'Lord' had been taken from us, beaten by the Roman soldiers, stripped of His clothing, and nailed to the cross. He was pronounced dead and was buried in a borrowed tomb.

"On the third day, while we still skulked about in fear and trembling, the women of our company went to perform the rites of the dead. When they arrived at the tomb, it was deserted; he was not there. Then they saw two men, if men they were, dressed in pure white clothing. One of the men spoke and said, 'Who is it you seek?'

"The women said they were there to perform the rites of the dead for Jesus. Then, the one who had spoken said to the women, 'Why do you seek the living here among the dead? He has risen, as he said he would. Go now, and tell his companions.'

"Peter, who stands before you, and another disciple ran to the tomb and saw nothing but his burial shroud. Later, while we were all discussing what this could possibly mean, there he was, standing in our midst, and we were stunned. Then he said, 'Do not be afraid. Did I not tell you that Scripture about me must be fulfilled?'"

At that moment, one of the men in the synagogue stood and angrily exclaimed, "Do you expect us to believe that this Jesus who was crucified and buried arose from his grave and appeared in your midst? This is madness, and we are fools for allowing Esdras to invite you into our company with such nonsense!"

But Andrew continued, "My brothers, everywhere we go, we first seek out the Jews to bring them the Good News that has taken place in our own time. The Scripture you read each Sabbath foretells the coming of the Messiah, and this is the hope we have all had in our hearts from generation to generation. It is that hope that has sustained us as a people. Now, when it is announced to you that the Messiah has indeed come as the prophets declared, you reject him and the salvation he brings, bought by him at such a great and terrible price. Now I solemnly warn you that you reject him at your peril, and we will go to the Gentiles, for the salvation he announced is intended for all men who believe in him."

Andrew accompanied his brother as they traveled to other towns that had synagogues. When they were invited to speak, many refused to listen, and each time the apostles announced that if the Jews would not listen, they would go to the Gentiles, for the Gentiles were anxious to hear about the Lord Jesus.

Andrew told Peter that he and Matthias, who had recovered from his injury, were anxious to undertake a mission to Scythia. The Scythians had long been known for their warlike character. They were renowned horsemen eagerly sought out by military leaders to serve as mercenary cavalry. Some even said the Scythians had not abandoned their ancient habit of eating human flesh. Peter agreed that the Good News should be made known to the Scythians and blessed both Andrew and Matthias. This was the last time the brothers were ever to see each other on this earth.

Andrew and Matthias sailed to far distant Olbia in Scythia. The city magistrate explained that most Scythians preferred to live outside the city in tents, as they herded livestock and moved with the seasons. He also cautioned the apostles to be careful and not insult the gods of the Scythians, for the tribesmen were barely civilized and easily provoked to violence. He warned them that, should violence occur, he would be powerless to take any action since the maintenance of peace with the powerful and warlike Scythians was the major priority of the governor of the region.

The apostles traveled several miles from the city to a large gathering of the Roxolani tribe. When he was invited to address them, Andrew said, "O, Scythians, what I have to tell you began during the dawn of history and has been told from one generation to another down through the ages since the earth was formed. When the Lord of the universe saw that man, his highest creation, was inclined to do evil rather than good, he looked around at all the tribes on the earth, the mighty and the weak, for he desired to make a covenant that would be a blessing for the whole earth.

"Finally, his eye fell on a small and insignificant tribe, and he selected that small, unimportant tribe out of all the world's inhabitants to be his people of the covenant. From this tribe would come many prophets and holy men, who would guide these people with the oracles sent down from the Creator himself from highest heaven. Through hundreds of years and through many generations, the prophets continued to say, once the time was right, the Creator would send the Anointed One, his only Son, to tell these people and all the sons of men how to gain eternal life.

"These oracles and promises of the Lord of the universe were written down to be passed from one generation of the chosen people to another. Many of their learned men spent their days searching these Scriptures, hoping to identify the time the Promised One would appear.

"Because they were few in number and weak, these people were frequent victims of stronger tribes, who enslaved them and took them away from their homeland in chains as slaves. Even during the long years of their captivity, these people still believed the Anointed One would come one day as the prophets had foretold. They held on to this promise down through the ages, despite great suffering and tribulation.

"Then, in our own day, the Promised One, the one our people call Messiah, did come and lived among these chosen people, but the leaders of his own people refused to accept him. Even though he cured the blind, the sick, and the lame, they would not acknowledge him. Even though he raised the dead, they would not believe in him. In fact, these leaders conspired against him, apprehended him, tried and beat him, and even had him put to death.

"But death could not hold the Promised One, for he arose from the dead in glory and announced that inasmuch as those to whom he had been promised had denied him, from that day forward, the Lord of Creation's kingdom in heaven was forever open for anyone from any tribe who would acknowledge him as the Creator's Son. This, then, is the reason why we have traveled so far and braved the storms at sea to bring you the Good News that Jesus Christ, the Anointed One, is Lord, and if you will acknowledge him, keep his commandments, and believe in him, life eternal will be granted to you."

Soriaca, chief priest of the Scythian god Ares, said, "And where is this Messiah you claim rose from the dead? Is he here in your company? Did he travel with you on the ship? Present him to us that we might see him for ourselves. We are servants of the great god Ares, and he is sufficient for us. By his command we sacrifice our enemies to his glory. What need do we have for new gods?"

Andrew answered, "Jesus Christ has ascended into heaven to sit at the right hand of his Father, but he offers a glorious salvation and eternal home in his Father's kingdom to all who believe in him. He came not to demand sacrifice and victims, but to teach men how to live more abundantly in this world and how to live with him forever in eternity. No man ever spoke the words of comfort and assurance that Jesus Christ did. No man ever loved others as Jesus did, so much so that he died to set us free from the bondage of sin. You ask what need do you have for new gods? I tell you, Jesus loved the Scythians enough for Matthias and me to come this great distance to tell you about him."

During the months that followed a large number of the Scythians gave up their fierce, warlike ways and became believers. Andrew named Argempta, one of the first converts, as bishop of the Scythian congregation. Then the apostles felt the Holy Spirit calling them to journey to Greece.

When they arrived in that land, Andrew and Matthias ministered first to the church in Thynias, then they established new congregations of believers in Enos, Pydna, and Lyrissa. They also ministered to the churches founded by Paul in Neapolis and Philippi and several of the islands in the Aegean Sea.

Andrew rejoiced to find Luke at Patrae in Achaea and decided to establish his base in that city while he worked with Luke bringing souls to Christ in the various towns and villages nearby.

Matthias felt called by the Lord to return to Jerusalem. He had been one of the Seventy, the first disciples who followed the Lord after the apostles had become his companions. Matthias had been a fisherman from Capernaum who had worked with James and John on the boat owned by their father, Zebedee. He was present when the Lord healed a blind man, and immediately left the boat to become one of the Seventy.

When he arrived in Jerusalem he found that the congregation of believers there had suffered terribly from the persecution of the Zealots, as well as from the enmity of the Sanhedrin. Several prominent Christian families had already departed for Galilee or Petra because of this persecution.

When he saw a group of Christians being verbally abused by Zealots, Matthias boldly proclaimed, "To believers and nonbelievers alike, I address you all in the name of Jesus the Messiah, who paid the full price for your salvation by his death on the cross." The murmuring stopped and everyone listened to the apostle.

"I remember as though it were yesterday when Jesus commissioned his earliest disciples to go forth to the Jewish towns and villages to announce the Good News. He told them to stay away from Gentile and Samaritan towns and minister only to the people of Israel, and he declared to all of them that the reign of God was near. Then he instructed his followers to heal the sick, the blind, and the lame and expel the demons; he told them to take no money or sandals on their journey to these towns, but to depend on the hospitality of the household that welcomed them.

"The Lord Jesus then said to them, 'I'm sending you like lambs into a pack of wolves. There are people who will take you before the judges or have you beaten wherever they find you. Because of me, you will be brought before authorities to tell them and the Gentiles about your faith.'

"'Brothers and sisters will betray one another and be responsible for each other's death. In those times parents will betray their own children, and children will betray their parents and even have them killed. Each one of you will be hated because of me. But if you are faithful until the end, salvation is yours.'

"My friends, the day the Lord described has come. It is as he said it would be, and if we remain faithful to him, no matter what forces are brought against us, we will enjoy eternal life with him in his Father's kingdom. Do not let others dictate where you will spend eternity."

Nathan, the leader of the Zealots, said in a loud voice, "You dare to call that one Lord? We who are the children of Abraham will restore the faith of God's chosen people to its pure and ancient form. That one was a heretic and was justifiably condemned for blasphemy. By calling him Lord and Messiah, you blaspheme also, and the punishment for blasphemy is death; but we are called upon to be merciful, and if you recant in our presence and acknowledge that one to be a traitor and a fraud to the true faith, you will be spared."

Matthias said, "He healed the sick, the blind, and the lame among our people, yet you cannot even say his name, but can only refer to him as 'That One.' There was a time when every one of his followers were frightened men and denied him, I among them, but he forgave us and sent the Holy Spirit to strengthen us and commanded that we take the Good News to all men, not only those of the Covenant. You ask me to recant in order to save my life. Never again! I testify that he is the Lord, the Messiah, the Son of the Most High, and the Savior of all who believe in him."

Nathan stood and announced, "So be it. You have condemned yourself."

Nathan and the other Zealots took Matthias outside the city walls to an abandoned cistern. The Zealots stood at the top of the cistern with stones in their hands, looking to Nathan for his signal. "I solemnly give you this last warning. Do you recant and live, or do you die?"

But Matthias answered, saying, "I pray that the Lord Jesus will forgive you for what you are about to do. In him and in no other can we possess eternal life."

Nathan raised his hand, and the Zealots stoned the apostle. He continued to pray for them until he lost consciousness. Later, members of the frightened congregation were told where to find his body, and they sorrowfully laid him to rest near the temple where they had buried Stephen and James.

Andrew and Luke continued to labor among the cities and towns of Achaia, and established churches in Limeira, Methone, Megalopolis, and Olympia; then Paul sent Luke a letter asking him to go and tend to the churches in Macedonia. When they parted, Andrew returned to Patrae.

Because the persecution of Christians ordered by the Emperor Nero after Rome burned was in full force at that time, the church began to meet in secret locations in different parts of Patrae.

Andrew was informed by several believers that a young Roman officer had attended church services. They were fearful that he was about to betray the congregation to the proconsul. Andrew took the young man aside and asked him, "My young friend, there are those among us who are afraid because they believe you plan to hand us over to the proconsul."

The officer, Varianus vigorously denied this, saying, "Servant of the Lord, my only intention is to beg you to baptize me, for I believe what you say, that Jesus the Christ is the Son of God."

Andrew reminded the young man that for a Roman soldier to

admit to being a Christian would almost certainly result in a death sentence. He advised the young man to take time to consider the consequences.

Over time Andrew became convinced that the young man's faith was sincere so he agreed to baptize him, and Varianus became the first of the Roman soldiers to abandon military service and follow the Lord.

Sometime later, the proconsul was away on imperial business in the north when his brother, Stratocles, arrived in the city after a voyage from Syria. In his company were his slaves, Gaiana and Eutychos. Now Stratocles dearly loved Gaiana, who had become gravely ill on the ship, and when they arrived at the proconsul's palace, doctors were summoned to attend her. Each day her condition became more severe, however, and the doctors advised Stratocles to prepare for the worst.

Kreon, who was a Christian and also a slave of the proconsul, seeing that Stratocles was in great distress over Gaiana's illness, told him that Andrew, a disciple of the Lord Jesus, had healed many of the sick in Patrae. Stratocles and Kreon went to visit the apostle, and the proconsul's brother said to him, "Please, sir. My slave is gravely ill and the doctors have given up on her. I beg you to come and heal her, and I will pay you whatever you demand."

Andrew looked at the anxious man and replied, "Friend, I have no need for your money. I follow the Lord Jesus and do his bidding. Now take me to the one you are concerned about. "

The apostle was taken to Gaiana's bedside where he knelt and prayed. He surprised Stratocles when he told him to have fresh fruit provided for the slave. When Stratocles returned from the kitchen, he was overjoyed to see Gaiana smiling and sitting up in her bed. When he asked about the apostle, one of the attendants told him Andrew had left the palace before the girl had revived.

About one month later, Maximilla, the wife of the proconsul, became ill, and the doctors were called in to attend her. Over the next several days, her condition worsened, and Stratocles again went to Andrew and asked him to use his power to heal the proconsul's wife. The apostle responded and said, "My friend, it is through no power of mine that healing occurs, but only through the grace of Jesus Christ, my Lord and Savior. It is he whom I serve, and it is he who heals not only the sick in body but the restless soul that seeks eternal life. Now let us go and visit the proconsul's lady."

When they arrived at the palace, they went to Maximilla's bedside where Andrew knelt and prayed. When he stood up, the apostle told Stratocles his sister would be well that very night. Then he left the palace. Sure enough, when nightfall came, Maximilla suddenly regained her health, and she and Stratocles rejoiced and resolved to learn all about this Jesus, whom the apostle said he served.

From that day forward, both Stratocles and Maximilla met with the believers and listened as Andrew told them about the sayings and works of our Lord. Before the proconsul returned, and despite the persecution of Christians ordered by Rome, they became believers, gave much of their wealth to support the poor among the Christians, and were baptized by Andrew.

When Proconsul Aegeates returned, both Stratocles and Maximilla met him and described the marvelous recovery of both the slave Gaiana and Maximilla, and their own newfound devotion to Jesus the Christ. Hearing this, Aegeates was greatly alarmed.

"Do you not know," he said, "that Nero has commanded his officials to arrest all Christians as enemies of the empire? Do you not know that you have put me at great risk of being removed from my position here in Achaia should your affiliation with Christians be brought to the emperor's attention? Have you no idea of the danger you've put this family in? I order you to abandon these Christians. We will say no more about this unfortunate episode and hope that no word about your participation has been dispatched to Rome."

But Maximilla said, "My husband, as a dutiful wife, I've always deferred to your judgment, even when I haven't agreed with you. But in this instance, you must understand that during the time of your absence, I was cured of a serious malady by the grace of Jesus Christ, and, moreover, my soul has been cleansed of all unrighteousness by the power of his name. I cannot and will not renounce him, whatever the cost."

Before the proconsul could respond, Stratocles said, "My brother, you do not know what you ask. We are witnesses to something greater than mere human experience. We were witnesses to acts of divine healing, and we can never again be as we were before. My slave could not be healed by the best physicians in the city. She was at the point of death when, as a last, desperate measure, I sought out Andrew, a servant of Jesus Christ. He agreed to see her and told me the Lord Jesus would cure her, and it was as he said. She was completely cured and radiant with good health, and your wife's situation was much the same. She worsened under the doctors' care until I implored Andrew to intervene. He told me to return to the palace and Maximilla would be well by nightfall, and she was completely cured and up from her bed that night. What we experienced was not of this world. Do not ask us to renounce what we have been witnesses to."

When Aegeates found that no amount of argument could persuade either Maximilla or Stratocles to abandon their belief in the Christian faith, he threw up his hands in despair and retired to his quarters. His aide, Carinus, brought him even more ominous news.

"Sir," Carinus began, "there has been a report that your former officer, Varianus, was observed attending a Christian meeting. In your absence, I dispatched several of our soldiers to investigate. They confirmed that not only was he attending Christian services, he was an ardent believer and an enthusiastic assistant to their leader, Andrew, a Jew from the province of Judea.

"Since the imperial decree ordered the arrest and imprisonment of followers of this Christ, I thought it best to take into custody this Andrew along with Varianus and hold them for your judgment. Unfortunately, Varianus has disappeared, but Andrew has been apprehended and is being held for your ruling. I took the liberty of sending a dispatch to the attention of the Praetorian commander in Rome that this arrest had been made and you would pronounce judgment upon your return."

Now Aegeates considered what the emperor would expect of him. Nero would naturally be informed about this situation by the Praetorian commander and would demand that his proconsul take decisive action. Nero was suspicious, cruel, and vengeful; those who angered him usually forfeited their lives. It was far better to get this matter settled and the emperor informed of the results without delay. He did not trust his aide, Carinus, for the man had friends at court, and he would not hesitate to notify Rome should Aegeates hesitate to take action. The proconsul ordered Carinus to schedule the trial of the apostle for the next day.

When Andrew was brought before the proconsul in chains, Aegeates said to him, "You are accused of being a member of that sect of believers the emperor has condemned. Furthermore, you are accused of harboring a Roman soldier who has abandoned his comrades in order to embrace this cursed sect. How do you plead?"

The apostle answered, saying, "Esteemed Proconsul, I am privileged among men to have been a follower of Jesus Christ during the three years of his earthly ministry. I witnessed firsthand the wonderful miracles he wrought in Judea. I am proud to be the servant of the one who opened the gates of paradise to mankind by his death on the Roman cross. Concerning the Roman soldier, all those who are baptized into the faith of Christ belong to Christ alone. Varianus made his decision to follow Christ rather than Caesar."

Knowing that Carinus was listening to every word, the proconsul exclaimed, "You have the gall to say that a soldier of Rome has abandoned his duty to the emperor to follow an eastern mystic who was executed as a common criminal? And you say you are proud to belong to a loathsome sect the emperor has condemned? Very well, since you so admired this Jewish criminal, you will share his punishment. This day, you will be crucified, and you will remain on that cross without food or water until death takes you." This trial took place during the consulship of C. Socinus Italicus and P. Galerius Trachalus.

Carinus fastened Andrew to a cross, not with nails, but with ropes. Four soldiers were left at the site to prevent anyone from bringing him food or water. Each day, an increasing number of people appeared at the site. Andrew continued to tell the growing multitude all about Jesus Christ, recounting his miracles, and a number of pagans, seeing how the apostle suffered, resolved to be baptized into a faith that even death on the cross could not subdue. Finally, his voice becoming too weak to continue, Andrew bowed his head, saying, "Lord Jesus, receive my spirit." Shortly thereafter, he died, and his followers received permission from the proconsul to bury him.

Varianus continued to minister to the Christians in Patrae and in other regions of Greece, and many came to know the Lord because of him until he was caught up in the persecutions of Emperor Domitian many years later. Like so many others, he died in the Coliseum in Rome, professing Christ with his last breath.

CHAPTER 16

Father Michael finished his oral reading, removed his glasses and said, "Mr. Monroe, we've long known or suspected that Andrew was at first one of John the Baptist's disciples before he left to follow Christ. What we hadn't known until now is that earlier he was an associate of the Essenes. This group was a strict Jewish brotherhood that lived a virtual monastic existence in the Judean wilderness near the Dead Sea. They didn't participate in temple worship, but they observed the Sabbath with rigorous formality. They washed often, as personal cleanliness was virtually sacred to them. They fasted often, lived simply, and had little fear of death, for they believed the soul would live forever.

"They were," the priest continued, "compassionate, took excellent care of their sick and infirm, and were renowned for their kindness to strangers. They held all things in common and were forbidden to eat anything prepared by outsiders. I tell you this since it would appear so much of their spiritual behavior was adopted by early Christians, probably influenced by Andrew. As far as we now know, Andrew was the only member of Christ's inner group who had an active association with the Essenes.

"We were also struck by Ignatius's account of Andrew's preaching, first to the Jews, then to the Gentiles. Until now, most biblical historians have attributed this style of ministry solely to Saint Paul. Now it appears from Ignatius account this was a common practice among the early disciples.

"Church tradition has long held that Andrew traveled as far

as Scythia to preach the Gospel, but there's been little evidence available to substantiate this. What wasn't known was that Matthias was Andrew's companion on this journey."

Doctor Bankkour added, "Let me supplement what Father Michael is saying by pointing out what a dangerous trip this could have been. The Scythians were wild and fierce nomadic horsemen who roamed the plains of today's Ukraine. They were eagerly sought as mercenaries by kings who valued their expert ability to shoot arrows accurately while riding their horses at a full gallop. They had a justified reputation for being cruel masters, showing little pity to conquered tribes. Several reports of the ancient Greeks painted the Scythians as wild cannibals who killed, then ate their victims. Whether or not these tales were true, travelers were warned of dire consequences at the hands of the Scythians should they venture into that forbidding land."

Father Michael smiled as he added, "It seems that the warnings of the Greeks made little impression on Andrew and Matthias, for they worked hard to secure passage to the Scythian homeland. Historians have long held that the Christian conversion of substantial numbers of Scythians didn't take place until late in the second century, but Ignatius writes that their initial conversion took place during the age of the apostles. We do know there was a tribe among the Scythians called the Roxolani, and it seems the two apostles met with great success in establishing missions among these people, regardless of their fearsome reputation.

"Despite the historians' view that Scythian conversion to Christianity didn't take place until the second century," the priest continued, "the great church historian Eusebius identified Scythia as the mission field for Andrew. Ignatius's assertion that Andrew joined his brother, Peter, in Asia Minor also makes perfect sense. This was the area that accounted for so much of the growth of the Christian faith in the early years. It seems natural that Peter would call on his brother for assistance while they were meeting with such evangelistic success. Now, perhaps Doctor Bankkour had best continue our report."

After a brief glance at his notes, Bankkour remarked, "Eusebius also is one of the few who mention anything about Matthias outside his brief introduction in the book of Acts, where he was chosen by lot to succeed Judas Iscariot. Eusebius simply says that Matthias was one of the Seventy, those original disciples in the infant church after the apostles were called.

"Matthias has long been something of an enigma in church history, little being known either about him or his ministry. Ignatius tells us that Andrew and Matthias returned to Greece after the Scythian mission and how they later parted, with Andrew remaining in Greece while Matthias returned to Jerusalem. He goes on to tell us that Andrew was crucified during the consulship of Italicus and Trachalus, which would be in 68 AD, when various factions of the Zealot party were struggling for control in Jerusalem, and the Roman legions were moving south from Galilee toward the Holy City.

"Ancient tradition tells us the early church suffered greatly from both orthodox Judaism and the Zealots, since Christians were perceived as heretics. The first-century Jewish historian Josephus described bands of Zealots roaming the streets of Jerusalem, severely punishing and even killing those who were not ardent followers of temple worship.

"It seems to us to be quite likely that Matthias was martyred by the Jewish Zealots in Jerusalem as revealed by Ignatius" Bankkour continued. "No doubt many believers were killed for the faith in those tumultuous days. The *Acts of the Apostles* tells us about the death of the first martyr, Stephen, years earlier. Stoning was a routine punishment for heresy in those days.

"It was at about that same time that most Christians decided to leave Jerusalem in fear for their lives. It was fortunate for them that they set out for Pella when they did. Shortly thereafter, the Zealots gained full control of the city and refused to allow anyone to leave. Those who remained suffered greatly from harsh food restrictions imposed by the Zealots, and later, from starvation when the Roman legions surrounded Jerusalem and cut off the city's meager food supply.

"Church tradition has consistently claimed that Andrew ministered in Greece and was martyred there by crucifixion," said the linguist. "It's most interesting that a man named Varianus, whom Ignatius claimed was a Roman soldier, embraced the Christian faith. There is an ancient legend about a Bishop Varianus who had once been a soldier and who was swept up in the persecution of Christians by Domitian some years later. It would seem this is the same man.

"There's a persistent early church tradition that mentions the Roman Proconsul Aegeates, his wife Maximilla, and his brother Stratocles. In this tradition, Andrew indeed met his death by being tied to a cross and left to die after having cured Maximilla of a disease. In Ignatius's account, Aegeates was intimidated by the officer who reported directly to Nero's imperial palace in Rome. Nero's cruelty was legendary, and most of his officials tended to look over their shoulders at who might be reporting on their actions to the emperor as Aegeates certainly did according to Ignatius.

"Mr. Monroe, did you have a question?"

"I was wondering," said Ken, "isn't the emblem on the flag of Great Britain referred to as the Cross of Saint Andrew? Is this the same Andrew, and is there any record of the apostle having visited the British Isles?"

"As far as we know," responded Bankkour, "there's no generally accepted tradition of Andrew ever visiting Britain; however, in the eighth century, Scotland's King Hungus had a dream in which that apostle led Scottish soldiers to victory against the English. When his men triumphed, Saint Andrew was declared the patron saint of

Scotland. The present-day flag of Great Britain reflects the union of Scotland and England, which took place immediately after the reign of the first Queen Elizabeth.

"Several traditions support the claim of Ignatius that Andrew converted the first Christian Scythians in southern Russia. Because of the strength of these traditions, he was also declared patron saint of Russia in the time of the Tsars.

"And now, my friends," the linguist announced, "let me suggest if we talk much longer the good Father and I will miss our flight back to Charleston."

The three of them took a taxi to the airport, Ken to fly to Augusta and deliver a copy of today's presentation to Charles, while Doctor Bankkour and Father Michael were to return to West Virginia. Before leaving, the scholars agreed to meet with Ken in Atlanta the following month after the next chapter of Ignatius's work had been translated.

CHAPTER 17

At precisely ten o'clock p.m. on a Tuesday evening, an international phone call was made from Atlanta, Georgia, to Tikrit, Iraq.

Amir: "Yes? What do you have to report?"

Sentry: "We've been encouraged by the good work of our contact in West Virginia, sir. He's familiar with the name we found on the brother's desk calendar and confirms that it refers to a community of infidel Syrian Christian monks located in the mountains of that state."

Amir: "I see. So, what is it you plan to do about this?"

Sentry: "We leave Atlanta tonight in separate cars and will arrive in Charleston tomorrow. One of our brothers there owns a warehouse where we plan to meet tomorrow night. Our Charleston members are familiar with these accursed Syrians and will brief us on whatever security arrangements they have and on the general layout of the monastery.

"Our next step will be to gain access to the monastery and determine the location of the package and how it might be retrieved and what, if any, resistance we might anticipate from the Syrians."

Amir: "I caution you to proceed with great care. We don't want, by any means, to bring public attention to this subject that might hamper our efforts to return the package to its rightful place. At the same time, those individuals in high places here are anxious that your mission be concluded quietly as soon as possible."

Sentry: "I understand their concern, but I must confess that if we proceed with caution and restraint, our mission will not be concluded as swiftly as those worthy personages expect. I seek your advice and counsel on how we're to proceed."

Amir: "I'll present this concern of yours to them and will explain as best I can that you and your associates plan to proceed with caution to avoid public scrutiny, while at the same time you plan to move with deliberate speed to complete this mission.

"Do not fail in this matter, my son. It will not go well with me or you should you be unsuccessful. Nor, may I say, with your family here in Tikrit. I will await your call next week."

CHAPTER 18

O n a rainy Saturday afternoon in August, Ken, Doctor Bankkour, and Father Michael gathered again in the offices of Ken's company to review the next section of the recently translated manuscript. Ken explained that Charles's infirmities kept him confined to his bed for the time being, but he would continue to keep his brother informed about the team's progress. Doctor Bankkour began the session by asking Father Michael to lead them in prayer, then the linguist gave each of them a copy of the team's most recent translation before he began to read aloud.

It was unfortunate that I never met the blessed apostle Matthew, for it was his mission to remain in Jerusalem and in other cities in Judea ministering to the Jews while the other apostles traveled to do the work of the Lord in distant lands. I rely heavily on the reports submitted by Agabus and Quartus, early disciples of the Lord, who were companions and fellow workers with the apostle for a great many years, not only in Judea but in the lands he visited in later years.

It is amazing, dear daughter in Christ, Dorothea, how the divine will of our Lord confounds all the conventional wisdom of the world. Of all the apostles, Matthew labored longer and harder among the Jews of his native land than did any of the others, in spite of the fact that, in earlier years, he was the most resented among those who followed the Lord. He was a Jew from Capernaum in Galilee and grew up with Peter, Andrew, James, and John, but early on, he determined to work for the governing authorities as a despised revenue collector.

Matthew was not among those who submitted bids to the Romans for the privilege of collecting taxes; he served as a minor employee of a Greek named Lykos, who was the successful bidder for taxes collected in Capernaum. Since much of the tax revenue in that city was based on collections from the fishing fleet, Matthew was well known to the fishermen, including those who were called to follow the Lord. All of them loathed him. Andrew has even reported that Matthew would come down to the docks in the worst weather for fear of missing out on the collection of revenue from even one fishing boat's catch. The Jews fervently hated Matthew as a collaborator with the Romans, and Matthew detested the Jews in return.

Peter confided to me that it came as a great shock to him and the others when Jesus called on Matthew to forsake his tax collecting booth and join his disciples. When Peter explained that he and the others considered Matthew to be a traitor to his people, Jesus said, "This man, who once only wrote accounts of taxes collected, will one day write an account of what he has seen and observed in your company. Many will confess their sins and receive the gift of salvation because of what he has written, and they will call him blessed." Of course, our Lord was referring to the wonderful 'Sayings of the Lord' composed by Matthew now in common use in many of the churches, especially among Jewish converts he ministered to while he was in Judea.

Agabus informed me that Matthew was a good businessman and took over as treasurer for the apostles after Judas's betrayal. Despite his past work as a hated tax collector, Matthew eventually won over his companions with his piety and devotion to the Lord Jesus. His work and care for the sick and helpless later endeared him to the Jews.

Matthew was in Jerusalem at the time Emperor Claudius restored Herod Agrippa as King of Judea. Not long after, to gain favor with the Sanhedrin, Herod began to persecute the Christians, and among his first victims was the apostle James, son of Zebedee and the brother of John. During this persecution, Matthew remained in Jerusalem and arranged the escape from the city of many Jewish believers.

Because Matthew's ministry was almost entirely to the Jews, he began most of his preaching by pointing out how Jesus was the fulfillment of prophecies regarding the coming of the Messiah. Once he was invited to address the synagogue in Emmaus, and the leader said to him, "Sir, you have declared in the past your belief that Jesus of Nazareth is the long-awaited Messiah, but our teachers tell us he had little regard for the Law or its consequences. How can one who has little love for the Law claim to be Messiah? Can you enlighten us on that matter?"

Matthew answered, "My friends, the Law had no greater champion than my master. Only those who feared his message would accuse him of having little regard for it. Let me tell you what I once heard him say to the Pharisees who accused him of not following the Law. Jesus said, 'It would be wrong for you to think that I have come to abolish the Law. No, I have not come to do away with the Law, but rather to completely fulfill it. For I tell you, until heaven and earth disappear, not one word or even a small letter of a word in the Law will disappear until all has been accomplished.

'As you know, there are those among the Pharisees and Scribes who teach that several of the commandments are of less importance than others, and the penalty for breaking one of them is less than to break one of the major commandments; but I solemnly tell you that anyone who breaks a single one of these commandments and teaches others to break them will be called least in the kingdom of heaven, but whoever keeps and values each and every one these commandments will be called great in the kingdom of heaven.'

"Brothers," Matthew continued, "you yourselves know that our religious teachers have laid heavy burdens on the poor among us. They tell us to be patient and God will provide, yet they make no attempt to share their own wealth with the poor. They never tire of reminding us that one day, God will send us the Messiah, but when the Lord Jesus came and walked among us, working miracles only the Messiah could perform, they not only refused to acknowledge him, but had him put to death by Pilate's soldiers.

"Brothers, here is the Good News that will transform the world. By the miracle of God's grace, death could not hold Jesus, and three days later, he arose from the grave and appeared to his disciples, charging them with declaring his Gospel before all mankind, Jew and Gentile alike. It is in keeping with his will that I stand before you this day to announce that the kingdom of heaven is near."

Later, Matthew was in Joppa, and had occasion to speak to the Jews of that city. One of them, Elhanan, a Zealot who strictly observed the Law, said to him, "We believe that our people are the chosen of God, and the Messiah will restore us to a position of importance before all the Gentile nations; yet you say that this Jesus, whom you call the Promised One, instructed his followers to take his message of salvation even to the Gentiles. How can this be and that you, a Jew, can even repeat this claim?"

Matthew responded, "There is no argument when you rightfully say God set apart the Jewish people and established a covenant with them, but you must also admit that our people broke his commandments, scorned the prophets, and even killed some. We have been neither a faithful nor an obedient people. Let me share a parable I once heard my Lord Jesus use regarding this subject.

"Once, a man planted a vineyard and carefully tended the young vines, then he built a watchtower, winepress, and outbuildings and constructed a wall to enclose the vineyard; then he rented the vineyard to farmers and left for a distant place. Now, when it was time for the grapes to be harvested, he sent his servants to the tenants to collect the rent.

"The tenants laid hold of the servants, beating and stoning them until one was killed, then the owner sent other servants to the tenants, but they, too, were treated as harshly as were the first. Finally, the owner decided to send his only son to collect the rent, believing that the tenants would treat his son with proper respect and dignity.

"When the owner's son arrived at the vineyard, the tenants saw him and said, 'This is the owner's only son. If he dies there will be no one to inherit the vineyard, so let us kill him and enjoy his inheritance for ourselves.' So they laid hands upon him and killed him.

"Then Jesus asked his listeners, 'What do you say the owner will do to the tenants when he himself comes to the vineyard and finds that they have killed his son?' And they answered him saying, 'He will take his revenge on those evil tenants, and he will find other people to whom he will rent the vineyard.' It is with this parable in mind that the disciples of the Lord have resolved to take the Good News of the Way first to the Jews, the people of the covenant, but if the people of the covenant do not believe him to be the Messiah, we will then take his message to the Gentiles, for they will rejoice when they hear it."

Matthew then felt the Lord calling him to journey to the distant Kingdom of Axum. After a long and arduous journey he arrived in the capital of that nation and was invited to address the Jews in the synagogue there.

On the first Sabbath, Matthew said to those gathered in the synagogue. "My brothers," he said, "you have asked me to tell you about the wondrous things that happened in recent memory in Jerusalem, indeed, things that are still occurring. You are aware that Scripture describes the long history of our people from Abraham to Moses.

"You will no doubt recall from Scripture that Moses announced shortly before his death that in a time and place of his own choosing, God would send one like Moses to bring God's word to the Hebrew people. Since that time down through the ages, our people have longed for this Promised One, the Messiah, to deliver us from our sinful ways.

"My brothers, I am here to tell you that, in our own time, the day of the promise has been fulfilled, and the one foretold by Moses, Jesus of Nazareth, has brought God's message of salvation to our people. He was greeted with great joy by our fellow countrymen in Judea, who flocked to hear him. He cured many of the sick and the lame, even giving sight to the blind. The people began to hail him as king, but those in authority in the Sanhedrin feared and rejected him and prevailed upon the Gentile governor to nail him to a Roman cross.

"My brothers, I cannot begin to describe for you the grief of his disciples after this cruel deed, but to our great wonder, three days after his death on the Roman cross, he appeared among us, not as a spirit, but in the flesh as he had told us he would, and our sadness turned to great joy. Many others, even unbelievers, saw him and were astonished, and most of them live to this day and can verify that I am telling you the truth. I stand before you today in response to his command to his disciples that his glorious message of salvation be carried even to the ends of the earth. I call on you to rejoice, for in God's good pleasure, the great promise made by Moses that a savior would be born among our people has taken place in our own time."

Some of the Jews believed, but Matthew and his companions found the Gentiles to be more anxious to hear the Good News. Matthew healed the sick and the lame, and many who came to be healed remained to hear the apostle and his companions preach. A large number believed and were baptized.

Word about the apostle spread throughout the kingdom until it reached the ears of King Aeglippus. Now Aeglippus had a daughter, Ephigenia, who had been sickly from birth and was now confined to her bed. Since she was her father's favorite child, the king dispatched his soldiers to bring the apostle to him. When Matthew came before him, the king pleaded with him to heal his daughter.

"I will make you wealthy beyond all belief if you will heal my daughter," the king said.

Matthew responded, "Give your treasure to the many in your kingdom who are poor and destitute, o king. I am a servant of Jesus Christ, the Son of Almighty God. It is solely in his name that healing takes place, not through any power I possess. Take me to your daughter, and when she is healed, give praise to him who is Lord of all."

At the king's command, guards escorted Matthew to Ephigenia's bedside, and there the apostle knelt, took the girl's hand in his own, and bowed his head in prayer.

The next morning, Aeglippus found that his daughter was healed. In great joy and gladness, the king gave orders that the poor and destitute of Adulis be given food and money in thanksgiving. He ordered his soldiers to again bring Matthew before him, and when the apostle was in the king's presence, he announced, "See? I have done as you said and have commanded that the poor be fed at my expense. Had you not prevailed upon Jesus Christ, I might have lost my precious daughter. Now she and I both desire that we might be accepted as his followers."

For several years Matthew labored among the people of Axum, and ever increasing numbers were saved, but many continued to serve their pagan gods. The priests of these gods resented Matthew and his influence with the king and the loss of their god's worshippers to Christ so they plotted against him.

While in the city of Matara, Matthew and his companions

witnessed a religious parade honoring Astar, the god of war. Devotees of this god paraded naked down the main street, beating each other with lead-studded whips. Several participants were barely able to stand after this punishment, and if they faltered and fell, their feet were tied to horse-drawn carts, and they were dragged to the pagan god's temple to be sacrificed to Astar.

As the temple priests and their assistants carried the first of the severely injured young men up the stairs to the altar to be sacrificed, Matthew pushed his way to the front of the crowd. When a young man was placed on the altar, the high priest raised his ceremonial dagger and was about to strike when the apostle shouted, "Stop in the name of Jesus!"

The high priest turned and said, "Who dares to interfere in the sacred ritual of the great god Astar?"

Matthew answered, "What kind of abomination is this where the murder of youths is condoned as religious practice? What kind of faith is this that demands the blood of its own devotees?"

Many in the crowd agreed with the apostle, demanding that the young devotees be set free. From that day forward, the priests of Astar vowed to rid themselves of this man from distant Judea. Because Matthew was highly favored by the king, they conspired to seat Aeglippus's brother, Hyrtaeus, on the throne. With their active help, Hyrtaeus resolved to kill Aeglippus to have both the crown and his niece, Ephigenia.

Hyrtaeus invited the king to a feast. One of Hyrtaeus's servants, who had been bribed, filled the king's cup with poisoned wine. When the king fell violently ill at the table Hyrtaeus refused to call a physician. The next day, Hyrtaeus announced that his brother was dead and set out for Adulis with the high priest of Astar in his company to be crowned the new King of Axum.

Hyrtaeus summoned Ephigenia and announced to his court that he and the girl would be married within the week. With a boldness that surprised the new king, Ephigenia declared that upon becoming a Christian believer, she had vowed to live a life of chastity and to care for the sick and poor. Hyrtaeus swore the wedding would take place despite her protestations. He ordered the high priest to make preparations for the royal wedding and commanded his guard to confine Ephigenia to her quarters until the day of their wedding.

Ephigenia sent word of her situation through one of her maids to Matthew, who was aware of the holy vows she had made upon her conversion to devote her life to working with the poor.

On the day the marriage was to be performed, large crowds gathered at the palace. When the princess entered, onlookers were amazed to see that she had tied a rope around her hands to signify that she was being forced into this ceremony against her will. Hyrtaeus ordered his guard to cut the rope, but suddenly, from the rear of the palace, a voice shouted, "Stop! This shameful affair must end immediately!" Matthew walked down the center aisle toward the royal party.

The king spoke, "How dare you interrupt this royal marriage! Guards, seize that man and bring him to me!"

Unnoticed in the confusion, Ephigenia's maid led the princess out of the room and into the street. She was met by members of the Christian congregation, who quickly covered her royal garments with an old robe and hurried her away.

While the king fumed, Matthew said, "It is disgraceful and an affront before God for a man to force the daughter of his own brother into marriage. I call on all the people present to remember that less than a week ago, Ephigenia's father, your beloved former king, was alive and well, yet this day you have another king who demands to marry his brother's daughter against God's law and against her will."

The guard commander struck the apostle in the face with his fist. The infuriated king turned to the high priest of Astar and declared, "Away with him! Now take this foreigner and offer him to the god as a substitute for those he has stolen from you." Hyrtaeus then noticed that Ephigenia was no longer in the room.

And so it came to pass that the triumphant priests of Astar took a bound Matthew to their temple and built a roaring fire within the belly of their idol Astar. Matthew prayed aloud in the hearing of the priests, "O my Lord and Savior, forgive these men who are ignorant of what they are about to do, and receive your unworthy servant into your kingdom." Then, the followers of Astar cast the apostle into the blazing flames.

The king's soldiers were never able to find Ephigenia. When Hyrtaeus died in a drunken state less than a year later, Ephigenia was still working among the poor and the sick in the name of Jesus, always well-guarded by loyal believers. She never forgot the kindness of Matthew and how he had offered himself so that she could remain true to her Christian vow.

CHAPTER 19

After he finished reading aloud this most recent translated chapter of Ignatius's manuscript, Doctor Bankkour began by saying, "Of all the apostles, with the possible exception of Matthias, we know less about Matthew's activities after the Resurrection than any of the others. He has been an apostle shrouded in mystery, for there are a variety of conflicting accounts about where he went and what he did. A few of them point to Persia or India as locations for his missionary endeavors, while others say he worked in North Africa, Egypt, and Ethiopia. Ignatius writes that Matthew went to Axum, an ancient maritime kingdom in East Africa consisting of what we now know as Ethiopia and Somalia. But more about this later."

The linguist continued, "It has always seemed amazing to me that Jesus called a Jewish collaborator with the Romans, a despised tax collector, to be one of his intimate companions, yet that's exactly who and what Matthew was. A Jewish man would be considered a traitor to his own people to agree to serve as a tax collector for the hated Roman authorities, and this would have been sufficient reason for the Jews to avoid social contact with Matthew."

Father Michael smiled as he added, "You make a valid point, Doctor. Why, indeed, would our Lord pick a turncoat like Matthew to be a part of his inner circle? Perhaps Jesus saw in Matthew not what he was, but what he would become. Ignatius appears to confirm that Jesus saw in Matthew a man whose pen would, for all time in the Gospel named after him, reveal the written record of what Jesus said—those words that would inspire generations of Christians after the Resurrection right down to our own time."

"Father, I have a question," said Ken. "Do most scholars accept that Matthew was the author of the Gospel that is named for him?"

"All the early church fathers gave credit to Matthew for being the writer of the Gospel that's called by his name, Mr. Monroe, and this is the Gospel that takes great pains to point out how Jesus fulfilled the Old Testament prophecies concerning the coming of the Messiah. Many modern biblical scholars tend to agree with Ignatius that Matthew was the author of the Gospel. Perhaps our Lord saw in Matthew the tax collector the gifted penman he would become, one who would write about all these wonderful events several years after Jesus's earthly ministry ended."

Father Michael paused, then looked at Ken and said, "Do you not find it intriguing, Mr. Monroe, that Matthew, who had been an outcast among his fellow Jews, according to Ignatius remained longer in Judea ministering to the Jewish believers than any of the other apostles? Church tradition tells us that Matthew remained in Judea years after the other apostles had departed for other regions. And Ignatius's account confirms this tradition.

"Ignatius writes that Matthew went to the kingdom of Axum when he left Judea and ministered for a number of years in that land. What we know is that there's a tradition held in high regard by the Coptic Christians in Egypt, as well as in Ethiopia, that relates how the king of Axum, Aeglippus, knowing of the marvelous healing power of the apostle, pleaded with him to restore life to his son who had died. When Matthew did as the king requested, Aeglippus was overcome with joy and he, his daughter Ephigenia, and his court became Christians. Soon many others in the land embraced the new faith, which alarmed the pagan priests in Axum, who conspired to rid the land of the apostle. Ignatius omits any reference to a son of the king, but the rest of his account is remarkably similar to the Coptic tradition."

"Excuse me for interrupting, Father," said Ken. "Ignatius seems to always be referring to the Christian faith by using the term 'the Way.' Was that common practice in ancient times?"

"Throughout most of the first century, believers tended to refer to themselves as followers of the Way. Perhaps it was originally intended as a code word to help the Christians avoid persecution at the hands of orthodox Jews or the Zealot party members, who often were apt to physically abuse fellow Jews who followed the new faith."

"Please continue, Father. I'm sorry I interrupted you. I was just curious about what you were saying concerning the Coptic tradition."

The priest smiled as he said, "Feel free to interrupt at any time, Mr. Monroe. After all, that's the purpose of these sessions. We encourage you to ask whatever questions come to mind and at any time.

"Now, about that Coptic Christian tradition: This ancient tradition goes on to state that years later, when Aeglippus had died and was succeeded by his brother, Hyrtaeus, this king developed a fierce passion for his niece, Ephigenia, and he resolved to marry her. The niece appealed to Matthew to save her from this fate. Hyrtaeus sought the apostle's assistance in his quest to marry Ephigenia, but Matthew refused. The king went into a rage and ordered his soldiers to kill the apostle.

"I've always thought there was a lot more than scholars generally recognize as fact behind most Christian traditions," said Doctor Bankkour. "Ignatius reports that the king handed Matthew over to the pagan priests to be thrown into a flaming furnace, and he confirms much of the rest of this tradition. Although history tells us it was two centuries later that Christianity became the religion of Axum, this doesn't preclude missionary work performed by Matthew and other disciples as described by Ignatius. The fact remains that the Christian influence has always been especially strong in Ethiopia, and this could well be attributed to the early ministry of the apostle. Do you have a question, Mr. Monroe?"

"Not so much a question, Doctor," responded Ken. "Perhaps what I'm beginning to see for the first time is a new and personal revelation into the mind of Jesus. It makes perfect sense that Jesus would have enlisted a disciple who'd have the education and writing ability to record what he said and did during those three years of his earthly ministry. From what I remember of what the Gospels tell us, it seems that most of the disciples Jesus selected were fishermen from the Sea of Galilee, who more than likely weren't well-trained in writing skills."

"You make an excellent point, Mr. Monroe," said Father Michael. "It's fair to assume that few of the other apostles were equipped by training to write an account of the Lord's sayings. After all, Matthew and John are the only apostles to be acknowledged as authors of the Gospels, and there's even more on this subject that ought to be said.

"Of all the prophets in the Old Testament, none was quoted by Jesus more than the prophet Isaiah. In fact, the Lord began his ministry in Nazareth by reading from the book of Isaiah. Remember? *'The Lord's Spirit has come upon me, because he has chosen me to tell the good news to the poor. The Lord has sent me to announce freedom for prisoners, to give sight to the blind,'* and so on. I feel certain that as familiar as he was with the book of Isaiah, Jesus was equally familiar with the life of the prophet—how Isaiah, knowing that he would one day be put to death by a vengeful king, gathered a group of disciples who would record what the prophet said long after his death. Isaiah had even stated, *'I will bind up my testimony, and seal my teaching in the hearts of my disciples.'*

"I believe Jesus knew his ministry would be cut short after a scant three years. After all, he had witnessed the work of John the

Baptizer come to an abrupt end at the executioner's hands in the dungeon of Herod Agrippa. I believe this is the reason he chose an intimate group of disciples to carry on his work when he was no longer with them, but he surely knew that those disciples he called up to Matthew's selection were earnest, hard-working fishermen. Their talent lay in catching fish, not in writing manuscripts. Perhaps that's why, when Jesus saw Matthew at his tax collecting booth, he saw not the despised tax collector, but a skilled penman who would one day record what his Lord said and did during the next three years."

"Did you notice," said Doctor Bankkour, "that Ignatius suggests that Bartholomew contributed to the contents of Matthew's Gospel? This is certainly something no scholars suspected, and Ignatius also tells us that Matthew filled the role of treasurer after Judas betrayed the Lord. Ignatius continues to add new dimensions to our understanding of how the apostles organized and carried out their mission after the Resurrection."

And Father Michael added, "Since Ignatius was martyred during Trajan's reign, his mention of Matthew's Gospel certainly closes the door on biblical critics who maintain the Gospels were written late in the second century."

Both Father Michael and Doctor Bankkour expressed concern about Charles's state of health. Ken thanked them for asking about his brother and told them that Charles was grateful for the continued enthusiastic support of this project demonstrated by all team members. He also told them that Charles had undergone a series of operations to remove shrapnel from various parts of his body and had experienced an infection that had resulted in a setback for several weeks, but that Charles looked forward to rejoining the group as soon as he regained a little strength.

As they drove to the airport, the linguist described the mounting excitement the team felt as they were beginning the translation on

Ignatius's account of the travels of the Apostle Thomas, for the churches in the East for centuries maintained that this apostle had established the faith in distant India, despite doubts expressed by Western scholars.

When Ken remarked that Charles was still not strong enough to make the trip to Atlanta, Father Michael suggested they might meet at Charles's home in Augusta. Ken declined, explaining that his brother was about to undergo a rather extensive operation on the stump of his right leg at the Veterans Hospital in Augusta and would require extensive bed rest. Instead, Ken suggested they once again use his office in Atlanta, which they agreed to and decided to schedule during the latter part of September.

CHAPTER 20

An international phone call was placed from Charleston, West Virginia, to Tikrit, Iraq, at ten o'clock p.m. on the third Tuesday of the month.

Amir: "I've been anxiously waiting for your call. What do you have to tell me?"

Sentry: "I know you've been concerned with our progress, sir. I think you'll be pleased with this report. We've been successful in our effort to gain access to the Syrian monastery. One of our associates, posing as a destitute Iraqi Christian immigrant, was given a room within the monastery and was provided with a job as a groundskeeper.

"He had only been working on the grounds for two days when he noticed that each morning a group of civilians, not always the same individuals, gathered at the monastery library. When he asked the monk supervising the grounds crew who these men were, he was told they were scholars from various universities who were working on old Syriac documents from the monastery's vast library. He was also told that it wasn't unusual for scholars to come to the monastery, for the resident librarian and linguist was recognized as a world-class translator of Middle Eastern manuscripts. Does this information not please you?"

Amir: "It would please me and the distinguished leaders of our movement even more were we to hear that you've made plans to retrieve what was lost and safely conduct it back to its country of origin."

Sentry: "Then I'm pleased to report that the security of this monastery is primitive. Our associate in place will unlock the small gate at the monastery after midnight this coming Friday. We've selected this time because most of the senior monks will have left for the different churches where they will conduct Sunday services, and the civilian workers at the monastery will have returned to their homes for the weekend. At that time, two of our associates will join the one in place and proceed to the library, where we believe the package is located. They plan to enter and remove the package and transport it back to Charleston before dawn to our warehouse. From there we plan to disguise the package and arrange for it to be flown back to its native land."

Amir: "This plan seems reasonable, and I think the others here who are following your progress with great interest will agree. However, a word of caution. You must impress upon your associates that we don't want any type of action that will have repercussions in the land of the infidels. What is required is stealth. Do you understand?"

Sentry: "I understand perfectly, sir, and I'll advise them of your concerns."

Amir: "Then I'll expect your next call will be to advise me that the package is safely on its way home."

CHAPTER 21

Doctor Bankkour began by asking about Charles's family. He suggested that they begin immediately with the next chapter in Ignatius' manuscript since he would need to catch the last flight back to Charleston. He explained that a group of Orthodox nuns were expecting him to show them the library's extensive collection of ancient Syriac documents. Then he began to read the latest completed translation aloud.

All of these apostles were wonderful and godly men, and each had many attributes worthy of our attention and imitation, Dorothea. One I recall with great personal fondness was the apostle Thomas Didymus. I first met him when he, Jude Thaddaeus, and Bartholomew, as well as several other disciples of the Lord, were on their journey from Jerusalem to the kingdom of Osroene. Before setting out to that kingdom, however, they traveled to Antioch to confer with Peter. It was Peter's practice to have the disciples meet with him before undertaking their missionary journeys so they could coordinate these trips with the activities of other apostles and disciples in the mission fields.

This planned journey to Osroene by Thomas and his companions was not the first mission to that kingdom. Earlier, both Thomas and Jude Thaddaeus had labored successfully in the Lord's work in the capital city, Edessa, where a large colony of Jews lived. In fact, King Abgarus of Osroene was the first ruler to invite the apostles to present the Good News before his court not long after the

Resurrection of our Lord.

It was with sadness and reluctance that the apostles at an earlier time had, at the request of Peter, cut short their mission to Edessa to go to Jerusalem. He had asked them to join the other apostles to hear the plea of Paul and Barnabas regarding the Gentile converts. The decision was made to refrain from applying the Jewish practice of circumcision to Gentile converts.

I was still a young man, both in age and in my conversion to the faith, when these apostles reported to Peter. When Peter introduced me to them, Thomas gave me a most enthusiastic greeting and surprised all of us by placing me on a table top where he announced to all present, "Behold! This lad, in God's own time, will become a much-revered leader of the faithful and will bring many lost souls to Christ our Lord." I was embarrassed to be singled out in this manner, but Peter later told me that ever since the Resurrection of the Lord, Thomas had been perceived as a prophet among the brothers, and I should treat his pronouncements with proper esteem and respect.

Of all the apostles, Thomas stands out in my mind for having the highest developed gift for languages. When Thomas made his way into India, he picked up the many diverse tongues spoken by various tribes and used this skill to tell them the Good News in their own languages.

Peter asked me to conduct Thomas to the house of the merchant Clement, where a number of our newest converts were receiving instruction in the faith. Thomas told me he had once been a follower of John the Baptizer before John bade him to go and follow Jesus. When he told the Baptizer that he preferred to remain with him, John said, "Will you then follow me to Herod's prison? Why would you remain with the servant when the Anointed One has made His appearance?"

I introduced Thomas to the converts and asked him to share whatever the Holy Spirit put on his heart to say. The apostle began by saying, "Dear friends in Christ, I rejoice with you in your newfound faith in our Lord Jesus. You have not seen him, yet you believe in him. I pray you will always believe in him, no matter what the world might say or do to disturb your belief. I tell you this as one who was with him from the beginning, yet even in his presence, my faith was not strong enough to reject the wiles and snares of Satan. Even after I witnessed his raising to new life of the dead Lazarus, my weak faith caused me to abandon him to his enemies in the Sanhedrin. I confess to you, I was paralyzed with fear that the other disciples and I would suffer that same punishment when he was tried, beaten, and led to the place of the Skull where he was nailed to the Roman cross.

"My friends, I did not believe it when my fellow disciples told me he had arisen from the dead three days after being laid in the tomb, even as he had told us he would. I did not believe them when they said he had appeared in their presence in the flesh. No, I told them I would never believe unless I could place my finger where the nails pierced his hands and the spear punctured his side.

"It was only later, when we had gathered together, that he suddenly appeared and said, 'Thomas, come and place your hands on my wounds and cast all your doubts aside.' When I had done so I fell on my face and worshipped him, but he said to me, 'Now you have faith because you have seen me. Far more blessed are those who will follow me in the future. They will not see me, yet they will believe.'

"And now here we are, long after he has ascended to God his Father. Though I was with him for three years, witnessed his miraculous healings, and heard his matchless words, you are far more blessed than I, for you believe yet you have not seen him.

"Be on your guard lest the evil one cause you to doubt as he did me. Pray often for the faith that will remain your constant companion as you go about your daily work. If, in days to come, your faith should ever falter, think of Thomas and what I have told you this day."

Thomas, Jude Thaddaeus, Philip, and Bartholomew accompanied Peter and me for several months as we visited the churches in Galatia. With each congregation, Thomas repeated this message and encouraged those who were present to resist every doubt, for doubts were the weapons of the evil one. All during this time, he continued to discuss his plans for carrying the Good News to the East. Peter encouraged the four disciples to visit the Jewish settlements in Armenia before continuing on to Osroene.

I continued to grow close to Thomas, and he shared many things about our Lord's ministry during those precious months he was with us. Before he departed, Thomas gave me his blessing, saying, "Ignatius, one day soon believers will look to you for leadership. Those who love the Lord have already faced persecution from the Jews in Judea. Now there are reports that the Romans have determined to imprison Christian believers who refuse to openly worship the emperor. When the wrath of Rome is fully aroused, I fear the believers will be sorely pressed. You, and others like you, will be called upon to hold the church together in the face of relentless oppression. The Lord has impressed upon my heart from the first day I met you that you would be equal to that challenge. May God's richest blessings be upon you."

Sadly, I never saw Thomas and Bartholomew again. It was more than a year later that Hyllos, one of the Seventy, returned to Antioch and told us what happened on that momentous journey.

When the disciples of the Lord reached Artaxata, the city of Armenia's king, they found a large settlement of Jews there. Samuel, the leader of the synagogue, invited Bartholomew to address the congregation.

Bartholomew said to the Jews, "My countrymen, there is no need for me to tell you of the many prophets who have foretold the coming of the Messiah. You have the record of their prophecies here in the Holy Scriptures. These scrolls describe the great yearning of these holy ones and our forefathers to see the day when the Messiah would come.

"My purpose today is not to recount the longing of the prophets and patriarchs, for God did not ordain that they would live to see the day of the Messiah's coming. Their mission was to simply announce that he would come. Scripture records that Moses foretold the coming of the Messiah when he said, 'The Lord your God will raise up for you a prophet like me from among you and him you shall heed.' For God had spoken to Moses saying, 'I will raise up for them a prophet like you from among them, and I will put my words in his mouth and he shall speak to them all that I command.'

"The prophet Isaiah said that when the Promised One came, 'The eyes of the blind shall be opened and the ears of the deaf shall be unstopped, then shall the lame man leap as a hart, and the tongue of the dumb shall sing.'

"Today, my brothers, I declare unto you with great joy that the day of the prophets' longing has been fulfilled in your time, for this Jesus who healed the sick, the blind, and the lame is the long-awaited Messiah, the Promised One of God.

"I was with him when Jesus received word that his friend, Lazarus of Bethany, was gravely ill. Several days later, he resolved to go to Bethany, even though his disciples warned him that the authorities in nearby Jerusalem were waiting for a chance to arrest him. When we arrived in Bethany, we were met by Lazarus's sister, Martha, who fell at his feet and announced that Lazarus had died and was now four days in his tomb.

"Jesus declared to all those present that Lazarus would live again, and Martha thought he was speaking of Judgment Day when all the dead would rise, but Jesus declared in a bold voice, 'I am the Resurrection and the life. Those who believe in me will never die, for they will inherit eternal life.' Then Jesus asked Martha, 'Do you believe what I say?'

"And Martha replied, 'Yes, Lord. I believe you are the Promised One, the Son of God.'

"Then Jesus told those present to roll away the stone that sealed the tomb. Holding their cloaks to their faces against the stench of death, several of the young men rolled the stone away, then Jesus stepped forward and, in a loud voice commanded, 'Lazarus, come forth!' My friends, Lazarus came out of the tomb, his hands and feet still bound in the wrappings of the dead. Jesus said, 'Unbind him and let him go.' Where there had been weeping and mourning, there was now great wonder, joy, and gladness, for the one who had been dead for several days was now among the living."

For a number of months thereafter, the disciples were invited to address the Jews, and many, including the leader, Samuel, became believers. Others, however, refused to accept Jesus as the Messiah.

The apostles and members of the Seventy began to minister among the Gentiles, and many Armenians received the faith and were cured of their illnesses. The preaching of Bartholomew and the others found great acceptance of the faith among the common people, and many of their number begged the disciples to visit nearby towns and villages to carry the message of salvation to their friends and relatives.

One of the converts to the faith was Abbanes, a Jewish merchant from India. Abbanes was a wealthy man who conducted a thriving trade between Armenia, Parthia, and India. He described many wonders and customs to be found in India, and Thomas and Bartholomew became convinced that the Lord wanted them to take the Good News to that land. Leaving Philip and Jude Thaddaeus to minister to the Armenians, Thomas and Bartholomew made plans to travel to India.

After talking to Abbanes, it was decided that Thomas would go to the city of Andrapolis, a highly advanced city in northern

India, while Bartholomew would preach the Good News in Kalyana, a kingdom located near the coast.

Thomas learned that King Gundaphorus, who ruled Andrapolis, had returned from visiting his cousin, who was heir to the throne of Parthia. Thomas and the disciples were summoned to court to meet the king.

Gundaphorus invited Thomas to describe what his mission was in the king's land. Though the king seemed to have little interest in religious matters, he was impressed with the apostle's faith and saw in him a man of integrity. He had been told that the apostle had been a skilled carpenter back in his native land.

Gundaphorus declared that he was so impressed with Thomas that he would give the disciples permission to minister among his people on the condition that the apostle would supervise the construction of a palace he intended to build near the southern border of his kingdom. This supervision of this project would include handling payment from the royal treasury for the materials and labor used in construction.

While Gundaphorus was preoccupied with leading his troops in skirmishes with rebellious tribesmen in the north, Thomas continued to draw funds from the treasury for the project, but, distressed by the poverty and misery of the native people in the region, he distributed these funds to the needy instead of for work on the new palace. The king sent a message to Thomas inquiring about the progress of construction. The apostle replied that the roof was not yet built, so the king ordered that additional gold and silver be sent from the treasury to be used for construction of the roof.

When the king returned to Andrapolis, he asked his nobles about the progress of his new palace. They responded that, to their knowledge, no construction had taken place, but instead that Thomas had distributed all the gold and silver intended for the construction of the palace to the poor while he spent his time healing the sick and lame and preaching about a foreign god. Gundaphorus, seething with anger, sent his soldiers to bring the apostle and his companions to court.

The king declared, "Is the construction of my palace complete?"

Thomas replied, "Yes, your Majesty."

Then the king said, "Come, I would have you accompany me, and we will view the completed palace together."

The apostle said, "The palace has been completed in heaven; therefore, you cannot see it now but only when you have departed this life."

Seething with anger, the king ordered that the disciples be chained and confined in prison until the new moon, when they were to be flayed alive at the place where the new palace was supposed to have been built. On the night Gundaphorus imposed this sentence, the king's heir and favorite son, Ganapati, was stricken with a fever, and the king feared for his life.

Despite the best efforts of the king's doctors, for two days the king's son grew weaker, and the king had given up all hope for his recovery. Professional mourners were summoned, prepared to accompany the young prince on his last journey to the grave.

It was at this time that Abbanes, who had been away, returned to Andrapolis and heard about Ganapati's illness. "Your Majesty, I have heard you have condemned Thomas and the others, but I must tell you that, over the past year, I have witnessed amazing healings by this man. Your son is gravely ill. Would it not be wise to summon Thomas and see if the God he worships can heal your son?"

Gundaphorus sent for Thomas, told him about the prince's fever, and led him to Ganapati's bed. The apostle felt the young man's forehead, then knelt by the bed and prayed. The boy opened his eyes and called for his father. The overjoyed king embraced his son and thanked the apostle for restoring Ganapati's health; but Thomas said, "It is the power of the Lord Jesus that cured your son, O King. I am only his servant. Give all your praise to him." Gundaphorus then ordered that the companions of Thomas be released from prison.

In the days and months that followed, the king's son became a follower of Thomas and accompanied him as he healed the sick and taught about the Lord Jesus. Ganapati confided in his father that he had asked the apostle to baptize him, and Gundaphorus went to Thomas and asked to be baptized along with his son. Many of the members of the king's court came to the river to watch as Gundaphorus and Ganapati were baptized by the apostle. A number of them approached Thomas and the disciples and asked to be baptized as well.

Thomas and his companions labored for many months in Andrapolis and the surrounding territory, preaching and healing the sick among the people, and many came to believe in the Lord Jesus. But the time came when the disciples decided that they must travel to other places in India to spread the Good News.

After a journey that took many weeks, the party arrived in the Pandyan kingdom, the home of those converts who had convinced Thomas to venture south. These men had created a commotion when they joyfully announced to their fellow countrymen that they had been redeemed from an endless rebirth on earth, which was the common belief among the people. They declared that they hoped to enjoy eternal life in heaven through the merits of the Lord Jesus, the only Son of the true God. The people demanded to know more about this new faith, and even the priests and members of the king's court joined them in requesting that Thomas tell them about God's only Son. The murmur of the crowd ceased when the apostle raised his hands for silence.

Thomas spoke, "Good people, I stand before you to proclaim not another god, but to declare solemnly that there is but one God who made the earth, the moon, and the stars. After God created the earth, he created man and gave him dominion over it. It was God's plan that men would live in peace with one another, but he gave man free will, even if in exercising that free will would lead man to grievous sin and error. When men decided to depart from God's plan and follow their own evil inclinations, theft, murder, and cruelty became common. God was saddened at what man had become, so he determined to set aside a tribe of people to whom he would reveal his commandments and to whom, one day, he promised to send his only Son, a savior who would liberate men from their sins.

"Down through the centuries, this tribe chosen by God remembered his promise to send a savior, but they failed to keep his commandments so God decided that it was time for this long-promised savior to be born among these people he had chosen. God, therefore, sent his only Son, but when God's beloved Son, Jesus Christ, came into the world, the people to whom he had been promised refused to accept him. Not only did they refuse to accept him, they turned him over to outsiders to be put to death. He was scourged like a common criminal, nailed to a cross, died, and was buried in a borrowed tomb, but death could not hold him. He arose from the grave and appeared to his disciples, and instructed them to announce the Good News of salvation to all men everywhere. Those who heard and believed in his Son were promised eternal life with him in his Father's heavenly kingdom.

"Now this is the word I proclaim to you. Jesus Christ, who is the Promised One, the Son of God, came to redeem you from your sins. I am one of his disciples. I knew him and loved him and followed him during the years of his earthly ministry.

"It is because of him and God's great love for you that I have traveled so far to bring this wonderful message of salvation to you. If you will ask forgiveness for your sins, believe in his Son, and proclaim this belief with your mouth you will enjoy paradise with him in eternity."

Then the lead priest, Lokesh, said, "Are you telling us that this man called Jesus died, then arose from the dead and appeared to you?"

The apostle replied, "It is with much sadness that I must say I was not there when he first appeared to the other disciples. Not only that, I am compelled to admit when they told me he had been in their presence, I refused to believe them, and told them I would not believe unless I saw him face-to-face. Furthermore, I told them I would refuse to believe unless I could put my hands in his wounds.

"Several days later, I was with the others when Jesus appeared in our midst. I was astonished, and when he invited me to touch the wounds in his hands and side, I did. I fell to the floor and worshipped him. It was then that he said, 'Thomas, you now believe because you have seen me and felt of my wounds. How blessed are those who believe in me yet have not seen me.'

"It is I, his most obstinate servant, who has come these many leagues to proclaim that he did indeed rise from the dead and ascend to his Father and, obedient to his command, I invite you to believe in him and enjoy eternity in his loving presence."

People, even from kingdoms near and far, heard of the miracles of healing and the apostle's powerful preaching, and journeyed great distances to hear Thomas and the other disciples. Within the king's court, however, there was anger and hostility regarding the disciples.

The Brahmins, who were the highest order among the rigid classification system that separated all people in India from one another, feared that the disciples' preaching encouraged the people to abandon the ancient social structure, especially the lowest caste, called the untouchables.

King Misdeus called the leading Brahmins to discuss the matter. The king thus far had been impressed with Thomas's message.

Daksha, the most vocal foe of the disciples, spoke to the court, composed entirely of members of the priest and warrior castes, telling them that Thomas and his disciples were encouraging the untouchables to ignore class distinctions. Should this teaching prevail, Daksha warned, who would perform the tasks of emptying the slop jars that had been the traditional role of the untouchables? Even Lokesh, the priest, who from the beginning favored the apostle and his teaching, was won over to the side of his fellow Brahmins by the force of Daksha's argument.

The king, seeing that his court was of this mindset, ordered that all teaching against local custom temporarily cease until further notice. He then summoned Thomas to appear before the court.

When the disciples and the court were assembled, the king said, "There are those among our Brahmins who are angry that what you teach goes against the custom of our people and the traditions of our ancestors. It was our pleasure to allow the captain of our guard, Daksha, to prepare a preliminary decree for my consideration at this meeting. It is my desire that he read this proposed decree aloud."

Daksha cleared his throat and began to read in a loud voice, "To all who live within the realm of our sovereign lord, King Misdeus, greetings. It has long been the custom of our people that all men and women are born into one of the separate categories of our caste system, which are mentioned in our ancient holy texts and were granted by the gods to our ancestors. Our prosperity, our happiness depend upon this system, and we give thanks to the gods for their enlightened gift that has been an integral part of our culture for ages.

"It has come to the attention of our beloved sovereign that foreigners in our midst have spoken against the time-honored ways of our fathers. His Majesty has, therefore, decreed that from this date forward any effort, word, or act, public or private, to diminish, dissolve, or in any way to interfere with these established Varnas, or castes, will be severely punished."

The king said to Thomas, "Tell us about this teaching of yours that has so troubled our court. What are your views on our Varna, or caste system, and why do you seek to alter it?'"

"O King, I thank you for the gracious hospitality shown to me and my companions by the people of your kingdom, and I thank you for allowing me to address your court. I can appreciate the Varnas, or castes, that define your people, for I come from people where a similar rigid class system is a part of everyday life.

"In my homeland, those born of my Jewish race are forbidden to have dealings with foreigners. To even enter the house of a foreigner renders a Jew 'unclean,' and of all the foreigners who reside in adjacent communities, none are more reprehensible to my people than the Samaritans. These Samaritans are considered by my people to be a cursed race. No self-respecting Jew will have anything to do with them. In your Varnas, or classes, the Samaritans would be comparable to the untouchables, the lowest step in the caste system.

"But Jesus, the Lord I follow, led his disciples one day deep into the heart of Samaria. Sending them on ahead to the town, he sat down by a well where a Samaritan woman had come to draw water. 'Will you give me a drink?' Jesus said to the woman.

"'How is it,' the woman replied, 'that you, a Jew, ask a Samaritan woman for a drink?'

"Jesus answered, 'If you were aware of God's gift and who it is that asks you for a drink, you would have asked him and he would provide you with living water. Everyone who drinks water from this well will become thirsty again, but whoever drinks from the water I give will never be thirsty again. The living water I give will become for those who drink it a way toward eternal life.'

"Then Jesus asked her to summon her husband, but she said, 'Sir, I have no husband.'

"Jesus said, 'You were right to say you have no husband. You have had five husbands, and the man in your house is not your husband.'

"Surprised, the woman responded, 'Sir, I can see you are a prophet. We believe when the Promised One comes, he will explain everything that has been hidden.'

"Jesus said, 'I am the one you are waiting for.'

"Jesus spent two days ministering to the Samaritans, and many believed he was the long-awaited Promised One. They marveled that Jesus, a Jew, sought them out and spoke to them of love and salvation. It was a message not only for the Samaritans, but for us as his followers.

"The Lord Jesus Christ taught all of those, Jew and Samaritan, that salvation begins with love for our fellow man. He taught us that it was not enough to love those close to us, our family and friends, but that we are required to love even our enemies. Now it is not Thomas who has come this great distance to bring you this message of salvation, it is Jesus Christ who lives in me."

Thomas and the disciples were dismissed from the king's court. Daksha said, "O King, this foreigner dares to upend the tradition of our ancestors. He would have us abandon the system that orders the lives of all our people. Should he have his way, the untouchables would be sitting in this court judging Brahmins! It is unthinkable! Who, then, would perform the disgusting chores of emptying the latrines to fertilize the crops? What this man says is madness. He must be silenced, or our entire social system will be overturned." Many of the other Brahmins joined him in calling for the decree to be enacted and rigidly enforced, and much animated discussion followed.

Finally, the king announced, "Your concern for the traditions of our fathers is clearly evident and is of great value to me, but the teaching of this Jesus that Thomas preaches about touches my heart. Perhaps a modification of our caste system is called for. I intend to carefully consider the matter and then have a private conversation with Thomas before considering the issuing of this decree." Dismissing the court, he retired to his chambers.

Daksha gathered those who agreed with him and said, "The

king is almost persuaded to allow this foreigner to continue with his radical teaching. Already, this teaching has stirred unrest among the untouchables, and turmoil will only increase if this Thomas is permitted to continue his preaching. I say we must put an end to this matter, here and now. The foreigner must be silenced once and for all."

There were vigorous nods of agreement; however, one Brahmin spoke up and said, "Wait! Let us continue to present our concerns to the king. Surely, if we are persistent, he will see the danger in Thomas's preaching and issue the decree."

Disdainfully, Daksha said, "In the meanwhile, you will, of course, have your sons empty your latrines since the untouchables will be away listening to the foreigner."

Another man said, "What do you propose to do to stop this Thomas from preaching to the people?"

Daksha responded, "Do not concern yourself. I promise before this night is over, our problems with this foreigner will be resolved." When the others had gone, the captain of the guard sent for his lieutenant and gave the man instructions.

At midnight, a guard detail was sent to the house where Thomas was staying, and Thomas was instructed to dress and go with them. When his disciples protested, Thomas urged them to be calm; then he left.

The disciple Hyllos, unknown to the guard, followed them as they marched several miles outside the town where Thomas was confined in a hut. Daksha was waiting for him. The Brahmin spoke, saying, "This is my final word to you, foreigner. My men are prepared to put you aboard a nearby ship should you agree never to return to this land under pain of death. If you refuse, you will die. What is your answer?"

Thomas replied, "Do you think after I have witnessed the glory of my risen Lord that I could so easily turn my back on his command and sail off out of harm's way? Do you think I consider my life worth more than the Lord's work? Do what you will. I for my part will pray for you and for others who think like you."

Then Thomas knelt down, bowed his head, and began to pray. Daksha nodded to the guard commander, who drove his spear through the apostle's body.

When the king learned that Thomas was dead, he was overcome with emotion. He tore up the decree composed by Daksha and exiled the Brahmin to a distant city. He ordered that the apostle's body be buried and the burial site marked with an inscribed stone. The king and Lokesh, the high priest, became Christians, and many Brahmins as well as members of other castes were converted to the faith. Most of the disciples remained in India preaching the Good News, but Hyllos decided to return to Antioch to inform the faithful about what had transpired in India.

CHAPTER 22

As he finished reading, Doctor Bankkour said, "Perhaps, Mr. Monroe, you might have questions regarding this extraordinary account? If so, I'll ask Father Michael to respond while I rest my voice for a while."

Marshalling his thoughts and questions, Ken asked, "Father, I had absolutely no idea that Thomas, the one the Gospels claim demanded to put his fingers in Jesus's wounds before he would accept the Resurrection, would later travel so widely in the East, even as far as India. And I must confess, I've never heard of a country called Osroene. Where is this place, and what was its significance?"

Father Michael laughed as he replied, "I can well believe you have never heard of Osroene, Mr. Monroe, for it hasn't existed in more than eighteen hundred years. In the age of the apostles, Osroene was a small, ancient kingdom located between the Tigris and Euphrates Rivers, across the southern frontier of modern Turkey and the northern frontier of Syria. Its capitol city was Edessa, now known as Urfa, Turkey. Because Osroene controlled parts of what was known as the Old Persian Royal Road, it was in a strategic position when the giant empires of Rome and Parthia clashed. The kings in Edessa maintained a tenuous balancing act, aligning the country first with one, then with the other.

"Osroene was important in the early history of the Christian faith," continued the priest. "Interestingly, the church historian Eusebius, writing in the fourth century, assures us that he was shown documents in the Edessa archives confirming that King Abgar V had written a letter to Jesus imploring our Savior to come and cure the king of a lifelong illness. Eusebius went on to say that Jesus replied that his work in Judea was of paramount importance, but that after his Resurrection, he would send his disciples to the king and they would cure his affliction.

"Eusebius writes that after the ascension of our Lord, the apostles Jude Thaddaeus and Thomas went to Edessa, cured the king, and made many converts there. The Eastern Church has long maintained that these two apostles spent years ministering in Osroene and that thousands were converted as a result. Many historians, however, claim that it wasn't until the reign of Abgar IX, around the year 200 AD, that the king and the country professed Christianity. In any event, the Roman Emperor Caracalla abolished the kingdom in 216 AD, and it became a minor Roman colony.

"For my part," said Father Michael, "I was surprised that Ignatius mentioned the collection of Jesus's sayings by Matthew, which obviously referred to what we now call Matthew's Gospel. This would indicate that a form of this Gospel was in circulation in India during Ignatius's era. This would appear to validate an ancient church tradition that tells us when Christian missionaries arrived in India in the third century, they were astonished to find native Christians there who had a copy of Matthew's Gospel written in Aramaic."

Ken thought for a moment, then asked, "Father, do you think it's even likely that Thomas could have traveled as far as India converting large numbers of people to the Christian faith? Seems to me, if this were true, there would have been many Christians around when the British gained control of India hundreds of years ago."

"Well," said Father Michael, "first of all, Great Britain wasn't the first European power to establish colonies in India, though they did arrive there in the 1600s. More than a hundred years earlier, Vasco da Gama, the Portuguese explorer, landed on the Malabar

Coast of India. It is said that he and his men were dumbfounded when they were met by Indians who professed to be Christians. When questioned by Portuguese priests, these Indians claimed they had been Christian since the Apostle Thomas converted their ancestors around the year 60 AD.

"For many years, scholars disputed that claim, maintaining that Syrian Christian missionaries only arrived in India around the year 400 AD to introduce Christianity. But the Indian Christians persevered in their belief that the Apostle Thomas introduced Christianity to the subcontinent, and an increasing number of modern-day scholars are now beginning to accept that claim. Now, in his manuscript, Ignatius confirms this tradition."

Doctor Bankkour then said, "Mr. Monroe, did you notice that Ignatius frequently refers to Peter's role as leader among the Christians? Early in this account, he mentions that Peter suggested that Thomas, Jude Thaddaeus, Philip, and Bartholomew visit the Jewish settlers in Armenia first before going on to Osroene as they had planned. Throughout Ignatius's manuscript, the other apostles and disciples seem to rely on Peter for counsel and guidance."

"Yes, I've noticed that, too," said Ken. "Peter seems to have been the guiding figure for the missionary activities undertaken by the others. I suppose he was seen by them as the 'Rock' he was called by Jesus. The others certainly seemed to defer to him concerning their missions. But, what continues to amaze me," Ken continued, "is Ignatius's account of the widespread colonies of Jews so far from their homeland. Apparently, according to Ignatius, there were Jewish settlements even in far-off India, which prompted Thomas to undertake that distant journey.

"Why do you suppose," Ken continued, "so many Jews settled in so many distant places, since we've always heard about their yearning to return to their homeland? In any event, I had always understood that the Jewish dispersion took place after the Romans destroyed Jerusalem and the temple, which would have been during Ignatius's lifetime. I wouldn't have thought so many colonies of Jews could have been established in such a short time."

"Good question, Mr. Monroe. Let me try to explain," said Father Michael. "It's certainly true that the Roman victory and their destruction of Jerusalem in 70 AD that ended the Jewish revolt resulted in the widespread dispersion of thousands of Jews, many of whom were sent as slaves to construct the Coliseum in Rome.

"The Jewish Diaspora, however, began more than seven hundred years earlier, when the kingdom of Israel was conquered by the Assyrians. The inhabitants of Israel, the northern kingdom, were dispersed throughout the Assyrian empire and completely disappeared from history as a distinct people. The southern kingdom of Judea was conquered little more than a hundred years later by the Babylonians; Jerusalem and the first temple were left in ruins, and most of its inhabitants were taken to Babylon as slaves. Later, when they were freed by the Persian Cyrus and allowed to return to Judea, only a few of them decided to go. Most remained in Babylon.

"All during these tumultuous years," the priest continued, "groups of Jews continued to migrate to distant cities in order to avoid the unrest and warfare in Israel and Judea. There is archaeological evidence of Jewish settlements throughout the Mediterranean and Black Sea regions, and even on the Malabar Coast of India dating from before the time of Christ. So there were substantial Jewish settlements all over the known world during the time of the apostles."

"We also shouldn't forget," suggested Doctor Bankkour, "that the Jews were a prolific race, and Judea then, as now, was, for the most part, arid desert and could not sustain an increasing population. It was evident that the Jews would need to emigrate in order to survive, which they certainly did. They became skilled traders and merchants, and many of them became successful and wealthy, and their success encouraged more emigration on the part of their fellow countrymen.

"We must also remember that the Jews' deeply rooted religious observances continued to set them apart from their neighbors' pagan practices, and they never became assimilated among the Gentiles. They maintained this separateness and were usually granted permission to erect their own houses of worship. It was to these distant synagogues that the apostles journeyed to preach the Good News, first to the Jews, then to the Gentiles."

Father Michael then added, "The *Acts of Thomas*, Mr. Monroe, which is a Syrian document dating from around 200 AD, an ancient type of novel, recounts the experiences of the apostle in India. It was the earliest bit of information placing Thomas in the Indian kingdom ruled by Gundaphorus before the Damascus Testament was discovered.

"It is a matter of historical record that scholars denied for years that a king by the name of Gundaphorus ever lived and ruled in India, until late in the nineteenth century when coins bearing his name and image dating to the first century AD were discovered in India. Subsequent research has revealed that a King Gundaphorus of Persian descent did in fact rule a kingdom in Northern India around 50 AD.

"Several scholars who now are disposed to accept Thomas's mission to India have suggested that the apostle may have ventured far inland to the city of Taxila, which, in apostolic times, was referred to as the Athens of India. It's known that there was a renowned university there at that time where Greek, Persian, and Indian scholars were in residence. It's certainly reasonable to suppose that if Thomas journeyed there, he could have learned the Punjabi language, enabling him to communicate freely with the Indian inhabitants of the kingdoms he visited while, at the same time, becoming familiar with the various customs of the Indians, their religious practices, and the caste system.

"There is another ancient Syrian document called the *Doctrines of the Apostles*," declared Doctor Bankkour, "written in the third century that provides additional evidence of Thomas's presence in India. In it, the author boldly proclaims that '*India and all its own countries and those bordering even to the farthest sea received the apostles' hand of priesthood from Judas Thomas, who was guide and ruler in the church which he built there and ministered to there.*'

"I believe the preponderance of evidence, now confirmed by the *Antioch Testament* of Ignatius, points to the validity of the apostle Thomas having ministered in India," said Father Michael. "Several of the ancient church traditions associated with Thomas depict him as having been martyred by means of a spear near Mylapore, in India. There's a cathedral in Mylapore, by the way, that is identified as being the traditional spot where the apostle was killed.

"What we haven't known until Ignatius' revelation is that Thomas was first a disciple of John the Baptist. And, speaking of that, please be sure to tell your brother, Mr. Monroe, that, according to Ignatius, John the Baptist twice confirmed Jesus as being the Messiah. He will also be interested to note that Thomas, as well as Paul, stated that Christians should believe in their hearts and confess with their mouths that Jesus is God's Son."

"I think it is highly significant," suggested the linguist, "that Ignatius claims Thomas foretold that Ignatius would become a prominent figure in early church history and subsequent events have proved this point."

When Father Michael and Doctor Bankkour completed their remarks, the three men discussed the current work of the team for more than an hour. Bankkour suggested that Ken talk to Charles about his thoughts regarding a permanent home for the original document when the final translation had been published. All agreed that this should occur as part of the publicity concerned with publishing the team's findings.

After they set a date for meeting in the following month, Father Michael and Doctor Bankkour left for the airport, while Ken remained to attend to a few brokerage matters. Later that evening, he drove to Augusta to spend the weekend with his brother and share the latest translation of the *Antioch Testament*.

CHAPTER 23

At the appointed time on the following Tuesday evening, another phone call to Tikrit, Iraq, was placed from Charleston, West Virginia.

Amir: "Well? Don't keep me in suspense. Is the package safe and in your hands as you virtually assured me it would be when we talked last week?"

Sentry: "Unfortunately, we have run into a complication through no fault of our own."

Amir: "I am not interested in talk of failure. Our brothers in this organization will decide whether you or any of your associates will be held blameless in whatever has happened, but go ahead with your report."

Sentry: "Of course, that's understood. In any event, all went smoothly at midnight on Friday. One of our companions, the one who managed to be hired as groundskeeper by the monastery, was able to unlock the small gate, allowing two other associates to join him on the monastery grounds late in the evening.

"The three of them approached the library and weren't observed. Then, one of our companions, who is gifted and skilled in such things, easily opened the locked library door and the three of them went inside. Using flashlights, they searched throughout the library and concluded that the package wasn't there. The search did reveal, however, a reinforced steel door inside the librarian's office, which must lead to another room. As our skilled associate began to work on one of the locks, suddenly the lights went on, and one of the monks entered the library.

"Quickly, the three associates headed for the exit and, when the monk attempted to stop them, our recently hired groundskeeper struck him a hard blow with his flashlight, and all three ran out through the gate and down the road, where their car had been concealed. Unfortunately, we have discovered that the monk who was struck has been hospitalized with a serious concussion, and news of the attempted break-in has even been printed in the Charleston newspapers. According to radio news, the police are searching for the former groundskeeper.

"Mindful of your warning about creating a public issue in this mission, we've disciplined the associate who struck the monk and await your counsel on what we're to do next."

Amir: "The damage is done. No doubt the groundskeeper was recognized. Do you know whether photos were taken when the monastery hired him?"

Sentry: "He says all employees of the monastery are required to be photographed, and this photograph is laminated on his identity card."

Amir: "Is this associate within hearing distance of this telephone?"

Sentry: "No. He's still somewhat the worse for wear after we disciplined him. Are we to release him to his family?"

Amir: "No, of course not, you fool. All we need is for this imbecile to fall into the hands of the infidel police. No, he must be eliminated. Have the other associates take the groundskeeper to an isolated spot. Execute him and bury the body. Will this pose a problem with the other associates?"

Sentry: "They've assured me that they're willing to die for the cause of the Martyr's Revenge, and I believe them, but may I suggest we not test their loyalty with so drastic a measure?"

Amir: "Why? What is it you propose?"

Sentry: "These men were born here in this infidel country. I do not fully trust them to take drastic measures. I suggest that we allow them to keep this man under close watch in this remote, rural residence where we have him presently. At this moment, his guards are diligent, angry, and disgusted with his carelessness, for he has endangered this entire operation."

Amir: "Let it be as you say, for now. Guard him carefully. Later, we'll see. As for your next course of action, since the groundskeeper has been thoroughly secured and closely guarded, have all the rest of the associates go back to their homes and resume normal living. This unfortunate altercation means we will have to postpone the retrieval of the package until the publicity dies down. I would suspect the authorities will believe it was a simple burglary gone wrong, so it should not be a long wait before we can again work to retrieve our objective."

Sentry: "It will be done as you say."

Amir: "In the meanwhile, you'll travel back to New York and remain there until we deem it safe to resume our mission. We will continue our conversation next Tuesday evening."

CHAPTER 24

octor Bankkour was alone when he next met with Ken at the Brinkley and Todd offices. He explained that Father Michael had been called back to Syria to attend the funeral of his eldest brother.

"Mr. Monroe, it's my prayer and the hope of this entire team that your brother is progressing satisfactorily with his rehabilitation," said the linguist.

"It's kind of you to ask about Charles, Doctor Bankkour. Truth is, this has been a trying month for him. He continues to have these terrible headaches and has undergone several additional surgeries to remove bits of shrapnel. I'm worried that he continues to lose weight despite the best efforts of his wife. Anne is one of the best cooks in Augusta, and she prepares meals including his favorite foods, but all to no avail. All we can do is hope for a positive change."

"We can do much more than that, Mr. Monroe. The abbot and all the monks remember your brother daily in their prayers, and the abbot has requested that the congregation at Saint Matthew's Orthodox Church join the monks in special prayers for Reverend Monroe."

"I thank you for that, Doctor, and I'll inform Charles and his family that so many are praying for his recovery."

After they had visited awhile, the linguist removed a thick file of papers from a large brown briefcase and suggested they begin reviewing the latest translation of the manuscript. He said he'd like to get started, for he was scheduled to fly to California that afternoon to attend a conference dealing with the most recent persecution of the Eastern Church in Muslim countries.

"Could I ask whether the conference you plan to attend has anything to do with what newscasters have been calling the Arab Spring?" asked Ken.

"Indeed it has," responded Doctor Bankkour. "Since the first Egyptian uprising took place at the first of the year, we Eastern Christians have been dreading the consequences. No matter what name Western journalists give it—Arab Spring, Democracy in Action, and so forth—we cringe, for our experience tells us it is only a matter of time before the anger of the Muslims will be turned against Christians and our churches.

"By the way, I must tell you, Mr. Monroe. There was a break-in at the monastery library this week. As far as we can determine, nothing was taken and the robbers were observed by one of the brothers, but he was hit on the head before he could raise the alarm and is now in the hospital for observation. He recognized one of the robbers as a man recently hired as a groundskeeper, but he wasn't able to identify the others. I mention this primarily because of the recent break-in you experienced in Atlanta. Perhaps the two incidences might be connected to Ignatius' book. "

"I'm so sorry to hear about the monk who was injured and hope he recovers quickly. You're right. Perhaps these two events are related. This would mean someone else has an interest in the book, someone who doesn't want to be seen or identified. We should be more cautious in light of these incidences. Who do you think it could be?"

"Let me share one fact with you based on our preliminary investigation of the attempted robbery, Mr. Monroe. Though we are not absolutely sure yet, there is evidence that the men were Arabs. Our secular leaders, members of Saint Matthew Orthodox Church, plan to initiate a better security situation on the monastery grounds beginning immediately."

"Well, I'm certainly intrigued, Doctor, and I'd like to explore this further with you, but we'll do it at a later date when more information is available. But, getting back to the matter of the Arab Spring. What's your take on the events taking place in the Arab world? All I've read about lately in the news or heard on TV is the media's excitement over the Arab desire to replace dictators with elected representatives."

Doctor Bankkour smiled sadly while answering, "As is usually the case, I'm afraid you're not getting the full impact of what's going on. You're getting a rather sanitized version, based mostly on wishful thinking of certain politicians and their willing allies in the press rather than the hard reality of these events. With respect, Mr. Monroe, the American media seems to have a preplanned agenda, where events contrary to their expectations are ignored, while those incidences in line with their progressive views are given extensive coverage. In my opinion, they repeatedly make the mistake of looking at events taking place in the Near East through the prism of Western culture, which is one hundred eighty degrees different from the culture of the Muslim world. I'm afraid the problem is not only the wishful thinking of the media, but also is too frequently mirrored in the mindset of Western policy makers.

"But that's a matter we can discuss at length at a later time. I'm sure you are interested in the team's latest translation."

Ken replied, "I believe you told me when we talked on the phone that our subject today concerns the apostle Nathanael."

"Yes, that's right," said the linguist. "Our subject is indeed Nathanael."

CHAPTER 25

After they both were comfortably seated, Doctor Bankkour began to read aloud.

You will recall, dear Dorothea, that Thomas and Bartholomew left Jude Thaddaeus and Philip in Armenia when they set out for India. I must tell you that, although he was known among the disciples of the Lord as Bartholomew, which simply means 'son of Tolmai,' the apostle preferred to be called Nathanael, since that was the name given to him by his father. Inasmuch as the members of the Seventy who accompanied him to Armenia always referred to him as Brother Bartholomew, and the Armenians and the Indians knew him only by that name, he will always be referred to as Bartholomew in my letters to you.

Bartholomew had come to our Lord as a young man. With the exception of John, he was the youngest among the apostles, and he was one of the best educated, since his father had sent him to be instructed by a renowned Greek tutor while he was still a small boy. Bartholomew was charged with looking after the welfare of the apostles' families while they accompanied Jesus on his ministerial travels. Simon Peter once told me that, after the Resurrection of our Lord, Bartholomew helped Matthew compile the recollections of the Twelve about Jesus's ministry.

Remember, Dorothea, at an earlier time, I told you that Bartholomew accompanied Thomas when the disciples set out for

India. You will also recall that I told you Bartholomew took with him Matthew's work containing the wondrous sayings of our Lord to the Indian kingdom of Kalyana. Both apostles journeyed to the city of Nanyati, where they located the Jewish community. Anxious to hear the latest news from their native land, they were invited to address the synagogue.

The leader said to the congregation, "My brothers, you are aware that much commotion was created in Judea in the not too distant past when the Galilean named Jesus was arrested, tried, and executed on the charge of blasphemy. You were told that this Jesus had a number of disciples who continued to proclaim that he was the Messiah even after his death as a condemned criminal on a Roman cross in Jerusalem. I have read a letter to you from the Sanhedrin in Jerusalem that demands all descendants of Abraham shun those who advocate for this Galilean to avoid being led astray.

"In spite of the Sanhedrin's demand, Bartholomew, one of the Galilean's disciples has come to us and wishes to make the case for this Jesus here in your hearing. Shall we allow him to speak?" With the approval of the congregation, the leader motioned for Bartholomew to address the members.

"My brothers, I come to you today bearing glad tidings that the great event you and your forefathers longed for these many years has come to pass in your lifetime. Since the time of the great lawgiver Moses, our people have looked forward to the great day of our salvation. The prophets and patriarchs have proclaimed the coming of the Messiah in Holy Scripture, and every Sabbath, your teachers read these passages to remind you of the coming of the Promised One. I stand here today in your presence to proclaim that the Messiah has indeed appeared in our midst as foretold by the prophets. Your hopes and prayers have been answered, and Scripture has been fulfilled.

"The prophet Isaiah prophesied the time of his coming when

he wrote, 'Then the eyes of the blind shall be opened, and the ears of the deaf shall be unstopped.' Ask anyone who happened to be in Galilee in those days, and he will surely tell you that Jesus healed the blind, the deaf, and the lame many times, and thousands witnessed these marvelous healings. Everywhere he went in Galilee, the multitudes gathered, bringing their sick and lame for his healing power. He cured them all, and none were turned away.

"Your leader of this synagogue introduced me by saying that the Sanhedrin condemned the one I call Lord for blasphemy, and that is indeed what the Sanhedrin did. Jesus called God his Father, and for that they condemned him; then they took him to the Roman governor, where he was humiliated, spit upon, severely beaten, and nailed on a Roman cross to die; but did not Scripture predict that this would happen? In Isaiah, we read, 'I give my back to the lash. I do not hide from shame while they spit in my face.' And the Book of Psalms foretold the manner of his death where it says, 'For they have pierced my hands and my feet.' True to the prophet's prediction, he died as a common criminal, but he had committed no crime. He suffered all this to fulfill what had been prophesied about him when Isaiah wrote, 'He was wounded for our transgressions; he was bruised for our iniquities; the chastisement of our peace was upon him, and with his stripes we are healed.'

"My brothers, by his death on that cross, he gained, for those who believe in him, eternal life in his Father's kingdom. It is for this purpose that I and his other disciples have come these many miles to proclaim the Good News of his coming and salvation for those who will hear and believe."

A handful of the most prominent members of the synagogue became believers, but others remained unconvinced. It was among the Indian converts to Judaism that the disciples experienced much greater success.

Once, when Bartholomew was visiting the house of Kumar

the merchant, one of the guests asked, "Sir, we have heard from our relatives who attend the synagogue that the Jewish Scripture holds if a man gouges out the eye of another, he must pay with his own eye. Is this also the teaching of Jesus?"

In reply, Bartholomew said, "On one occasion, I heard Jesus tell the crowds that followed him, 'Do not be misled. I have not come to cancel the words of Moses and the prophets. I have come to fulfill them, to bring them to completion. You have heard it said, "An eye for an eye and a tooth for a tooth." But I say to you, do not resist violence. If someone strikes you on the right cheek, turn the left one to him also. If a man sues you in court in order to take your tunic, give him your cloak as well.'

"Jesus went on to say, 'You have heard it was said "You shall love your neighbor and hate your enemy." But I say to you, love your enemies and pray for those who persecute you. When you do this you are acting as true sons of your Heavenly Father, for does he not make the rain fall on the just as well as the unjust and the sun to shine on both the righteous and the evil alike? So I say to you strive to be perfect as your heavenly Father is perfect.'"

Throughout the kingdom, many among the Indians became committed to Christ, for they heard what the Lord had said with gladness in their hearts.

At the beginning of the consulship of Publius Marius Celsus and Lucius Afinius Gallus, news was received from Artemus—one of the Seventy who traveled with the apostles to Armenia—telling of the great chaos and turmoil in that land brought about by the warfare between Rome and Parthia. You will remember, Dorothea, when Bartholomew had left Armenia only six months previously, Philip and Jude Thaddaeus had remained in that kingdom to minister to the new believers.

In his letter, Artemus wrote that shortly after Bartholomew and his companions departed for India, Philip was summoned back to Galatia by Peter, who was preparing to go to Rome and needed Philip to minister in Pontus. The letter also said that Jude Thaddaeus, who had ministered earlier in Osroene, received word from King Manu that he was urgently needed in that land so he, too, left Armenia. The letter also informed them that King Tigranes VI had been forced to abandon his throne since the Roman legions that supported him had been defeated by the Parthians under King Vologases.

An interesting fact about this Tigranes, Dorothea, is that he was a direct descendant of Herod the Great, being that man's grandson, but Tigranes had been raised in Rome and had been confirmed as king in Armenia by Nero.

Tigranes, despite his Jewish heritage, had given himself over to pagan gods, but nevertheless, had allowed all faiths to flourish without interference. During his benevolent but short reign, many of the Armenians had become Christian believers, but now, according to the urgent letter from Artemus, all converts faced imminent danger since Vologases had placed his brother Tiradates on the Armenian throne. Both Vologases and Tiradates were followers of Mithra, a pagan religion based on worship of the sun.

Bartholomew immediately took leave of the Indians and set out for Armenia. When he arrived in that country, he found that many of the new converts were terrified and in hiding, for the new king had let it be known that any religion other than the one he followed would no longer be tolerated in Armenia.

The new ruler, Tiradates, ordered that leaders of all religions in Armenia were to appear before his counselor, Babak, at the royal palace. Bartholomew, along with Artemus and Norayr, an Armenian convert, attended to represent the Christian community.

Babak, who had been a Parthian general during the war with Rome, commanded all the leaders to kneel. Then he said, "It has come to the attention of the great Tiradates, king of Armenia, that your former ruler, Tigranes, was lax and lenient and allowed you to assemble and worship however you pleased. You are gathered here now to understand that day is over, and you will find absolute obedience will be required in the matter of religious worship. You will obey the dictates of your king in all affairs: civil, military, and religious. Henceforth, you will only worship the god Mithra. The price for disobedience is not a simple chastisement; it is death. Now go back to your followers and convey this message to them. You will assemble here again two weeks from this day at this same time to receive further commands."

Two weeks later the leaders again assembled in the king's palace, but this time Bartholomew was not present. Babak called for the palace guard to locate the apostle. Several hours later, the guard brought Bartholomew, bound in chains, into the king's presence long after the other religious leaders swore fealty to the new religion and had been dismissed.

The guard captain announced that the apostle had quietly submitted to arrest. Intrigued by Bartholomew's calm demeanor, the king said, "You were here when Babak announced that the worship of Mithra would henceforth be the faith of the Armenians, weren't you? And you were told that the penalty for noncompliance would be death? And were you not commanded to be present this morning?"

The apostle answered him, "I did hear the general, O King. His message was quite clear."

Puzzled, the king demanded, "Then why did you not attend the meeting with the others this morning?"

Bartholomew responded, "I was leaving last-minute instructions to those who follow Christ, O King, for I indeed heard your general declare that all must follow Mithra or death would be their lot. I thought when your soldiers came, it was to carry out your orders, and I would be executed."

The king was mystified at the apostle's willing embrace of

anticipated death, for he had never met one who seemed to be so lacking in fear. "Tell me about this God you worship," the king said.

Bartholomew responded, "There is but one God, O king, who is the creator of the world and all that is in it, and he sent his Son as a ransom for the sins of all men. It is that God and it is that Son whom I serve."

The king could not help admiring the apostle for his boldness. He said, "I can see you are a man dedicated to the one you serve, and I can appreciate that kind of loyalty. It is for that reason that I will make an exception and explain the reason I command full obedience to Mithra.

"There has long been enmity between the Armenians and Persians. Generations of men from these countries have fought and killed each other, and the mutual hatred is intense. Ever since Rome has inserted itself into our quarrel, the hatreds and killings have increased dramatically, fanned as they were by Rome, which seeks to dominate both nations.

"This is a new day. Now that I am king in Armenia, I've determined that one faith, the faith of Mithra, will unite the Persians and the Armenians and help us to keep the Romans out of our affairs. My brother and I are of like mind in this regard, for the enemy of both our people is Rome. You don't have to personally believe in Mithra if it offends you. Your conscience is of small matter to me. What I look for is your loyalty.

"You prove your loyalty to me by publically proclaiming your belief in Mithra before your people," continued the king. "I admire your frankness and will delight in honoring you as one of my advisors here at court. You will find that the reputation for being a trusted advisor to the king brings much wealth and esteem in my kingdom.

"Go back to your fellow believers and proclaim Mithra, Bartholomew; then come to my court and receive the honors that will be your due from a grateful king."

Babak ordered that the apostle be freed from his chains, and said, "Take this bag of gold and return to your people. Remember what the king demands of you."

Soon after the apostle left the king's palace, he distributed the gold coins to eager beggars who were always present in the palace courtyard, then he returned to his residence where he was joyously greeted by the community who had greatly feared the new king's anger.

"My children," said Bartholomew, "I do not wish to have you ignorant about what soon will take place. It's true that the king has released me, but he did so expecting that I would urge you to abandon what we've taught you about the Lord Jesus and instead turn to the false worship of Mithra. This I will not do, for what we have brought to you is the Good News that Jesus came to redeem all men who acknowledge him as God's only Son. No matter what evil the future holds, remember, Jesus Christ died for your sins, and the gates of paradise have been flung open for you, but only if you persevere in your faith in him."

The leaders among the converted urged Bartholomew to flee, but Bartholomew had no intention of leaving. When he heard that Bartholomew refused to instruct his followers to embrace Mithra, a furious king ordered his soldiers to arrest Bartholomew.

Once more, the apostle was brought before the king in chains, and this time many of his followers were arrested and brought before the king with him. "You dared to accept my gold, then defied me by continuing to preach about this Jesus! You did this knowing that I have the power of life and death in Armenia. Are you such a fool that you believe you can disobey my command and escape my retribution? Speak, I command you! This will be the last time you're permitted to speak in my presence or in the presence of those Christians with you."

The apostle said, "King Tiradates, it is true you provided me with gold that I gave to the poor beggars in your courtyard, for they were hungry; but those who have committed themselves to Jesus Christ, my Lord and Master, are hungry too. They hunger for the word of God. They hunger for the truth, but what you wanted me to do was to lie to them, and this I will never do. I serve the Lord Jesus with all my heart and soul."

Turning toward those who had been arrested with him, Bartholomew said, "Years ago I heard my Lord say, 'My friends, be not afraid of those who desire to put you to death, for they can only kill the body. They have no power over your souls, which are eternal; but fear God, who has the power not only to kill, but to cast your souls into hell for all eternity.'

"It is true that persecution arouses fear as its closest companion," continued the apostle. "Those of us who were the Lord's first disciples experienced panic in Jerusalem when Jesus was arrested by the temple guard. And all during the time he was being mocked, scorned, and nailed to the cross, we trembled in fear that we would share his fate. We were so paralyzed by our fears that on the third day after his death on that cross we dared not leave the cellar we were hiding in to anoint him in his tomb. I am ashamed to say, we allowed the women believers to go to the place where he was buried in our stead.

Everyone present was amazed at the apostle's calm and steady manner as he continued to address the king. "As they approached the tomb of Jesus, bringing spices to anoint him, the women's concern was that no one would help them roll away the heavy stone at the entrance to the tomb. When they arrived, they were startled to find that the stone had been rolled away. When they entered, they found that our Lord's body was not there, but instead two angels they mistook for men, dressed in sparkling white robes, stood before them, saying, 'Why do you seek the living here among the dead? Do you not remember that he told you that he would be delivered into the hands of those who hated him; that they would crucify him, but on the third day, he would rise from the dead? As you can see, he is not here, for he has risen, as he promised he would.'

"The women came back and told us this amazing news," said the apostle, "and we rejoiced, for suddenly our fears left us as we remembered the many times he had told us that he would die and rise again. While we were rejoicing, our Lord appeared to us, chiding us for our fears and for not believing what he had told us. Then he said to us, 'Go into every nation and preach the Good News to all people. And this is my solemn promise. Those who believe in me and are baptized will be saved, but those who do not believe will be condemned. Now go, and never be frightened again, for I am with you even unto the end.'"

Bartholomew concluded, saying, "My friends and fellow believers, I say to you again, have no fear, for no matter what men may do to the body, no one, king or commoner, has the power to destroy your immortal soul."

The king screamed, "Not only do I have the power to kill you, I have the power to make you die a thousand deaths!" Then he turned to his chief executioner and said, "Take this wretch and apply the ancient Persian punishment reserved for those who dare to defy the king. Flay him alive!" Even the courtiers flinched when this most hideous of punishments was decreed, for this meant that the executioner would apply the whip until the skin was peeled from the apostle's body, and he would not let up until Bartholomew died.

The apostle was taken to the courtyard where he was stripped of his clothes, and his hands and feet were tied to wooden posts. The royal executioner brandished a leather whip studded with bits of sharp metal. With each crack of the whip, the executioner peeled the skin from the apostle's body, strip by strip. After more than an agonizing hour of this torture, Bartholomew looked toward heaven and exclaimed, "Lord, forgive them and receive my spirit into your Father's kingdom."

For the next two years, the king tried to force the believers to abandon the Way, but most remained faithful, and a great many were executed for their belief. When Tiradates was confirmed as king by the Roman emperor, the persecution of Christians diminished. In the period of relative peace that followed, a large number of Armenians were baptized. And to this day, many among them are faithful believers even in the face of renewed persecution.

CHAPTER 26

"Mr. Monroe," said Doctor Bankkour at the conclusion of the reading, "do you have any questions? I noticed you were writing while I was reading the text."

Looking at his notes, Ken said, "I was struck by the emphasis that Bartholomew, as well as other apostles, placed on messianic prophecies when speaking to their fellow Jews. I have to confess my ignorance here, for I guess I never knew there were so many expectations of a coming Messiah included in the Old Testament; I was equally surprised by the revelation that Bartholomew assisted Matthew in gathering the recollections of the apostles, which were apparently utilized when the Gospel according to Matthew was written. I know Charles will be interested in this bit of news."

"Perhaps you might be interested in knowing there are at least 360 prophecies in the Old Testament foretelling the coming of a Jewish Messiah, Mr. Monroe," explained the linguist. "It was quite a natural thing for the apostles to match these predictions with Jesus's ministry here on earth. All of these prophecies were written hundreds of years before our Lord's birth. These were specific predictions that gave the Jewish people a way to measure whether any man met the criteria for being the Messiah. Imposters could be easily identified and dismissed. Today, a number of modern biblical scholars have come to the conclusion that Jesus and only Jesus met all the criteria for being the Anointed One.

"About the writings of Matthew," continued the linguist. "We've already noted that Ignatius's report mentions that Matthew's

Gospel was carried by the disciples into India, but, like you, we were surprised to learn that Bartholomew contributed to Matthew's work. It makes perfect sense when you think about it, though. Can't you imagine one apostle asking another what it was Jesus did or said at certain times to confirm the matter? I certainly can."

Then Ken asked, "What about that kingdom Ignatius mentions, Kalyana? Do we know anything about it?"

"What we know is that Kalyana was a small Indian kingdom, or city-state, known to have a large Jewish population," Doctor Bankkour said in response. "It was known to the Romans as 'India Felix' or 'Happy India,' and many Roman merchants made their fortunes by trading with the people of Kalyana.

"It's interesting to note that the great historian Eusebius claims a second-century scholar named Pantanaeus visited the Christian communities in India in the year 180 AD, and while there, he was given or saw a copy of Saint Matthew's Gospel written in Aramaic which the Christian community claimed had been left to them by Saint Bartholomew.

"Now, as to Armenia. Throughout the centuries, Mr. Monroe, the Armenian Church has claimed its founders were the apostles Thaddaeus and Bartholomew. To this day they are called the First Illuminators, the first to bring Christianity to Armenia, and the Armenians have remained fiercely Christian through the centuries, despite the intense persecution they have endured because of their faith."

"Does it seem probable," asked Ken, "that the new king, Tiradates, forced the Armenians to worship Mithra, and is that the same faith I've read about that was so popular with Roman soldiers?"

"I suspect," said Bankkour, "that Tiradates used the religion of Mithra primarily to consolidate his rule. In any event, during the first century, Mithra was a Parthian god, the son of the god Ahura Mazda, who was charged with keeping the universe in order. In the

Zoroastrian scriptures, he was described as having ten thousand eyes and ears. Later, Mithra evolved into a Roman religion popular among the Roman legions until the reign of Constantine the Great, whose conversion to Christianity resulted in its death knell.

"I believe that Bartholomew's refusal to worship Mithra was typical of the fortitude of the apostles so well described by Ignatius. The idea, though, that he defied King Tiradates as the new king was trying to establish his control over Armenia might come as a surprise to most biblical scholars.

"We do know that, for a while, during those years, the Romans did in fact lose Armenia to the Parthians, Mr. Monroe," the linguist continued. "We also know that the Parthian king, Vologases, did manage to install his brother, Tiradates, on the Armenian throne. The historical record affirms that after a few years of inconclusive battles between Parthia and Rome, Nero decided to recognize Tiradates as ruler of Armenia as a kind of face-saving acknowledgement of events on the ground. In fact, Nero insisted that Tiradates journey all the way to Rome so that a big show could take place with Nero crowning Tiradates and confirming Rome's approval of the new ruler."

Ken looked at his notes for a minute, then said, "I want to be sure I'm clear on these things before reporting on our meeting to Charles. I know you have said that the Armenian Church is one of the oldest Christian communities in the world, but I wondered whether the first-century Christian movement in Armenia survived Tiradates' persecution, or did it need to be revived later?"

"That's a good question, Mr. Monroe. What we know is that Armenia has long claimed the title of being the first country in the world to adopt Christianity as its state religion; however, that didn't come about until the year 301 AD. The Armenian Church steadfastly maintains that Christianity was first introduced into the country only thirty years after the Ascension of our Lord by his disciples Bartholomew and Thaddaeus. In the Armenian faith, these two disciples are known as Illuminators of the Armenian World.

"Ignatius claims that Artemus's letter from Armenia arrived during the consulship of Celsus and Gallus. That would be in 62 AD, and that would confirm the timeframe as Ignatius indicates, thirty years after the Resurrection of our Lord.

Referring to his notes once more, the linguist continued, "Historians tell us that Christian believers in Armenia were forced underground for the first two centuries due to persecution by their Parthian line of kings and various Zoroastrian sects, and Mithra was certainly one of these sects.

"Despite so many years of persecution, especially by the Muslim Turks, Christianity has remained the predominant faith of the Armenian people, and today, the visitor will find thousands of monuments to the faith among the many monasteries and churches secluded in forests and located on high mountain tops in that nation.

"One event that Armenian Christians take great pride in is their claim that the first book ever written in the Armenian alphabet was the Holy Bible. In their faith, the Bible is referred to as the Breath of God."

"Here's another thing I'd like to be clear about," Ken remarked, looking again at his notes. "Did I hear you correctly? I believe I heard you say something about Tigranes being the grandson of King Herod?"

"That is correct, Mr. Monroe," the linguist answered, smiling. "It was the practice of the Romans to have the children and grandchildren of their client kings sent to Rome, the better to guard against their clients' change of heart and loyalty. The fact that these dependents were being educated and raised in the Roman culture frequently resulted in them being more Roman in outlook than their elders. Tigranes was Herod's grandson, but he had been raised in Rome and more than likely considered himself a Roman."

After they finished discussing the most recent chapter

translation, Ken invited Doctor Bankkour to dine with him before heading back to the airport. While they ate a late lunch, he explained that even though Charles's health showed little improvement, his brother remained vitally interested in the progress being made on deciphering the manuscript. Ken even suggested that progress on the manuscript was one of the few things that kept Charles's mind occupied during his struggles to overcome his injuries.

The linguist replied by reiterating his and the team's concern, and assured Ken that he would keep the team informed about the situation, encouraging them to redouble their efforts to complete the task in a timely manner. He also said he would call Ken as soon as the next section of the translated manuscript was completed.

"A thought occurred to me, Mr. Monroe," said Doctor Bankkour. "Have you considered a computer-generated conference call that would allow your brother to participate personally in our discussions even from confines of his bedside?"

Ken brightened at the suggestion and said, "Doctor, that's a marvelous suggestion. Here I've been involved in dozens of conference calls, and not once have I even considered including my brother in one. I suppose I've been so concerned with his physical condition I've neglected to think how pleased he would be to be right back in this unfolding story. I think this is a splendid idea, and I'll get to work on the mechanics right away so we can be ready when the team is prepared to share the next episode."

When Bankkour telephoned almost six weeks later to tell him that the next chapter had been translated and was ready to be explored, Ken informed him that he had familiarized Charles and his family with the techniques of setting up the equipment and the mechanics of conference calling. He suggested that the linguist give him an hour to contact Blake, Charles's son, who would set up the equipment. The linguist agreed to call back within that timeframe.

When Doctor Bankkour called a little more than an hour later, Ken assured him that Charles was online and they were ready to proceed.

Chapter 27

"Reverend Monroe, we are delighted you are with us today. We have missed you these past few months. All the team joins with me in welcoming you back amongst us as we proceed with this marvelous testimony of Saint Ignatius," said Doctor Bankkour. "Today we have his account of the activities of John's brother, James. As you know, James was the first apostle to give his life for the Lord while John outlived all the others. So, with your permission, I've invited Doctor Sabha to conduct today's reading."

Doctor Sabha welcomed Charles to the electronic conference and began to read.

James, the son of Zebedee and the brother of the apostle John, had remained in Galilee long after most of the others had departed for foreign places. Much of his ministry occurred in and around those towns and villages where our Savior had first proclaimed the Good News, and many of the people of Galilee continued to welcome those who followed the Way.

Galilee was, at that time, the most troublesome region governed by King Herod Agrippa. The Emperor Claudius had not only made Herod king over his uncle's previous domains; he favored the king with additional provinces, including Judea and Samaria. Even though Herod had been raised in Rome, he was, nevertheless, the grandson of Herod the Great, and his reign saw the temporary end of the Roman procurators. It was suggested that Herod strongly supported the imperial candidacy of Claudius before the Roman Senate, thereby gaining the favor of Claudius toward all the king's territorial desires.

For the most part, Herod was regarded with affection by the Jews, for his ascent to the throne resulted in the recall of the hated Roman governors, at whose hands the Jews had endured years of brutality, and for a short while, it seemed that prosperity, peace, and tranquility had returned to Judea. In Galilee, however, there was still turmoil, and many Galileans shared the Zealots' view that Herod was little more than a proxy for the hated Roman emperor.

Though Herod maintained his residence in the palace built by his grandfather in Caesarea, he continued to curry favor with the Jews by contributing many riches to the temple in Jerusalem and by supporting the Sanhedrin in its persecution of the Christian believers.

Herod also maintained a palace in Jerusalem for those times it was important for him to reside in the city. When he perceived that his support of the Sanhedrin won him favor with the Jews, he authorized his military forces to apprehend Christian believers throughout his realm and had them brought before the Sanhedrin for trial.

It was during Herod's persecution that Peter was arrested and would no doubt have faced execution had he not been freed by an angel of the Lord. Peter's escape so infuriated the king that he resolved to eliminate the Christian faith by arresting all its leaders and forcing them to renounce their belief in our Lord or be executed.

During the tumultuous period that followed, a number of Christian leaders in Jerusalem were seized and brought before the Sanhedrin for judgment.

News of the king's persecution spread swiftly to all the lands under Herod's control, including Galilee. James was in Capernaum when word reached the believers that Peter and other leaders had been arrested. James's companions, Baram, Ehud, and Chanan, urged the apostle to flee to the mountains, but James insisted on speaking to the members of the synagogue in Capernaum.

Honi, a member of the Zealots, demanded to speak first. "How is it, my brothers," said Honi, "that you can ignore the fact that our nation is still under the domination of foreigners? How can you not see that Herod is no more than a willing tool of the Romans, like his grandfather? How is it that, knowing all of this, you still invite one to speak who prattles on about loving those who despise the customs of our forefathers?

"I have heard this man call on our brothers to love their enemies in the synagogue in Magdala. The one he follows, Jesus of Nazareth, said this same thing when he was among us. Love your enemies, indeed! I'm sure he will deliver this same message to you today. But I say to you, if there is even an ounce of the blood of your fathers in your veins, the blood of David, Joshua, or Samson, you will rise up, take up your scythes, and kill every Roman and Jewish traitor you can find. Only then will our land be free and David's kingdom restored!"

James then spoke. "How soon we forget, my brothers. How soon the marvelous things Jesus said and did in Galilee pass from our memory. Are there not here in your midst friends or relatives who were cured of their illnesses by Jesus, the one I follow? Are there not men and women you know who were blind or lame whom he healed? Did not many of you mingle with the thousands who gathered to hear him speak those wonderful words of spiritual consolation? And did not at least a few of you partake of the miraculous food he had his disciples distribute to you in the desert?

"Is that not Amos, son of Haskel, I see sitting in your midst? Are there those here in this gathering who can remember the little crippled boy who had never taken a step in his life until Jesus laid his hands on him and told him to rise and walk? And here in your company is Nadab, who was born blind. Now he sees as well as anyone, do you not, Nadab? Tell this congregation, who did this wonderful gift of sight come from?"

Nadab shouted, "Jesus of Nazareth!"

James continued, "Now David and Solomon were great kings, but does Scripture tell us that either of them ever made the lame walk or the blind see? When Peter, Andrew, and my brother John first began to follow Jesus, our thinking was like that of Honi. We thought that he was going to restore David's kingdom.

"I confess that each of us harbored sinful ambition and conspired against each other to hold places of high honor in this revived kingdom. Yes, we shared Honi's view that, at all cost, the Romans must be driven from the land. My friends, we didn't understand what Jesus's real mission was all about, even though we eagerly followed him and observed how powerful his influence was over all who gathered to hear him speak. No, he is truly the greatest of kings, but his kingdom is definitely not of this sinful world.

"Still, brothers, the people in Jerusalem saw in him a new David; he could have been king of Israel had he so desired. Have you not heard how the people of Jerusalem hailed him as king when he rode in triumph down the Mount of Olives, across the Kidron Valley, and up to the Gate of Mercy before the temple? The crowd was poised to make him king, but instead of claiming a crown, he walked away from them. Less than a week later, the same people who offered him the crown lined the streets of the city, jeering at him as he carried the cross on which he was to die.

"He had told us on many occasions that his kingdom was not of this world, but we didn't understand. He came only to offer himself as a sacrifice for those who would accept him and believe he was God's only son.

"My brothers, I am but one of many witnesses who can testify that after Jesus had been in his tomb three days, he rose from the dead, exactly as he had promised he would, and hundreds in

Jerusalem saw him in the flesh after his death on the cross." James paused, looked up, and declared in a loud voice. "I testify that Jesus is the one and only Son of the Most High, and he was sent to ransom us from our sins. Furthermore, he has promised that if we believe in him, though we die, we will rise to live with him in his Father's kingdom forever."

Suddenly, the door of the synagogue was thrown open, and Herod's soldiers marched in. Their captain, Benoni, marched up to the apostle and announced, "Your words have condemned you. You are a follower of that one the Sanhedrin put to death as a blasphemer. In our hearing, you have claimed that one is the Son of the Most High. That is blasphemy! Now you go to the Sanhedrin for judgment."

The crowd watched in fearful silence as the guards placed chains on James and led him out. Then Honi spoke, "Now do you see what you have become? You are nothing but sheep, and Herod, along with his Roman masters, are the wolves among you. They snatch away James, and no one says a word in protest. Yet James prattles on about Jesus refusing a crown. Who wants a king who loves his enemies? Give me a king who will slay his enemies! Give me a king who will kill those among our people who serve the Romans and will drive the hated foreigners from this land!"

Jonathan ben Anon was the high priest, having been appointed to that position by King Herod Agrippa. When James was brought to Jerusalem in chains, Herod was still angry that Peter had escaped from his clutches and had not been recaptured. He sent word that James must be condemned to death by the Sanhedrin. Dutifully, the Sanhedrin accused James of blasphemy, condemned him to death, and sent him to Herod for execution.

It was during the consulship of Titus Statilius Taurus and P. Calvisius Sabinus Pomponius that James was brought before the king. Herod dismissed everyone in attendance except the commander of the guard, who forced the apostle to kneel before the throne. "Where is this Simon, your leader, the one I cast in prison, but who escaped? Tell me truthfully where he is and I might allow you to live, even though the Sanhedrin has condemned you to death."

"Wherever Simon called Peter might be, he is serving my Lord Jesus," responded James. "He is preaching the Good News about the redemption of sinful man through the sacrifice and death of Jesus, God's only Son, on the cross of Calvary. Why, O King, are you persecuting those who do no harm but only desire that all men be saved? Why do you support those Pharisees and Sadducees who lay impossible burdens on the shoulders of the poor while they excuse themselves from these burdens and enjoy lives of comfort and wealth?"

Herod answered with a laugh, "I didn't expect you to tell me where Peter was hiding. Do you fools who believe in this Jesus still not understand the realities of power here in Judea? Do you not yet realize that the Sanhedrin and I retain what little power we have at the sufferance of Rome? The Zealots among the people rage and complain that we are puppets of Rome, and they foolishly call for rebellion against the Roman legions. They still do not realize that the Sanhedrin and I remain in office only at the pleasure of the emperor. Should we allow these radical elements among the people, including your fellow believers, to stir up trouble, the emperor will send in the Roman legions to crush us all.

"No, we dare not allow you and those like you who refuse to worship the emperor strain our relationship with Rome," the king exclaimed. "And I, as tetrarch, do not intend on being summoned by the emperor to answer for the likes of you or the Zealots. It is far better to calm the nervous brows of the Roman Senate with an occasional execution of a troublemaker than to risk the displeasure of Rome.

"Now, would you like to know who gave you up to our soldiers?" Upon this announcement Honi, the Zealot, walked into the room.

"This man," said the king, "is a paid informer who poses as a Zealot leader in order to gain information on the unrest in Galilee. Honi informed us you were scheduled to speak, so we sent our soldiers to arrest you, and here you are in chains. Honi, meanwhile, gets a purse of gold for his work and will return to Galilee pretending to be a Zealot to ferret out more of your delusional fellow countrymen who bring disgrace upon us by refusing to worship the emperor."

Honi fell to his knees and cried, "King Herod, I have done wrong before God by betraying this good and decent man. While being present here in your palace, I have found that even members of your own household have embraced the Way of Jesus, and they have made it a point to forgive me for betraying James. I have learned much about Jesus and his miraculous ways from them and from the many Galileans who were cured of various illnesses by him. Now I'm persuaded that he is truly the long-awaited Messiah. I beg you, release this man, for I am sick at heart at what I have done and pray that Jesus will forgive me for this and many other transgressions. I will gladly return your purse of gold."

Herod looked at his agent with contempt. "You fool. You, too, have fallen under the spell of this Jesus. You, a man who would even betray your own mother for a few gold pieces. How dare you make this request of me? If I didn't have use for your devious skills of deception, I'd send you to the executioner as well."

"King Agrippa," exclaimed James, "before your eyes, you have seen the work of my Lord Jesus take place. Now Honi understands from the Lord's followers the miracle of forgiveness for evil acts and the salvation of his immortal soul. Do you not also long for forgiveness, peace, and rest for your soul?"

"How dare you question me and even suggest that I require forgiveness for any of my acts! You forget who I am and who you are. Only fools and idiots could believe this Galilean carpenter and rabble-rouser was the Son of God. You and all your deluded followers are the scum of the earth—troublemakers who, along with the Zealots, will bring down the might of Rome on our heads!"

"Are we troublemakers?" the apostle replied calmly. "Have any of the followers of the Way demonstrated anything other than love and concern for our fellow Jews lest they miss out on the hope of salvation? We have simply proclaimed that the long-awaited hope of our nation, the Messiah, has come in our own time. We have only carried out our Lord Jesus's command to proclaim the Good News of forgiveness of sins to all who will listen. It is those who violently oppose this proclamation who create trouble."

"You are so naïve," the tetrarch said with exasperation. "Even in the midst of your blasphemy, you still fail to understand. It is your opposition to the traditional rabbinical teaching in the temple and the fact this man Jesus had the gall to chase the moneylenders and sellers of sacrificial animals out of the temple that has so stirred up the scribes and priests. You represent a direct challenge to the authority of the Sanhedrin, the priests, and scribes, and their livelihood. It is precisely because the Sanhedrin represents the majority view of the people, and continues to bask in the favor of the emperor, that you are here before me now and stand condemned. It is precisely because I, too, intend to remain in the emperor's good graces that I will enforce the Sanhedrin's judgment against you."

Herod looked at the two men. "The Sanhedrin and I will make an example of you as a leader of an heretical sect, and I'll ensure that a report will go to Caesar that, once again, his loyal and faithful tetrarch has executed another troublemaker. You will die, Rome will be satisfied, and the Sanhedrin and I will no doubt be congratulated by Emperor Claudius himself for having removed yet another menace to peace and tranquility in the empire."

The king turned to Honi and asked, "Well, what about you, fool? What is your decision? Do you intend on going back to Galilee as my agent, or do you prefer to accompany this man to the executioner?"

Honi rose from his knees and replied, "The disciples of Jesus have forgiven me for my acts of betrayal. I now believe that Jesus was indeed God's Son. If James will allow me, I will accompany him wherever he is to go."

King Herod spat in disgust. Turning to the commander of the guard, he said, "So be it. Benoni, take these two fools to the public square. James, you can count yourself fortunate that the Sanhedrin did not order you to be scourged first before execution like that Jesus you call 'Lord.' Benoni, have the soldiers assemble a crowd to witness the punishment in store for all heretics who defy the teachings of the Sanhedrin and the Law of Moses, then behead them."

James and Honi were led to the execution block where James addressed the crowd, "People of Jerusalem! Remember how the Lord Jesus wept for you and the burdens laid upon you by those in authority. Remember how much he loved you and went to his death so that your sins would be forgiven. Now Honi and I go to join him in the kingdom of his Father, which was his promise to all who believe in him. What joy awaits us! Farewell to you in the name of the innocent one who was crucified!"

Then he knelt down, placed his head on the block, and said, "Lord Jesus, I come to you!" The commander raised his sword, then swiftly brought it down.

I never knew James, Dorothea, but several of the disciples have told me that he was known early on for his fiery temper and argumentative behavior. All of that, I'm told, changed after the Lord's Resurrection. He became quiet and contemplative, often for days at a time. He had great affection for his brother, John, and was modest and discreet, except when talking about the Lord. He was brave and determined and was never afraid to speak out about the Savior, regardless of the danger.

CHAPTER 28

Doctor Bankkour was alarmed when he saw Charles's image on the TV monitor. The chaplain had obviously lost much weight and appeared to be in some physical discomfort, but the linguist managed to keep his demeanor neutral, working hard at not showing his concern.

"Reverend Monroe, it is so good to be in contact with you once again, even though we're several hundred miles apart. We're in each other's presence through what seems to be the magic of electronic transmission. Your brother has kept us up to date on your progress, and we hope we'll all be together in the flesh in the near future."

"Thank you, Doctor," Charles replied. "I'm pleased to be able to be a part of this discussion once again, by whatever means. Though Ken has kept me fully informed after each of your sessions, I'm looking forward to getting back into the mainstream of the discussions rather than hearing about them secondhand."

The linguist smiled as he responded, "We're as pleased as you are to have you back with us. Today I'm delighted to have with me both Doctor Sabha and Doctor Allen Morse. You'll remember Doctor Morse from our organizational meeting several months ago. He is a professor of Oriental and Near Eastern history at William Wallace University, and he has been vitally important to our work with this manuscript. I've asked him to be with us, for he has a personal interest in the brothers, Saints James and John, and has written several books on their contributions to early Christianity.

Perhaps I neglected to say at that early date that Doctor Morse is a fairly recent convert to the Christian faith, but I'm sure he'll tell you more about this later on. So without further ado, he will present our most recent findings."

"Good day to the both of you, and let me add that it is good to see you once again," Doctor Morse said to the brothers. "I hope your presence today, Reverend Monroe, represents a large step forward in your rehabilitation and that you will continue to make progress in the days and months ahead. As Doctor Bankkour said, I do have a personal interest in the two brothers who were intimate companions of our Lord. I think it's quite remarkable, as Doctor Bankkour points out, to note that James was the first apostle to die, while his brother, John, was the last survivor of that extraordinary group of twelve men charged with spreading the Good News to the world.

"As you'll recall, these two brothers didn't start out as stalwart believers," Morse continued. "In fact, according to Matthew's Gospel, they were consumed with ambition to become leaders in what they thought would be a restored earthly Jewish kingdom with Jesus as its king. I'm sure you'll recall from the Gospel account how their mother, Salome, approached Jesus on the way to Jerusalem on that last journey and asked a favor of him. When he asked what she wanted, she said, 'See to it that my sons, James and John, will sit one to your right and one to your left in your coming kingdom.' Jesus said in reply, 'You do not know what you are asking. Can your sons drink from the cup I must drink from?' And they eagerly responded, 'Yes we can!'

"Then Jesus, thinking of the struggles that lay ahead for the early church in general and the sacrifices that lay ahead for his apostles in particular, answered, 'You will indeed drink from my cup, but to sit at my right and sit at my left are not mine to grant, for this decision is left for my Father to determine.'

"Of the twelve original apostles, James and the traitor Judas Iscariot are the only ones whose deaths are recorded in the New

Testament. By the way, a growing number of biblical historians suggest that the Gospels were written much earlier than previously thought, for it would seem only natural the Gospel story would account for something as significant as the deaths of the other apostles.

"According to the most reliable information we have, the next martyrdom among the apostles was that of Bartholomew in 62 AD. In this scenario, the Gospels might have been written between the years 44 AD, the year Ignatius cites as the year of the consuls Taurus and Pomponius when James was killed and 62 AD, the year Tiradates assumed the crown of Armenia and ordered Bartholomew' martyrdom.

"Again, Ignatius continues to date events he writes about by following the usual practice in that day of naming the two consuls for that year. This date, by the way—44 AD—certainly is in accord with early church tradition as being the date of James's martyrdom."

Observing on the computer screen that Charles was trying to get his attention, Doctor Morse asked, "Reverend Monroe, did you have a question for me?"

"Yes, thank you. I had always understood that Herod Agrippa was rather kindly disposed toward Paul when he heard the apostle explain his case in Caesarea as recorded in Acts. Ignatius, on the other hand, presents him as a complete tyrant. Do we have other information that might shed a little light on his actions?"

"I can well understand your point, Reverend Monroe. In Acts, Luke presents a picture of Herod Agrippa, who appeared to be charmed by Paul's explanation of the charges made against him, but we must keep in mind that, above all things, Herod was an astute politician. He spent long years in Rome, where he is believed to have had significant influence with Claudius and was even instrumental in helping him gain the throne as emperor.

"Herod Agrippa also knew that his grandfather, Herod the Great, was generally despised by the Jews. So, being the consummate politician, he probably set out intentionally to win popularity among the Jews while, at the same time, cementing his relationship with his friend Claudius, the Roman emperor. He knew the success of his reign was based on the backing of the Roman legions while he devoted time to cultivating the approval of his Jewish subjects. Like politicians of any age, his first priority was to remain in power, and he was fully capable of doing anything to achieve this.

"I don't believe he had any personal animosity toward the Christians. Quite simply, he saw the apprehension and sacrifice of James as a means to solidify his political relationship with his orthodox Jewish subjects, including the Sanhedrin, while at the same time showing Rome that he wouldn't tolerate troublemakers who might upset the status quo."

Morse paused to drink a sip of water, then continued, "We should also remember that Saint Luke told us in Acts that Herod persecuted the Christians, executed James, and when he saw how this pleased the Jews, he sent his soldiers to arrest Peter. I'm convinced that Herod did what he did solely to cement his hold on power. What his true convictions were, no one knows.

"I think it's significant, Reverend Monroe, that Ignatius informs us Herod preferred to spend his time in Caesarea rather than in Jerusalem. As we know, Caesarea was the seat for Roman power in Judea, and Herod must have felt much more secure being close to the Romans than he did in unpredictable Jerusalem. Remember, these were tumultuous times, and there was growing resistance toward Roman rule. Zealots in the countryside were already murdering Roman merchants and isolated Roman sentries, events that were growing in number and intensity, and would culminate a few years later in the open Jewish rebellion that was so bloodily crushed by the Roman legions under Vespasian and his son, Titus.

"Among the historical revelations new to us in Ignatius's account dealing with James, is his observation that the Galileans for the most part continued to admire and respect Jesus, even after his execution as a criminal in Jerusalem. Ignatius has James point out there remained many in Galilee who had been cured of various physical defects by Jesus, and many among them had heard the wonderful pronouncements of our Lord during his three years of teaching.

"Because his ministry after our Lord's crucifixion lasted only for approximately ten years," said Morse, "it's instructive to discover from Ignatius's account that James appears to have spent most of his time in Galilee, where all the apostles except Judas came from. I think from what Ignatius tells us, we can deduce that James's ministry consisted for the most part in retracing the steps of Jesus in the towns and villages where the Gospels tell us our Lord made such a great impact."

Doctor Morse pointed out another remarkable revelation of Ignatius that coincided with ancient tradition. "Early Christian tradition tells us that the individual who denounced James was present when Herod condemned him. He was so overcome with contrition that he begged James to forgive him and insisted that he be executed with the apostle. Ignatius names this individual, Honi, and tells us he was an informer for Herod and that he pretended to be a Zealot, but was overcome with remorse and accompanied the apostle to the place where both of them were martyred."

As their discussion drew to a close, Doctor Bankkour told them that the next transcription, concerning the apostle Philip, was taking longer to develop because in the distant past something had happened to several pages of the manuscript that caused the text to fade. He said he was confident, however, that with the modern electronic devices at the team's disposal, they would be able to successfully transcribe the manuscript.

CHAPTER 29

Six weeks later, the linguist contacted Ken and informed him that the team had been successful, and the chapter concerning the apostle Philip was now translated and ready to be shared. Ken agreed to set up another computer-generated conference call so that Charles could again be involved, and a mutually convenient date was set for this event.

At the agreed upon date, Doctor Bankkour first made sure the computer connection was working properly before he spoke." Reverend Monroe, we hope your rehabilitation is progressing satisfactorily and that you are getting your strength back," he said.

"Thank you, Doctor," Charles replied. "I appreciate your concern and trust you'll convey my sincere thanks to the abbot and monks at the monastery for all their prayers for my recovery. I'm eager to hear Ignatius' account of the life of Saint Philip and I see you have your notes ready so please begin."

The linguist looked at his notes and began to read.

Enoch, the father of the apostle Philip, was a prosperous owner of a number of fishing boats on the Sea of Galilee. It was his custom to take Philip with him when he conducted business in the cities and towns along the shore. In Tiberius, he met the Greek merchant Diodorus, and the two became good friends, as did their two sons, Philip and Timon.

In time, Diodorus persuaded Enoch to allow Philip to remain in Tiberius and attend private lessons with Timon. Because so many

Gentiles were moving into this area, Diodorus convinced Enoch that it would be advantageous to his business to have his son learn to read and speak Greek. Enoch was to be deeply disappointed years later when Philip abandoned the fishing business as a young man and went off to join Andrew and follow John the Baptizer along the banks of the Jordan River.

Philip was among the early ones called to follow our Lord. He and Matthew frequently spoke with the Gentiles who were increasingly drawn to the Lord during the last year of his earthly ministry, since both of them were fluent in the Greek tongue. It was his responsibility during the apostles' travel with our Lord to arrange for food and shelter for the group. It is said Jesus fondly referred to him as 'Old Reliable,' for Philip took this responsibility with great seriousness.

Philip was the first apostle we know about to venture from Jerusalem after the Resurrection to carry the Good News to Samaria. His wife was a faithful disciple, but she died early in the apostle's ministry, leaving him with several young daughters who were raised by his sister. Philip was a gentle person much loved by the poor, in whom he took a great interest.

Shortly after the Resurrection of our Lord, the people from Samaria, no doubt remembering the Lord's visit with them earlier, asked Peter to send one of the disciples to their land, for many there had seen and heard the Lord speak when he walked the earth, and they desired to learn more. When Peter brought this request before the others, he suggested that either Matthew or Philip undertake the journey because of their proficiency in Greek. In those days, many of the Samaritans conducted business with Gentiles in the Decapolis, so they spoke only Greek. Philip volunteered to go to Samaria, while Matthew elected to remain in Jerusalem.

Philip was accompanied on his mission to Samaria by the oldest of his daughters, Hermione. Hermione shared the gentle nature of her father and gained the respect of the disciples of the Lord for her gift of prophecy and the care and concern she had for the poor, the sick, and the lame. She was especially popular among the women, for they felt they could speak freely to her, and she answered many questions they had about our Lord and his mission.

When Philip and Hermione arrived in the city of Sebaste, they were greeted by Mattan, a leader among the Samaritans. A large crowd descended on the town, anxious to hear what the apostle had to say.

"Men of Samaria, in former times you would never have summoned a Jew, a member of the race you hate and despise, to come to you and talk about religious matters. You have your own beliefs, and they are entirely different from the beliefs of the Jews. Neither would any Jew consent to answer a summons from Samaritans, a people the Jews hate and despise. The fact that Samaritans have appealed to a Jew and a Jew has come to you is a clear signal that these are not normal times, that something of great magnitude has occurred to cause Jew and Samaritan to gather in friendship, for what binds Jew and Samaritan together in these last days is none other than Jesus, my Lord and my Redeemer.

"You will find it in the Scriptures of both Jew and Samaritan that one day, in God's own time, he would send an Anointed One, a Messiah, to rescue men from the wiles and snares of the evil one. For ages, both Jew and Samaritan have cried out to God, praying that day would soon come. Now it is with great joy that I stand before you to proclaim that the prayers of both Jew and Samaritan have been answered, for the Anointed One, the Messiah, has come and even, for a few days, was present in the flesh in Samaria. Jesus is the only reason Samaritans requested that a Jew be sent to them, and Jesus is the only reason that I, a Jew, stand here before you this day."

A man stood and said, "You do rightly say that Samaritans and Jews despise one another and it has ever been so. Now you tell us that this Jesus was the Expected One and you come in his name. You tell us that the barriers that separated Jew and Samaritan have been removed, but did not your people condemn and execute this Jesus? Do you expect us to believe in and follow a dead man? And what did this man, a Jew, ever say about Samaritans that would cause us to believe in him?"

Philip responded, "One day when Jesus was teaching, a man, an expert in the Jewish Law, asked him what one must do to inherit eternal life. Jesus said, 'You are a teacher of the Law. You must know the Law says, "Love the Lord your God with all your heart, soul, strength, and mind, and love your neighbor as well as you love yourself." Then the man said, 'But who then is my neighbor?'

"Jesus answered, 'Once a Jew was traveling from Jerusalem to Jericho, but along the way he was set upon by thieves. They beat him and stripped him, took his money, and left him for dead. Then, along came a priest from the temple, who saw the bleeding man lying unconscious in the road. The priest did not stop and passed him by on the other side of the road. Next, a Levite came down the same road, but he, too, hurried along the way and quickly passed by him without stopping. The next traveler to come along the road was a Samaritan, who saw the Jew lying in the road and took pity on him. He stopped, ministered to him, pouring oil and wine on his wounds. Then he put the man on his donkey and took him to an inn, where he arranged accommodations for him and made him comfortable for the night. The next morning, he gave the innkeeper some money and told him to look after the wounded man, saying he would return and reimburse the innkeeper for any additional expense. Now I ask you, which of these three was a neighbor to the man who was left for dead by the thieves?'

"The man, who was an expert in the Law, replied, 'The one who had pity on him.'

"Jesus then said, 'You have your answer. Be on your way and do likewise.'

"Men of Samaria," Philip continued, "you have heard of the miracles performed by Jesus, and there are some among you who saw him and heard him preach when he passed through your land. Jesus's ministry was all about love, forgiveness, and acceptance. As his follower, I watched him break down barriers everywhere he went. When he looked into a man's heart, he did not see him as Jew or Samaritan for anyone who truly repented, asked God for forgiveness, and earnestly loved and cared for his neighbor was acceptable in his sight. 'Go into all the world and preach repentance and forgiveness in my name,' Jesus said. So here I am, a Jew, bearing this message to the Samaritans. And I tell you, those of us who followed him every day, heard him speak, saw him heal the sick, the blind, and the lame and were present when he raised the dead, believe salvation is found in no one else but Jesus Christ.

"Those who believe do not follow a dead man, but a risen Savior. It is true that the Sanhedrin condemned Jesus and the Romans crucified him, but three days later, he rose from the tomb as he promised he would and appeared in the midst of his disciples. There are many in Jerusalem who saw him after his death on the cross, and they still live and can testify to this. In the days that followed his glorious Resurrection, he commanded us to take his message of salvation to all men who truly repent of their sins.

"Yes, my friends, he is the Savior both Jew and Samaritan have longed for."

A great number of the Samaritans were saved that day and in the days that followed, dear daughter Dorothea. Nicholas from Antioch, one of the seven deacons chosen by the first community of believers to assist the apostles, was a longtime companion and fellow worker in the Lord's vineyard with Philip throughout the apostle's ministry. I knew Nicholas when he was an old man and had returned to Antioch. He told me Philip was a powerful preacher proficient in the Greek tongue who won many converts, first among the

Samaritans, then among the Gentiles in Caesarea in Judea, where he also ministered for a number of years. Nicholas accompanied the apostle and his daughter when they left Judea and traveled to distant Hierapolis at about the time the Jews rose in revolt against Rome.

Nicholas told me that if Philip had a limitation it was his inability to find any fault with those with whom he came in contact. He was such a generous and gregarious man and always seemed to search for the good in people even among those who were not worthy of his trust. One example of this was Philip's acceptance of Simon Magus into the community of faith when he still ministered to the Samaritans.

Previously, I described Simon Peter's confrontation with Simon Magus in Rome and how that wicked man deluded followers of the Way with his magical tricks. Many years earlier, he had been in Samaria performing these evil arts with a growing following at the time of Philip's visit. Observing how eagerly the Samaritans received the Good News preached by the apostle and the extraordinary healing power of his daughter Hermione, the Magus pretended to accept the Way of the Lord in order to acquire the marvelous powers granted to the Lord's true followers.

Hermione mistrusted the Magus and, several times, she warned her father that the man was a conniver and insincere in the faith. Each time Philip reminded her of the Lord's injunction to judge not that you also might avoid judgment.

It wasn't until Peter and John responded to Philip's call for assistance because the spiritual harvest among the Samaritans was so great, that Simon Magus's true evil nature was revealed. When Peter and John healed the sick and the lame among the Samaritans, the Magus approached them and offered to purchase their healing power. The apostles assembled the Samaritan believers with Simon present and publically admonished him for attempting to buy what the Lord so freely gave to his disciples. Disgraced, Simon Magus fled

Samaria, and Peter gently reminded Philip to be on guard, for even in the last days, Satan would do all in his power to hinder the Lord's followers.

Peter and John returned to Judea while Philip and Hermione continued their ministry among the Samaritans. For more than a year father and daughter labored in that country, and many came to Christ through their efforts.

Now, at about that same time, the Roman centurion Cornelius, the one Peter had converted to the Way, was being recalled to Rome. Cornelius informed Peter that he was soon to depart and asked Peter to send a disciple to minister to the believers in Caesarea. The number of believers had greatly increased since Peter and his companions had baptized Cornelius's household, most of them being Gentiles. Caesarea was the administrative center in Judea for the Romans, and most government agencies were located there. After the household of Cornelius had been converted, the centurion opened his house to believers, and through his efforts, many among the Gentiles became believers. Among these were soldiers, merchants, and slaves.

In response to Cornelius's plea, and knowing that Philip was proficient in Greek, Peter sent word to Philip that he was needed in Caesarea, so the apostle and his daughter took leave of the Samaritans and journeyed to that city.

Philip and Hermione were well received by the believers in Caesarea, and the church there continued to grow and prosper, with most of the converts coming from the Gentiles. Many of the new believers had first been attracted to the faith through the marvelous healing power of Hermione. Even when relations between the Jews and Romans deteriorated due to the atrocities committed by the Jewish Zealots and the increased cruelty among the Romans in Judea, the church continued to grow. Philip and his daughter worked tirelessly among the Gentiles, and many among the soldiers stationed in Caesarea became believers.

The brutalities of the Zealots in the countryside continued despite efforts by King Herod to contain them. Then, quite unexpectedly, the king died and the emperor once again added Judea to the Roman province of Syria. He sent M. Antonius Felix, a freedman and former slave, to Caesarea as proconsul. Felix soon became notorious for his great cruelty and avaricious nature. He openly solicited bribes and relentlessly punished what he saw as offenses against Rome. At first Felix punished minor offenses with the sentence of death, but then, finding it profitable to have the offender and his family sold as slaves, he sent many Jewish families to toil in the mines of Macedonia and Gaul. Instead of reducing the insurgency of the Zealots, his avarice, combined with his cruel and unjust acts, had the opposite effect, causing many among the Jews to join the Zealots. The increasing depredations of the Zealots later became the impetus for the Jewish revolt against Rome.

Some Romans thought that soldiers who became believers in the Way were being corrupted by the Jews. They did not differentiate between Jews who followed the traditional path and Jews who had become believers in the Lord. These men worked tirelessly to convince Felix to arrest those Jewish leaders who, in their view, were leading the soldiers astray. Their influence only became stronger when a new military tribune, Lucius Dalmaticus, arrived from Rome. He soon became a willing tool of those who desired to arrest and condemn any disciple of the Way working among the soldiers.

Several members of the army who had been converted by Philip came to the apostle and warned him that Lucius Dalmaticus was determined to expose and prosecute any Jew convicted of proselytizing among the legionnaires. Philip was just as determined to remain in Caesarea to be with those he had led to the faith, but Simon Peter, having been warned of this impending persecution, wrote to Philip and Hermione, requesting them to immediately undertake a journey to Hierapolis in Phrygia.

Philip considered any request from Peter to have the Lord's blessing, so he and his daughter reluctantly took leave of Caesarea, bidding goodbye to those believers who followed them to the harbor. "Remember, brothers, the Lord has promised to be with you always, and I will carry you forever in my heart."

Hierapolis was known as a "sacred city" because of the many temples built to pagan gods, but it was dedicated especially to the god Apollo. The warm springs that bubbled up in several locations around the city attracted many from distant places seeking to be healed of various diseases. When the sick and infirm would gather at the warm waters, they would pray to the god Apollo for healing. Knowing they would meet disappointment when praying to a god made of stone, Hermione would walk among them and invite them to attend worship services with the Christians. Those who did were often cured of their diseases and would loudly and joyfully proclaim that their healing came through the wonderful ministrations of Philip and Hermione through prayer to Jesus the Christ.

Philip continued the practice of the apostles of first taking the Good News to the Jews in the synagogues of the area. When he was well received, he would return and inform the congregation about the marvelous teachings of our Savior, but if they refused to hear him, he would take the Good News to the Gentiles.

The church experienced remarkable growth under Philip's leadership. At the end of the apostle's first year in that city, the Christian community was three times larger than before he came, and the church continued its growth not only in the town, but in the surrounding countryside. As those seeking cures continued to flock into the city, and more specifically, to the house of Philip, the physical demands on his and Hermione's time in ministering to these became so great that Philip sent word to Caesarea for his other daughters to join them in this mission.

Shortly after the arrival of Hermione's sisters, Hierapolis was extensively damaged in an earthquake, and many of its injured people sought out the daughters of Philip, who were known for their gifts of healing. Seeing that the apostle's house was far too small to accommodate all those seeking the attention of Philip and his daughters, Archon, a wealthy merchant convert, offered one of his warehouses to serve as a hospital and meeting place for the faithful.

Philip's work in Hierapolis was interrupted for a short while when he accompanied Jude Thaddaeus and Bartholomew to Edessa and to Armenia. While he was in Armenia, however, his daughters wrote to him, pleading with him to rejoin them quickly, for the church in Hierapolis continued to grow rapidly and the apostle was sorely needed. Jude Thaddaeus encouraged Philip to return, so he bade farewell to the Armenian converts and returned to Hierapolis.

As the church continued its amazing growth, a number of congregations were formed in and around the city. Philip felt called to name several presbyters to provide leadership while he continued to evangelize the region. In fact, the church was growing so rapidly, he traveled to Ephesus to meet with the Apostle John, and the two of them developed a strategy for spreading the faith that resulted in dramatic church growth in Asia during the next several years. In fact, this phenomenal growth was interrupted only when Domitian, the Roman emperor, became consumed with hatred because Christians refused to worship him.

Domitian succeeded his brother, Titus, on the imperial throne, and there are those who maintained he murdered his brother to become emperor. Domitian completed the Flavian arena in Rome begun by his father, Vespasian. It was constructed by Jewish slaves who were captured by Titus after the conquest and destruction of Jerusalem. Ever since the death of Nero, the emperors who followed him had been more or less content to leave the church unmolested, but Domitian was an entirely different kind of man than was his father or his brother Titus.

He was the first emperor to have himself proclaimed a god, insisting upon being addressed as "master and god." He instituted an imperial ban on Christian or Jewish practices. His cruelty knew no bounds, and it is said that no fewer than six consuls or former consuls were executed during his reign. Consuls, generals, senators—no one was safe from his depravity, and his insistence on personal worship spread from Rome to the Roman provinces.

In the province of Asia, imperial orders went out to Domitian's military leader, L. Volusius Saturninus, to institute the Emperor's Feast, honoring Domitian as master and god. These orders required that anyone who did not adore the emperor's image at this feast would be summarily executed. I am sad to say, Dorothea, that a few poor souls who had professed faith in Christ were unable to stand up under this pressure and gave in to the worship of the emperor, but others remained strong and persevered.

When Saturninus journeyed to Hierapolis to arrest and judge those accused of atheism for failing to worship Domitian as master and god, he was delighted to learn that Philip, the leader of the Christian faithful, had not attempted to escape punishment, but rather, had been easily identified and arrested by the soldiers. Saturninus was disappointed, however, seeing that the apostle was an old man.

Desiring to make an example of Philip's arrest and win influence with and the favor of the emperor, Saturninus ordered that a trial be held immediately and demanded that all government officials and Christian believers be present to witness the proceedings. Accordingly, the members of the church were rounded up and marched to the city prefect's palace. With these Christians and town officials assembled before him, the general gave an order, and the prisoner Philip was led in chains to stand before Saturninus, who was seated on a raised platform.

The general announced, "The proclamation of the Senate and the people of Rome to all provinces; be it known that inasmuch as it has pleased us to declare our gracious Emperor Titus Flavius Caesar Domitianus Augustus master and god, we therefore mandate his worship to all peoples and regions of the empire. Further, a feast in honor of our master and god will be held on the first day of the first month each quarter in perpetuity in commemoration of this our joyful proclamation in each city and town of the empire. Any individual who willfully refuses to worship our deified emperor shall be considered a traitor, subject to judgment and death."

Then he rolled up the scroll, handed it to the commander, looked at the crowd gathered before him, and said, "This man who stands before you, a member of an accursed race and an abominable religion, has dared to treat our emperor with utter contempt. He refuses to worship the emperor, thereby, he has condemned himself." Turning to Philip, he said, "Now, I ask you once again and for the final time, Jew, will you acknowledge our gracious emperor as master and god?"

Seeing in the crowd those he had converted and brought to the faith, Jews and Gentiles alike, Philip said, "We, as believers, have always endeavored to observe all aspects of the law. We are among the first to pay our taxes. We teach our children to respect the emperor and all the government officials he places over us. I see you have city officials here in this room. Ask any of them if our members are known for disobedience to the rightful laws of Rome."

Saturninus shouted, "Who are you to decide which of our laws are rightful? You have refused to worship the emperor as master and god, and that is what condemns you! Do not try my patience. Is there anything at all you have to say in your defense?"

In his usual calm voice, Philip responded, "General, if you will indulge me, I will tell you of another situation similar to this one that is part of my nation's history. It is written in our Scriptures and recalls an event that took place more than five hundred years ago. At that time, our people had been conquered and carried off into slavery to Babylon, where King Nebuchadnezzar determined to select promising youths from among our people, have them brought to his royal palace, and trained for high government roles in the future. Three of these youths were called Shadrach, Meshach, and Abednego, and they were among the most promising of all.

"King Nebuchadnezzar made an image of gold, erected it in a field, and summoned all the officials of his kingdom to hear a proclamation, which said, 'As soon as you hear the sound of musical instruments, you and all the people of every province must prostrate yourselves and worship the image set up by King Nebuchadnezzar. Anyone who does not immediately fall down and worship the image will be thrown into a blazing furnace.'

"Now it happened that agents of the king discovered that, although obedient in every other way to the king's commands, Shadrach, Meshach, and Abednego would not fall down on their knees and worship the golden image, for they worshipped the Lord God of Israel and him only.

"When these agents next met with the king, they denounced the three youths by saying, 'O King! Your decree says that whoever hears the musical instruments must fall down and worship the golden image or be thrown into a fiery furnace, but the Jewish youths you have trained for government positions defy your proclamation and will not worship the golden image.' Upon hearing this charge, the king was furious and demanded that the three youths be brought to him.

"When they came into his presence, the king exclaimed, 'Is it true you do not abide by my command and worship my golden image? Do you know that the penalty for your refusal will result in your being thrown into the blazing furnace? If you persist in this disobedience, what god can save you from my wrath?'

"The three youths replied to the king, saying, ' The God we

worship alone can save us if saving us is his divine plan. However, even if he does not save us, we will not worship your golden image or any other god than the one true God.'

"Nebuchadnezzar ordered the guards to bind the three youths and throw them into a blazing furnace. The flames were so hot the guards themselves were burned alive as they cast the youths into the fire, but when the king looked into the furnace, he was astonished to see the three of them walking unharmed in the flames, and with them was a fourth person who looked like the Son of God.

"The king shouted, 'Servants of the Almighty God, come out!'

"When the three emerged from the furnace, all who were there with the king saw that they were not harmed and their clothing was not burned. Nebuchadnezzar said, 'All praise to the God of Shadrach, Meshach, and Abednego, for he has sent his spirit to rescue his servants who were willing to give their lives rather than worship any other god!'"

Frowning, Saturninus said, "Now what is the point you wish to make telling us this story?"

Philip answered him, saying, "O General, this has been a part of our Holy Scripture for over five hundred years. I believe the fourth person that the king saw in the blazing furnace was Jesus Christ, the only Son of God. It is the God of Shadrach, Meshach, and Abednego, and him alone I worship, and I am the servant of his Son. I can worship no other."

Saturninus said, "By your own lips you stand condemned. You will be crucified as the one you followed was crucified. Guards, take this man outside the Frontius Gate, scourge him, and nail him to a cross." The guards took him and tied him to a post, and Philip bravely withstood the lashes of the Roman whip.

A crowd of believers followed Philip and the soldiers to the hill of execution outside the Frontius Gate, weeping as they went, but Philip said to them as he was made to lie down on the cross,

"Do not weep, but give praise to the Lord that he has allowed me to serve him these many years. Though I am unworthy, I count myself fortunate that I am to be crucified like my Savior. Now I go to join him in his Father's kingdom." And so it was that in the fourth year of Domitian's reign that Philip went to be with the Lord.

CHAPTER 30

It had been late on a Wednesday afternoon that Charles and Ken gathered before the computer for this conference call. Doctor Bankkour had noticed that Charles did not appear to be much improved physically from their last session. Deciding not to comment on Reverend Monroe's health, he began by saying, "Reverend Monroe, I'm pleased to say that Father Michael as well as Doctor Morse are here with me today. Father Michael insisted on being here and flew in from Chicago for this session, for he plans to fly back tonight to participate in a lecture at Saint Arcadius Seminary. I'm pleased to call on him to discuss this chapter

Moving in front of the camera, Father Michael said, "Reverend Monroe, I am so pleased to be with you and your brother again even if we're together only in an electronic sense. I especially wanted to be present during this session, for our translation of Saint Ignatius's account of Saint Philip's ministry adds so much to the tapestry of the life of the apostles that we had so little information about previously.

"Let me begin by citing a few of those things early church tradition informs us about Saint Philip, Reverend Monroe. First, tradition says that Philip ministered in Scythia, yet Ignatius neglects to mention that as a place of Philip's ministry. We have no explanation for this gap between tradition and Ignatius's account other than to speculate that whoever was providing the information about Philip to Ignatius didn't have details to share about this portion of the apostle's ministry. An alternate explanation might be that when this part of the document was damaged in earlier years, the monks charged with its upkeep removed a few pages for repair and neglected to replace them afterward.

"Tradition also tells us that Philip was assisted in his ministry in Hierapolis by his four daughters, who were gifted with prophecy and the healing arts. Ignatius does prominently mention Hermione, Philip's older daughter, being an integral part of the apostle's ministry, and when their ministry there resulted in a great number of converts, he tells us that Philip summoned his other daughters to assist in their work. Church tradition maintains that Hermione was martyred much later during the reign of Hadrian when she was very old."

"Forgive me for interrupting, Father," said Charles, "but Ignatius also seems to confirm again Peter's leadership role when he describes how Peter determined where the disciples needed to minister. We Protestants have not always felt comfortable in dealing with this issue."

"It's interesting to note in this and in other sections of Ignatius's account how the other apostles looked upon Peter for leadership and direction," replied the priest. "Ignatius writes that Peter 'suggested' that Philip go to Samaria because of his ability to speak Greek. Then Peter 'asked' Philip to go to Caesarea for that same reason and 'requested' that Philip go to Hierapolis, and Philip did, for the account claims he considered a request from Peter to be inspired by God. Indeed, Peter was the rock upon which Christ founded his church.

"It's also revealing that the early church leaders, all of whom were Jews, abandoned the deep-seated, traditional Jewish hostility to the Samaritans and were willing to go and work among them. Also, it's illuminating to find that Ignatius mentions a 'weakness' Philip has in accepting everyone at face value, as in the case of Simon Magus, a charlatan, imposter, and self-centered magician in Samaria. You'll recall that Peter had to deal with this evil man in Samaria, then later in Rome.

"Early church tradition does indicate that Philip spent his last years of ministry in Hierapolis, a city known as a health resort in Phrygia, which is in modern-day Turkey. The city was Greek in culture, and again, Philip's understanding of Greek would have suited him well for ministry there. Since Hierapolis was only a short distance from Ephesus, and since the Apostle John was believed to have made his home in that city, it would have been convenient for them to meet, as Ignatius informs us, to plan evangelical missions for that entire region.

"Along those lines, Ignatius tells us that Philip named presbyters or assistants to aid him in ministry, with so many converts coming to the faith, much as the apostle Paul did in his own ministry."

Again, Charles indicated he had a question. "Father, did the persecution initiated against the early Christians by Nero ease off after his death?"

"Yes, Reverend Monroe," answered Father Michael. "It's believed by modern scholars that persecution of the early church diminished considerably with the death of Nero. Neither Vespasian nor Titus, emperors who followed Nero, were known to instigate or continue Christian persecution. It remained for Domitian, son of Vespasian and brother of Titus, to start all over again the monstrous cruelty reminiscent of Nero. This depraved emperor insisted that he be worshiped by everyone in the Roman Empire as master and god just as Ignatius informs us.

"It's known historically that Domitian hated Jews and anything having to do with Jewish culture. Since he considered Christians to be nothing more than a cult of the Jews, he persecuted both with enthusiasm. Christians considered 'emperor worship' a betrayal of their faith, and many refused to honor the emperor's command. What further infuriated Domitian was finding out that there were Christians among even his own family."

"In a rage," the priest continued, " Domitian condemned his own cousin, Flavius Clemens, a former consul, to death on the charge of atheism. This was the charge brought against Christians for refusing to worship the emperor. To the Romans, atheism meant that an individual refused to worship either the emperor or any of the pagan gods of Rome."

"Father Michael," said Charles, "was this General Saturninus, the man Ignatius claims arrested and tried Philip, a character known to us in history?"

"Ignatius does attribute the arrest and trial of Philip to L. Volusius Saturninus as being the Roman ordered by Domitian to persecute Christians in Phrygia. Yes, this man was a military leader believed to have been assigned to the Roman province of Asia by the emperor. Since this Saturninus shortly afterward became consul under Domitian, we can safely assume he was eager to comply with the emperor's demands.

"I think I should point out that Domitian's persecution was, in large measure, driven by the man's natural inclination toward cruelty. Quite a few historians believe he poisoned his brother, Titus, to gain the throne. His cruelty terrified his subjects, for he put to death anyone who displeased him, whether senator or commoner, and if anyone had a possession he desired, that person was in serious danger of being eliminated. In Domitian's view, Christianity was an unlicensed religion that taught defiance of established Roman religions and customs as well as a personal insult to his dignity.

"Here's an interesting tidbit of history for you, Reverend Monroe. It had long been the practice in Rome that an emperor would acquire divinity after death, probably more of a patriotic gesture than a religious one. Domitian wanted to speed up the process by insisting that he be recognized as divine prior to his death. Domitian's persecution varied in intensity from region to region. Whether out of personal fear of the emperor or out of desire for personal advancement, as in Saturninus's case, officials might actively participate in the harassment; in other regions, little persecution was reported."

When the priest finished speaking, Doctor Bankkour said, "Ignatius confirms the Gospel account that Philip was first a disciple of John the Baptist before he left to follow our Lord. He also enlightens us that the Roman centurion Cornelius, the first Gentile converted By Saint Peter, was a leader of the church in Caesarea and prevailed upon Saint Peter to send someone to guide the church after he departed for Rome.

"Let me ask you this," continued the linguist. " Do you feel up to reviewing another chapter? If you do, our group has prepared an additional one for discussion, but we certainly respect your rehabilitation, Reverend Monroe, and we'll only continue should you so desire. We'll be content to schedule another date should you say so."

"No, let's continue," responded Charles. "I appreciate so much the effort you and the other team members have made to keep this project moving steadily onward. Ken has kept me well informed about these activities, and I'm so grateful for all you've done and how much has been achieved to this point. So, please, by all means, let's continue."

CHAPTER 31

A t precisely ten o'clock p.m. on the following Tuesday evening, another international phone call was placed from Charleston, West Virginia, to Tikrit, Iraq.

Amir: "Do not waste my time. This entire venture has been jeopardized by the attack on the monk in the monastery library. There are people here, important people, who haven't been fully committed to this project from the beginning. Now they're calling this entire episode a disaster, and they have the attention of those who were formerly my allies in this project. If you don't succeed in obtaining the package by the time of your next phone call to me, this project will be terminated. Now, quickly, tell me, what are your plans?"

Sentry: "It's my duty to report that the monks have enlisted the active support of Christian Syrian laymen who have vowed to protect the monastery from what they call 'unbelieving Zealots.' Several of these men were recently discharged from the American army and saw military action in our country. Each evening, at least six of them show up and divide into pairs and patrol the monastery grounds. It's obvious they employ military tactics by varying the times of their patrols so that there is no fixed time schedule for when they'll appear."

Amir: "So, what do you propose? Are we to abandon our mission after that one paltry attempt? Do you expect me to go before our illustrious leaders and all our brothers and confess that this entire mission has been botched by you and those worthless scum working with you after one puny attempt?"

Sentry: "That is certainly not my intent. I am convinced we'll succeed. My plan is for our associates to set a fire at the monastery library; not a large fire, but one serious enough that the monks will want to transport the package to a safer environment. We'll carefully observe what the plans are for the removal of the package and will arrange to either halt the vehicle in which the package is being transported before it arrives at its new destination, or we'll lie in wait at the new destination and take it while it's being moved inside. There's a bit of risk in this, but I see no other alternative at this point."

Amir: "This seems much too risky. There is a good chance people will get hurt and draw too much attention from the American authorities. No, I believe you should make another attempt to retrieve the package while it is still in the monastery library. You must challenge your associates to make one final and successful effort. This time you absolutely must succeed!"

Sentry: "If that is your decision, we'll do as you say and attempt the retrieval from the library."

Amir: "Do not say 'attempt.' Be positive and convince your associates to be positive. I will expect nothing but your success. You must convince your associates that success is within their grasp. Now get busy and make your plans. Do not disappoint me in this matter."

CHAPTER 32

After assuring himself that Charles felt strong enough to review another chapter, Father Michael opened his notes on Ignatius' account of the life of Saint James, son of Alphaeus. Adjusting his glasses, the priest began to read aloud.

When news reached Peter in Antioch that James the son of Zebedee had been martyred by King Herod Agrippa in Jerusalem, he sent a message by one of the disciples to James the son of Alpheus, who, at that time, was ministering to the believers in Joppa. The message asked James to immediately set out for Galilee to continue the work of the son of Zebedee among the people there.

James was a cousin to Matthew, for whom he once worked. He arrived first in Capernaum, which had once been their home and had been the home of many of the Lord's first followers. Indeed, the believers there were, at that time, meeting in what had been Peter's house since the synagogue no longer welcomed them. When it was reported that James had returned to Capernaum, many townspeople turned out to welcome him, including a number who were supporters of the Zealot party. You see, Dorothea, James had been a member of that party early on, but the teachings of the Lord had convinced him that an armed struggle against the Romans was not the path one should take.

During our Lord's earthly ministry, James had been the one most responsible among the disciples to maintain order among those who came to hear the Lord speak. He was known to have been quite successful as a fisherman and was greatly missed when he abandoned fishing to take on the Lord's work.

Because of James's impetuosity and physical size, Thomas Didymus teased him and gave him the nickname 'Little James' to differentiate him from the much smaller but more somber James, the son of Zebedee.

When the believers in Capernaum next met in Peter's former house, members of the Zealot party were also present.

"My brothers," James said, "I thank you for welcoming me to the place I fondly remember as home. It is so good to see among you those I grew up with including many who heard my Lord Jesus proclaim salvation to those who confess their sins and believe in him. He, too, called Capernaum home for he loved you as you loved him, and he always seemed refreshed when he returned here after being away for many weeks.

"I know you are anxious to hear news about what is happening in the regions outside Galilee, especially in Judea and Samaria. The work of the Lord progresses well in Joppa where numerous Gentiles, as well as our fellow countrymen, have come to believe in him. Many even in Samaria have put their faith in Jesus and have become believers, and each day more and more of your brothers in Judea renounce their sins and believe in him. Peter, in whose former home we are meeting, sends word that hundreds of the Gentiles in Asia have forsaken their pagan ways and have become believers in the Way."

One of the Zealots present asked, "Why should we care about the Samaritans and Gentiles who have become believers in Jesus? We do not associate with any of them. None of them are from our race, the Chosen Ones."

James answered, "Chosen? Indeed, we are chosen! But what are we chosen for? Remember what Isaiah wrote about concerning being chosen; 'I am the Lord God and I have called you in righteousness; I have sent you to bring light and my promise of hope unto the Gentiles.' And again, Isaiah wrote in another place, 'It is such a small thing for you to be my servant to restore the tribes of Jacob and bring back those of Israel I have kept. I will also make you a light for the Gentiles so that you may bring my salvation to the ends of the earth.' I remember these words, for my Lord Jesus said much the same thing when he commanded us to take the Good News to all people everywhere in the world.

"At this moment, many of the apostles, members of our circumcised race, are at work keeping this commandment of our Lord in the lands of the Gentiles. Yes, it is as Isaiah says, 'too small a thing' to simply restore the tribes of Jacob. We're called to a higher task than that, for Jesus's sacrifice has enabled us to be 'a light to the Gentiles,' presenting a path to salvation to all those who seek it, Jew and Gentile."

Another of the Zealots said, "What kind of sacrifice was this? Was not this Jesus crucified by the Romans? Do you expect us to believe in the teachings of a man who died the death reserved for criminals?"

James responded, "If he were merely a man, he would have died and been buried and that would have been all there was to it. Many times when he was still with us he said, 'Destroy this temple and I will raise it up again.' Surely, there are those of you here who heard Jesus say this. He was not speaking of Herod's temple; he was speaking about his own body. Don't take my word for it. Ask the brothers gathered here who heard him say it. What I testify to is that he was crucified and died on the cross, yet he rose from the grave and appeared to many in Jerusalem. The book of Psalms says this about him: 'My heart is glad and my tongue rejoices, for God will not abandon me to the grave nor will he allow his Holy One to see corruption.'"

For a number of years, James continued preaching about forgiveness of sins to the people in Galilee. For a while he was joined by the apostles Simon and Jude Thaddaeus, who had also been Zealot sympathizers before they became followers of Jesus. All three were now repelled by the bloodthirsty actions of many among the Zealots, and they urged the Jews to abandon this group that openly called for rebellion against Rome.

These three apostles ministered in Nain, Nazareth, Cana, Chorazin, and Magdala in Galilee, as well as in Caesarea Philippi, Bethsaida, and Gadara among the towns of the Decapolis. Many came to Christ through their earnest efforts and healing power, and they appointed and laid their hands in blessing on a number of presbyters in these towns. Then Simon and Jude Thaddaeus were called to distant mission fields, while James continued to minister in the towns of Galilee from his base in Capernaum.

No one could have foreseen the horrors about to descend on this land. Even those who embraced the Zealot party were surprised when an even more radical element made its presence known. They were called Sicarii, named after the short daggers they concealed in their clothing. It was their custom to mingle with the crowd in full daylight, select a victim, strike quickly, then as quickly blend into the crowd and join them in screaming, "Help, murder!"

Incidences of this kind became so common and created such panic that ordinary people began to suspect and shun their neighbors and lifetime friends. Though many of these attacks took place in the towns of Galilee, one of the most prominent victims was the former high priest in Jerusalem, Jonathan, son of Ananus. He was attacked and killed one day in the shadow of the temple itself.

Each year the terror in Judea grew worse. Isolated Roman sentries would be found in the mornings with their throats cut. The same was true with Roman and Greek merchants. The Zealots and the Sicarii grew bolder by the month, each trying to outdo the other. Class warfare broke out in Galilee and Judea, with bandits breaking into the homes of the wealthy, killing the occupants and stealing their valuables. The wealthy, in turn, were successful in prevailing on the soldiers to execute large numbers of suspected brigands. The nobles and merchants who were in power oppressed the common people, while the common people envied the rich and were eager to destroy the powerful.

Then, in the twelfth year of Emperor Nero's reign, open violence broke out in Caesarea between the Gentile population and the Jews. Shortly after, the temple was invaded by Roman soldiers sent by the procurator, Gessius Florus, and temple funds were confiscated in the name of the emperor. When word of this atrocity reached the people, military weapons were distributed to the masses, and open rebellion broke out in many parts of the land, especially in Jerusalem. Florus responded by sending soldiers into the city to arrest a number of its prominent leaders. Several of these were whipped in public, then crucified. The outraged populace responded by taking up arms and quickly overcoming the Roman garrison in Jerusalem. Herod Agrippa II and his family fled the city, remaining loyal to Rome. His army, however, went over to the side of the Jewish rebels.

When he read reports of the unrest in Judea, Cestius Gallus, the Roman governor of Syria, dispatched a military force of thirty thousand soldiers to deal with the rebellion. This army recaptured Caesarea and a number of other towns that had sided with the rebels and even entered Jerusalem. When the Romans started back to Caesarea, however, they were ambushed by Jewish rebels, and more than six thousand were killed. Gallus abandoned his men and fled back to Syria. The Jews were overjoyed with their success, believing they had freed themselves from Roman rule, and they declared Jerusalem to be their national capital.

I can assure you, Dorothea, in Rome there was shock and dismay. Never had a rebellion against Roman authority been successful. Meanwhile, in Judea the Jewish rebels began creating several armies, for they knew Rome was not about to concede defeat.

One of the Jewish armies sent to Galilee was commanded by John of Gischala, a fanatical Zealot who was as committed to stamping out Jewish heresies as Paul had been before his conversion in front of the gates of Damascus. When John entered his hometown of Gischala in northern Galilee to prepare its defenses, Dovev, a friend from his youth, told him that a Christian teacher named James was at that moment speaking in the synagogue, trying to convince the people that Jesus of Nazareth was the Messiah.

John of Gischala and his fellow Zealots were fanatical Jewish nationalists who fiercely condemned any religious view that deviated from the orthodox Jewish faith. They hated the Christian movement, which they considered heretical. Furious that a Christian was preaching in the town of his birth, John sent his soldiers to arrest James and bring him back for judgment.

After the apostle had been apprehended, he was brought before the general and was brutally sent sprawling into the dust. When he tried to rise, he was again compelled to kneel at the feet of the general. "Are you a follower of this Nazorean named Jesus?" John asked. When James attempted to rise once more to respond, John kicked him in the face and told him to remain in the dust. "Do you know what we do with heretics now? We don't reason with them. We simply ask them to recant. If they do, they may go in peace. If they don't, we kill them. We have no time and energy to deal with heresy. We will shortly have Romans to contend with, and I will not leave heretics behind to disturb the minds of the people during our struggle.

"Are you a follower of this crucified madman, Jesus, or do you recant and renounce him? Do you sincerely believe that the Messiah who will redeem the Jewish people and drive out the oppressor would ever be nailed on a Roman cross to die as a criminal? What prophet ever taught such nonsense?"

Bleeding from a large cut on his face, James replied, "That

is a fair question, General. I believe you'll agree that no prophet of our people is more honored than the prophet Isaiah. Surely you remember how he described the Messiah. He wrote, 'He was despised and rejected by men, a man of sorrows and familiar with suffering, but it was our grief he bore, our sorrows that wore him down. He was wounded for our transgressions; he was bruised for our inequities, the punishment that brought us peace was upon him, yet by his wounds we are healed, and the Lord has laid on him the inequity of us all. He was oppressed and afflicted, yet he opened not his mouth; he was led like a lamb to the slaughter, and as a sheep before its shearers is silent, he did not open his mouth.'

"That is the Lord I follow, General. He is the one who was crucified and died and took all our sins on his shoulders so that all who believe in him might live forever. That is the Messiah we have long been waiting for."

"Stop! I will hear no more! That man was not the Messiah! He did not drive the Romans from our land!" shouted the general. "He was condemned as a blasphemer, and rightfully so. He got exactly what he deserved. You are a deluded fool, and you will follow your so-called Messiah to the grave. You'll be escorted outside the city walls. There, a detachment of my special guard will fasten you to a post, and you will suffer the death by stoning proscribed for heretics. Each man will vie with his companions to be the one to deal the death blow, for the one who succeeds will receive a purse of silver from me."

James was led outside the city gate and tied to a post. A squad of soldiers pulled a cart containing rocks and dumped the load before John's eager special detachment. Each man looked forward to claiming the general's prize, but before the first stone was thrown, James looked toward heaven and said, "Lord, forgive them for what they are about to do and, in your mercy, deliver them from their sins."

CHAPTER 33

When he finished reading, Father Michael turned the discussion over to Doctor Bankkour, who began by saying, "I believe I'm more excited by what we've learned about James the son of Alphaeus than about any of the other apostles, since our knowledge concerning him has been so limited.

"Church tradition about this apostle is so imprecise. We do understand that he and Matthew were natives of Capernaum, where Peter and Andrew also were from. The New Testament tells us that Jesus resided for a while in Capernaum. We also know that the early church fathers referred to this James as James the Less, but this was thought to be because he was a smaller man than Zebedee. Ignatius reports that the apostle Thomas teasingly gave him the nickname.

"Scholars have long believed James and Matthew were related," continued Bankkour. "Several have even suggested James worked under Matthew's supervision as a tax collector. Ignatius confirms the family relationship and also claims that James worked for Matthew, but the truth is, there are so few traditions about this apostle that we have, up to this point, known almost nothing about his activities after Pentecost; and this James is scarcely mentioned in the New Testament, except in the listings of the names of the apostles. In fact, one of our team members had given him the title James the Mysterious before we translated Ignatius's account of his life after our Lord's Resurrection.

"There's an Eastern Church tradition that James was the first bishop of Syria, but that's been discounted because of the much firmer tradition that Peter consecrated Evodius as the first bishop in Antioch. Other than that, there is little else to go on. Ignatius's revelation about James's ministry beyond Pentecost is the first evidence we've had since apostolic times. Reverend Monroe, I see on the screen that you have a question."

"Yes, I do," said Charles. "I seem to remember from my studies at Emory that there was an ancient church tradition that James the son of Alphaeus remained in Jerusalem and was martyred there. Am I remembering correctly?"

"You certainly are, Reverend Monroe, and please forgive me for neglecting to mention that particular tradition. There is the early church tradition that James remained in Jerusalem after Pentecost and was stoned by a mob there for professing Christ. Ignatius has him being martyred in Galilee by Jewish soldiers before Vespasian's legions attacked Gischala, which took place around 67 AD. Since most historians are of the opinion that the Christians had left or were driven out of Jerusalem at about that time, I think we could give much more credence to Ignatius's account of where, how, and when James's death took place. It's interesting, however, that both accounts testify to the apostle being killed by stoning."

Then Ken asked, "I'm afraid all of you are a step or two ahead of me in the matter of historical events taking place in that era. Would you enlighten me on who this John of Gischala was and the matter of Roman response to the Jews who were in rebellion?"

Father Michael was eager to respond, so at a gesture from Doctor Bankkour, he replied, "This era is a particular interest of mine, Mr. Monroe, so let me begin first with the Jewish rebellion, then we'll get to John of Gischala.

"Josephus, the Jewish general who was spared by the Romans after he was captured, has been noted throughout history as the most prominent and reliable historian of the Jewish rebellion. He said open war broke out after the Greek population in Caesarea provoked the Jews by mockingly sacrificing birds in front of a synagogue. Despite Jewish appeals, Roman authorities didn't take any action, and the long-simmering animosities between Jew and Greek exploded."

"But what I don't understand is why the Romans didn't immediately retaliate," said Ken. "I would have thought they would be ready to come down hard on the Jewish rebellion. After all, their whole empire must have been watching what was happening in Judea."

"The Romans didn't wait long to respond," Father Michael replied. "The local procurator, Gessius Florus, marched into Jerusalem and occupied the temple in defiance of Jewish sensitivities. Not only that, but he expropriated fourteen talents of gold from the temple treasury that he claimed he did on behalf of the emperor. Several years back, I recall someone suggesting that a talent of gold at that time was worth about a half million dollars, so Florus made away with over seven million dollars. The next day, the Jewish crowd mocked and jeered the Roman forces, so Florus sent his soldiers back into the city to arrest the Jewish leaders; they publicly whipped and even executed a few of them.

"In retaliation for Florus's theft of the temple funds, one of the Jewish temple clerks ordered that customary prayers and sacrifices on behalf of the emperor be halted. Then protests over taxation were added to the mix, while attacks on Romans living in Jerusalem were on the increase. Jewish leaders who were seen as too close to the Roman authorities were denounced as traitors, and a number of them were murdered.

"Josephus explained what happened next. The enraged populace, led by the Zealots, overwhelmed the local Roman garrison and took over the government, proclaiming Jewish independence. Then Jewish rebels surprised and defeated Roman forces outside the city and sent the survivors hastily retreating to Caesarea."

"That must have caught the interest of the other captive peoples in the empire," Charles said. "I'd imagine most of them would've loved to be free of Roman domination."

"How right you are, Reverend Monroe. When the news of this catastrophe reached Rome, there was shock and dismay, for this was one of the most devastating defeats ever suffered by Roman troops up to this time. Moreover, it could not be allowed to stand. The empire was built on the success of the Roman legions who subjugated the people of many nations. The fact that a Roman legion had been all but destroyed by Jewish nationalists would send a clear signal to other conquered people within the empire that they might do likewise.

"Earlier, Ignatius informed us that Nero ordered Titus Flavius Vespasian, one of Rome's most distinguished generals, to crush the revolt. Historians tell us that, sailing with two legions, Vespasian landed at Ptolemais in Galilee. There he was joined by his son, Titus, also a renowned military general, who brought another legion with him from Egypt. With a combined force of over sixty thousand soldiers, Vespasian left Ptolemais on the coast and began a steady advance into Galilee.

"Anticipating the arrival of the Roman legions," continued the priest, "those who had seized control of the government in Jerusalem appointed several generals to defend Judea. Josephus, the future historian whose account of the Jewish war is the classic account of that conflict, and John of Gischala were given command of the Jewish forces in Galilee. These two men were bitter personal enemies and did little to cooperate in resisting the Romans. This is the same John that Ignatius claims was responsible for the martyrdom of James, the son of Alphaeus.

"Meanwhile, Vespasian's legions slowly but relentlessly began the campaign to regain control of Galilee. Town after town fell to the Romans, and thousands of Jews perished. Josephus was captured and became a favorite of Vespasian by prophesying that the general would soon become emperor of Rome. John, on the other hand, fled from Gischala before it was captured and, with several thousand Zealots, made it into Jerusalem where he soon assumed a leadership role.

"It took two years for the Roman legions to conquer Galilee and other regions of Judea, but by 70 AD, Jerusalem alone held out. That same year Titus, the son of Vespasian, appeared with his legions and completely surrounded the city. Vespasian had meanwhile become emperor in Rome."

Father Michael paused for a moment apologizing for this rather long account of the Jewish rebellion, but said he felt it necessary in order that Charles and his brother could appreciate the enormity of the Jewish struggle to be independent. Then he continued, "For over seven months, the siege isolated Jerusalem. Confusion and turmoil reigned inside the city. Factions were at each other's throats. Food that had been warehoused was destroyed by the Sicarii to force the people to fight rather than consider surrendering to the Romans. Hunger and pestilence weakened the populace, but they continued to resist.

"The Roman historian Tacitus estimates that at the height of the siege, over six hundred thousand Jews manned the walls to resist the Romans, but in the summer of 70 AD, the Romans finally breached the ramparts and poured into the city, looting, killing, and burning everything before them. Herod's magnificent temple went up in flames, and its remaining treasures were looted.

"At the end of the rebellion, Josephus wrote that over one million Jews had died during the siege. When the dust of battle had settled, almost one hundred thousand Jews were enslaved and sent to Rome to construct the Colosseum, and Jerusalem lay in complete ruin."

"What a tragedy!" Charles exclaimed. "And it was about this terrible event that Matthew quoted Jesus as saying, 'Do you see all these buildings? I tell you the truth that not one stone shall rest upon another. Every stone shall be cast down.'"

"No doubt you noticed that Saint Ignatius claims the Christians had gathered in Capernaum at Peter's old house since they were not welcome in the synagogue," said Father Michael. "I think it's worth noting that when archaeologists were exploring the remains of a fifth-century church in 1968 in Capernaum, they discovered ruins of a much older church beneath it. This older church enclosed an even more ancient private dwelling that had been used as a meeting place for Christian gatherings from early in the first century AD.

"The archaeologists found that the walls of this building had been plastered, and first-century visitors had scratched prayers mentioning the name of Jesus on the walls. Many of these first-century etchings indicated that this building was Peter's house, and Peter's name was included in several of these scratched prayers on the plaster walls.

"Today, a modern church has been erected over the foundations of the house, but the visitor can still view the remains of this ancient first-century house."

Ken noticed that even in his present weakened state, Charles was thoroughly enjoying this presentation brought about through the use of computer conferencing. Because of his brother's precarious health, he resolved to continue with the computerized presentations in the immediate future.

CHAPTER 34

S everal weeks later the group again assembled for a computerized conference, and Ken thought he could begin to see a slight improvement in Charles's health, and for that he was extremely grateful.

Doctor Bankkour also thought Charles looked stronger than he had at their earlier presentation. After exchanging a few pleasantries with both brothers, the linguist said, "I gather you are ready, Reverend Monroe, to hear our latest revelation from Saint Ignatius. I think you might be surprised by what we have learned about this next apostle.

"We're pleased to have Doctor Martin Szabo again with us today who will read through this chapter. Doctor Szabo, will you please begin?"

As I mentioned earlier, Dorothea, it was quite common for the apostles to be accompanied on their journeys by other disciples of the Lord. One of these, Parmenas, was a lifelong friend and companion of Simon, called the Canaanite, and the other was Stachys, a former coworker with Parmenas on one of the fishing boats from Capernaum. Both these men were early disciples of the Lord and were among the Seventy. Parmenas, who was lost to us in the terrible persecutions of Tiradates in Armenia, has left us a written record of Simon's ministry as well as that of Jude Thaddaeus, which I have used to compile this letter. I never knew Simon personally, nor, in fact did I know Parmenas, but I did know Stachys, who returned from Armenia to live in Antioch as an old man and left this account of the apostle's ministry.

Stachys and Parmenas worked closely with other apostles and disciples in Armenia, but Stachys was away on a mission to Pontus Cappadocicus when the troubles in Armenia first began. When the persecution left most of the disciples in prison or executed, Stachys continued to minister in secret in the mountains of Armenia and was successful in winning souls for the Lord there for many years. I met frequently with Stachys in Antioch, and each time, I questioned him closely about this record, due to his great age, but he remained intellectually keen right up to the end and insisted that he had discussed the contents extensively with Parmenas, who had declared that every word in the record reflected what occurred, and it is this record I rely on.

Stachys assured me he had been with Simon on each of the apostle's journeys, even to his final mission which ended in a far distant land. It was only after this mission ended so abruptly in the turmoil there that he returned to Bithynia, then on to Armenia.

Simon was another of the Twelve who had initially become attracted to the Lord because he thought Jesus was about to restore David's earthly kingdom. Indeed, Simon was known far and wide as the Zealot for many years, for he had a deep-seated hatred of the Romans and the Jews he considered to be collaborators with the Romans. It was not until he saw our Savior raised from the grave that his zeal was transformed and he abandoned the Zealot party. Where he had first concentrated on vengeance, he now devoted his vast energies to spreading the Good News.

Stachys told me that Simon had developed a reputation as a fierce agitator early in life and had been profoundly affected when the wine shop where he was employed by his uncle had been destroyed by drunken Roman soldiers and his uncle was killed during the melee that followed. Seething with rage, he began following our

Lord because he thought Jesus would drive the hated Romans from the land, but Jesus won him over with his ministry of great love and compassion. Simon loved Jesus so much that he abandoned his Zealot tendencies and became a devoted follower. Early on, he had been a companion of John of Gischala, who you remember was one of the leaders of the Jewish rebellion against Roman authority.

After Judas Iscariot's vacant position among the Twelve had been filled by drawing straws to select Matthias, Peter summoned all the apostles for the purpose of allocating mission areas to each one. Simon was assigned coastal Egypt and other North African regions. Peter insisted all disciples bring the message of salvation to the Jews first wherever they ventured. Then, and only then, would they take their message to the Gentiles.

When they arrived in Alexandria, Simon and his companions sought out Nechemia, one of the leaders of the largest Jewish community, and asked permission to address the synagogue. Nechemia informed the brothers that both the Sanhedrin in Jerusalem and officials in the Alexandrian synagogue were in full agreement that deviant and heretical teaching should not be allowed during any of their sessions.

"Deviant and heretical teaching?" Simon replied. "Do the Jews of Alexandria believe that the coming of the Messiah, the Promised One, is deviant teaching? Are the prophecies of his coming that are written in Scripture heretical beliefs? Was Moses guilty of deviant teaching when he foretold that one day another leader like himself would appear among the people? How well the prophet Isaiah knew this people when he wrote, 'Go and tell the people ever hearing, but never understanding; be ever seeing, but never perceiving. Make the heart of this people calloused; make their ears dull and their eyes closed, lest they see with their eyes and hear with their ears and understand with their hearts and turn and be healed.'

"We have come bearing a message of great joy to tell the

people that the Messiah they have long awaited has come and that salvation of their souls is at hand, but they have determined not to hear us. Very well, we will go where we can be heard; we will go where this message will be welcome."

So Simon and his companions left Alexandria and ventured to the cities and towns in the Egyptian delta. The Jewish communities in the small towns of Naueratis, Prosopis, Tanis, and even the larger city of Heliopolis were much more hospitable than was Alexandria, and the disciples were given a warm welcome in the synagogues in those places. Some among the Jews believed, and many of the Gentiles came to the faith during their ministry. Simon was the primary spokesman, and he frequently greeted the gatherings of both Jews and Gentiles with the same message.

"Friends and brothers," he would say, "I stand here before you as a repentant Zealot. A Zealot, because I believed with all my heart that the Romans must be driven from Judea. It was precisely because I was so committed to the Zealot cause that I became a follower of Jesus, confident that he would restore David's kingdom and drive out the Roman occupiers. Indeed, I was deeply disappointed on numerous occasions when Jesus spoke to thousands of our countrymen and insisted that they must forgive their enemies rather than to hate them. I remember when Peter asked the Lord, 'How many times must I forgive someone who wrongs me? Is it enough that I have forgiven him seven times?' Jesus responded by saying, 'Not only seven times, but seventy times seven times!'

"My friends, I didn't understand. My hatred for all things Roman consumed me. The fact the Lord commanded his followers to forgive hurts and insults time after time was beyond my understanding. Whenever I saw a Roman mistreating one of our people, I wanted to strike him down, but Jesus would not tolerate retribution among his followers. 'I have not come to redeem the just ones, for their salvation is already assured. No, I came to redeem sinners,' he said. 'The man brimming with good health has no need for a physician, but the sick man does. Model your behavior after mine, for I seek always to do as my Father commands. You must forgive and love your enemies as I forgive and love those who hate me. Do this, and you will be welcomed in my Father's kingdom.'

"None of us fully understood him during all the years we followed him, but we knew there was something extraordinary about him. For how could a mortal man feed thousands with a few morsels of bread and a few fish? How could the sick be cured simply by touching his garment? How could the dead arise from the grave at his command? It was only through his death on the cross and his glorious Resurrection that we finally knew beyond all doubt that he was not only extraordinary, he was who he said he was, the Son of the living God."

By all accounts, Simon was a inspirational speaker, and many came to serve the Lord by his efforts in Egypt. A number of these were Jews, but most were Gentiles, even including a number of soldiers from the Roman legions. One of these converted soldiers had been recently discharged after serving more than twenty years in the legion. This man was especially useful to Simon, for he spoke Greek, Egyptian, and other tongues in use along the North African coast. His name was Gaius Publius, and he was well respected among the Gentiles for he had a distinguished record as a soldier. Simon frequently used him to translate when he spoke before gatherings of recently arrived Gentiles, including military recruits from Italy, Greece, and Dalmatia.

After several years of fruitful ministry in Egypt, Simon decided to accompany Gaius Publius on the long voyage to the soldier's home in Mauritania. For more than two years, the disciples labored to bring the message of salvation to the cities and towns along the coast. They boarded ship at Alexandria and sailed first to Darnis and Cyrene in Cyrenica where, through Gaius Publius, they met with a number of former soldiers and their families. Many along the way believed and were baptized, and Simon arranged to take young men of the community aboard ship to train as presbyters. When Simon was satisfied with their preparation, they were sent back to their cities and towns.

As they continued to make their way west, they stopped at Euphranta in Syrtica, Oea and Zitha in Tripolitana, and Bararus in Africa Vetus before ever reaching Mauritania. At each port, they attempted to address first the Jewish settlers before taking their message to the Gentiles.

When they arrived in port at Cartenna where Gaius Publius's family was living, the former soldier was prepared to remain there, but Simon, filled with the spirit, persuaded him to accompany them on an even farther journey. The ship captain, converted by Simon, told the apostle he was preparing to undertake a long voyage to Britain to deliver a cargo of olive oil so Simon's party, including Gaius Publius, sailed to Tingis, where the ship picked up casks of olive oil. Simon spoke to the Jewish community there, and the leader of the synagogue, along with several other members, embraced the faith and asked to be baptized.

They crossed the sea to Barcino, the port in Spain where Paul had established a church. Simon was met by Arpagius, the nephew of Marta, who was now the leader of the church. Marta was the woman who had invited Paul to establish the church at Barcino in her home when he was no longer welcome in the synagogue. Arpagius introduced them to his friend Tullius, a merchant who had recently returned to Barcino after having lived for years in that country.

Tullius warned the disciples not to continue their journey, for the tribes of Britannia were restless under Roman rule, and friction was building between Romans on one hand, and the Iceni and Trinobantes tribes on the other. These two tribes were the largest in that country and had previously lived in peace. He said there had been several instances where Britons had murdered isolated Roman soldiers and merchants, and the situation appeared to be getting worse before he departed. Most of the disciples wanted to heed Tullius's warning and remain in Spain, but Simon, Gaius Publius, and Stachys set sail for Britannia.

They arrived at the Roman military base and commercial settlement known as Londinium. Many merchants had established warehouses there under the protection of the Roman legion for the purpose of engaging in the tin trade. Among these merchants were Jews, and Simon and his companions spoke to them in the synagogue, but they were not well received. Leaving Gaius Publius to minister among the Roman legionnaires, Simon and Stachys made their way northward to the city of the Iceni, one of the largest of the British tribes.

Prasutagus, the king of the Iceni, had died some time before Simon's visit, leaving his great wealth to be divided between his two daughters and the Emperor Nero. Prasutagus's wife, Boadicea, was to rule the tribe until the daughters, Airic and Maerica, came of age. Nero was displeased that not all Prasutagus's wealth was left to him, so he ordered the governor of Britannia to send soldiers under Petillius Cerialis to impound all Prasutagus's treasure. Queen Boadicea and her advisors protested, but they were humiliated by the soldiers, who flogged Boadicea openly before her tribe and raped her two daughters before departing with the Iceni treasure.

When Simon and Stachys arrived at the Iceni encampment, they encountered great hostility toward outsiders, and the Druid priest, Caedmac, agitated to have the apostle and his companion put to death. Fortunately, Laeg, one of the commanders of the Iceni guard, interceded on their behalf and arranged for them to have a hearing before Boadicea. The queen, along with other tribal leaders and a number of Druid priests, gathered to hear what Simon had to say.

Simon addressed Boadicea, "O queen of the Iceni, I grieve for the great injustice that has been done to you and your daughters. I, too, come from a land that has suffered much from the Romans. Once I was called a Zealot because of my hatred for these Romans. It was my greatest desire to kill them and drive all who worked for them from the land.

"I began to follow one whom I thought would restore freedom to our people, but instead, by his life, his teaching, and his death on a Roman cross and his Resurrection from the grave, he taught me to release the shackles that bound me to this hatred. Now my only desire is to announce the Good News of his coming and what that coming means for the world. For the Good News is in fact his promise to provide salvation from sin and an eternal home for all who believe in him."

For more than a week, Boadicea invited Simon to address the Iceni, and many were impressed by his preaching, but the Druid priests reminded the people of the great indignity committed by the Romans on the queen and her daughters, and the desire for vengeance inflamed the tribe. Finally, the queen invited Simon and Stachys into her presence and announced, "Your hearts are good, so we bear you no ill will. I was almost persuaded by your words, but my people would disown me should I not declare war on the Romans. My people will never forgive the Romans for what they have done to me and to my daughters. This land will run with blood, for I have sworn I will drive these Romans back into the sea from whence they came. No harm will come to you from the Iceni, but I cannot speak for other tribes. The Romans are already preparing for war, and you can be sure spies will tell them you have been in our company. I strongly advise you to leave Britannia."

Despite this warning, Simon continued to minister among the Iceni, winning a number of them to Christ. Nor did he pause in these ministrations when word reached the tribe that the Roman legions were marching north from Londinium. His courage and bold preaching not only reached the hearts of the Iceni, but the Druid priest, Caedmac, the one who had originally sought the death of the disciples, became first an admirer, then asked to be baptized by the apostle.

The Iceni prepared for war as the Roman legions drew ever nearer, so Simon sent Stachys by a safe route back to Londinium while he alone remained among the tribesmen. Even though he urged the Iceni to abandon their armed resistance to the Romans, they persisted in preparing for war. Finally, the queen ordered Simon to depart.

Simon and an Iceni guide made their way south, but they were observed by a Roman scouting party, apprehended, and taken into custody. Perceived as spies, they were handled roughly by the Roman soldiers, who bound them and marched them back toward the advancing Roman legions.

When they reached the Roman encampment, the prisoners were taken to the tent of Catus Decianus, the Roman prefect of Britannia. This was the same Catus Decianus who had confiscated the wealth that Prasutagus had left to Boadicea and her daughters, the same man who had looked on and laughed as his men raped the queen's daughters.

The two prisoners were made to kneel before the prefect. A soldier announced that these men were suspected of being spies sent from Boadicea's camp. Decianus asked a question in the language of the Iceni, "What do you expect to learn from sneaking around our camp? Do you not know that when Romans march, they expect all to flee from their fury?"

Simon responded, but in the Latin language, "Are you the Roman whose greed for the treasures of the Icini has caused all this hatred? Are you the individual who has caused the friendship between Rome and the queen to be broken through your thievery?

Are you the one responsible for the humiliation of Queen Boadicea and the disgraceful violation of her daughters? In the name of God, stop this madness right now and beg the queen for forgiveness."

Surprised to be answered in his own tongue, Decianus replied, "And who might you be to dare question the actions of the Roman prefect of all Britannia?"

"I am Simon, a disciple of the Lord Jesus Christ, and I came to win souls for him among the Iceni, but I find that the disgraceful insults, theft and rape by you Romans have inflamed the passions of the Iceni, who now seek vengeance rather than salvation."

Decianus said, "And who is this Lord Jesus Christ you claim to follow? What country does he rule? How many legions does he command? Or is he that common criminal who was crucified in Judea? Was he not the fool whose claim to be a son of God caused him to be nailed to a cross? Are you indeed a disciple of a dead man?"

Simon replied, "I am a disciple of Jesus Christ, the one you Romans put to death on the cross, but the grave could not hold him. Three days later he arose in glory. I know because I saw him in the flesh. It is in his name and his cause that I am here in this land, ministering to the Iceni."

"Well, you will minister no more to the tribesmen," replied Decianus with a laugh. "Our soldiers are in need of entertainment on this tiresome march, so we will crucify you and see if you can rise from the grave like your master." He ordered that Simon be nailed to a cross in front of the legions, then he freed the young Iceni companion of Simon and told him to return to his queen and tell her Simon's fate would be the lot of the Iceni if they did not lay down their arms and surrender to the Romans.

For one full day Simon suffered on the cross while the assembled legionnaires mocked and made fun of him. When the legions received the order to march onward, one of the soldiers came forward with a hammer and broke the apostle's legs, then another pierced his chest with a spear. So it was that Simon died as his Savior had, nailed to a cross and pierced by a spear.

CHAPTER 35

When he had finished reading, Doctor Szabo looked at the image of Charles on the monitor and said, "Reverend Monroe, I know you share the excitement that we've all experienced as the details of this manuscript have unfolded. As a researcher I would never have thought it possible that I would have the honor and pleasure to have been involved in something as historically significant as this project. For my part, I want to thank you again for rescuing this priceless document from the hands of those who wanted to defile or destroy it.

"Now, if you'll permit me, I'd like to bring to your attention several of the notations we've made as we translated this chapter.

"First of all, as New Testament researchers, we knew nothing about Simon the Zealot as an apostle. Nothing has come down to us in sacred Scripture but the mention of his name. We have no reference of his having uttered a word, and Scripture doesn't mention anyone addressing him. Nor does Scripture note that he ever asked a question. In short, he was a nonentity as far as Scripture is concerned.

"You probably noticed that at the beginning of this chapter, Ignatius clearly stated that Simon Peter met with the apostles and made specific mission assignments for each of them. To the best of my knowledge, this is the first ancient document that confirms Peter's leadership role in dispatching the others to various mission fields.

"Surely you also noticed that, according to Ignatius, Peter is the one who insisted that the disciples first preach to the Jews before taking the Good News to the Gentiles. That being so, Paul was following Peter's instructions when he preached first to the Jews in the dispersion before preaching to the Gentiles, as reported in Acts.

"As for Simon the Zealot, while we have no scriptural information about him, we do have a number of different legends taking him as far east as Persia and as far west as Britain. One says that he and the apostle Jude Thaddeus were martyred in Persia, and it even implies that the two were brothers. Another states that Simon died peacefully of natural causes in Edessa.

"There are, however, several more persistent and stronger traditions which inform us that his apostolic endeavors were in Egypt and Mauritania and other lands along the coast of North Africa and in far-off Britain," continued Szabo. "Ignatius gives credence to this area of the apostle's ministry."

"Please excuse me for interrupting, Doctor," Charles said. "This account by Ignatius is the first time I've ever heard that the Sanhedrin sent word to the Jewish communities throughout the empire not to allow Christians to address them. I didn't know the Sanhedrin had that kind of power."

"It's certainly a new revelation. It's instructive to note that Ignatius writes about the Sanhedrin in Jerusalem sending word to synagogues throughout the Roman world to deny those who followed Jesus permission to address the congregations. This appears to be the first confirmation of what biblical historians have long suspected to be the influence of the Jerusalem Sanhedrin over the disbursed Jews throughout the empire."

"Yes, Reverend Monroe," said Doctor Szabo. "Is there something you wish to add?"

"Doctor, I think it's important to underscore and emphasize what you mentioned earlier. Ignatius places Peter firmly in the leader's role in describing how Peter assigns specific mission areas to the various apostles and disciples. Apparently, his leadership was accepted without question from the first Pentecost onward."

"That's definitely a valid point, Reverend Monroe. Certainly, as Ignatius describes it, Simon didn't hesitate to accept the assignment of Egypt and other parts of North Africa as his mission field. I think we can also understand from this chapter that while Peter assigned the specific mission areas for each of the disciples, once they were in a particular mission field, they allowed the grace of our Lord to direct them farther to other mission fields. In Simon's instance, this was first Mauritania, then on to Britain. Perhaps the great distances involved prevented more communication with Peter, who more than likely by this time was heavily involved in his own mission field of Asia Minor or perhaps even in Rome.

"There's another issue that seems quite clear from Ignatius's account of the Jewish rebellion," the former dean continued. "That's the persistent hatred the Zealots had for nonconforming Jews such as the Christian converts. Simon, himself a former Zealot, makes this plain in his preaching both to orthodox Jews and to the pagan Britons."

Charles indicated he had another question. "Isn't it true that there are ancient traditions claiming other apostles ministered in Britain? Ignatius, thus far in his manuscript, mentions Simon as the only one who made it to that country."

"Yes, there are ancient traditions placing several of the early disciples in the British Isles. Eusibius, the great historian, wrote that apostles did in fact reach Britain, but he didn't identify which ones. Another tradition claims that Peter ministered both in what is now France as well as in Britain. Yet another tradition states that Paul not only visited Spain, but went on to Britain. There is also a persistent tradition that says that Joseph of Arimathea, the member of the Sanhedrin who furnished the tomb for Jesus, founded the British church not long after the crucifixion, but Joseph wasn't an apostle. We certainly should include here yet another tradition that claims that Andrew ministered in Scotland.

"If we accept Ignatius's account as being the benchmark for validating the mission areas of the apostles, Simon is the only one Ignatius confirms to this point as having ministered in Britain. There's also this: his account of Simon's preaching before Queen Boadicea and her Iceni tribesmen is the first instance we've yet discovered that an apostle did minister to the Iceni."

"What ever happened to Queen Boadicea and her people?" Charles asked.

"The queen and her Iceni warriors went on to destroy the Roman army under Decianus, the Roman officer who had crucified Simon, and then marched south to London. They burned down the whole town, and reports are that they massacred upward of twenty thousand Roman soldiers and citizens before the Roman governor, Gavius Paulinus, gathered all the Roman soldiers remaining in Britain and attacked the Iceni in a narrow valley, defeating them with great slaughter. It's been claimed that more than eighty thousand Iceni and allied tribesmen, men, youth, and women perished in the battle. The queen and her daughters took their own lives rather than be captured. Paulinus was succeeded by Publius Turpilianus, who had the good sense to treat the remaining British tribes with respect. They were allowed to follow their own customs and laws so long as they acknowledged Roman authority, and the tribes remained loyal to Rome until the Western Empire ended several hundred years later."

Doctor Bankkour suggested that Simon's instruction of young men as prospective presbyters aboard ship as they sailed from one North African port to another might well be the first written account of seminary training in the early church.

Charles remarked that he was amazed over Ignatius' account of how Peter established the initial mission fields for the apostles as well as his insistence that the disciples first approach the Jews before taking the Good News to the Gentiles.

Since Doctor Szabo was scheduled to take an early flight to Chicago to attend a symposium in which he was a featured speaker, Ken suggested they adjourn early. They agreed that Doctor Bankkour would contact Ken to set up the next telephone conference when the translation of the next section was ready for review.

CHAPTER 36

Several weeks later, Doctor Bankkour called Ken, and the next computer conference was scheduled. Ken was in Augusta with Charles on the day of the presentation. After greetings were exchanged, Charles said, "I'm still in awe of Ignatius's account of Simon the Zealot and his ministry in the British Isles, Doctor Bankkour. I never would have thought Christianity reached the Britons as early as Ignatius indicated."

"I think you will be equally surprised when we cover this next chapter, Reverend Monroe. I have found it to be fascinating," replied the linguist. Then he began to read aloud.

Before you were born, dearest daughter, your late father invited Jude Thaddeus to reside in his home at the time the apostle passed through Antioch on the way to Edessa, his intended destination. This was not long after the glorious Resurrection of our Lord and Savior, Jesus Christ. As it so happened, this was one of the first apostolic missions to lands outside Judea, and it came about in a way that can only be described as miraculous.

Edessa was the capital of the small kingdom of Osroene and was at that time ruled by a king known as Abgar V the Black. The king had suffered from a disease that had caused him great agony since his youth, and it was his custom to seek out remedies for this disease whenever news reached him about new healings taking place.

Receiving news that many miraculous cures were occurring in Judea, he sent agents to investigate and report back to him whether or not these cures were genuine and worthy of his attention. Before long, his agents sent messages back to the king saying that a Galilean rabbi, a teacher, was indeed healing many from all sorts of physical sicknesses. They even reported that a few claimed to have received sight after having been born blind, while still others maintained that their withered limbs had been restored by the teacher. The king was greatly interested and sent word for his agents to invite the rabbi to visit his kingdom.

Several months later, the agents appeared before the king and reported that the teacher insisted that he must remain in Judea to perform the tasks appointed by his Father. He even claimed he soon would be put to death by the ruling authorities, but he advised the king to take heart, for after his death, one of his followers would come to visit the king, and the disease he suffered from would be cured.

Jude Thaddeus was not only an apostle, but had also been one of the Seventy the Lord had dispatched to the cities of Judea to announce the glorious news of salvation to those who sincerely repented and to heal the sick. Because of his earlier mission with the Seventy, Peter selected him to complete the Lord's commitment to the king in Edessa. When he undertook this mission, Jude Thaddeus was accompanied by Silvanus, Herodian, and Sosipater, all of whom had been his companions among the Seventy. Your late father, Theophilus, kindly opened his home to them when they arrived in Damascus, and they remained there with him for several days before setting out for Edessa.

Jude Thaddaeus had earned the reputation of being the best fisherman among the apostles, even better than Peter himself. After the Resurrection, however, he abandoned fishing and became renowned for his ability to heal the sick and the lame. His compassion and love for the poor made him a favorite in large gatherings. He was also a gifted preacher, and many came to the faith through his ministry.

After his arrival in Edessa, the apostle was invited to speak about recent events in Judea in the local synagogue. "My brothers," he said. "I know you have already heard about the recent crucifixion of the one we follow, Jesus the Nazorean. We are his disciples and have witnessed the mighty things he did and said while he was with us. I bear witness that he is the long-awaited Messiah, and he came to dwell among us as the prophets foretold. We were eyewitnesses to his restoring sight to the blind, strength to wasted limbs, and life to the dead. We also witnessed the hatred and enmity of the religious authorities in Jerusalem, who conspired with the Romans to bring about his death on the cross.

"The boldest among us were present when Jesus was brought before the governor Pontius Pilate, who examined him and announced to the authorities that he could find no fault in him and desired to set him free. The members of the Sanhedrin and their followers, however, clamored for his death, saying Pilate was no friend of Caesar if he released Jesus from custody. They said Jesus claimed to be their king, but the authorities protested that they had no king other than Caesar. Then, because of the procurator's fear they would denounce him before the emperor, Pilate washed his hands of the whole affair, saying he was innocent of the blood of Jesus.

"The authorities then answered the governor saying, 'His blood be upon us and upon our children.' So Pilate gave him up to the soldiers, who beat him mercilessly before taking him through the streets of Jerusalem to Golgotha, the place of the skull, where he was crucified. There at the foot of his cross, the authorities and onlookers heaped scorn and ridicule upon him. When the legionnaires confirmed he was dead, he was taken from the cross and buried, and the tomb was sealed and guarded by a squad of soldiers.

"I was one of his first followers, and I shamefully confess we all said we would die for him, yet when the time came to stand up

322 — DONALD JOINER

for him, we all ran away, " said the apostle with a sad smile. "We were cowards; afraid we would suffer his fate so we hid ourselves in the cellars of Jerusalem. I confess also that the women who followed him were more courageous than we were; so early on the third day several of them went out to his tomb to anoint him. To their amazement, the guards were asleep, the gravestone was rolled back, and Jesus was not there. Then, an angel of the Lord appeared and said, 'Why do you seek the living here among the dead? Did he not tell you death could not hold him? He has risen as he said.'

"While they pondered this, Jesus appeared to them, and a bit later, he appeared to Peter and John and then to the rest of us." Now the smile on the face of the apostle was radiant as he announced in a strong voice, "This, my friends, was no spirit, for he appeared among us in the flesh. Several of his disciples even examined his wounds, and we were all present when he sat down at table and took his meal with us. We were not the only ones to see him. Before he ascended into heaven to be with his Father, he was seen by hundreds of people in Jerusalem, many of whom were not his followers.

"Before he left us, he forgave us for our shortcomings and promised that the Holy Spirit would be sent from heaven to strengthen his disciples, and guide and inspire us so that we would proclaim the Good News of salvation to all nations and peoples; and to all those who confess their sins and believe in him he has promised eternal life."

While some wanted to debate the matter, a few believed and asked the apostle to tell them more about the Savior.

Within a week of his arrival in Edessa, a message from the king arrived, summoning Thaddeus to the palace. The Apostle Thomas joined the brothers and the disciples continued to minister in Odessa for many months, even after Thaddeus left for other mission fields.

When Thaddeus arrived at court, the king rushed forward to greet him, saying, "Just as soon as word reached me that one of his disciples was nearing the city to fulfill the Lord Jesus' promise, the terrible disease that has plagued me throughout these many years abruptly vanished. I am whole again, and no trace of my former condition remains. It is only through the power of Jesus, the one you call the Messiah, that this could come about, and it has only happened because you were sent to me by his command. I welcome you and your companions who come in his name. Tell me what I can do to honor him. What treasure I have is yours."

"We have no need for your treasure, O King," said Thaddeus. "Surely there are many in your kingdom that are ill or destitute and hungry. You can relieve this suffering with gold and silver. Your belief in our Lord is sufficient, but if you will allow us to preach the Good News to your people, you will reveal to all men that you have faith in our Lord and in his promises."

The king then said, "Gladly do I grant your request, and I will give orders that silver and gold be distributed among the needy as you suggest. Furthermore, I will announce my own belief in Jesus to my court, and the word of my faith will quickly spread."

And so it was that Thaddeus and his companions, including Thomas, brought the Christian faith to Edessa during the reign of Abgar the Black. True to his vow, the king did announce his faith in Jesus before his court, and most of that group believed and were baptized. The disciples found that many among the common people were anxious to hear about Jesus after they heard about the king's conversion.

This was the first time, dear Dorothea, that a member of a ruling class confessed faith in our Lord, and word quickly spread to surrounding areas. Inquiries from neighboring kingdoms began coming to the apostles and disciples of the Lord, inviting them to bring the Good News to the lands of the East. In Edessa hundreds became believers, and the disciples were kept busy strengthening the faith among the new converts.

For the next few years, the Christian faith grew and prospered. Many received Jesus Christ in their hearts. Thaddeus and his companions traveled throughout Osroene, and the harvest was bountiful. The apostle Bartholomew wrote to Thaddeus, saying that because of the success of the faith in Osroene, the road to Armenia had opened to the disciples. He urged Thaddeus to join him, and after much prayer and deliberation, the apostle took leave of Thomas and his other companions and set out for Armenia.

You will recall, Dorothea, that at the time Bartholomew brought the word of the Lord to Armenia, the armies of Parthia and Rome were engaged in brutal warfare to determine which empire would control that nation. While these battles raged, Bartholomew and Thaddeus worked tirelessly among the Armenians, and many came to Christ as a result of their labors.

It was only after the Parthians were victorious that Tiradates, the brother of the Parthian ruler, became king of Armenia. As I mentioned earlier, he sought to impose the religion of Mithra on the Armenians and ruthlessly suppressed all other faiths. While Bartholomew was almost immediately caught up in Tiradates's persecution and soon gave his life serving our Lord, Thaddeus was ministering in the remote mountain areas of Armenia, where many continued to be baptized in the name of Christ.

While the ongoing conflict between Parthia and Rome distracted Tiradates from his cruel suppression of Christians for a short time, Thaddeus and the other disciples worked diligently to increase the number of converts throughout the country. When he determined that the disciples would continue to be successful in his absence, Thaddeus decided that the time was ripe to extend the reach of the Good News to the land of Parthia in spite of the enmity of the Zoroastrians and the followers of Mithra in that land.

Several Armenian converts tried to dissuade the apostle from undertaking this venture. At this time the king of Parthia was invested with the robes of the high priest of Mithra, an offshoot of the Zoroastrian faith. There were those among the converts who described the punishments meted out by the Parthians as horrible beyond all comprehension, but Thaddeus was adamant about undertaking this journey, for he believed the Lord Jesus intended him to minister in Parthia.

Traveling with two Armenian disciples, Anag and Sarven, the apostle first visited the synagogue in Tabae; then he journeyed to Hatara and Arbela, preaching the Good News first in the synagogues, then going to the Parthians in those regions, most of whom were adherents of the Zoroastrian faith. He healed many of the sick and lame and became much revered by the people.

Knowing that Zoroaster held there to be two gods, one good and one evil, Thaddeus always began his preaching with the following message: "My friends, you have been taught that there are two gods, one of good and one of evil, both of whom strive for men's souls. You have been taught that only through mankind's good deeds can chaos and destruction in the world be avoided.

"I stand before you to proclaim that there is only one God, the creator of the universe and all that is in it. The evil that exists in the world is not a creation of another god, for the Lord God is one and inspires only good. Evil was introduced to the world through the acts of one of God's fallen angels, one who aspired to take God's place, even though he was but a creation of God. Now evil is alive and flourishing in the world because of man's desire for sinful pursuits. In this pursuit of evil, man is tempted and encouraged by Satan, the fallen angel; but today, my friends, we have an advocate before God. This is a mighty advocate, one who is highly favored by God, for God in his infinite mercy took pity on all of us who were mired in sin and sent his only son to pay the penalty for our transgressions and restore us into God's favor.

"It is in the name of Jesus, God's only son, that I stand before you this day and proclaim that he has paid the penalty for our sins by his death on a Roman cross, and all who confess their faith in him are forgiven their sins and will live forever with him in his Father's kingdom."

Papak, a Parthian noble, asked Thaddaeus, "Sir, I am perplexed. You would have us believe that a man condemned to die on a Roman cross is the only son of God. I see the great work of physical healing you bring to the sick and lame here, and it is truly amazing, but to claim that a man condemned as a criminal is the son of God and expect us to believe it is too much to ask. What proof do you have that this Jesus is who you claim him to be?"

Thaddeus replied, "You are right to ask for proof. Wise is the man who requires validation. Tell me, in the Zoroastrian religion, who among its devotees are considered to be the most greatly respected and learned?"

Papak, who was highly placed in the government, answered, "Without question, the Magi are the most holy and respected of all Ahura Mazda's servants, but what does that have to do with this Jesus? Why do you ask?"

"Because you asked for proof that Jesus was indeed the son of God. Surely important evidence should lie in the royal Parthian archives. You are an official of the king. You have the authority to review the archives. Go, then, to the records in the archives and search for a great journey undertaken by the Magi to a distant land in the west during the reign of King Phraates."

Sometime later Papak returned and, when Thaddeus saw him in the crowd, he asked the Parthian official to join him. "Many of you will remember," said Thaddeus, "that the noble Papak asked me to provide evidence that Jesus was the son of the living God. I advised him to seek an answer in the royal archives. I must tell you, dear people, you are not the first of Zarathustra's servants to bear witness to the events I have told you about that took place in Judea many years ago. Now that Papak has returned, I invite him to share with you what he discovered in the royal archives."

Papak spoke, and all present listened to him earnestly. "As Thaddeus said, I did indeed go to the archives to see for myself whether there was any information concerning a great journey undertaken by the Magi during the time mentioned by Thaddeus. The records clearly state that during the thirty-fourth year of King Phraates the Great, Magi Gushasaph, the king's advisor and cousin, informed the king that a vision had come to him in which he saw a newborn baby boy in a land far to the west who would one day show all men the right path to paradise. The king then urged Gushasaph to gather his companions and undertake a journey to find this child and present him with gifts on behalf of the king.

"For most of a year, Gushasaph and his companions studied their maps and prepared for this great journey. Gushasaph had another vision, and in it he was told this child was the son of the Most High but was not to be found in a palace or manor of a rich man. He was told in a dream that one day this child would rule all nations. The Magi were urged to begin their journey and to not fear getting lost, for there would be a divine light that would guide them to the place where this child would be found.

"The Magi were gone for many months," Papak continued. "When they arrived in Judea, they called on King Herod, but he professed not to know where this marvelous child could be found. He asked them to return and inform him when they located the child so he, too, could go and honor him. The light continued to lead the Magi onward to find the child, not in a palace or grand manor, but in a humble dwelling in a small village in Judea.

"When they arrived where the light led them, they were awestruck by the child's beauty and bearing, and they were compelled to fall on their knees to worship him. Gushasaph said to the child's mother, 'The child you hold will one day rule the nations, but I see much suffering for him and those who follow him before that day arrives.'

"On their homeward journey, all they could talk about was the feeling of great joy that overwhelmed them in the presence of the child. When they finally arrived back in Parthia, they reported to King Phraates that they had presented his gifts to the child's mother before setting out on the long journey home. They also reported that in a dream one of them had, they were advised not to return to King Herod, but to return to their country by another route.

"My friends," concluded Papak, "these things are in the archives, and they include all the evidence necessary for me to announce here before you that I believe this marvelous child was Jesus, and that he is the very son of God whom Thaddeus claims him to be. Else why would our Magi have undertaken such a long and perilous journey?"

Then the apostle said, "Now do you see that you are not the first of Zarathustra's servants to profess faith in God's only son? Many years ago when Jesus was but a babe in his mother's arms, God removed the scales from the eyes of your own Magi, your wise ones, and they followed a bright light for many months to search for this child. When they found him, they fell on their knees before him, laying treasures before him and worshipping him. Jesus, who is the only son of God, requires no treasure from you save only your belief in him."

This powerful message and Papak's testimony convinced many of the Parthians to become believers—so many, in fact, that one of the chief priests of Zoroaster, Arfaxat, swore to destroy Thaddaeus who was leading so many away from their ancient faith.

Arfaxat took into his confidence Bozan, one of the king's royal guards, and said to him, "You know how our Great King, Vologases, hates the Romans. He has waged victorious war against them in order to place his brother Tiradates on the Armenian throne. Now consider, Bozan, this foreign preacher who is called Thaddeus, the one who goes among our people spreading lies about our Magi, convincing many to adopt his foreign religion. You might believe him to be a simple servant of his god traveling through our sovereign's land. Most of our people think this is so, but what if I were to tell you a secret about him? A secret that would result in your basking in the esteem of our gracious king?

"It has come to my attention that this Thaddeus is an agent of Rome," Arfaxat declared. "It is true. At the moment I am the only one privileged with this information, but I am obligated to inform the king, and I plan to do so this evening. Then the thought occurred to me, what if you, Bozan, were to discover this information before I meet with the king? What if this Thaddeus resisted your effort to apprehend him? Think how much it would mean to the king to know that his faithful guard removed a Roman threat to his life. And if the man is killed attempting to escape, he will no longer be a threat to the king nor lead any of our people astray. Need I tell you how much the king rewards those who gain his favor?"

Eager to bask in the acclaim of the king, Bozan went to the house where Thaddeus was preaching. He waited until the apostle had finished speaking, and when Thaddeus walked out into the street, the guard shouted, "Stop, in the name of the great king!" As Thaddeus turned toward the guard, Bozan impaled him on his spear in front of the horrified crowd. One of his disciples ran up to Thaddeus as he lay on the street in a pool of blood, knelt by him, and lifted up his head.

The apostle looked up at him, smiled, and said, "Do not grieve for me, for this day I will be in the presence of the risen Lord Jesus."

Then his eyes closed, and his earthly mission came to an end, but the power of the Holy Spirit lived on, and many came to Christ in the following years.

CHAPTER 37

When he had finished reading, Doctor Bankkour noticed that Ken was anxious to get his attention. "Mr. Monroe, I can see you have a question."

"I know you told us earlier that Osroene was an ancient kingdom that early on had embraced the Christian faith, but I've never heard that a king had sought out Jesus for his healing power before the crucifixion. Can you enlighten us on that matter?"

"It's a fascinating part of early Christian history, Mr. Monroe," replied the linguist. "I had anticipated both of you might want to know more about this matter, so I copied what Eusebius had written in his fourth-century history concerning the Christian mission to King Abgar to share with you. Eusebius writes, and I quote,

'King Abgarus, who ruled with great glory the nations beyond the Euphrates, being afflicted with a terrible disease which it was beyond the power of human skill to cure, when he heard of the name of Jesus, and of his miracles, which were attested by all with one accord, sent a message to him by a courier and begged him to heal his disease.

'But he did not at the time comply with his request; yet he deemed him worthy of a personal letter, in which he said that he would send one of his disciples to cure his disease, and at the same time, promised salvation to himself and all his house.

'Not long afterward, his promise was fulfilled. For after Jesus' Resurrection from the dead and his ascent into heaven, Thomas, one of the twelve apostles, under divine impulse, sent Thaddeus, who was also numbered among the seventy disciples of Christ, to Edessa, as a preacher and evangelist of the teaching of Christ.

'And all that our Savior had promised received through him its fulfillment. You have written evidence of these things taken from the archives of Edessa, which was at that time a royal city. For in the public registers there, which contain accounts of ancient times and the acts of Abgarus, these things have been found preserved down to the present time. But there is no better way than to hear the Epistles themselves, which we have taken from the archives and have literally translated from the Syriac language.'

When he finished reading, Bankkour said, "Then, Mr. Monroe, Eusebius includes both a copy of what he calls a letter from the king requesting healing and a reply from Jesus, saying he would send a disciple after his Resurrection to heal the king and grant salvation to his family.

"Most modern historians discount the authenticity of these letters, but, nevertheless, Eusebius claims he personally looked at the letters in the public archives of Edessa and translated them from Syriac to Greek. Since all these records disappeared centuries ago, there's no way to verify Eusibius's account. What we do have, however, is Ignatius's testament, which appears to verify that both Jude Thaddeus and Thomas were in Edessa during the reign of Abgar, and the king was cured of his illness when the apostle first approached the city.

"Now, as to the king mentioned in Eusibius's history, most historians agree that Abgar the Black ruled from 13 AD to 50 AD, so these dates would fit in quite nicely for a mission of Jude Thaddeus and Thomas to Osroene.

"If we accept Ignatius's account as factual," continued the linguist, "Abgar and his court would be the first of the ancient ruling class to embrace the faith. Virtually all of the earliest Christian converts were from among the poor and dispossessed, so Ignatius would be correct in saying this episode was the first conversion among the ruling class."

Charles said, "Doctor, I had never given much thought to it, but I can't see anything that would have prevented a disciple among the Seventy from also being an apostle. Apparently, Ignatius thought the matter wasn't important since he made no comment other than to announce that Thaddeus had originally been among the Seventy before being elevated to the apostleship."

"You are quite right, Reverend Monroe," the linguist replied. "The term 'apostle' was more broadly interpreted by the early church than it is in modern times. Many of the early disciples were considered to be apostles. We know that Paul always considered himself an apostle even though he wasn't among the Twelve. In the broadest sense in ancient times, an apostle was considered to be a messenger spreading the Good News of salvation to all who would listen.

"While it was certainly interesting reading about the historian Eusebius visiting the archives of Edessa, wasn't it incredible to read Ignatius's account of the Parthian archives holding information concerning the visit of the Magi to Judea and bearing gifts to the infant Jesus in Bethlehem?"

"I'd have to confess that, to me, that was one of the most exciting revelations we have yet seen from Ignatius's book," said Charles. "To think that the ancient Parthian archives contained evidence giving credence to the story of the Magi visiting the baby Jesus as recorded in Matthew's Gospel is simply astounding. One question I'd like to ask, however. Can we substantiate that a king named Phraates ruled Parthia around the beginning of the first century?"

"That's a great question, and our team delved into that matter," replied Doctor Bankkour. "It seems there were a series of Parthian kings named Phraates, and we have confirmed that

Phraates IV most likely was the reigning monarch during the time of Jesus's birth.

"It is true that in our own time, liberal biblical scholars have discounted the visit of the Magi and have said it was a pious invention, but Ignatius appears to have validated this part of the nativity story."

Before they adjourned, Doctor Bankkour mentioned that the last portion of Ignatius's manuscript was almost ready to be shared. Ken asked if it would be convenient for the full company of those who worked on the manuscript to be present at his office for this presentation since Charles had recently made remarkable progress, was stronger now, and would like to meet with everyone involved in the project. Doctor Bankkour was pleased with Charles's recovery and said he would check with each member and notify Ken as to the date and time everyone could be present.

CHAPTER 38

O
n a bright Sunday morning in the first week of March, the good people of Harkins Corner, West Virginia woke up to find that their local newspaper, *The Tri-County News Courier*, had published a startling headline and story about a fire and burglary at Saint Matthew's Syriac Monastery.

ARSON AND THEFT AT SAINT MATTHEW SYRIAC MONASTERY

Despite increased security established by parish members at St. Matthews, thieves managed to distract the volunteer guards by setting a fire in a garage that housed maintenance equipment this past Friday.

While the volunteer guards joined in to help the monks fight the fire, thieves managed to break in to the library and stole a valuable ancient manuscript that scholars had been translating. Father Anselm, spokesperson for the monastery said he was not at liberty to discuss the contents of the ancient manuscript, but he did say a number of scholars from across the country had been working on it for several months.

Sheriff's department spokesman Sergeant Lou Casey said every effort would be made to apprehend the thieves and bring the stolen manuscript back to the monastery, but he acknowledged the department had few leads at the moment.

The fire was eventually contained, but it caused extensive damage to the garage and to equipment stored in it. The monks were able to remove a lawn tractor and a few tools, but it appears the garage and most of the contents will have to be replaced. Father Anselm indicated the monastery had already notified its insurance company and an investigator was being sent out from Charleston.

CHAPTER 39

At ten o'clock p.m. the following Tuesday evening, a phone call was placed from Charleston, West Virginia, to Tikrit, Iraq.

Amir: "What is your report?"

Sentry: "Allah has smiled on us, worthy Amir. We managed to retrieve the package and it is safely housed in our associate's warehouse. We were able to accomplish our objective despite the increased security established by the infidels. We set fire to an outbuilding that drew everyone's attention and one of our associates was able to open the lock on the steel door to the room I told you about. We quickly grabbed the package, which was right there lying on a linen sheet on a large table, and were able to run through the woods to our van without being seen.

Amir: Praise Allah! This is wonderful news, Sentry, and will be the talk of our entire organization. You must convey the sincere appreciation of those of us who battle the infidels daily to your associates. Now, I must plan how to get the package back to our country without raising the suspicions of the American authorities. You, my son, will now be numbered among the brotherhood's heroes and you will be suitably rewarded upon your return.

Sentry: Your approval is my reward, beloved of Allah.

Amir: We will discuss final plans for the recovery of the package next Tuesday.

CHAPTER 40

On the same afternoon that the fire and theft occurred, Doctor Bankkour called Ken to report the incident. The first thing that crossed Ken's mind was recollection of the earlier break-in when the monk was injured. "Doctor, there has to be a connection between these two break-ins. This just can't be a coincidence. It's obvious to me the manuscript was the target in both."

"I concur fully. Mr. Monroe," responded the linguist. "The abbot has many friends in the Syrian community in this country, Muslims as well as Christians, and he is reaching out to them as we speak. I can confirm that this deplorable theft does not sit well with our Syrian fellow immigrants and a number of well-connected individuals are getting the word out even to the less respectable elements of our community.

"Local, state and federal authorities are investigating the incident, but since we suspect an Arab involvement, I tend to think our Syriac community will stand a better chance of finding out who the thieves are.

"Mr. Monroe, do you see any reason we should delay the team's report to you and your brother in light of this regrettable incident? We had talked about perhaps meeting at your place of business with the whole team to discuss the final chapter of the manuscript. We can hold off, however, until something more is discovered about the theft if you'd rather."

Though still shocked by the theft of the manuscript, Ken immediately responded, "No, I think we should go ahead as planned. Just let me know when you'd like to meet."

Three weeks later, the entire project committee, along with Ken and Charles, gathered for the final reading at the offices of Brinkley and Todd. Ken had arranged for a catered meal to be served before the last session began. The silence during the meal was clear evidence that the team and the brothers were still distressed by the impact of the theft.

After they finished the meal, Doctor Bankkour stood and began to speak. "The consequences of the loss of the manuscript are deeply felt by each member of the team, Reverend Monroe, and I know how difficult this must be for you for it was only by your superb effort that it was saved from destruction and brought here for study by these distinguished scholars.

"I think it only fair that I point out the immense academic problem we face going forward. You might not be aware of it, but distrust and professional jealousy are pervasive in the academic world. Without the actual ancient document itself as proof, critics in our respective fields will be eager to scorn our finished work as fraudulent, a hoax. Some of our team members are unwilling to attach their names to our work for they feel their academic careers will be threatened as a result of the theft of the original source. I, myself, do not share that concern and other team members agree with me that the work should be published and defended. It will be left up to you to decide how we proceed under these circumstances.

"Now, enough said about team concerns. With your permission I will read aloud the final chapter in Ignatius' manuscript which deals with Saint John the Divine.

Now we come at last, Dorothea, to the one often referred to by the other disciples as Beloved of the Lord, the Apostle John. It is fitting that John is the final apostle I write to you about, dear sister in Christ, for through the incomparable mercy of God, he is indeed the last of our Lord's twelve companions still alive and is with us to this day in Ephesus. He is an old man, it is true, but is held in the greatest esteem by all the faithful and especially those in Asia, where John remains the patriarch. He is still fondly remembered as the one who took care of the Lord's mother, first in his house in Jerusalem, and then later when they took up residence in Ephesus.

It was because of this special responsibility he undertook to care for the Lord's mother that John confined his preaching at first to the regions around Jerusalem; he also frequently visited Lazarus and his sisters, and the faithful in nearby Bethany. John had, and still has to this day, a great love and concern for the poor and the sick. Everywhere he went, crowds gathered, bringing their afflicted with them, and many were cured at the apostle's touch. Multitudes came to the faith by virtue of the kindness, healing power, and generous spirit of John.

He had been the youngest of the apostles and a favorite among the Lord's earthly family. He, along with Peter and his own brother, James, were three of the most intimate companions of the Lord. He is truly gifted; able to write in both Aramaic and Greek.

Andros, one of the Seventy, recently related how John often reviewed his recollections of the Lord with the other disciples. He was revered as the first apostle to believe in the Resurrection of our Lord.

For many years the authorities were reluctant to lay hands on John for fear of the crowds, for the apostle, in his healing of the sick and lame, made no distinction between honest, God-fearing people and the most violent of the Zealots. It is rumored that the captain of the Sanhedrin's guard was informed by certain Zealot leaders that should any of his soldiers lay hands on the apostle, the captain himself would suffer the consequences. Of course, John knew nothing of this matter and continued his ministry unaware of the Zealots' warning.

For many years John continued his ministry in and around Jerusalem, and it was not until the Jewish rebellion against Roman authority brought forth the invasion of Vespasian's Roman legions that any thought was given that his place of ministry should change. However, with the advent of rebellion in the Holy Land and the increasing fanaticism of the Jewish Zealots in the city, the situation in Jerusalem became ever more dangerous for Christian believers. Though you are no doubt aware through your studies of these terrible years, Dorothea, you were not born until after the Roman conquest of Jerusalem during the first year of the reign of the Emperor Vespasian.

The seeds of this rebellion were sown from the beginning of the Roman conquest of the Holy Land under Pompey the Great, more than fifty years before our Savior was born. Not only did Pompey's soldiers slaughter thousands of Jews, but succeeding Roman generals violated the temple and ruthlessly put down Jewish efforts to gain freedom by crucifying thousands of young Jewish men and selling their wives and children to slave dealers. The crushing taxes imposed on the Jews by the Romans and their appointed Jewish princes only added fuel to the fire of Jewish resentment.

As the years passed, Jewish Zealots who took refuge in the barren mountains began to prey upon isolated Roman military outposts, as well as upon Roman merchants. You may recall that our Savior was crucified between two men who had been condemned as Zealots. It was a normal occurrence for the Romans to publicly crucify captured Jewish Zealots to intimidate the general population.

Taxation and violence grew together, and pleas for relief by the Jews went unanswered until Jewish religious leaders of the temple halted public prayers and sacrifices for the Roman emperor. In the countryside, and now in the cities, violent protests and murder of both Romans and those Jews who worked for them became commonplace.

Before the Zealots took complete charge of Jerusalem, James, the brother of the Lord and head of the church in Jerusalem, was brutally murdered by Jewish authorities who threw him from the precipice of the temple when he refused to abandon his faith in Christ. When the believers turned to John and begged him to succeed James as leader of the Jerusalem church, he refused, believing his primary role was to care for Mary, the mother of our Lord, who was in advanced age and remained part of his household. John then endorsed Simeon, the son of Cleophas, who became the second bishop of Jerusalem. A short while before the Romans subdued Galilee, John took Mary and other members of his family and traveled north to Ephesus.

After John left the city, it soon become apparent that, were the Christians to remain in Jerusalem, the fanatics who were now fully in control of the city would kill them all. Consequently, before the Roman army completed its last victorious conquests in Galilee, Simeon led the surviving Christian believers out of the city and north to the city of Pella in the Decapolis where they could dwell in comparative safety.

Not long after the Christian exodus, conditions in Judea continued to decline precipitously. In Jerusalem, anarchy reigned in place of order. The radical elements, the Zealots, and their even more fanatical companions, the Sicarii, now controlled the city, and they executed anyone within Jerusalem who advocated surrender to the Roman army. The fanatics even burned the city's large supply of food to force the people to resist the Romans who, after completing their task in Galilee, had begun to choke off supplies to Jerusalem.

Meanwhile, dramatic events were taking place in Rome. During the fourteenth year of his reign, Nero's behavior, always unpredictable, worsened considerably, and many prominent Romans were accused of treason and swiftly executed. In fear and exasperation, the Roman Senate declared Nero an enemy of the people and ordered his arrest. Abandoned by his friends, and now in despair, Nero committed suicide, and for more than a year the empire was in turmoil, with several generals claiming the imperial throne. Order was restored only when Vespasian was hailed as emperor by the legions under his command. Before he began the long journey back to Rome, he turned over the command of the legions and the prosecution of the Jewish War to his son and future emperor, Titus.

Titus brutally conducted the war in Judea, capturing towns and villages on the way south toward Jerusalem. Ahead of the relentless legions, waves of terrified Jewish refugees streamed into Jerusalem. Finally, Titus brought his victorious legions to the Holy City itself and surrounded it. Any Jew caught attempting to escape from the city was caught and crucified facing the population of the city.

As I explained earlier, for seven long months the siege continued, until finally, the Romans succeeded in breaching the walls. The city and the temple were destroyed, thousands of Jewish soldiers were crucified, and the men, women, and children who survived were enslaved. Many of them were transported to Rome, where they were put to work building the Flavian Colosseum, where so many of our fellow Christians have since lost their lives because of their faith.

Although a number of the Christian exiles were allowed to return to the ruined Holy City, John remained in Ephesus, supervising the churches in Asia. He was the revered leader of the faithful not only in Asia, but in many other regions as well, for he was among the few intimate companions of the Lord still among the living.

One day in Ephesus, while John was preaching, a man asked, "Beloved of the Lord, why is it that so many hate us for following the teachings of our Savior? We desire only to live in peace."

John answered, "I remember it as clearly as though it were yesterday. Once, a disciple asked this same question of our Lord, and he responded, 'I am the light of the world. Many who live in the world prefer to live in darkness. You will be hated by multitudes because you live in my light. I am the way, the truth, and the life; no one can come to the Father except through me. Always remember, when those in the world hate you, they hated me first. If you were still a part of the world, the world would love you, but because you follow me in the light, the world will hate you. I have chosen you out of the world, and for this reason the world hates you. And not only does the world hate you, you will be persecuted because you are my disciples and believe in me and the one who sent me. I have told you all this so you will not stray from the truth. A time is coming when men will believe they serve God when they persecute you, but do not be afraid, for I will be with you always.'"

John's own disciples marveled at these words and prevailed upon him to record all these sayings and actions of the Lord so they might be sent to the churches in Laodicea, Pergamum, and the other cities in Asia where the believers were suffering persecution. John agreed, and Marcellus, who was the apostle's favorite scribe, wrote as John dictated, and these letters were sent to the Christian communities in Asia.

It was at about this time that the apostle was made aware of the collected writings of John Mark and Luke. After he had carefully reviewed these works, his disciples asked if they were faithful to what had transpired. John said they were accurate accounts, but they reflected only a small portion of what had transpired during our Lord's ministry. From that time onward, Marcellus kept copies of all the letters John wrote to the faithful in Asia.

When several in John's audience scoffed at his descriptions of our Lord's teachings, the apostle quieted them by saying, "I remember once hearing the Lord saying to a large crowd gathered around him, 'A farmer went to the fields to sow his seed. In the process of sowing, some of the seed fell on a well-worn path, where it was trampled on, and the birds came and quickly ate all the seeds. Some of the seed fell on rocky ground rather than good soil, and when the seed sprouted roots, they quickly withered away because they found no moisture. Other seeds fell in the midst of thorns, which matured with the seeds and smothered them. But still other seed fell on recently plowed soil, where it matured and produced a crop many times greater than all the seed that the farmer had sown.'

"While the crowd pondered what the Lord had said," John continued, "his disciples gathered around him and questioned what he meant, for he had spoken in a parable, and we did not understand it. The Lord explained that he spoke in parables so that believers and unbelievers could make of his teachings what they willed. In this manner he avoided the traps set for him by the Pharisees and lawyers who sought to destroy him.

"When he saw that we still didn't understand, he explained the meaning of the parable. He said, 'The seed is the word of God. Those on the path hear, but the devil quickly comes and removes the word from their hearts so they will not believe and be saved. The ones on the rocky ground receive the word with gladness when they hear it, but they have no root, so they believe only for a short time, and when they are put to the test, they fall away. Those among the thorns hear but are preoccupied with the concerns of the world, including wealth and pleasures, so they lose sight of the word. The ones on the good soil, however, are those who receive the word gladly and keep it through perseverance and bear fruit a hundredfold.'"

John met frequently with Philip in Asia, and during their time of harvesting souls, many of the Gentiles were brought to the faith. On several occasions, I was privileged to meet with these two blessed disciples of our Lord to discuss the progress of the faith, and I remember them with great fondness. Soon it was common to find households of the faith in virtually every town and village in Asia.

During the relatively peaceful years of the reigns of both Vespasian and his son, Titus, the conqueror of Jerusalem, the church continued to grow and prosper, but when Titus was succeeded by his brother Domitian during the consulship of L. Carminus Lusitanicus and M. Petronius Umbrinus, the church suffered fearfully, and many good and faithful Christians lost their lives because they persevered in serving the Lord, while others, to their eternal shame and damnation, abandoned the faith under threat of death and confiscation of property.

I have already told you, Dorothea, about the circumstances that led to the martyrdom of Philip, how he was cruelly put to death because he refused to worship the Emperor Domitian as master and god. It was well known that the emperor loathed the Jews. He considered the Christians to be little more than a Jewish sect. It is ironic that both his father, Vespasian, and his brother, Titus, both of whom ruled before him, harbored no compelling grudge against either Jews or Christians, and yet both these men led the legions that had crushed the Jewish rebellion. Domitian, on the other hand, never faced the Jews in battle, yet he openly despised them and went out of his way to torment and persecute Jew and Christian alike.

When Philip and a number of Christians in Hierapolis had been arrested and put to death by the cruel Roman general Saturninus for refusing to worship Domitian as a god, their brothers in faith in Ephesus swiftly took John into the remote mountains until the savagery of Saturninus passed. When the general and his retinue left Hierapolis and traveled farther east to carry out the emperor's orders, the brothers in Ephesus brought the apostle down from the mountains and back into the city. All during the time he had been in the mountains, John had remonstrated with those who had taken him there, saying he never intended to leave those of the faith remaining in the city to the wiles and snares of Satan.

As time went on, it became apparent to the emperor that this mass killing of Christians was economically unproductive. Indeed, slaves condemned to work in the lead and silver mines in Asia had short lifespans, and replacements were always in high demand. Domitian gave orders to sentence those who refused to worship him to life terms in the mines.

In Ephesus, the emperor's law courts were kept busy as the soldiers continued to round up and condemn Christians whose intransigence in the face of persecution remained firm. John insisted on accompanying a group of believers to the imperial court. So it was that among those brought to judgment was the Apostle John, now an old man. His voice was still strong and as firm as that of a young man. The Roman judge sentenced him to a life term on the prison island of Patmos.

It is the handiwork of God that even among the Roman soldiers charged with operating the emperor's prisons, there were Christian believers. Though this fact was widely known among the believers, the pagan Romans were largely ignorant of this matter, and Koios, one of the leaders of the church in Ephesus, managed to get word to his kinsman, Lykomedes, a believer and chief physician on Patmos, that the apostle was on his way to the island as a prisoner. Lykomedes made arrangements that the old disciple be escorted to the medical facility, where he would be in the care of the chief physician.

When the apostle arrived on the island, Lykomedes informed him that he was to work in the medical facility as an assistant, thereby remaining out of the general prison population and the more stringent labor required of the other prisoners. John responded, "Though you mean well, brother in Christ, I intend to remain with the others who refused to worship the emperor and share their workload so long as any of us remain on this island."

Since the prison population had grown enormously, emergency provisions for housing these prisoners were required. Having few alternatives, prison officials were compelled to reopen nearby abandoned mines. These mines were utilized as living accommodations for the newest prisoners.

John and a number of the believers from Ephesus were sent to the deepest and darkest of these former mines. Several of his fellow Christian prisoners have since reported that the apostle kept their spirits bright by recounting the wonderful sayings and acts of our Lord while they labored in the mines. The aged disciple was inspired to write an account of the visions he was having about the future of the church.

One day, the commander had all the Christian prisoners brought to the central assembly area where he announced that Domitian had been murdered in Rome, and that his successor, the Emperor Nerva, had signed a decree commuting the sentence of all believers whose only offense had been a refusal to worship Domitian.

Set free a little more than eighteen months after he had been sent as a condemned prisoner to Patmos, the apostle and many of his fellow believers set sail for Ephesus. There they were met at the docks by joyous throngs of Christians who scattered flowers in their path. Many felt that the age of persecution was finally over and they would be free from the terrors that had haunted them during the years that Domitian sat on the throne. In this, they were sadly mistaken.

After he rested for a few days, John summoned Marcellus and Diodorus, who were known as the best scribes among the believers in Ephesus. You will recall, Dorothea, Marcellus had long been engaged as a scribe for the apostle. In that capacity, he had written and made copies of those letters John had written to the churches in Asia and other places. Now John requested that Marcellus provide him with copies of these letters and, after he had reviewed them, he announced what he intended to do.

"Brothers," he began, "during the months I was confined on Patmos, I had time to reflect on the fact that I am the last alive of those who were the Lord's companions. While deep in the caves of that island prison, I had a vision about what is to come in ages not yet born, but there is more that must be accomplished while I yet live. The Lord is not finished with me yet, even though I am old and worn. Since I am one of the few left who knew the Lord, heard him preach, and witnessed his miraculous acts, it will be my task now to relate what the Lord said and did in those precious few years he was among us. It will be your task, Marcellus, for you and Diodorus to take turns and write down my recollections. Because my time is short, you must be vigilant and work with me day and night to see this task to completion."

Marcellus replied, "But sir, we already know of these sayings and works of the Lord from the writings of John Mark and Luke. They have left us with a full record. Why exhaust yourself with this repetitive task?"

John answered, "Repetitive task, Marcellus? Did you not hear me telling our people about the Lord's receiving word that his friend Lazarus lay gravely sick in Bethany, how he traveled there only to find that Lazarus had died and lay four days in the tomb? Have you not heard me tell how the Lord commanded Lazarus to come out of his grave, and to the shock of everyone present, Lazarus obeyed and came forth?

"Have you not heard me tell the people how so many of our Lord's early followers abandoned him when he told them unless they would partake of his body and drink of his blood they would not have eternal life? And were you not present those times when I told them how the Lord reminded all his followers that the world would hate them as it first hated him, how they would be expelled from the synagogues, and even killed for being his followers?

"Did you not hear me tell the people, Marcellus, how our Lord said that he must ascend to his Father so that the Holy Spirit would come to his followers, filling them with the strength to resist the wiles and snares of Satan and the world? Finally, did you not hear me repeat the words of our Lord when he prayed not only for those of us who were his disciples, but for all who would come to believe in him through our ministry?

"Repetitive? I think not, Marcellus. You will not find these things in the writings of John Mark and Luke, nor will you ever know many other things our Lord said and did unless I recall them and you record them."

The apostle remained in his quarters for the space of two months, dictating first to Marcellus, then to Diodotus. Even when a number of his disciples wanted his advice on questions concerning church administration, he bade them to be patient a little while, telling them that his present task must be completed soon, for great age was upon him, and his days were surely numbered. Sometimes the dictation went on far into the night, while at other times, John would rouse one of the scribes to write down a recollection that came to him as these men were trying to sleep.

When John reviewed the completed work, he insisted that certain changes be made to reflect a more accurate description of what the Lord had said and done. Finally, the work was concluded, and to the great relief of Marcellus and Diodorus, the apostle was satisfied.

Old and tired, having outlived his contemporaries, John was now more than ninety years old. He remained in his bed most of the time, but finally gave in to the entreaties of his disciples and agreed to preach to the Ephesus community of believers one final time. When word reached the community of the faithful that their beloved apostle was going to address them one last time, great joy swept the congregation, and they gathered in large numbers at the church to hear him.

As the faithful sang a hymn of praise, John's disciples carried him to the front of the building, for he no longer had the strength to walk. When the hymn ended, there was absolute silence as the old apostle began to speak. "Little children, I implore you to love one another." Then he sat down and bade his disciples return him to his room.

As they put him in his bed, Diodorus said, "Master, many of our people had gathered to hear you recall the wonderful message of the Lord Jesus, and they were perplexed that you only said, 'Love one another.'"

John responded, "That is the heart of the message of our Lord Jesus, Diodorus. Many were the times I heard him say that the world would recognize his followers by the love they bore for one another."

When last I heard from Ephesus, John was confined to his bed. He grows weaker by the day. When he goes to join our Lord, the Age of the Apostles will close, and it will be up to those of us who were inspired by them to continue to present the Good News to a hurting and anxious world. I pray God will grant us the strength to imitate their fortitude and devotion.

So there you have it, dear Dorothea, the wonderful ministries of our Lord's companions after his glorious Resurrection and ascension. Each one was committed until the end to carry out our Lord's command that repentance and forgiveness of sins be preached to people everywhere, no matter what tribe or nation. So modeling ourselves on their fortitude and devotion, we go forth likewise, even in these perilous days when, at the inspiration of Satan, persecution of believers has again reared its ugly head.

CHAPTER 41

At 5:15 pm on the next Monday evening, an unexpected phone call was placed from Charleston, West Virginia to Tikrit, Iraq.

Amir: "Why are you breaking our protocol and calling me on a different date and time?"

Sentry: "Because things have gone very wrong here, Amir. At this moment I'm in the associate's warehouse, but the local police have surrounded the building and have demanded that I come out.

Amir: "How did this ever happen? I thought you and the others had successfully eluded pursuit from the monastery and were in the clear. What happened?"

Sentry: "You will recall the associate who injured the monk and we had confined under guard? Well, it has turned out that his guard was his cousin and he convinced the cousin that the others were going to kill him so the cousin released him and both of them went to the infidel police and told them about the warehouse location. The police had this traitor call me to demand I surrender and bring the package out with me."

Amir: "You must destroy the package, Sentry. Under no circumstances should it be surrendered to the infidels. I know you were trained to have a contingency plan. What is it?"

Sentry: "Gasoline soaked rags have been stuffed in various places in this old wooden building and the package is in a paper box with a large quantity of soaked rags. Within seconds this building will be fully engulfed in flames. Amir, take care of my family for I will remain in the building."

Amir: "Have no fear, little one. Your family will be well provided for and your name will be remembered as a hero of the faith by the Martyrs Brigade. May Allah guide you on your journey to paradise?"

Sentry: "There is no god but Allah and Mohammed is his prophet!"

CHAPTER 42

The following Thursday morning in the town of Harkins Corner, West Virginia, the *Tri-County News Courier* carried the following headline and story:

WAREHOUSE FIRE AND MONASTERY BURGLARY CONNECTED

Acting on a tip from an informer, Charleston police surrounded a warehouse in Charleston registered as *Yazen's Fine Oriental Rug Cleaning* this past Monday in which the perpetrators of the recent fire and robbery at Saint Matthews Syriac Monastery were alleged to be present. Police found the building locked and called for those inside to surrender and come out.

Several attempts were made by the police to contact anyone inside the warehouse to no avail. At the direction of the police, the informer called someone he said was connected to the crime, but it is unknown what was said since they apparently spoke in Arabic. As police prepared to storm the building, smoke and fire was seen coming from several places in the building and within moments the entire building was ablaze. Within five minutes Charleston firemen were on the scene, but the building was completely enveloped in flames. While police and firemen stood by helplessly, the roof collapsed and by daybreak the warehouse was a smoldering ruin.

Investigators are on the scene, but there is no word yet on any casualties. The building is owned by foreign investors and efforts are currently underway to get in touch with the rug merchants who have rented the building for the past year. Though their report is tentative, the investigators believe arson was involved.

A spokesman for the Charleston police said that a member of the Iraqi refugees who have been resettled in Charleston claimed to have been kidnapped by the thieves who recently burglarized the monastery and was held captive for several days before being able to escape. He told authorities that his captors had in their possession an ancient manuscript believed to have been in the warehouse at the time of the fire. Police are continuing to question the informer and believe he knows more about this theft and fire than he has previously disclosed.

When asked about the stolen manuscript, Father Anselm, Saint Matthew Monastery's spokesman, said a group of internationally recognized scholars had been working on translating the ancient document over the past year. He said he was not authorized to discuss the contents, but he believed a full report would be made available soon.

CHAPTER 43

"Reverend Monroe, the chapter on the Apostle John completes our work on this amazing book," Doctor Bankkour said. "I've asked Doctor Morse, who is nationally recognized as one of the leading modern scholars in Roman history, to comment on Ignatius's account of the Jewish rebellion and its consequences. Doctor Morse, the floor is yours."

Doctor Morse stood and said, "We've all continued to be astounded by the revelations of this quite remarkable book, and perhaps no one more so than me. In this last chapter particularly, I was simply amazed at how much Ignatius's description of the turbulent years of the Roman conquest of Galilee, as well as the portrayal of the fall of Jerusalem, mirrors the history left to us by Flavius Josephus, the former Jewish general who became the foremost authority on the Jewish War.

"Might I add that I am deeply saddened by the theft of this manuscript? It is a tragedy of monumental proportions for without it, we can expect to find more doubters than believers among the world's scholars. Be that as it may, however, I am prepared to add my name publically to the list of those who want to see it published."

"Now, back to this final chapter of Ignatius' manuscript. When the Jewish rebellion in Galilee collapsed, the more radical Zealot leaders managed to escape to Jerusalem. They quickly took control of the city and proceeded to massacre the more moderate leaders who had endorsed and supported the revolt only a few years before. The fanatics in charge then initiated a virtual reign of terror within the city, destroying the vast quantities of food that had been carefully stored in anticipation of a long siege, and killing with impunity anyone who advocated surrender to the Romans. There was incredible suffering in Jerusalem during those final months of the siege. Many died of starvation, while those caught trying to escape from the city were killed by the Zealots.

"During the summer of 70 AD, the Romans succeeded in breeching the walls and drove the remaining defenders back into the temple with great slaughter. Finally, the temple complex was set on fire, and the last defenses of the Jews collapsed. Josephus's history estimates that as many as one million Jews died during the rebellion, and many thousands of captives were taken back to Rome or condemned to the mines as slaves.

"It would appear that John traveled less than most of the other apostles. Ignatius writes that he refused the church's leadership role in Jerusalem so he could devote the time to looking after our Lord's mother who was a member of his household in Jerusalem. Later, he took Mary with him to Ephesus. Perhaps Doctor Szabo will describe for us the importance of Ephesus in the early church."

"It's my pleasure," the young historian said. "As you no doubt know, Reverend Monroe, Ephesus's greatest claim to fame in antiquity was its magnificent temple devoted to Artemis, the Greek goddess of the hunt, and one of the most popular pagan deities in Asia Minor. This temple complex was considered one of the Seven Wonders of the World in ancient times.

"During the apostolic era, the city was one of the major seaports in the Roman Empire—its harbor crammed with ships to be loaded with the produce of Asia. It was a vital component of the imperial food supply system to various cities on the Italian mainland. Reliable historical estimates inform us that Ephesus, during this period, had more than a quarter million inhabitants.

"The New Testament tells us that Paul and Barnabas lived

and preached in Ephesus, and their success in attracting converts among the people resulted in a riot among the silversmiths, who felt that this success threatened their income, which came from making statues of the goddess Artemis.

"After Paul had departed for other mission fields, Ignatius informs us that John brought Mary to Ephesus and established his ministry headquarters there. It was from Ephesus that John supervised the churches in the province of Asia, including those in the cities of Pergamum, Sardis, Philadelphia, Thyatira, Laodicea, and Smyrna, all of which the apostle addressed when he wrote the book of Revelation. It's interesting to note that a building still in existence in Ephesus is said to have been the residence of the Virgin Mary. Now, I can see that Father Michael is anxious to tell us about John's later years."

The priest smiled as he turned toward Charles and said, "Reverend Monroe, of course you know that during the final years of the first Christian century, John was the last apostle left alive. Ignatius informs us that all the others by this time had given their lives for the Gospel.

"Historians maintain that during his final decade as ruler, Emperor Domitian decided that everyone was to address him as lord and god, and he began all his correspondence invoking this form of address. When the Christians refused, they were singled out for persecution. At first, those accused of insulting the emperor by refusing to address him as he desired were put to death so vividly described by Ignatius when he wrote about the persecution of Philip, but finally, it is believed the emperor's staff suggested that instead of death these Christians could be imprisoned and made to work in the mines and on other imperial projects. The emperor apparently agreed, and Ignatius's account seems to validate this point.

"Ignatius explains that John was an old man by the time of his imprisonment and that he was sent to the mines on Patmos. It was on this island, you'll recall, that most biblical historians believe the book of Revelation was written. Ignatius says the apostle was sent to the deepest and darkest mines on the island where he had the visions of the End of Days.

"Now we come to what will be of great interest to biblical historians. Ignatius tells us that John reviewed the Gospels of Mark and Luke when he returned to Ephesus from Patmos. According to Ignatius, it was in Ephesus that he was persuaded to complete the Gospel story, since the other Gospel writers had confined their written accounts to what Jesus said and did during only one year of his ministry.

"I do so like the way Ignatius describes the last preaching of the aged apostle, for many have long called John's Gospel the Gospel of Love. Clement of Alexandria, a doctor of the Church from the first century, confirms that Ignatius was correct in saying John was still alive during the reign of Emperor Nerva. Clement said that John lived on into the reign of Trajan who became emperor in 98 AD. Ironically, it was Trajan who later condemned Ignatius to death in the Colosseum."

Doctor Bankkour then said, "Reverend Monroe, would you like to add to this discussion?

Charles looked fondly at his brother as he addressed the team, "This entire experience has been a tremendous blessing to me. For many hours, I've remained awake at night in the hospital or at home, thinking about Ignatius's account of the ministry and later lives of the apostles, and I've written a short summary of what I've learned, for fear I'd leave something out that was revealed in this incredible manuscript. Before I get to that, however, please let me say to each one of you how thankful I am for your expertise, your talent, and your dedication. Without you, this project would have never gotten off the ground.

"I'd like to take this moment to say that regardless of the theft and perhaps the destruction of the manuscript, my brother and I have agreed that it will be published and we will be happy to include the names of any of you who desire to be associated with the publication. I for one see the hand of the Lord in the fact that you as a team were able to completely translate it before the theft occurred. I know there will be sceptics who will doubt that a manuscript ever existed, but we know the truth so we will proceed with publication.

"I'd now like to share with you some of what I've learned from Ignatius's incredible account of the lives and missions of Jesus's first followers.

"First, we have Paul who, Ignatius says, did indeed minister in Spain before finally ending his marvelous missionary travels in Rome. It's ironic that, according to Ignatius, he once was declared innocent by one Roman prefect only to be arrested, tried, and condemned by another. Because he was a Roman citizen, he could not be crucified, so the soldiers took him to a place of execution, where he was beheaded.

"Peter, the one designated by our Lord to be the leader of the early church, planned and managed the missionary journeys of the apostles and disciples; directed the journeys and activities of the other apostles, cared for the church in Judea, Asia Minor, and finally, in Rome where he was arrested, chained to a dungeon pillar for many months, then condemned and crucified, head downward, on Vatican Hill.

"Matthias, the last apostle, the one chosen to replace the turncoat, Judas Iscariot, was a missionary in Greece and southern Russia only to return to Jerusalem, where he was stoned to death by fanatical Zealots who considered him a heretic because of his faith in Christ.

"Andrew, Peter's brother, whose quiet presence and organizational gifts were of immense value to his brother during the earliest days in guiding the young church, served as a missionary in

Asia Minor and southern Russia before journeying to Greece where he was crucified by the Roman governor.

"Matthew, author of the Gospel that goes by his name, the former tax collector, cared for the Christians for many years in Judea before traveling to Egypt, and then south to the ancient kingdom of Axum on the southeastern coast of Africa, where he brought many to Christ before an angry king ordered him to be thrown into a blazing furnace in the iron belly of a pagan god.

"Thomas, who traveled farther than any of the other apostles, the one who had once doubted the Resurrection of the Lord, was successful in baptizing a sitting king in Osroene, helped found the church in the Middle East and Armenia, then traveled a great distance south to both coasts of India, making many converts before being run through with a spear for daring to preach against the caste system.

"Jude Thaddaeus, the first to convert a member of a royal family in Edessa, co-founded the church in Armenia before journeying on to Persia where Ignatius says he discovered evidence in the royal archives of the wise men's visit to the infant Jesus in Bethlehem before he was stabbed to death by a Persian guard.

"Nathanael, also called Bartholomew, the one chosen to care for the families of the other apostles as they accompanied Jesus on his travels throughout Judea, ministered first in Armenia and then India, where Ignatius credits him with introducing Matthew's Gospel. From India, he journeyed back to Armenia, where he was apprehended and scourged to death on orders of the king for his refusal to abandon his faith in Jesus Christ.

"James, the brother of John, the first of the apostles to die, cared for the infant church in Judea and Galilee before being condemned by the Sanhedrin for blasphemy and executed by King Herod Agrippa, but not before converting to the faith the man who had betrayed him to Herod's soldiers.

"Philip, called the 'Old Reliable' by Jesus for his ability to find food and shelter for the disciples as they accompanied our Lord on those journeys around Galilee and Judea, ministered to the Samaritans, the Judeans, then to Christians in Asia Minor before being tried, condemned, and crucified by the Romans for refusing to worship Emperor Domitian.

"James, son of Alpheus, a former Zealot like several of the apostles, gave up this radical cause to follow Jesus and ministered to the people of Galilee even after the Jewish revolt against Rome. Apprehended in Galilee and condemned as a heretic by John of Gischala, a Zealot general, he was stoned to death shortly before that region fell to the victorious Romans legions commanded by Vespasian.

"Simon the Canaanite, another former Zealot who abandoned this fanatical cause to follow our Lord, was a missionary in North Africa before undertaking the long journey to Britain, where he proclaimed the Good News to Queen Boadicea and the Iceni tribe before being captured and crucified by the Romans.

"Finally, there was John, called the Beloved of the Lord, the last apostle remaining alive, who was condemned in his old age to the penal island of Patmos by Emperor Domitian, where he wrote the book of Revelation. Freed upon the death of Domitian, he returned to Ephesus where according to Ignatius, he wrote the Gospel that is called by his name.

"This entire experience has been a wonderful blessing to me, but the greatest blessing of all has been what my brother told me as we traveled here today. I've urged him to share what he said with you, and he has reluctantly agreed." Charles gestured for Ken to address the group.

"This is difficult for me, for I am by nature a deeply private individual and am uncomfortable sharing anything about my personal life," said Ken as he stood before the group of scholars. "But this is important to Charles, so I'll forge ahead.

"During the time we've been together on this project, I've never tried to hide the fact that I've been a longtime unbeliever in this whole matter of religion. All through my adult life I've questioned the idea of there being a deity of any kind. The only reason I ever got involved with this book project was because of Charles's injuries and his request that I at least deliver the book to Saint Matthew's Monastery. It was there, Doctor Bankkour, that my curiosity was aroused by your initial assessment of what the book seemed to contain, and I was hooked, at least for the short term, but purely in the historical sense. I was still definitely an unbeliever.

"Charles's slow recovery from his injuries, combined with my increasing curiosity, kept me involved far longer than I had anticipated, but, despite my inhibitions, this curiosity took on a more profound meaning as we progressed through Ignatius's account of the many travels and extraordinary experiences of the apostles. I even went back and, for the first time ever, read through the four Gospels at one sitting. I was struck by the fact that, according to the New Testament, these men had been so self-seeking, so blinded by their misperception that Jesus had come to establish a revival of David's earthly kingdom, and their ambitions for prominent positions in it. For the three years they followed him and witnessed his many miracles, they still were beguiled by dreams of an earthly Jewish kingdom, with them as favored advisors and administrators.

"These expectations were crushed, of course, by Jesus's arrest, crucifixion, and death. Now in great fear, they skulked about in their hiding places in Jerusalem, hoping against hope they would manage to escape Jesus's fate and that, somehow, it would be possible that they could make it back to safety in Galilee and resume their careers as fishermen. But something extraordinary happened after the Resurrection. According to the New Testament, the apostles and disciples were completely and miraculously changed when the risen Jesus appeared in their midst.

"No longer were they the self-absorbed men who had banked on becoming high officials in a new, worldly kingdom. Now they went boldly out into the streets of Jerusalem, proclaiming that Jesus was the long-anticipated Messiah, and that was their first step, for as Ignatius tells us, they dedicated the rest of their lives to fearlessly proclaiming to the whole world, regardless of the dangers involved, that Jesus was the Son of God. Now they truly became the fishers of men that Jesus had promised to make them when he first invited them to follow him.

"I was struck by the fact that they were so different from men my firm and I deal with in today's world. According to Ignatius, not a one of them was ever concerned about a retirement plan, took a vacation, or were concerned about an investment plan or saving money for a rainy day. They set out with only one thought in mind: to take the Good News, the message of salvation, to the far corners of the world. This they did, no matter what the cost, and no matter what dangers lay in their path. They didn't end up in assisted living, nursing homes or in comfortable retirement, either. Their travels, their preaching, and their lives came to a close only, as Charles has summarized for us, when they were either stretched out on a cross, stoned to death, thrown into a blazing furnace, pierced with spears, or forced to bend their necks before an executioner's sword.

"So, gentlemen, as I shared with Charles, I now see that faith can come to men through many avenues. For me, personally, it was through Ignatius's chronicle of the lives of the apostles. These men started out believing that Jesus would reestablish a worldly kingdom, then had that belief shattered by his arrest, trial, torture, and death on the cross. Here the story of Jesus and the Good News he proclaimed should, by all rights, have come to an end. But it didn't. It had only just begun.

"When Jesus appeared to them after his Resurrection, then came their moment of discovery. To their astonishment, he appeared to them in the flesh. And not to them alone. He was no ghost. Many others in Jerusalem saw him also. He had risen from the grave as he had told them, for death couldn't hold him. They were convinced he was the Son of God by the power of his Resurrection and their presence at his ascension to God the Father. They were completely transformed men. They spent the rest of their lives sure of Jesus's divinity and proclaiming his message of salvation, all because they were convinced they had once walked the roads of Judea in the presence of the Son of God.

"Because they were totally changed from being grasping, selfish men angling for a position in a worldly kingdom and were now absolutely convinced that Jesus was who he said he was, the Son of the living God, I too have become persuaded by their transformation, and I now believe. Furthermore, if I'm permitted to make a prediction concerning the future, I will say this: many of those who read Ignatius's account of the lives of the apostles in the days ahead will marvel at their complete transformation and will come to believe, as these apostles did, that Jesus was indeed the Son of God."